PRAISE FOR
BRIAN FREEMAN'S BOURNE BOOKS

"This is a tightly plotted, complex yarn with the fast pace that will keep readers flipping the pages. . . . This may wind up on the big screen, but don't wait for the movie. It's a fun read."
—*Kirkus Reviews*

"Freeman has a firm grasp of Bourne's tangled background, plus the skills to keep the action front and center. Bourne fans will hope for an encore from this talented author."
—*Publishers Weekly*

"Yet another nonstop thrill ride. . . . In the hands of Brian Freeman, [Bourne] is not only as alive as ever, he jumps right off the page. . . . Everything you have come to expect from a Bourne novel, and more."
—Bookreporter.com

"Freeman . . . is an excellent storyteller. . . . His two Bourne novels—and we hope there will be more—take a much-loved character and breathe new life into him, giving him new energy and a renewed purpose. Fans of Ludlum's iconic character will definitely want to read this."
—*Booklist*

"It's been a while since Jason Bourne sat atop the thriller genre, but with Brian Freeman at the helm, he retakes his seat among the best in the business. Bottom line: Jason Bourne is back and better than ever."
—The Real Book Spy

THE BOURNE SERIES

ROBERT LUDLUM'S
THE BOURNE SACRIFICE
(by Brian Freeman)

ROBERT LUDLUM'S
THE BOURNE TREACHERY
(by Brian Freeman)

ROBERT LUDLUM'S
THE BOURNE EVOLUTION
(by Brian Freeman)

ROBERT LUDLUM'S
THE BOURNE INITIATIVE
(by Eric Van Lustbader)

ROBERT LUDLUM'S
THE BOURNE ENIGMA
(by Eric Van Lustbader)

ROBERT LUDLUM'S
THE BOURNE ASCENDANCY
(by Eric Van Lustbader)

ROBERT LUDLUM'S
THE BOURNE RETRIBUTION
(by Eric Van Lustbader)

ROBERT LUDLUM'S
THE BOURNE IMPERATIVE
(by Eric Van Lustbader)

ROBERT LUDLUM'S
THE BOURNE DOMINION
(by Eric Van Lustbader)

ROBERT LUDLUM'S
THE BOURNE OBJECTIVE
(by Eric Van Lustbader)

ROBERT LUDLUM'S
THE BOURNE DECEPTION
(by Eric Van Lustbader)

ROBERT LUDLUM'S
THE BOURNE SANCTION
(by Eric Van Lustbader)

ROBERT LUDLUM'S
THE BOURNE BETRAYAL
(by Eric Van Lustbader)

ROBERT LUDLUM'S
THE BOURNE LEGACY
(by Eric Van Lustbader)

THE BOURNE ULTIMATUM

THE BOURNE SUPREMACY

THE BOURNE IDENTITY

THE TREADSTONE SERIES

ROBERT LUDLUM'S
THE TREADSTONE RENDITION
(by Joshua Hood)

ROBERT LUDLUM'S
THE TREADSTONE TRANSGRESSION
(by Joshua Hood)

ROBERT LUDLUM'S
THE TREADSTONE EXILE
(by Joshua Hood)

ROBERT LUDLUM'S
THE TREADSTONE RESURRECTION
(by Joshua Hood)

THE BLACKBRIAR SERIES

ROBERT LUDLUM'S
THE BLACKBRIAR GENESIS
(by Simon Gervais)

THE COVERT-ONE SERIES

ROBERT LUDLUM'S
THE PATRIOT ATTACK
(by Kyle Mills)

ROBERT LUDLUM'S
THE MOSCOW VECTOR
(with Patrick Larkin)

ROBERT LUDLUM'S
THE GENEVA STRATEGY
(by Jamie Freveletti)

ROBERT LUDLUM'S
THE LAZARUS VENDETTA
(with Patrick Larkin)

ROBERT LUDLUM'S
THE UTOPIA EXPERIMENT
(by Kyle Mills)

ROBERT LUDLUM'S
THE ALTMAN CODE
(with Gayle Lynds)

ROBERT LUDLUM'S
THE JANUS REPRISAL
(by Jamie Freveletti)

ROBERT LUDLUM'S
THE PARIS OPTION
(with Gayle Lynds)

ROBERT LUDLUM'S
THE ARES DECISION
(by Kyle Mills)

ROBERT LUDLUM'S
THE CASSANDRA COMPACT
(with Philip Shelby)

ROBERT LUDLUM'S
THE ARCTIC EVENT
(by James H. Cobb)

ROBERT LUDLUM'S
THE HADES FACTOR
(with Gayle Lynds)

ROBERT LUDLUM'S

THE

BOURNE
SACRIFICE

BRIAN FREEMAN

G. P. PUTNAM'S SONS
NEW YORK

PUTNAM
— EST. 1838 —

G. P. PUTNAM'S SONS
Publishers Since 1838
An imprint of Penguin Random House LLC
penguinrandomhouse.com

The Library of Congress has catalogued the
G. P. Putnam's Sons hardcover edition as follows:

Names: Freeman, Brian, 1963– author.
Title: Robert Ludlum's the bourne sacrifice / Brian Freeman.
Description: New York : G. P. Putnam's Sons, 2022. | Series: Jason Bourne ; 3
Identifiers: LCCN 2022026952 (print) | LCCN 2022026953 (ebook) |
ISBN 9780593419854 (hardcover) | ISBN 9780593419861 (ebook)
Subjects: LCGFT: Mystery fiction. | Novels.
Classification: LCC PS3606.R4454 R669 2022 (print) |
LCC PS3606.R4454 (ebook) | DDC 813/.6--dc23
LC record available at https://lccn.loc.gov/2022026952
LC ebook record available at https://lccn.loc.gov/2022026953

First G. P. Putnam's Sons hardcover edition / July 2022
First G. P. Putnam's Sons premium edition / May 2023
First G. P. Putnam's Sons premium edition ISBN / 9780593419878

Printed in the United States of America
1 3 5 7 9 10 8 6 4 2

ROBERT LUDLUM'S
THE BOURNE SACRIFICE

THE YOUNG WOMAN CLIMBED OUT OF A TAXI NEAR THE FDR memorial in West Potomac Park. It was almost midnight, and she zipped up her blue nylon jacket against the cold spring air. When she dug in her pocket, she found that she had only enough dollars to give the driver the exact fare, so she offered him a twenty-euro note for the tip.

"Es tut mir leid," she murmured, apologizing.

The driver replied with a grumble of annoyance. Even so, he snatched the crumpled foreign bill from her outstretched fingers, then screeched away from the curb so quickly that she had to jump back to avoid the vehicle running over her toes. The cab's tires splashed through a pool of muddy water, which sprayed the cuffs of her red jeans and the suede tops of her Morgen Trainers.

She waited where she was and didn't move until the taxi had disappeared. Those were her instructions, which she'd followed precisely since landing at Reagan National two hours earlier. Take a cab, not an Uber. Don't take the first one in line; skip the first two, and take the third. Give your destination as the National Archives, and when you get there, cross the mall on foot. Leave your phone on, but hide it near the fountain where it's not likely to be found. Then take a second cab to the FDR memorial.

Only a paranoid mind would insist on those precautions, but the man she was meeting believed in conspiracies. His whole life had been about creating fiction that was more real than the so-called truth. That was why she'd chosen him for her story. She needed someone who was willing to reject the lies that everyone else believed.

Meine Lügen, she thought. *My own lies! The lies that kill!*

When the taxi was gone, the woman—she was twenty-eight years old—shoved her hands in the pockets of her jacket and marched quickly into the park. She was tall, with a thin, gangly frame and messy black hair parted in the middle. Her face was elongated and narrow, her chin making a deep U, her small nose sculpted with sharp ridges, her pale skin dotted with freckles. She had thin lips and a mouth not easily given to smiling. Her dark eyes always studied the world with a grim stare, but they were also eyes that missed very little.

She crossed the plaza, where she spotted FDR's famous saying carved into a stone wall: *The only thing we have to fear is fear itself.* But Roosevelt had been wrong. She knew there was plenty to fear.

As if to prove that was true, a sharp metallic click stopped her in her tracks. It sounded to her ears like the cocking of a gun somewhere in the darkness. She studied the gnarled tree trunks and looked for the source of the threat. She didn't see anyone else, but the sickly sweet smell of marijuana and the low rattle of a cough told her there were unseen strangers watching her in the park. The street people hid in places like this, but they weren't the ones who frightened her.

It was the others. The men from the Pyramid.

Had they found her?

Hurrying now, the woman continued to the paved sidewalk that ran beside the Tidal Basin. Cherry blossoms blew off the trees in clouds like pink snow. The overhead lights cast strange shadows and made her body look like a giant. She was in the open now. A target. But *how* could they even know where she was? How could they already know she was planning to betray them? She'd been so careful. She'd told no one what she was going to do.

Except for Oskar. She couldn't leave him behind and not explain why. But even her message to him had been hidden, left behind with a friend, and she doubted he would find it until long after this night was over.

Even so, her instincts told her that she was being watched. She looked nervously behind her to make sure she was still alone, and then she followed the path beside the glistening water. She passed several empty benches until she found the one she wanted—the one that had a small *X* scratched on the seat in white chalk. Another precaution—a way to make sure she really was the woman he was expecting to meet.

She took a seat, checked her watch, and saw that it was five minutes until midnight. Five minutes until he was supposed to join her.

Across the water, the tower of the Washington Monument glowed like a rocket ready for launch. Stars gleamed over her head in the cloudless, moonless sky. It was a beautiful night. Perfect. She wished that Oskar could be with her now. She remembered all the times he'd talked about the two of them taking a trip to America to see things like the Smithsonian, the Golden Gate Bridge, and the Grand Canyon. He'd said they could go together, maybe even as a honeymoon trip, which was his way of hinting that a proposal was coming soon. He had no idea that she'd been to the U.S. many times, that she'd done missions for the Pyramid all over the country for several years.

The lies that kill!

Her last trip had been in October last year. Ever since then, flashbacks of that terrible night had tormented her memory. She still shivered as she pictured the thousands of people in the Atlanta streets, the screaming and chanting, the Molotov cocktails, the clouds of tear gas. And the fire. The fire was what had pushed her over the edge. They'd sworn to her that the building was empty. They'd insisted that no one would be hurt. The fire was supposed to be a symbol and nothing more; that was enough. Instead, she'd watched them drag out nine dead bodies, nine zipped vinyl bags lined up on the street.

Including three children.

That was when she'd made her decision. That was when she'd realized that she had to stop the lies.

She checked her watch again, and worry crept through her. Too much time had passed. It was 12:07 a.m. Where was he? She looked up and down the trail, hoping to spot that familiar face, which she'd recognized on the back covers of books since she was a teenager. She'd devoured all of them, even the ones that went back long before she was born. On the plane from Germany, she'd read his latest—a novel called *Serpent!*

But there was no sign of the writer anywhere. Her heart began to sink as the reality hit her. He wasn't coming.

Had he betrayed her? *No!* Not him, *never* him!

Or was he already dead?

In the dark woods behind her, she heard a violent disturbance. Instantly, she jumped to her feet and spun around. Between the twisted trunks of the cherry trees, a huge, unkempt man stumbled drunkenly down the dirt slope directly toward her. At first, he was nothing more than a giant silhouette, but when he came into the light, she saw that his face was wild, his mouth open in silent agony, beads of sweat running down his forehead. He came at her like some kind of overgrown monster, then shuddered to a stop, his body contracting with spasms. He toppled like a tree, jerked several more times, and lay still.

She ran to the dead man and looked down at him. It

was not the man she'd been hoping to see here. This man lay on his back, eyes fixed and open. He had greasy black hair and pockmarked skin, and the dark stubble on his face indicated that he hadn't shaved in days. He wore a dirty white T-shirt that stretched over his huge frame and jeans that were torn and caked with mud and stains. A potent smell of sour body odor made her cover her nose and mouth to block out the stench.

A homeless man. An addict suffering an overdose. She could see the bruises in the seam of his arm where he'd injected himself again and again. The European newspapers told her that deaths like this happened all the time in American cities.

But it was too much of a coincidence that he would die here and now.

She glanced at the man's giant right hand and saw something clutched between his fingers. It was a woman's leather purse, compact and expensive. She knelt by the man and separated the purse from his hand and opened it. Inside, she found a wallet, and when she opened the flap, she saw several hundred dollars in cash, along with credit cards made out in the name of Deborah Mueller. A stranger's name. Someone she'd never met.

There was also a German passport in the purse.

With a strange sense of horror, the woman opened the pages of the passport and had to stifle a scream. The name on the passport was the same as on the credit cards. Deborah Mueller. But the face was all too familiar. It was *her* face.

The photograph of the woman called Deborah Mueller was a photograph of *her*.

Another lie!

She knew what it meant. She knew they were coming for her. She dropped the purse and turned to run, but she was already too late. When she looked both ways on the path, she saw two men closing on her from each side. They were dressed identically in black, their faces hidden behind cartoon masks. With only one direction open to her, she sprinted up the slope where the homeless man had run to his death, but as she neared the cherry trees, a third man emerged from the darkness immediately in front of her.

The dogs had flushed the prey to the hunter.

The man wore a dark suit with a tweed wool coat down to his ankles. He had blond hair and a ruddy face and the ugly red gash of a scar down one cheek. What drew her eyes was the knife in his hand, an old, dull, dirty knife, the kind a homeless man would carry as a tool. But in the hands of this man, it was a deadly weapon. She froze in despair. She couldn't move or run. The man's lips pursed, and, oddly, he whistled the fragment of a Beatles song. Just a short fragment, but enough for her to recognize it, like one last bitter joke.

"I Should Have Known Better."

Yes, she should have known better. She should have known how this would end.

"Liebst du der Beatles, Louisa?" the man asked with a cruel smile as his fingers tightened around the knife handle.

She sighed with a whimper of regret. The blade would come next. The blade and the blood. In the last seconds of her life, she realized that she would never have the chance to come back to America with Oskar.

She'd lost, and the Pyramid had won. Varak had won.

The lies would continue.

PART ONE

1

JASON BOURNE CROUCHED BEHIND THE STONE WALL THAT ringed the little black church. A bitter wind blew across the lava fields, and slate gray clouds clung to the dark tips of the mountains. With his Swarovski binoculars, he zoomed in on the twin white buildings of the oceanfront hotel below him. There were no other structures around for miles, just the simple black church and the elegant hotel amid the landscape of strangely sculpted volcanic stone. The only sounds were the fierce whistle of the wind and the thunder of waves crashing from the Atlantic onto the shell beach.

He'd watched the men of the protection detail arriving separately over the past hour. They'd staked out different locations around the hotel, blending like locals into the remote Icelandic countryside. They were obviously waiting for someone. If Bourne was right, that meant that the assassin known as Lennon would be arriving soon.

There were five killers serving as Lennon's advance team. One was a man in overalls who'd parked his truck off the shoulder of the single lonely road that led to the coast. He'd opened the hood and was pretending to tinker with the engine. Two others shared pints of beer at a picnic table behind the hotel and joked with each other in loud voices. Another was just a speck of camouflage in the distance, but Bourne had spotted him stretched out in the wavy grass of the lava field, with the scope of a long gun trained on the hotel.

The fifth man lay on the ground at the base of the wall next to Bourne, his skull crushed by a slab of volcanic stone, his VP40 pistol and two extra magazines now in Bourne's pocket. Jason listened in on the man's radio receiver, but so far, there had been no communications among the team.

The next hour passed slowly. The dark afternoon bled into early evening, and the brooding mountains on the horizon grew shrouded by mist. The air got colder, wind roared in ripples through the tough scrub brush, and drizzle spat across Bourne's face. He remained motionless, his binoculars propped on the wall, his black wool cap pulled low on his forehead. His hands were covered with black nylon gloves. The naked eye could perceive the tiniest movement or color even from long distances, so he took care to avoid both. Then again, if one of the advance team spotted someone hiding near the church, they would assume it was the man who was dead at Bourne's feet.

Finally, he spotted a car approaching on the single-lane road. It was a red dot on the curving gray highway. As the car got closer, he recognized it as a compact Citroën C3, which was not the kind of vehicle he expected Lennon to use. The Citroën parked at the rear of the hotel, and when the driver's door opened, he saw a woman get out. She was alone. Quickly, Bourne grabbed a camera from his leather jacket to magnify her face and snap multiple photos. She was in her late twenties, slim and attractive, with shoulder-length blond hair. She wore a navy blue Icelandic wool sweater over khakis and hiking boots, and she carried a leather pack slung over one shoulder. Rather than go into the hotel, she lit a cigarette and wandered away toward a shallow slope overlooking the beach.

The two killers drinking beer at the picnic table pretended to ignore her. She ignored them, too, but Bourne suspected that was because she didn't realize she was being watched. Instead, she stared out at the whitecaps on the ocean while the wind mussed her hair. When she finished her first cigarette, she lit another, with the jerky motions of someone who was trying to calm her nerves. Her demeanor told him she wasn't a pro.

Not long after, Bourne saw two more cars approaching at high speed. Both were gray Range Rovers with smoked windows. He tensed, his senses alert now as he watched the men of the protection detail stiffen with anticipation. The man in overalls slammed shut the hood of his truck. The two men on the bench put down their beers and slipped their hands into their pockets in order to ready weapons.

A single clipped sentence in Icelandic crackled through the radio receiver in Bourne's ear.

"Það er hann."

It's him.

The two SUVs braked hard and stopped behind the hotel. No one got out. The engines kept running. But the blond woman crushed out her cigarette and immediately headed for the Range Rovers.

Bourne held his breath.

It all came down to this.

One year. One year of hunting across Europe for the killer known as Lennon. A killer who'd eluded Treadstone and Interpol. A killer who claimed to hold the key to Bourne's missing past.

The last time they'd clashed had been during a fight to the death on a Northern California beach, but Lennon had managed to escape on the water. Ever since, Bourne had tracked the assassin from mission to mission, always one step behind, always too late to grab him and interrogate him. And then kill him. Until last week. Last week, he'd located a corrupt banker in Barcelona with ties to Lennon, who'd told him about a meeting coming up on the Snæfellsnes peninsula, two hours from Reykjavík. This time, Bourne was ready.

The back door of the first Range Rover opened. A man got out.

Through the binoculars, Bourne studied him. He saw a man with cropped blond hair and diamond earrings in both ears. His eyes were hidden by sunglasses, but he had thick, pale brows. His nose was broad and prominent, his chin strong, with a red, horizontal scar making a seam down one cheek. He was tall and wore an expensive gray wool coat that draped to his ankles. Below the coat, he wore a collarless white sweater, black slacks, and dress shoes.

Was it him?

This man looked nothing like the killer Bourne had met in California, but appearances didn't matter. Lennon was a master of false identities; he could change his face, his hair, his eyes, his language, and his accent, and never appear the same way twice. He took over other people's identities and left their dead bodies behind.

He was a mystery. A ghost.

The man signaled to the blond woman with a slight tilt of his head. The two of them walked side by side to a dirt path that led into the lava fields. *That walk!* Bourne had seen it before, in London last year when Lennon was mounting an elaborate assassination plot at a meeting of the WTO. He'd seen it on that beach in California. And he'd seen it somewhere in the fog of his own forgotten past.

Behind every disguise was the same casual, graceful walk, as if his torso and powerful shoulders were floating above rigid hips.

Lennon.

The blond woman accompanied the assassin into the

field of black stones. Through the binoculars, Bourne saw strain on her face, and he knew she was scared. She didn't like the loneliness of the meeting ground, and regardless of his disguises, she didn't like seeing the killer's face. People who saw that face didn't usually live to tell about it. The woman let the leather pack slide off her shoulder, and she handed the strap to Lennon. He could see her arm sagging with the weight. The killer unzipped the top a few inches, took a glance inside, and zipped it up again. He looked satisfied with the contents.

A payoff. It was definitely a payoff.

But for what?

When he had the pack over his shoulder, Lennon's hand slid into the pocket of his wool coat. The woman flinched, expecting a gun, expecting a kill shot. By instinct, Bourne reached for his Sig Sauer, but he was too far away to intervene. It didn't matter. Lennon's hand reappeared, not with a gun, but with a coin that glinted with a flash of gold. He flipped it in the air with his thumb, then grabbed the woman's hand by the wrist and deposited the coin on her open palm.

He murmured something, and Bourne could read his lips. *"For you."*

Then Lennon folded the woman's fingers shut over the coin. He patted her cheek, the signal that the meeting was done.

The blond woman stumbled back to her Citroën. She couldn't get away fast enough now. The engine fired with a cough, and the little red car shot down the highway. From the trail, Lennon watched the car until it disappeared, then shifted his gaze back to the rugged panorama around him. He was perfectly in view through Bourne's binoculars. The ocean wind ruffled his blond hair. In the low light, he was barely more than a shadow, and his eyes were still hidden behind sunglasses. However, his gaze seemed to focus on the little black church, as if somehow he knew Jason was there.

Lennon's face broke into the tiniest smile. Then he returned to the Range Rover, and the two SUVs drove away toward the mountains.

AN HOUR LATER, IT WAS NIGHT, AND NIGHT IN ICELAND WAS utterly black.

Jason followed the Range Rovers on a Kawasaki motorcycle, which he'd acquired from a dealer in Reykjavík when he'd arrived in Iceland three days earlier. He stayed back at a considerable distance, only occasionally seeing red taillights ahead of him. He wasn't worried about losing them out here because there were no other vehicles and almost no crossroads on the barren stretch of highway.

He was more worried about the weather. As the light rain continued, and the temperatures fell, ice was a threat, particularly if the SUVs turned north. Through the motorcycle's single headlight, he could see the wet shine of the pavement. Around him, the rest of the world was dark. The rushing air was cold even through his rain suit, but they'd trained him not to notice the cold.

Separate your mind and your body.

Treadstone.

Bourne was just over six feet tall, and his frame didn't advertise his physical toughness, but the men who knew such things—the men who killed for a living—always recognized the danger he represented. It wasn't just his experience and background; it was also the intelligence in his cool blue-gray eyes. He analyzed people and situations in a split second, assessing the risks, strengths, and weaknesses. Then he acted without hesitation.

He was also self-aware enough to recognize his own greatest weakness. He was a man with no memory of his past.

Years earlier, a bullet to the head on a Treadstone mission had nearly killed him. He'd survived, but the trauma to his brain had erased who he was. He'd come back to consciousness as a stranger to himself, and he still was. Most of the first three decades of his life remained lost in a fog, with nothing but a few photographs to prove that he had any past at all. He knew that meant there were threats out there that he would never see coming. What he didn't know could kill him. If he was going to stay alive, he needed answers.

Lennon claimed to have those answers. In California, the assassin had bragged about being a part of Bourne's missing life. Maybe it was nothing but a lie, but Jason needed to know for sure.

The dark Icelandic countryside passed around him. He was an extension of the bike as he drove. He was hunched forward, feeling every vibration of the machine.

At thirty-six years old, his body couldn't completely escape the aftereffects of the fights and assaults he'd endured. But during his search for Lennon over the past year, he'd followed an intense regimen of workouts and martial arts training, because he knew that the assassin was doing the same. Whenever they met again, Bourne needed to be ready.

And that would be soon.

Far ahead of him, he saw tiny flashes of white light. The SUVs had left the highway. The valley was perfectly flat, so he could easily track the headlights, but he saw no road signs denoting an intersection. Instead, as he drew close to the area where the vehicles had turned, he saw a dirt trail heading toward the hills. He followed, leaving his light on so he could see, but he drove slowly on the bumpy, rutted track. After several miles, with the slopes of the mountains looming larger in front of him, he saw that the SUVs had stopped. Their lights vanished. Bourne stopped, too, seeing nothing but darkness. There seemed to be no buildings out here, no reason for Lennon to come to this place.

The open fields were quiet except for the soft patter of drizzle. He was still a mile from the vehicles, too far away for his night vision monocular to be of use. Instead, he waited to see what would happen next. Only a few minutes passed, and then he heard the distant growl of engines again, and the headlights came to life like eyes. The SUVs had turned around; they were heading his way, heading back toward *him*.

Jason quickly rolled the bike off the dirt road and laid it sideways in the brush. He stretched out along the ground, covered by the tall grass. The vehicles roared by, kicking up spray and mud, and they didn't slow down as they passed him. They didn't know he was there. When they were gone, he stood up, eyeing the taillights heading back toward the main highway. This was a rare moment when his instincts did battle. Follow them, or investigate the meaning of their brief stop in the middle of nowhere. If he lost them now, he risked losing Lennon altogether after a year on his trail.

And yet.

He fired up the motorcycle again and sped down the dirt road toward the hills. He didn't bother turning off his headlight because he knew that the throb of his engine would give him away if someone was listening. He drove to within a short distance of where he estimated that the SUVs had stopped, and then he shut down the bike and retrieved his night vision monocular and focused on the landscape. The fields and hills all bloomed to life through the single lens in eerie shades of gray.

There it was.

Dark, small, and virtually invisible in the mist was a cottage, built where the mountains began to rise immediately behind it. It was a single-story farmhouse, and Jason could see the frames of multiple tall windows that took advantage of the views across the countryside. He saw no light to indicate that the house was occupied, but he needed to see what was inside.

Bourne unzipped his rain suit and quickly stepped out of it. With his Sig in his right hand, he sprinted through the wet grass, and less than a minute later, he crouched beneath the tall windows of the cottage. He made a circuit around the house, and on the other side, the dark foothills rose sharply from flat, open fields. From inside, he heard no sounds, and no lights were on behind the windows.

When he got back to the front door, he turned the knob silently. The door was open. Still crouched, he crept inside. The interior was cool and completely black, and he realized that all the windows had been covered over with blackout curtains. It was impossible to see anything. With his breathing hushed, he listened, and he heard the faint sound of someone moving in a different room near the rear of the cottage. His gun level at his waist, he took a careful step in the darkness.

Then a voice spoke, as if someone were standing next to him.

A whisper hissed through speakers somewhere in the room.

"Cain."

Jason backed away. He stayed close to the wall, where he could feel his way forward. When he glanced at the ceiling, he spotted a single red dot of light, which told him that cameras were pointed at him, seeing in the dark. He needed light himself, so when he felt one of the blackout curtains on a window frame, he tore it down, ignoring the noise. Then he found another and tore that down, too. At least he could see enough to realize that the room was empty, just the furniture of an ordinary Icelandic cottage.

But he knew there was nothing ordinary about it.

The voice spoke again.

"You were at the black church, weren't you? Strange, isn't it? I could feel you there. We're connected, you and me. But that's as it should be. We have history."

Bourne heard the voice in stereo. Yes, it was coming through the speakers, but he could hear the voice from the back of the house, too. Lennon was *here*. He headed that way, but he knew that the assassin could see him coming, so he took his Sig and fired at the camera mounted in the corner of the ceiling. In the stark silence, the gunshot was as loud as a bomb.

"Both of us in darkness," the voice went on in the aftermath. *"It's better that way. But I have an advantage. I can kill you, Cain. It doesn't matter to me if you die. But you want me alive, don't you? You can't kill me until you know what I know."*

Lennon was right. Jason didn't want to kill him. Not yet. He wanted answers first. He'd tracked him across Europe to this remote cottage to find out the truth about Lennon's past. And about his own past.

Jason saw the outline of a doorway. It led him to a small kitchen, but before he went inside, he surveyed the ceiling and spotted another red dot of light. Another camera. He took aim and fired, and again the noise was explosive. Then he spun through the doorway and stayed low, tracking the border of the room to the other side.

Beyond the kitchen, he saw a faint glow, as if from a computer monitor, but then the glow disappeared. Everything in the house turned black.

They were both blind.

Bourne felt around the nearest counter for something, anything, he could throw into the next room. His fingers closed over a heavy ceramic coffee mug. Nearing the doorway, staying close to the ground, he heaved it into the room, hearing it land on a hardwood floor with a thud and a roll. Immediately, the house erupted with a burst of automatic fire from a machine pistol, and bullets cut through the walls and ricocheted into the kitchen. Sparks flashed. Smoke scorched the air.

His semiautomatic pistol was no match for that weapon.

"Do you remember, Cain?"

Lennon was close. Bourne could hear him speaking from the next room, and he zeroed in on the location of the voice.

"We were in a cottage like this once near the end. Before they sent you after me. The two of us were in darkness just like this. Staking out our victims. But no, of course, you don't remember. It's all gone."

Bourne slithered along the floor to the doorway. He extended just the barrel of the gun around the frame.

He thought: *Keep talking.*

"We were talking about sixties music. We were reciting lyrics from our favorite songs to pass the time. I did 'Maxwell's Silver Hammer.' No surprise in that, right? I was always a Beatles fan. You did 'Itchycoo Park.'"

Jason froze, his body stiffening on the floor. Even though he couldn't see, he squeezed his eyes shut, because a roaring took over his brain, like the growl of a jet engine. It happened that way when he felt memories pushing to come back in.

"Itchycoo Park."

Jesus, he *did* remember! Somewhere in the fog of his brain, he could hear himself laughing about getting high and touching the sky.

With this man? With *Lennon*?

He heard a smile in the voice in the other room. "Ah, so some of it *is* still there."

Bourne pushed the fingers of his left hand into a fist. With his right hand, he fired his Sig into the dark space. Once, twice, three times. He aimed for where he thought the voice had been coming from, and instantly, Lennon fired back, a burst from his machine pistol that threw up wood dust and forced Jason back into the kitchen. He touched his arm and felt blood. A bullet had nicked him.

Lennon kept firing, like an incessant cloud of violence, but then—with an impotent click—the man's weapon jammed. Jason heard a curse. He scrambled to his feet and surged through the doorway, firing his Sig in an arc around the pitch-black room. He pulled the trigger five, six, seven times, but he heard nothing, no cry of pain, no falling body. Then, from the darkness, Lennon threw himself at Bourne, and the two men landed heavily on the floor. A chop from Lennon's hand hit Jason's right wrist, and his Sig came loose and spun away, unseen. Wrapped up in each other's arms, they traded blows back and forth. He felt Lennon's hand slip down to one ankle, knowing he'd find a knife there, and the rush of air told Bourne that the blade was coming for his chest. He rolled. The blade clanged hard against the wooden floor, and Jason lashed out with his boot, feeling it connect under Lennon's jaw and spill him backward.

Bourne scrambled to his feet.

He heard Lennon do the same.

Like boxers, they retreated to opposite corners of the room. The open space seemed to go from one side of the cottage to the other, as if the house's individual bedrooms had been broken down into a single large space. He passed computer tables. The cool metal of filing cabinets. This was like a headquarters for Lennon's entire operation.

Then he felt the blackout curtains of one of the tall windows under his hand. If he ripped it down, he could see *something*. But so could Lennon. He left them in darkness.

The assassin spoke from the other corner of the room.

"You still haven't figured it out, have you, Cain? Why I know so much. You see, I was one of you. *I was Treadstone.*"

The roaring in Bourne's head came back. Empty memories crushed his skull like a vise. He was so *close*. If his mind reached out a little further, he could almost find what he was missing. But he didn't want this truth. He didn't want to believe that this man, this killer, was the same as him.

A lie! It was a lie!

"If you were Treadstone," Jason murmured, his voice raspy, his breathing ragged, "then what was rule number one?"

Lennon laughed. "You mean the rule you struggled with? The rule you always seem to break? *Never get involved.*"

Jason pushed his fists against his head. Yes! That was the rule! The first in the long list of rules that dictated how you lived your whole life as a Treadstone agent. Never get involved. As soon as your emotions came into play, you put yourself at risk, and you put your lover at risk. And Lennon was right about the rest, too. Jason had broken that rule too many times.

Marie.

Nova.

Abbey Laurent.

Bourne had so many questions about the past, but he'd run out of time. Not far away, he heard the throb of rotors outside the cottage, getting closer and louder. It came from the sky. A helicopter was descending from the hills.

"That will be my latest Yoko," Lennon said from the black room. "A fiery little girl I found in Barcelona. Her orders are to destroy the cottage, Cain, and Yoko always follows orders, whether I'm inside or not. So we can both die here together, or we can get out before that missile blows through the wall."

Bourne ripped down the blackout curtain near the window, letting in light. On the far side of the room,

Lennon did the same. The assassin was caught in a white glow through the glass now as the helicopter neared the ground. The engine shook the entire cottage like relentless, deafening rolls of thunder.

His Sig was in the middle of the room.

So was Lennon's machine pistol.

Both were too far away for either man to grab.

"Goodbye . . . *Jason*," Lennon told him. Then the killer dove through the glass and vanished.

Bourne took one step across the floor to chase him, but then he heard the high-pitched whistle of a round being fired from the helicopter. With only a split second before the impact, he threw himself through the window behind him. He landed hard on the wet grass and rolled toward the fields as an explosion ripped through the cottage, filling the world around him with heat and flame. Glass and wood pummeled his body. He got up and ran, but with another shriek, a second explosion followed the first, its shock wave punching him in the back and hurling him at least ten feet forward into the field.

He landed on his face. Air burst from his lungs, and he struggled to breathe. When he was finally able to turn over, he saw the entire cottage engulfed in flame, erasing whatever evidence Lennon had left behind.

On the far side of the house, in the shadow of the hills, the helicopter rose back up toward the sky like a black spider.

He was sure the assassin was on it. Escaping.

Bourne got to his feet. His face and clothes were a

mess of mud and blood. He staggered back toward the motorcycle he'd left on the dirt road. The drizzle continued to fall, cool rain on his hot skin.

He could still hear the arrogant hiss of Lennon's voice, and he wondered if it was true. Or was it another lie?

I was Treadstone.

2

ONCE A MONTH, ABBEY LAURENT DROVE FROM HER STUDIO
apartment in the wooded neighborhood of Mount Pleasant in Washington, DC, to the small town of Hyattsville,
Maryland. The point-to-point driving distance was only
half an hour, but Abbey took a different route each time,
randomly making multiple turns that seemed to annoy
the voice on her phone's GPS system. In the end, the trip
usually took her more than an hour.

When she got to Hyattsville, she always parked in a
different part of town. Today she used the empty lot of a
construction supply business that was closed on Satur-
day. She picked her way across railroad tracks and
emerged onto a sidewalk near the County Service Building. When the traffic thinned, she hurried across the
street and cut through a small park. Then she followed

an alley to the next street, passing an artisanal coffee shop, where she ducked inside and bought a latte to go.

As Abbey came out sipping her coffee, her gaze landed on a woman sitting at one of the outside benches. She was pretty sure the woman hadn't been there when she went inside. The woman took a longer-than-normal look at Abbey, then went back to her coffee and picked up a paperback book. It was actually the book, more than the woman, that drew Abbey's attention. She recognized the cover and title: *Serpent!*

Abbey had read the book. In fact, she was *in* the book. Or at least, there was a character named Phoebe Duchamp, a Montreal-based journalist, who bore an uncomfortable resemblance to Abbey Laurent. *Serpent!* was a novel, but the plot was closely based on the hunt for a technology group called Medusa, with which Abbey had been involved two years earlier. Fiction or not, some of the details hit awfully close to home, including Phoebe's relationship with an American intelligence agent who'd been framed by Medusa. It made her wonder about the author's sources.

The book had been a bestseller, so it wasn't unusual to come upon someone reading it. And yet it made Abbey nervous to see anyone with that particular book when she was on her monthly mission to Hyattsville. Because Hyattsville was where she made contact with Jason Bourne.

The woman with the paperback didn't look up again. Abbey continued past the coffee shop to the corner of the street, and then glanced back. The woman hadn't moved; she was still at the bench, her nose buried in the book. Abbey watched her for a few moments, then decided she was letting her paranoia get out of control. She crossed the street and went into the Hyattsville Post Office.

It was quiet inside, as it usually was. Her breath quickened. She felt a combination of fear and excitement, as she always did.

Would there be a message from Jason?

She found the post office box and used her key to open it, but when she looked inside, she slammed the metal door shut again in disappointment. The box was empty. It had been empty for every one of her last six visits. She knew the message he was sending her. She could hear his cool, hard voice in her head, explaining all the reasons they couldn't be together.

It's not safe.

When you're with me, you're in danger.

The people who come after me will come after you.

I'm a killer.

But Abbey didn't care. All she felt was anger that he was letting her twist in the wind, not telling her where he was or what he was doing. She'd sent him letters for two years—even sent him little maple candies from her hometown of Quebec City, because it was an inside joke between them—and for a while, he'd replied. But as time wore on, his notes had grown more infrequent and more distant as he pushed her away. Until, ten months ago, they'd stopped altogether. His silence was more eloquent than anything he could have said.

Stay away from me.

He wasn't dead. She was sure of that. She'd finally extracted a promise from him that if he got killed, someone would get in touch with her. If she could trust anything about Jason, he kept his promises. One day, some man she didn't know would come up to her and tell her that Cain was dead and then walk away without answering any of her questions. That was how it would go. But at least she'd know. Until that happened, he was still alive. He was just ghosting her.

Bastard!

Abbey went into the main part of the post office and bought a greeting card with no message inside. Before she had time to think better of it, she wrote a note on the card, scrawled Jason's mail drop address in Paris on the outside, and slipped it into the outgoing mail slot. As soon as she did, as soon as she thought of Jason reading what she'd written, she regretted it. But it was done. At least he'd know how she felt.

She left the post office into the warm morning air. A cloud of depression went with her despite the blue skies overhead. She retraced her steps into the alley, then sat down at one of the benches outside the coffee shop. The woman was still reading her book and didn't look up. Abbey drank more of her latte and gripped the cup so tightly that it began to crush in her fist. She was pissed at herself and pissed at Jason Bourne.

Two years. She hadn't seen him in two years, but she couldn't let go of him.

Abbey brushed away the deep red bangs from her

forehead. Her shoulder-length hair was always choppy and messy. Her lipstick was a slightly paler shade of red, but she didn't wear much makeup beyond that. She was who she was, and people could take it or leave it. She didn't think of herself as pretty, but Jason had told her that she was incredibly wrong about that. Her eyes were dark and smart, her mouth expressive and full. She stood just over five foot seven, a little taller in her suede boots. An unbuttoned, untucked purple blouse covered her white spaghetti-strap top.

She checked her phone. No messages.

She knew she should work. She had stories to write. Tom Blomberg at the *Washington Sentinel* had not so gently pointed out that she was late with her profile on the new DC mayor, which was mainly because the mayor kept ducking Abbey's calls. She owed *Vanity Fair* an article on the latest TikTok dance craze. The Verge wanted her to do an essay on the Prescix social media software that was rising from the ashes.

That was her life now. Two years ago, she'd walked away from her stable job at an online Canadian magazine called *The Fort* and signed on to do freelance work for less money and no benefits. She'd given up her studio apartment in Quebec City for an even smaller studio apartment in DC for twice the rent. She had what she wanted from her career. She was in the middle of everything going on in the world. But she still couldn't forget the sheer adrenaline she'd felt when she was with Jason. She missed it.

She missed *him*.

"Are you Abbey Laurent?"

Abbey looked up and tensed with surprise as the woman who'd been reading *Serpent!* slid onto the other side of the picnic table across from her. In her head, she heard the echo of Jason's warning. *The people who come after me will come after you.*

"Who are you?" Abbey demanded.

The girl held up both hands, palms outward, as if to prove she wasn't a threat. She had a different cheap ring on every finger. She couldn't be older than twenty, and she was stick-thin, with a buzz cut of black hair and nerdy round glasses that made her blue eyes look oddly large.

"I need to talk to you, Abbey."

"I said, who the fuck are you, and how do you know who I am, and how the hell did you find me?"

"My name's Iris," the girl said. "And we all know who you are. You're one of the few people who calls out the bullshit on both sides."

"Who's *we*?"

"An online group. Young people all over the country. We don't believe the lies we're being told."

"You're conspiracy nuts," Abbey concluded with a sigh.

"You of all people should know we're not nuts." Iris held up the paperback novel. "This is you, isn't it? The character in the book—it's based on you? You broke the story about Medusa and the tech cabal. That was no conspiracy, was it?"

Abbey glanced around the alley. She was unnerved by

the girl's fanatical intensity, and she wondered if Iris was alone, or whether there were others from her group nearby. "How did you find me? No one knows I'm here."

"I told you, we know who you are. One of our people, Jerry, works at the post office. He's seen you in there several times. So we know you come here regularly. I've been here for days, waiting for you to show up."

Abbey studied Iris over the top of her coffee cup. "Sure, nothing creepy about that."

"I'm sorry, but I needed to talk to you. I don't know why you come here, and I don't want to know, but you seem to be taking steps to keep it a secret. So this seemed like the safest place to meet, where no one would be watching us."

"And what exactly do you want from me?"

"I have a story for you."

Abbey rolled her eyes. "Yeah, everybody's got a story. QAnon. Pizzagate. Russiagate. Every online rumor will find somebody who believes it. But ninety-nine percent of them are complete bullshit."

"This is about a murder."

Abbey frowned. That wasn't what she'd expected. "Whose murder?"

"A tourist was killed in DC two weeks ago."

"Are you talking about the woman in West Potomac Park?"

"Yes."

"As I recall, that case sounded pretty straightforward. She was mugged and stabbed by a homeless man who was high on heroin."

"That's just the lie we've all been told. I know the truth."

"Yeah? So what's being covered up?"

Iris shook her head. "Not here. Too many people could be watching."

Abbey listened to her journalist's instincts about sources. Usually, it was easy to make a call: serious or not serious. But with Iris, she wasn't sure. At first, she'd consigned the girl to the fanatical fringes, but something about her earnest intelligence made Abbey reassess her opinion. Most conspiracists saw big plots. Fake moon landings. Stolen elections. They didn't waste their time on little things. Like murder.

"Okay, let's take a walk," Abbey said. "I'll give you ten minutes."

THE TWO OF THEM STOPPED NEXT TO THE WALL OF A CON-crete overpass near the railroad tracks. At Iris's request, Abbey turned off her phone.

"They can track phones," the girl said.

When Abbey had done so, Iris took out a joint and lit it, and after smoking for a couple of minutes, she looked more relaxed. She offered it to Abbey, who shook her head.

"Deborah Mueller," Abbey said, wanting to get back to the story. "That was the woman's name, right?"

Iris nodded. "Yes."

"German tourist flies in for a vacation, and two hours

later, she's dead. Murdered across the water from the Washington Monument."

The girl slid a phone from the back pocket of her jeans. "Have you seen this video? Actually, I know you haven't. Almost no one has."

"What is it?"

"An interview with a homeless woman who was in the park that night. She *saw* the murder."

Abbey's brow creased with surprise. "I don't recall there being any witnesses."

"I know. That's what the police said. That's what the media said. But this video is out there. One of our group filmed it a couple days after the murder. Except it's being censored. You can't find it online. Search for it on Google or YouTube, and it doesn't exist. And whatever you can't find online may as well not be real."

She held up the phone and played the video. The quality was bad, just an interview done with a phone. The sky looked gray, and Abbey could see the Jefferson Memorial in the background, as well as police tape surrounding the area where the body had been found. There were still a couple of cops on the scene, looking bored as they kept gawkers away. The woman in the video had gray hair and was in her fifties. She wore mismatched clothes and had a small terrier in her arms. Her voice was shrill, and she gestured over her shoulder at the police as she talked.

"I saw it!" she exclaimed. "I saw the whole thing, but they won't listen to me! I was hiding in the grass, didn't dare show my face, you know? They would have killed

me, too. There were three men. Three! Two of them
wore creepy masks, and the third, he just took a knife
and killed her! Stabbed her right there where I could see
it! They killed Leon, too! They must have shot him up
with H, you know? I saw him go down. He had nothing
to do with that woman, nothing at all."

Iris clicked off the video. "See?"

"I see a woman who probably has mental and sub-
stance abuse issues trying to get attention for herself."

"So she's got problems. That doesn't mean she's lying.
Don't you think people have a right to judge for them-
selves? We can't post the video anywhere. Google and
Facebook flagged it as misinformation."

"Well, it probably is. I mean, I don't agree with them
yanking the video. But I don't see any big conspiracy
here, Iris."

"There's more."

Iris tapped her phone and showed Abbey a photograph. "This is a picture that went viral. It supposedly
leaked, and nobody knows where it came from. Deborah
Mueller's body. You can see her face. Next to her is a
roller bag she brought with her on the plane, okay? According to the police, they found clothes, printouts
about DC tourist locations, postcards she bought at the
airport, personal stuff. All the shit an ordinary German
tourist would have, right?"

"So what?"

The girl played another video. "One of our people
works at the airport. He was able to grab a video of the
taxi line that night before the police confiscated it. See?

There's Deborah Mueller getting to the front of the line. She heads to the third cab, not the first, which pisses people off. Do you recognize the face? It's the same woman."

"Okay. That's her. What's the significance?"

Iris played the video again. "Where's her bag?"

"What?"

"Deborah Mueller doesn't have a roller bag with her."

Abbey took the phone from Iris and played the video again. And then a fourth time. She tried to think of an explanation that made sense, but Iris was right. The woman whose body had been found next to a travel bag in the park came out of the airport from an international flight and got into a taxi with no luggage.

"All right," Abbey acknowledged. "That's pretty weird, but there are probably half a dozen different explanations for it."

"Maybe, but don't you think it's worth looking into?" the girl asked.

Abbey hesitated. She played the video one more time, and then she studied the photograph of the dead woman in the park, comparing the faces. They were definitely the same. And she played the video of the homeless woman again, talking about three men converging on Deborah Mueller and killing both her and the man named Leon who got the blame for her death.

"Why do you need me?" Abbey asked. "Sounds like you've got a lot of sources in this group of yours."

"We have people but no platform, no way to get the word out. You do."

Abbey stared at the foliage around the railroad tracks and shivered, feeling an odd sensation of being watched. "Can you send me all of this?"

Iris gave her a tiny smile. "Yes."

"I'll see what I can find out."

"Thank you."

"Tell me something," Abbey said. "How did you find out about any of this? What made you think there was something weird about this woman's death?"

Iris opened up the pictures on her phone again. She showed Abbey another photo of Deborah Mueller lying dead in the park. Then she swiped to the next picture, which seemed to be identical to the first one. "The first picture was the one that leaked. The second one went viral, and the first disappeared. You can't find it anywhere online anymore."

"They're the same," Abbey said.

Iris shook her head. "No, they're not. Look closely. Look at the woman's arm."

Abbey did. When she studied the first picture again, she now spotted a small tattoo on the woman's wrist. It was the Eye of Providence—an eye within a triangle that appeared at the top of the pyramid on the backside of the U.S. dollar bill. And yet in the woman's tattoo, the triangle was upside down.

Then she swiped to the second photograph, the one that had gone viral. In that picture, the woman's arm had no tattoo.

"Okay, well, maybe the first is the fake," Abbey

pointed out. "Maybe someone added the tattoo as some kind of weird joke."

"Either way, we've seen that tattoo before," Iris said. "We think it's the symbol of an organization that has been spreading lies online. Manipulating the truth. Making sure people believe only what they want them to believe. If this woman was part of them, then that's the reason why she was killed."

Abbey frowned. "What is this organization?"

"We don't know much about them," Iris replied. "Just their name. They call themselves the Pyramid."

3

AS HE LEANED ON THE RAILING, JASON TURNED OVER THE
card from Abbey in his hand. The lights of Paris stretched
out below him, the city skyline mostly flat except for the
sparkling spire of the Eiffel Tower. Behind him loomed
the white domes of the basilica known as Sacré-Cœur. It
was almost ten o'clock in the evening, but there were still
plenty of people gathered in the courtyard of the church.
He heard half a dozen different languages being spoken,
most of which he understood. Automatically, he eaves-
dropped on the conversations, making sure there were
no threats nearby.

As it was, he'd already spotted three Treadstone agents
taking up position. One stood in the shadowy doorway
of the church. That man was in his twenties, wearing a
loose Jim Morrison T-shirt, but Bourne had spotted the
bulge of a weapon tucked in his belt. Another was a

thirtysomething man talking on his phone at the railing no more than twenty feet away. There was nothing overtly suspicious about him, but Bourne had been around enough agents to recognize the physical characteristics of a fighter.

The third agent stood below him on the sharp steps leading down from the basilica. She had kinky brown hair partly covered by a beret. He recognized her from a confrontation they'd had in the Tuileries the previous year. He stared at her until she broke cover and looked back at him, with a frown creasing her face that he'd spotted her.

All of that meant that Nash Rollins was coming soon.

As he waited for his Treadstone handler, he opened the card from Abbey. She had terrible handwriting; it was childish and almost illegible. And yet just the sight of that scrawl brought her face into his mind. The messy red hair. The flirty lips. The dark eyes that stared at him—at a *killer!*—with no fear. He hadn't seen her in two years, since he'd left her behind on the boardwalk in Quebec City. They'd slept together only once, in a motel outside Amarillo. They'd spent no more than a few days together while he was hunting the Medusa group, but she was still a woman he couldn't forget.

Part of him realized that Abbey was in love with him and that he was in love with her. Even if that was true, it changed nothing. He couldn't afford to be close to her. Bringing Abbey into his life was like signing her death sentence.

He read what she'd written on the card, and he could feel the heat behind her words.

Fuck you, Jason. Say something to me.

He wished he could do that. He'd kept up their secret correspondence even when he knew it was a risk. He'd allowed himself to believe that keeping thousands of miles between them was enough. But almost a year ago, everything had changed. He'd confronted the assassin known as Lennon on a beach in Northern California, and Lennon had said a name that turned Jason's blood cold with fear.

Abbey Laurent.

Lennon knew about her. He knew who she was. He knew about Jason's relationship with her.

So when Lennon escaped, Bourne decided that he had to cut Abbey out of his life completely. Immediately. No delays, no farewells. He couldn't continue to put her in jeopardy, not when Lennon might decide at any moment to use her as leverage against him. Just like that, he shut her out. He stopped writing. He ignored her letters, hoping that she'd get the message to forget about him.

Don't you understand? I don't want to get you killed!

But ten months later, she was still sending him notes. The tone of her latest letter made it clear that she was getting angry and frustrated, running out of patience with his silence. That was good. He needed her to be angry. He needed her to *hate* him. Then she'd finally walk away, and she'd be safe.

Bourne took a cigarette lighter out of the pocket of his jacket. He put Abbey's note back in the envelope, and with a flick of the lighter, he set it ablaze. He held the envelope aloft until the flame burned down to his fingertips, and then he dropped it on the ground and kicked away the black fragments of ash.

"Goodbye, Abbey."

He looked up and saw Nash Rollins leaning on his cane with a crooked smile on his face. The white façade of Sacré-Cœur was framed behind him. The senior Treadstone agent made the smallest gesture with his hand, a signal to the nearest member of his support team to give them space. When they were alone, Nash came up to the railing and stood next to Bourne. He used his phone to take a picture of the imposing cathedral, as if he were nothing but a Paris tourist out for a stroll.

Nash was a small man, knocking on the door of sixty years old, with the weathered exterior of ripe fruit left out in the sun for too long. His wiry gray hair was combed back over his head. In his prime, he'd been a great field man, but now he was like a chess grandmaster pushing pieces around the board. He left the wet work to his younger agents. Bourne's relationship with Nash went back years, to a time long before a bullet had erased Jason's memory. As a result, he only trusted Nash so far, because he had no way of confirming that the things Nash told him about his history with Treadstone were true. They were more than colleagues, but less than friends. Even so, they needed each other.

"I was surprised to get your message, Jason," Nash told him. "In December, you said you were out."

"I'm still out."

"And yet here you are looking for my help."

"It's a project for our mutual benefit," Bourne said.

Nash turned around, facing the glow of Paris below them. "I hope you appreciate that I've kept my end of the bargain since then. No minders. No missions. We've left you alone. But I assumed you weren't looking for retirement on the Riviera."

"I'm not retired, but I do things my way now."

"That includes hunting Lennon?"

"Yes."

"Fair enough. We need the help. We're no further than we were before. And if you catch him?"

"I'll hand him over to you."

"After you squeeze him for information, you mean."

Bourne shrugged. "I want answers. Lennon claims to be part of my past."

He didn't add the rest: *He claims to be part of Treadstone.*

"Jason, I told you before that Lennon is playing with you," Nash said. "He's using your past as a weapon. That doesn't mean any of it's true."

Bourne said nothing.

There had been too much water under the bridge for him to take anything Nash told him on faith. In the end, the senior agent's loyalties were always to the shadowy people above him. If Bourne became a liability, if the government wanted him gone, Nash wouldn't hesitate to have him eliminated. He'd proven that more than once.

"However, I appreciate the update about Iceland," Nash went on. "I had an interesting time explaining to the minister of justice in Reykjavík why she shouldn't worry too much about a remote cottage being taken out by an explosive round fired from a helicopter. The police turned the investigation over to Interpol, but there wasn't much left to find."

"I think that location was Lennon's headquarters. He ran his European operations out of there. I'm not sure for how long, but regardless, now he's moved on. That means I'm almost back to square one."

"Almost," Nash said. "In other words, you want to find the woman."

"Yes. I sent you her photo. The blond woman I saw at the lava fields in Búðir was making a payoff. I'm sure she was just a cutout, but she was scared that she was going to be killed once she handed over the money. That tells me she knew who Lennon was and may know what the job was. Either way, if I can find her, I can follow the chain to the higher-ups and hopefully find my way back to Lennon again."

Nash was quiet for a while. He took a tin of hard candies from his pocket, selected one, and popped it in his mouth. His breath began to smell of butterscotch. "My help isn't free, Jason."

"Except you want Lennon as much as I do."

"In normal circumstances, I might say that's enough, but the situation has grown more complicated than that."

Bourne hesitated. He had reason to distrust Treadstone's hidden agendas, but in this case, he knew Nash was holding all the cards. He needed his help. "First things first. Did you find the woman?"

"I did."

"Okay. What's the price for her name?"

Nash had the smug look of the cat who'd snatched a bird out of the tree. "If Lennon has uprooted his base of operations, it may be because he's changed employers. He's working with a new client."

"Lennon always worked directly for Putin," Bourne pointed out. "It's hard to believe either one of them would walk away from that."

"I doubt that it's a permanent divorce, but for the time being, Putin is focusing his craziness elsewhere. He's got his hands full. So Lennon is on hiatus from the Russians. But like you, he's not retired. We believe he's developed new affiliations. The payoff you saw was probably part of that."

"Who is he working for?" Bourne asked.

Nash's face took on a dark cast. "That's the problem. We don't know. Whatever group it is, they have to be extremely well funded to afford the services of a pro like Lennon. And obviously, if they have an assassin on the payroll, it means they're engaged in wet work. Maybe it's another government. Maybe it's a terrorist organization. There's a lot of chatter, but nothing that specifically ties Lennon to anyone's plans and no indication of *who* they've used Lennon to hit. Up until now, our attempts to find a connection have come up empty."

"Until I found the woman," Bourne said.

"Yes. That's our first lead."

"So while I'm chasing this woman to Lennon, you want me to figure out who Lennon is working for."

"Exactly," Nash replied. "Quid pro quo, Jason."

Bourne shoved his hands in his jacket pockets. The evening air was cool on the Paris hilltop. He knew the smart thing to do was walk away. Tell Nash what he'd told him six months ago: *I'm out*. Find the woman some other way. But he didn't know how long that would take, and by the time he did, the trail to Lennon would be as cold as the Iceland glaciers.

He had no choice.

He had to say yes. No matter how he tried, he couldn't fully escape Treadstone's web. The agency always pulled him back in.

"All right, who is she?" Bourne asked.

Nash smiled, knowing he'd won. "Her name is Kenna Martin. Twenty-nine years old. She works as a publicist at the Forster Group in Manhattan."

"And you're sure it's her?"

"It's her," Nash told him. "Kenna's passport clicked at JFK five days ago. She cleared customs on her way back from Reykjavík on an Icelandair flight. Happy hunting, Jason."

4

KENNA MARTIN LIVED WELL. TOO WELL.

When Bourne arrived in New York two days later, he staked out the Chelsea high-rise in which the public relations agency called the Forster Group was located. At almost seven o'clock that night, he spotted Kenna leaving the building. She was dressed in a conservative gray pantsuit and had her long hair tied in a ponytail, but he had no trouble recognizing the willowy blond he'd first seen handing a leather daypack to Lennon on the Iceland coast.

He followed her uptown to the Upper East Side, where she lived in a six-floor condo building only four blocks from the park. When she was inside, he saw lights go on in a top-floor unit, and Kenna came to the windows with a glass of white wine in her hand. Zillow told him that she'd purchased the unit for nearly two million dollars one year earlier. That seemed an unlikely transaction for a twentysomething publicist, unless she had resources from somewhere else.

Less than half an hour after arriving home, Kenna left again. She hadn't changed out of her pantsuit, but she'd loosened her hair. He tracked her on foot to a brasserie called Orsay five minutes away on Lexington. Inside, she met three other women of similar age, and Bourne arranged to get a table that was close enough for him to hear their conversation. Listening to the women talk over the next hour and a half, he concluded that none of her friends knew anything about Kenna's double life. She made no mention of her overseas travel the previous week. As far as her friends were concerned, she'd been home sick in New York for several days, not in Iceland.

When the party broke up, Kenna returned to her condo, and she didn't leave again.

The next morning, Bourne waited outside the building on 79th until he saw Kenna leave for work. He assessed the building security and noted that there was no doorman, but that the condos worked on a key-lock elevator system unique to each unit. To defeat it, he'd need a sample of one of the keys. So he waited until another resident left the building, then followed the man and pocketed his wallet while he was waiting in line at a coffee shop. Using a Treadstone device about the size of a credit card attached to his phone, he read the data off the magnetic stripe on the man's keycard and reconfigured it into a master key that would give him access to any of the units in the building.

Half an hour later, Bourne let himself inside Kenna Martin's luxury condo.

Somewhere in this woman's life was a connection to Lennon. It might be in her business life, her personal life, her family, or boyfriend. To the outside world, she looked like one more single New York professional, a woman right out of *Sex and the City*. But Kenna had a big secret, and judging by the fear he'd seen on her face in Iceland, she was a pawn in this game, not a professional. She was in over her head, and that made her vulnerable.

Quickly, Bourne searched the apartment. He saw family photos on a digital frame that made her parents look middle class; they weren't the source of her money or connections. He found condoms in her nightstand, but saw nothing to suggest that she had a steady boyfriend. In her closet, he saw expensive dance-wear, and hidden inside the toilet tank in her bathroom, he also located a small supply of cocaine. Kenna liked to party.

Was that how she'd been recruited? Had Lennon found a vice or crime he could use to manipulate her?

Everyone has a weakness to exploit.

Treadstone.

He located her suitcase under her bed. She'd removed the airline bag tags, and she'd destroyed any papers related to where she'd stayed or how she'd traveled, but he found a single fifty-krónur coin at the bottom of one suitcase pocket that she'd missed. That seemed to be the only evidence left of her illicit trip to Iceland. Otherwise, the condominium was clean. The gold coin Lennon had given her was probably already in a safe-deposit box somewhere.

This was the home of Kenna Martin, publicist, not Kenna Martin, spy.

Before he left, Jason checked the condo living room and found a vase filled with multicolored stones on a high shelf near the outside windows. He secreted a miniature camera inside the vase and positioned it so that it was invisible unless someone physically climbed to the shelf and took the vase down. On his phone, he checked that the app was receiving video and audio from the camera. The battery would last for a few days.

Then Bourne left the building, dropping the wallet he'd stolen inside the elevator.

His next stop was at the tower on 26th where the Forster Group was located. He found a table at a Starbucks that gave him a view of the tower entrance, and as he watched the people coming and going, he did research on Kenna's employer. The Forster Group had been founded twenty years ago and was still owned and led by Darrell Forster. The man was a longtime *New York Times* reporter who'd traded in his journalism credentials at age forty for the more lucrative business of helping corporations and nonprofits manage their media reputations. He now led a team of more than one hundred communication specialists. That included Kenna Martin, but based on her website bio, she was a low-level publicist, not one of the firm's account managers.

A website summary of the agency's credentials also drew Bourne's attention. The Forster Group handled

projects for an eclectic range of clients, including Exxon,
Tesla, the Varak Foundation, and a Russian software giant called 4Bear. Bourne had heard of 4Bear. They were
cloaked in respectability, but they'd been rumored to be
the brains behind a series of recent hacks of U.S. government agencies. Scratch the surface, and that meant 4Bear
had ties to Vladimir Putin, and Putin in turn had ties to
Lennon.

He didn't know exactly how Kenna Martin had found
herself in the middle of the assassin's operations, but he
suspected that the connection originated with her employer.

Bourne watched the building all day. Once again,
Kenna left the office at seven o'clock. This time, she lin-
gered outside long enough to smoke a cigarette and de-
flect come-ons from a few men on the street. Then Jason
followed her back to her Upper East Side condo. After
she went inside, he returned to the room he'd booked at
the Carlyle Hotel three blocks away. There, he ordered
Chinese food and booted up his computer to observe
Kenna Martin at home.

She was attractive but not in an intimidating way. Her
smile still had a girl-next-door innocence. The blond hair
came out of a bottle, but she didn't hide the dark roots.
After she took a shower, she wandered back into the living room wearing only a lace bra and panties, and she
stretched out on the sofa to watch TV, drink wine and
eat popcorn, and snuggle with a stuffed koala bear. Her
body was skinny, her legs long and smooth. If this had
been a cheap apartment in Brooklyn, she would have

looked right at home, but this was a multimillion-dollar condo, and Kenna was up to her neck in death.

During the evening, he expected *something* to happen to give him a clue to her other life. A call on a separate phone, a conversation about a secret meeting. A delivery of papers, drugs, or information. Instead, the only thing that happened was a call from a girlfriend in which Kenna talked about a club in a Tribeca warehouse, where there was a party coming up the next night. She giggled in a high-pitched voice, sounding even younger than she was, and described the hot new outfit she was planning to wear.

That was all.

At midnight, Kenna turned off the television and the apartment lights and went to bed. She took the stuffed bear with her. Bourne stared at a black screen streaming from the camera and tried to get inside her head. This was a girl who compartmentalized her life. In Iceland, she'd looked terrified about meeting an assassin, but in this safe compartment, she was relaxed, happy, and normal.

If Bourne was going to get her to talk, that had to change. He needed Kenna Martin off-balance.

He needed her *scared*.

ON FRIDAY, BOURNE ARRIVED IN THE TRIBECA NEIGHBORHOOD at midnight. Far down the cobblestoned street, he could see the lights of Jersey City on the other side of the Hudson. The location of the club was a four-story redbrick building with high metal doors covered with graffiti. There was no sign to identify it, but a bass drumbeat thumped through dark windows on the other side of the walls.

Bourne stayed in the shadows of a loading dock doorway as he examined his surroundings. The street was quiet at this hour but not empty. He kept an eye on a man walking the sidewalk by himself; he was tall, with a dark buzz cut, but Bourne saw no weapons. There was a group of women hanging out at the corner with drinks in their hands. A homeless man huddled near a building wall. An old man walked a miniature schnauzer. When he was satisfied that there were no threats, he crossed the street and went inside.

The club was crowded, lit by whirls of red and white strobe lights mounted on the high ceiling. A mix of dance music played through speakers at a staggering volume. He pushed through the crowd of twenty- and thirtysomethings, keeping an eye out for Kenna Martin. Bourne knew she was here; he'd watched her dress and leave on the spy camera from his hotel. But one blond girl in the chaotic crowd was hard to find.

He went to the bar and ordered a shot of Teeling whiskey. Then he turned around and studied the faces. He wore a leather jacket and a tight black jean shirt, plus caramel-colored sunglasses hiding his eyes. Standing by himself, he got plenty of attention from the women coming to order drinks, and he deflected them with a tight smile.

There!

There she was.

Kenna danced with two other girls not far away. He recognized the outfit she'd worn, a glittering aquamarine dress that showed off her legs and made a deep V over her breasts. In her heels, she was taller than most of the other women here. Her blond hair flew as she spun ungracefully on the dance floor. Her face had a loose, happy smile, and Bourne suspected that she was already a little drunk and that she'd tapped into the supply of cocaine hidden in her toilet before leaving for the party.

His eyes never left her, and he didn't hide his interest. That was a deliberate move. He was sending the unmistakable club signal that she was the one he wanted. It didn't take long for that sensation of being watched to penetrate her mind. Kenna glanced at the bar, spotted him, then looked away without catching his eye. A few seconds later, she took another look, as if to confirm that he was really focused on her, not one of the dozens of other women dancing close by. At that point, her gaze found his with interested blue eyes. Her innocent smile turned smoky, and he smiled back at her. Then, playing hard to get, she ignored him for a while, but he saw her whispering to her friends, and they both checked him out, too. They obviously approved.

Ten minutes later, her face flushed from dancing, Kenna finally came up to the bar. She ordered white wine, but before she could take money from her purse, Bourne signaled to the bartender that he would pay for her drink. As she sipped it, her head swiveled to stare at him, and she gave a little toss of her blond hair.

Thanks.

She had to mouth the word. They couldn't hear each other in the tumult of the club. So she leaned close, her lips brushing his ear.

"I'm Kenna."

Bourne leaned in, too. "Payton."

"Nice to meet you, Payton." She fluttered her hand near her cheek, as if she could dispel the warmth of so many people pressed together. She didn't bother with small talk or games; the drink and drugs had made her direct. "It's hot in here. I was going to head up to the roof for some fresh air. Wanna join me?"

"Why not?"

"Good."

She took his hand. Her long fingernails grazed his palm. They navigated the crowd, then climbed three sets of metal stairs to the roof, where they found the heavy door propped open. Outside, cool air washed over them, and the Manhattan lights glowed in the taller buildings on every side. A few other couples had already made their way up here, but there were plenty of isolated spots. Kenna went to the edge of the railing that looked down at the street. She drank her wine, and Bourne sipped his whiskey.

"Let's get the awkward stuff out of the way," she told him.

She put a hand around his neck and kissed him slow and hard. Her lips moved sensually on his mouth; her tongue played with his. When she was done, she giggled. "I find doing that breaks the ice and saves time."

"Yes, it does," Bourne replied.

The girl leaned against the railing, looking pleased with herself. She closed her eyes dreamily as the wind mussed her hair.

"Kenna," he said.

"That's me."

"Kenna Martin. Publicist with the Forster Group. Lives in a two-million-dollar condo when she should be struggling to pay the rent on a basement apartment in Queens. Makes overseas money drops to professional assassins."

Kenna's eyes flew open with terror. *"Fuck!"*

She turned to get away, but Bourne grabbed her wrist and held her where she was. "We need to talk, Kenna."

"What do you want? I can scream. If I scream, people will come running."

"You don't need to scream. I'm not going to hurt you."

"Who *are* you? FBI?"

"The bigger question is, who are you, and what the hell are you involved in? I know about Iceland, Kenna. I was there. I saw you."

The wineglass fell from her hand and shattered on the stone rooftop. Kenna's hand flew to her mouth. "Oh, my God. Oh, my God, I'm going to die. They're going to kill me. What do you *want*?"

"I want you to tell me about the man in the lava fields."

"I don't know anything about him!" Kenna hissed. "I don't know who he is or what he does! I don't know what was in the pack! I gave it to him, that's all. All I do is make drops. That's it!"

"You're going to have to do better than that," Bourne told her. "I need to find that man, and you're going to help me."

5

ABBEY DIDN'T WANT TO CALL TOM BLOMBERG AT THE *WASH-ington Sentinel* until she had a real story. Conspiracy theories from a girl named Iris weren't enough to place an article in a national newspaper. But she'd been digging into the murder of Deborah Mueller for days, and she hadn't made much progress getting past the official explanation. With every search she ran, she bumped into an internet wall, which made her suspect that Iris was right. Somehow, the facts of the Mueller case were being suppressed online.

Why?

The lights in Abbey's studio apartment were off, so the bright glow of the screen strained her eyes. It was already well past midnight, but she did her best work during the nights. Sometimes she stayed home and wrote; sometimes she found an all-night bar and nursed a beer while she worked. She was a morning sleeper, typically not going to bed until three or four o'clock.

With a sigh of frustration, she put the laptop on the sofa next to her, then got up and poured a cup of coffee from the pot in her efficiency kitchen. No single-cup coffee makers for her. She drank cheap Folgers in staggering quantity. She took her coffee mug to the fifth-floor window and stared down at the small park below her. It was dark except for a single streetlight near the alley that ran behind the building. Her red hair was dirty; she could feel the grease as she pushed the bangs out of her eyes. She hadn't showered in two days as she pounded on the keyboard, but she'd finally switched clothes and underwear to freshen up. When she was close to a story, she couldn't think about anything else.

Focus! What are you missing?

Abbey went back to the sofa. She'd already filled up half a dozen yellow pads with notes, and so she went back to the beginning and reviewed all the research she'd gathered for the past week.

She started with the video. Iris had shown her the interview with the homeless woman in West Potomac Park, who claimed to have seen three killers converging on Deborah Mueller. Abbey had the video on her phone now, and she watched it again just to confirm that it was real. But other than that, the video didn't seem to exist anymore. She couldn't find it online, not on YouTube, not on Twitter, not on Facebook. Searches came back empty. And yet it *had* been there, because Iris had done screen captures of the video in multiple locations.

When Abbey checked, all of those links now came back dead.

But it wasn't just the video that had disappeared. So had the woman in the park.

Abbey had gone to West Potomac Park to locate the witness. Everyone knew her. Her name was Retha, and she'd spent most of her days and nights in the park for as long as anyone could remember. But shortly after the murder of Deborah Mueller, Retha had suddenly stopped showing up. Nobody knew where she'd gone. Abbey had checked other homeless encampments nearby—plus local hospitals—but Retha was a missing person.

A coincidence?

She didn't think so.

Then Abbey began to dig into the story of the killer. Again, things didn't add up. According to the DC police, a homeless addict by the name of Leon had stabbed Deborah Mueller multiple times in the chest, probably while under the influence of heroin. He'd died of an overdose in the park, with Deborah's purse in his hand. Open and shut. But when Abbey talked to the people who knew Leon, they'd all been shocked that he would have committed a crime like that. He'd never had a history of violence. His nickname in the park was the Gentle Giant.

None of which, Abbey knew, proved anything at all.

When she'd brought her suspicions to a friend on the DC police, he'd laughed at her. She couldn't entirely blame him. She had no evidence to prove that the murder of Deborah Mueller was anything other than what the police said it was.

So for the last two days in her apartment, Abbey had been investigating the next piece of the puzzle, which was Deborah Mueller herself. The victim. That was when things got even stranger, because as Abbey researched Deborah Mueller, she found herself unable to confirm *anything* about her.

She called up the picture of Deborah on her laptop, which was the passport photo everyone knew from news reports: the twenty-eight-year-old German woman with the long, narrow face, intense dark eyes, and oh-so-severe expression on her mouth. A very German-looking girl. Abbey could recite everything she knew about Deborah, because she'd seen the same facts on every news website: Deborah Mueller had lived in an apartment in a small town outside Berlin. She'd worked as an IT analyst for a software company. She was single, her parents were dead, she had no siblings. She'd talked for months about taking a vacation to America, only to become the latest victim of the country's urban violence.

That was the portrait of Deborah Mueller that had appeared over and over on U.S. news programs and online.

It was very specific, until you realized it was completely vague.

A small town outside Berlin. Which town? Abbey couldn't find a reference anywhere to the actual place where Deborah had lived.

IT analyst for a software company. Which company? What industry? Abbey didn't know. No one knew.

She'd searched for the name *Deborah Mueller* in Germany and found more than two hundred women with the same name. But none of the profiles on social media matched the passport photograph of Deborah Mueller, and she'd found no accounts where anyone had posted their regrets about the woman's death. It was as if she'd been murdered, but no one in her life had even noticed.

Neither had the German press. In Abbey's mind, a German tourist stabbed to death in Washington, DC, should have been front-page news. But the only articles she'd found in Berlin newspapers were translations of wire stories that had been taken from Reuters International. No one in the German media had bothered to take a deeper dive into the life and death of Deborah Mueller.

Why?

When Abbey reviewed online news reports about the crime, she noticed something else that was curious. The so-called facts about the life of Deborah Mueller all seemed to come from the same two German women. Interviews with those women had been rebroadcast and reposted by multiple news outlets. Ursula Hopf said she'd worked at the same software company with Deborah for two years; she called her colleague smart and serious, a good worker. Trudy Weiss said she'd lived in the same apartment building with Deborah for nearly five years, and it was such a shock to think that her good friend was dead.

Ursula Hopf. Trudy Weiss.

Two real German women who claimed to know Deborah Mueller.

But Abbey had spent an entire day tracking *them* online, and she couldn't find any evidence of who they were or where they lived. Deborah was a ghost, and so were Ursula and Trudy.

Insane!

"Who *are* you?" Abbey said to the photograph on her screen, but the somber picture of Deborah Mueller didn't reply.

She got up with her coffee and went to the window again. With her phone in her hand, she rewatched the banned video of the woman known as Retha. The more she watched it, the less she thought the woman was mentally ill. She was scared, yes, but not crazy. *There were three men. Three! Two of them wore creepy masks, and the third, he just took a knife and killed her!*

Abbey let that idea sink into her head.

What if it was true?

What if the woman in the park *hadn't* been killed by a homeless man? What if she'd been assassinated? Targeted by three killers. A professional hit. That was the only explanation for the scenario Retha described.

A mystery woman killed by mystery men.

As Abbey stood by the apartment window, her phone began ringing. She was surprised; usually, she was the only one who worked crazy hours. She went to the sofa and grabbed the phone and noticed that the caller ID reflected an unknown number. Probably spam. But Abbey answered it anyway.

"Abbey Laurent."

"Abbey, it's Mike Parisi with ICE."

She recognized his voice, but she was surprised, because Mike was already in her contact folder. He should have showed up as the caller. The fact that he didn't meant he was reaching out to her from a different phone, and that told her he didn't want a record of the call showing up anywhere.

"Did you get that information I was looking for?" Abbey asked.

The customs agent hesitated. "Yes and no."

"What does that mean?"

"Yes, I was able to access the manifests on incoming flights to DC from Germany from the night you mentioned."

"And?"

"And there's no Deborah Mueller."

Abbey loaded the passport photo on her laptop. Then she played the video Iris had given her of the taxi line at Reagan National. There was no mistaking that it was the same woman's face.

"Mike, I've got footage of her at the airport that night. She was killed a couple of hours later."

"I know that."

"So what the fuck?" Abbey asked.

"All I can tell you is that no one named Deborah Mueller came into the U.S. from Germany on a flight that night. And I'm not just talking about DC. There's no match on any inbound flights. I checked on the off chance she'd cleared customs somewhere else."

"What if she was using a different name? Were you able to match her photo to someone else?"

"I looked," Mike replied. "Her passport photo doesn't show up anywhere."

"How is that possible?"

She heard a long pause before he answered. Mike was a serious man, and she'd used him as a source for years, but for the first time in their relationship, he sounded nervous about talking to her. "Well, if she did fly in from overseas that night, then the computer data was altered. Somebody removed her record from the system. To do that, you'd have to have access at a pretty high level."

"As in?"

"As in CIA. State. NSA. This is the kind of thing that gets done for operatives under cover."

"You think Deborah Mueller was some kind of spy?" Abbey asked.

"I have no idea what she was," Mike told her. "As far as I can tell, Deborah Mueller doesn't exist at all."

6

BOURNE AND KENNA CROSSED TO THE GREENWAY ON THE
Hudson at Laight Street. The river was agitated in the
wind and had a salty ocean smell. Lights glowed on
the Jersey side of the water, and the brightness of One
World Trade Center dominated the skyline directly
ahead of them. A few late-night bicyclists and joggers
passed them on the trail. Bourne kept his leather jacket
hung over his right arm, covering the Sig that was in his
hand. His eyes moved constantly, watching the shadows.

"So who are you?" Kenna asked.

She hadn't said much since they'd left the club together. She'd avoided talking to her friends, who obviously suspected that she was on her way to a one-night
stand. Her blue leather coat was buttoned to her neck,
and she kept her arms tightly nestled together. She

bowed her head and looked down at the sidewalk as they walked.

"You're not a fed," she went on. "If you were, I'd already be under arrest."

"Who I am doesn't matter. What matters to me is finding Lennon."

Kenna shook her head. "I don't know who that is."

"You can do better than that. I was watching you in Iceland, Kenna. That man scared you. That tells me you know who he is and what he does."

"Not necessarily. I'm scared of *you*, but I don't know who you are."

"Drop the little-girl innocence. I'm not buying it. Lennon kills people. You were terrified he was going to kill you."

Her blue eyes flashed with a momentary defiance. "What about you? Do you kill people, too?"

He shifted his jacket and let her see the gun. "Yes."

Kenna paled. Her makeup had run where she'd been crying. She veered to the railing at the water, and her knees buckled. He thought she might throw up. "Fuck all of this," she whispered. "I can't believe it's gone this far. I never wanted any of this. Just shoot me if you want. You're going to do it anyway."

"I told you, I'm not going to hurt you. But I need your help."

"And I told you, I don't know *anything*! That's deliberate. Don't you get it? They want me in the dark, so that when someone like you comes along, I don't have anything to give you. You called the man Lennon. That means nothing to me. Was I afraid of him? Yes. One look at that smile of his, and I was practically peeing myself. Believe me, I don't need to be a fucking spy to know what a killer looks like. But I don't know anything about him, or what he did, or how to find him."

Bourne sighed. He realized that Kenna wasn't lying. Underneath the games they'd forced her to play, she was still an amateur. They'd taken a sweet girl and manipulated her into being a courier.

"How did it start?" he asked.

"Why do you care? What difference does it make?"

"Because the more I know about what they did to you, the better chance I have of finding a connection to Lennon."

Kenna shrugged. "It was my fault. I fucked up."

"How?"

"I started at the Forster Group fresh out of grad school five years ago. Master's in journalism from Columbia. Darrell recruited me himself. He said they were looking for activist communicators, people who wanted to make a difference. That was me. I mean, working in New York right out of school, with a job at one of the top agencies in the country? I thought I was pretty hot shit."

"What happened?"

"Darrell sent me on a pro bono assignment to Minnesota. We were representing Native groups and environmental activists trying to stop a pipeline. I asked him about tactics, and he said not to waste his time talking to him about specific plans. My job was to *stop the pipeline*. He told me to get it done."

"And did you?"

"No. We lost. But a couple of the protesters who were really on the fringe wanted to stage a false flag incident. Create an accident that could be blamed on the construction company, and use that to halt the project. I was young and stupid, and Darrell said my job was to do whatever was necessary to stop the pipeline. So I helped them. They wanted to make it look like a propane explosion breached the line. Except it went wrong. They blew themselves up instead. Man and a woman, both dead."

"What happened to you?"

Kenna laughed sourly. "Nothing. My role in it never came out. I mean, I figured I was done. Prison for twenty years. Instead, I walked away free as a bird. Two people dead, and me, I got a bonus for getting the protests covered on *60 Minutes*. Darrell said I had a great future at the agency."

Bourne held up his hand to stop her. He heard something from the trees near the greenway. His finger slid onto the trigger of his Sig. He took a few steps away from the water, watching for movement in the shadows. Nothing caught his eye, and yet the sound recurred, a stifled whimper, like a dog being restrained.

He returned to the river, where Kenna breathed loudly and nervously. Her pretty nose had begun to run. "What is it?"

"Maybe nothing. I'm not sure."

"Sometimes I feel like people watch me," she said. "Is that paranoid?"

Jason wanted to laugh. This girl was paying off professional killers, and she wondered if she was crazy to think people were spying on her. "No, it's not paranoid. But go on. Quickly. What happened next?"

"Two years ago, they reached out to me."

"'They'?"

She shrugged. "Whoever they are. I don't know."

"What happened?"

"I was living in a cheap apartment in Newark. I came home and found somebody had broken in. They left an envelope for me. Documents, photos, screenshots of texts and emails between me and the pipeline protesters. It was everything the police needed to arrest me for murder. And there was a number for me to call. Believe me, I called."

Bourne shook his head. "A deal with the devil."

"Yeah. I have no idea who I talked to. Some man with a smooth voice. He sounded a lot older. He said I had a choice. Say yes, and I'd have plenty of money, and they'd buy me a nice condo in the city, and all I would have to do is make anonymous deliveries for them from time to time. Say no, and I'd be spending the next few years of my life in a federal prison. I didn't have to think about it. I said yes."

"How does it work?" Bourne asked.

Kenna opened her purse and produced a gold key about two inches long. "You know those Pop'n Drop stores around the city? They're like PO boxes for documents and packages. Open twenty-four/seven. They gave me this key. Every few days, I get a phone call, a wrong number, spam call, whatever. The caller gives me a code for which location to visit. The box number is always the same. One fifty-six. That box matches my key. As soon as I get the call, I go to the store, open the box, and there's an envelope waiting for me, plus a location and time. I go to the rendezvous, and somebody meets me. I give them the envelope, no questions asked. That's all I do."

"Is it the same person who meets you?"

"No. Never. They're always different."

"Have you ever opened the envelopes?"

"They're sealed. If I open it, they'll know. They made it clear that if I ever opened an envelope, that was the end of the arrangement and the end of me. I was pretty sure they weren't talking about prison at that point. They'd kill me."

"And you make these deliveries regularly?"

"Yes. Several times a month."

Bourne processed the strategy in his head. It was a standard cutout arrangement, using a go-between who had no knowledge of the sender or the recipient. If Kenna was discovered by anyone, she couldn't expose any part of the operation. On the other hand, the volume of deliveries didn't sound like it originated with Lennon. His involvement appeared to be the exception rather than the rule. That meant this scheme was likely being run by whoever had hired Lennon.

Hired him to *kill*, which was what Lennon did. But kill who?

"What about Iceland?" Bourne asked. "Was that a typical drop?"

Kenna shook her head. "No! I've never had to do

anything like that before. That's why I was so scared. I got the daypack, plus first-class airline tickets to Reykjavík and hotel and rental car reservations. There was a note explaining exactly what I had to do. The first time I laid eyes on this Lennon was when I met him at the lava fields. Don't you see? I can't help you!"

"Just keep talking. Do you have any idea who's behind this?"

The girl pushed up the sleeve of her coat. "The only thing I know about them is that they made me get this."

In the glow of the city lights, Bourne saw a small tattoo on the girl's inner arm, done in purple ink. He recognized the Eye of Providence from the top of the pyramid on the back of the U.S. dollar bill. But the triangle was upside down, the long base at the top.

"What does it mean?" he asked.

"I have no idea."

"Have you ever seen anyone else with it?"

Kenna shook her head. "No."

Bourne felt frustrated; the people behind this operation had covered their tracks well. "What about the drops? The materials they give you? Have you ever seen the person who places the envelopes in the boxes for you?"

She flushed and didn't answer immediately.

"Don't hold out on me, Kenna."

The girl chewed her lip nervously. "Yes, once. I got there, and the box was empty. Then as I was leaving, a bicycle messenger showed up. He went to my box, and he saw me watching him. We both knew the score. He was as scared as I was, like he thought he was fucked because he was late."

"Had you ever seen him before?"

"No. I don't even know what he actually looked like. I avoided looking too closely, you know? He had a helmet, bicycle shorts, sunglasses, the usual nightmare. Maybe a beard, but I'm not even sure about that. The thing is—"

Bourne gave her a cold stare. "The thing is?"

"He made a mistake."

"What kind of mistake?"

"He left something extra in the box. An envelope for somebody else, not me. It was sort of stuck to the back of my envelope, and he was in a hurry and didn't notice. I didn't open the box until he was gone, so I couldn't give it back to him."

"Who was the other envelope for?"

"I don't remember," Kenna replied. "When I got home, I burned it. I didn't even open it. I didn't want anyone to know I had it. It looked innocent enough, but I wasn't taking any chances."

"Do you remember *anything* about it?"

She nodded. "It came from a travel agency in the Bowery called Wolf Man Travel. Their logo has a wolf man on it, so it caught my eye. But for all I know, the travel agency has nothing to do with the people behind this. The messenger probably picked up deliveries from lots of different places."

Bourne frowned.

Was the travel agency part of the network? Maybe yes,

maybe no. *Wolf Man Travel.* But he had other priorities to check out first. He thought about Darrell Forster and the Forster Group and the client project roster he'd found for them online: 4Bear. A Russian software developer with ties to Putin, who had launched Lennon's career as an assassin.

Always follow the money.

Treadstone.

"Tell me about Darrell Forster."

Kenna's brow creased. "Why?"

Bourne wanted to shake the naivete out of this girl. "Because the odds are, he's the one who set you up."

"What? Darrell? No, that's crazy."

"Kenna, he recruited you himself. He sent you on that assignment in Minnesota. You think all of that happened by accident? He was looking to recruit a pawn for whatever operation he's running, and you fit the bill. An eager, idealistic young Columbia grad. He runs it all at arm's length, but he's been playing you since the beginning."

Her eyes widened, and she looked genuinely stunned. The idea that her boss was the mystery man behind the extortion had never occurred to her. "I can't believe that Darrell—"

"Believe it. Now tell me about him."

"He's a great man," Kenna protested. "No way he'd be involved in anything illegal. He was a *Times* reporter for years. I studied some of his journalism exposés at Columbia. The reason his agency is so successful is because of his reputation for integrity, for lack of bias. That new fact-finding institute? The one started by the Varak Foundation? Darrell is the chair. How often can you get the tech companies, the media companies, and the politicians to agree on anything? But they all said Darrell was the perfect choice."

Bourne was focused on Forster, but the other name that Kenna had given him suddenly made him pause. Darrell Forster's agency represented the Varak Foundation. He'd seen it on the client roster, too, but he'd glossed over it when he spotted 4Bear and made the connection to Putin.

Varak!

A billionaire investor who'd become one of the richest men on the planet. He'd established a charitable foundation that had more financial assets than most countries. There were only a handful of individuals who had the resources to hire someone like Lennon, but Varak was definitely one of them.

Varak, whose up-from-nothing personal story was legendary. He'd begun his online investment career thirty years earlier out of a barn on his parents' farm . . . in rural *Iceland.*

"I need to talk to Forster," Bourne said.

"Well, he's in town, but his schedule is always booked up weeks in advance."

"He'll see me. Talk to him tomorrow, and tell him I approached you. Say my name is Payton Griggs, and I told you I was an investigator working for the Senate Republicans. I was looking to get information out of you about the agency's representation of 4Bear. You'll look like a good soldier for telling him. Trust me, he'll put me on his calendar when I call."

Kenna hesitated. "Okay."

"If you see me in the office, look at me like you hate my guts."

"Trust me, that won't be hard."

Bourne ignored the girl's spark of defiance. Then he spun around, gun in hand, because he heard another noise from the shadows. It was the sharp yelp of a small dog, like a terrier or schnauzer. He wandered from the water, and now he saw the silhouette of a man hurrying away from the park, crossing at the light toward the city.

A man with a dog.

He'd seen a man with a miniature schnauzer outside the Tribeca club. Was it the same man? Were they being followed? It was too dark to be sure. A late-night dog walker in the city was common enough.

And yet.

Bourne heard Kenna coming up behind him. He turned around and surprised her by taking her chin between his fingers and squeezing hard. The girl's eyes widened with a new wave of fear, but he couldn't help that. He needed her to stay scared. Fear was the only thing that would keep her functioning, and she was right to be afraid. The bill for her sins was coming due.

"Listen carefully," he told her. "I'm going to give you a cell phone number. Memorize it, don't write it down. The next time you get a call about making a drop, call that number immediately. I'll follow you, and then I'll follow whoever is there to meet you. If you want to stay alive, *don't tell anyone*. Remember, I'll be watching you, Kenna."

THE WOMAN IN THE STOLEN F-150 CLIMBED DOWN FROM BE-hind the wheel of the truck to the street. She examined the houses in the quiet Friendship Heights neighborhood to make sure that no one had heard the thud of the collision or the brief cry of the victim. It was late, and no lights came on in any of the windows. The street was empty of traffic.

She walked behind the truck to where the twenty-year-old girl named Iris lay half on the pavement, half on the grass near the curb. She'd hit her at full speed, and the impact had tossed her like a doll, so she assumed the girl would be dead. But you could never be sure. A pro always checked before leaving the scene.

The woman squatted over her. The girl's eyes were closed, and blood pooled darkly in the green grass under her head. Ribbons of it smeared her buzzed black hair, and her round glasses lay broken in the street a few feet away. With a gloved hand, the woman checked for a pulse and found none.

Mission complete.

She walked back to the pickup truck. As she did, her phone began ringing. It was the second of her burner phones. *His* phone.

"Yoko," Lennon said when she answered.

"The job here is done," she told him. She spoke English, but her Catalan roots were in her voice.

"Excellent work, as always."

She reviewed the neighborhood one last time for witnesses, then got back behind the wheel of the truck and drove away at a calm speed. She put the call on speaker, enjoying the sound of Lennon's voice. It always excited her to hear that honey smoothness, and she felt arousal between her legs. Maybe tonight he'd come to her. She never knew when he would arrive. She always left the lights off in her hotel room in case he showed up in the middle of the night for sex.

But it was not to be. Not tonight.

"I have a new assignment for you," Lennon went on.

"Of course."

"You need to get to New York right away."

"Okay, I'll take the train in the morning," Yoko replied. "Will that be fast enough? Or should I drive there tonight?"

"Tomorrow is fine. Then await instructions."

"I will. What's going on?"

"*Cain* is back," Lennon told her, drawing out the name like it was fine wine on his lips. "He's still on the hunt. We need to act before he gets any closer."

7

TOM BLOMBERG OF THE *WASHINGTON SENTINEL* SAT ACROSS
from Abbey and poured sriracha ketchup over his scrambled eggs. He was a heavyset man in his early fifties, but
he looked older. He kept his stringy dark hair long
enough to cover his ears, where it began to curl upward
in small ringlets. Dark crescent moons hung in pouches
under his sunken eyes, and his face had the bloodshot
look of someone who'd spent too much time drinking
scotch and smoking cigarettes. In other words, he joked,
he was a newspaperman.

"Where's my piece on the mayor?" he asked between
bites of eggs, which he washed down with a Bloody
Mary. "You owe me three thousand words, Abigail, and
that was two weeks ago."

He always called her Abigail. Abbey wasn't short for
anything other than Abbey, but Tom had started calling

her Abigail shortly after they met. After correcting him a few times, she'd given up and let him keep doing it.

"Well, about that," she said.

She took a spoonful of her Greek yogurt bowl. They sat at an outdoor table at Bistro Bis, a restaurant at the George Hotel on E Street. The location was within a couple blocks of the Capitol, and Tom always wanted to sit outside to see which politicians passed by so he could take note of who was talking to whom.

"The mayor won't return my calls," Abbey went on. "The word must have gone out to his staff, too, because they're freezing me out."

Tom chewed on a piece of crisp bacon. It was early, and as the morning sun came from behind the clouds, he whipped out a pair of sunglasses and put them on. "Naturally. He's still pissed about that piece you did for Politico on the council's push to give the vote to sixteen-year-olds."

"It was a funny piece."

"You made them look like idiots," Tom said.

"Well, that doesn't take much work," Abbey replied. "Anyway, I don't *need* an interview with him to do the piece, but what's the point if I can't get one? This thing needs his voice. I hate to give it up, but I think you should hand it off to someone else."

"You mean, start over on a project that's already late? I don't like that."

"I know, but I can give a new writer all of my other research to get them up to speed."

Tom tapped a thick finger thoughtfully on the table.

He knew Abbey well enough to know there was more to her request than she'd admitted. They'd met years earlier when she was a journalism student at McGill. Tom had guest-lectured in Walden Thatcher's senior symposium shortly after winning his first Pulitzer, and Walden had insisted on introducing Tom to his star student. They'd clicked as friends, the chain-smoking senior reporter and the college writer bent on exposing political corruption. Tom was the kind of reporter Abbey wanted to be, and he'd served as a mentor to her more than once during her career. When she'd left the online magazine *The Fort* two years earlier, Tom had given her freelance assignments that helped build her name in the closed world of Washington media.

"What is this really about, Abigail?" he asked.

Abbey glanced at the other outside tables, which were all full. She recognized most of the people; this was a Capitol Hill power place. There were other reporters nearby, too, so she leaned forward and lowered her voice. "I want to pursue a different story."

"Ah. And what is that?"

"The Deborah Mueller murder."

Tom took off his sunglasses. His heavy eyelids narrowed. "Deborah Mueller? The woman in West Potomac Park?"

"Yes."

"I don't see any interesting feature angle there. Urban crime has been done to death."

"It's not about that."

Abbey took a breath. Either she believed in this story

or she didn't, but she knew she was crossing a line that could make or break her career. It was one thing to play around with conspiracy theories on her laptop in the middle of the night. It was another to pitch the story to a senior editor at one of the country's leading newspapers. But she did it anyway. In five minutes, she sketched out the story for him. The missing witness, the suppressed video, the interviews with two German women who didn't even seem to be real people, and the enigma of Deborah Mueller herself.

"I don't have all the answers yet," Abbey told him, "but I have a lot of questions. What do you think?"

Tom went back to his spicy eggs without saying anything. She waited impatiently for his reply, but he took his time. A couple of minutes later, he finally put down his fork and took another long drink of his Bloody Mary. He opened his mouth to say something, but before he did, his eyes drifted over her shoulder.

"Senator," he suddenly announced in a loud voice. "Good morning."

Abbey glanced at the sidewalk. She recognized Sadie Adamson, the junior senator from Georgia, who'd won a special election the previous year. She was a former mayor of Atlanta, which put her to the far left of just about everyone in an increasingly purple state. But her opponent, a moderate Republican cop, had self-destructed during the race. Since the election, Adamson had established a reputation as a progressive powerhouse in a closely divided Senate.

Adamson was in deep conversation with an aide, but

she stopped outside the restaurant when she heard Tom calling to her. She was a petite Black woman with short, curly hair, and she wore a burgundy dress with navy blue stripes.

"Tom," she said pleasantly. "It's good to see you. Nice piece on modular nuclear reactors this morning. Wrong, totally misguided, and deeply irresponsible, but very nice."

A smile creased Tom's face. "I do what I can."

Then the editor gestured at Abbey. "Senator, do you know Abbey Laurent? She's one of the top feature writers in the city."

Abbey noted that Tom used her correct name. He'd always known what it was; he just liked tweaking her by calling her Abigail.

The senator studied her with smart dark eyes. "A pleasure, Ms. Laurent. If Tom says you're good, I consider that high praise, despite his tendency to print warmed-over puff pieces that I'm saving for the next toilet paper shortage."

She winked at Blomberg, who chuckled.

"Do you happen to have a card?" Adamson asked Abbey. "I like to keep a close eye on writers in DC. Sooner or later, they all seem to write about me."

"I do," Abbey replied, digging in her purse and handing the senator a business card.

"Excellent. Well, Tom, I'm sure I'll see you later."

"Goodbye, Senator."

Adamson disappeared toward Capitol Street with her aide in tow. When she was gone, Abbey lifted her glass of orange juice toward Tom in a toast. "Thank you for the introduction. And the kind words."

"I meant what I said. You're one of the best. Walden told me about your potential all the way back at McGill, and he was right." Then Tom leaned back in his chair, and his eyes turned unhappy. "That's why I don't like to see you wasting my time and yours chasing bullshit stories."

"Tom, this isn't—"

He cut her off with a wave of his hand. "Hang on. Listen to me. Sadie Adamson is smart and tough, whether or not you agree with her politics. You know why she's in the Senate? Because reporters in Georgia didn't take her opponent at face value. Because they dug into his background and realized he was a hard-core white supremacist. They found people who'd seen how he treated suspects as a cop. The story exploded all over the state, and he was forced out of the race."

"He was forced out because a fire broke out during the protests," Abbey pointed out. "Nine people died."

"Yes, I'm aware of the tragedy. The point is, that story began with reporters doing their job. Pursuing the truth. Asking hard questions. *Not* running after fringe con- spiracy theories."

"Tom, all my instincts tell me there's more to this murder than what's come out in the press so far."

He shook his head. "Who's your source? Where did you get this?"

"A woman approached me," Abbey replied, hesitating because she knew how it sounded. "She's part of an on- line group—"

"Oh, for fuck's sake, Abigail," he interrupted her. "An online fringe group? Conspiracy nuts? Are you kidding?"

"Everything she told me checks out," Abbey protested. "Didn't you hear what I said? I've got a source at ICE who can't even confirm that this woman Deborah Mueller exists. So who the hell got killed in that park?"

Tom pushed away his plate. "I'm disappointed in you. You know the old saying, right? When you hear hoofbeats, think horses, not zebras. If you get a reputation for going after too many zebras as a reporter, you lose your credibility. I don't want to see that happen to you, Abbey. You're too good for that. If you respect me and respect my advice, you'll drop this. Do the piece I gave you. Get the mayor to talk to you, even if he hates your guts. That's what it means to be a journalist."

Abbey felt as if she'd walked into the crosscurrents of a hurricane. She'd never heard Tom talk to her like that, and she felt a sting of humiliation and embarrassment. "Look, I understand what you're saying. It's just that—"

Tom didn't listen. He took out his wallet and slapped a bill on the table. "Finish your breakfast. I have to go. I'll give you one more week to get me the profile. Get it done, or I can't send anything else your way in the future."

He got up from his chair and walked away, leaving Abbey alone.

WHEN TOM BLOMBERG REACHED THE PARK ACROSS FROM THE Capitol's white dome, he saw Sadie Adamson sitting by herself on a bench underneath the trees. Her aide was gone. None of the handful of tourists in the park seemed to realize they were sharing the space with a United States senator. Adamson had her phone in one hand, and she sipped a cup of coffee with the other. She didn't look up as Tom sat down next to her, but she spoke to him under her breath.

"So she's the one?" Adamson asked.

"Yes."

"Pretty. And you're right, she's obviously smart. You can tell by the eyes."

"She's very smart."

"Did she mention the Mueller incident?"

"Yes, she did. She's already gone pretty far in her research. Abbey doesn't miss much. She knows that Deborah Mueller was a false identity. She even figured out that the Germans we used to establish Mueller's background were both plants."

"Does she know who Louisa really was?"

"No. Not yet."

"Well, did you shut her down?"

Tom hesitated. "I'm not sure. I made it clear that if she pursued it, her work for me would dry up. That's an incentive, because she doesn't have a lot of money. But I've known her a long time. She's stubborn. When someone tells her there's no story, she works even harder to find it."

"Her original source has been dealt with," the senator told him. "There won't be any more leaks there."

"And Abbey?"

"I'll call Varak," Adamson said. "He'll take the appropriate steps."

Tom stood up from the bench. His face was pained. "Is that absolutely necessary?"

The senator gave him an exasperated look from over the rim of her coffee cup. "Would you rather she find out about the Pyramid? Or about the bot farm in Frankfurt?" Adamson paused. "Or the truth about the fire?"

"Of course not. God, of course not!"

"Then don't worry about things above your pay grade, Tom. Varak will deal with Abbey Laurent."

8

"MR. GRIGGS, IS IT?" DARRELL FORSTER ASKED AS BOURNE was shown into the top-floor office in the Chelsea tower.

"That's right."

"Well, have a seat, won't you? Would you like a drink?"

"No. Thank you."

Bourne took a chair in front of the man's high-tech desk. There were no drawers, no shelves, just aluminum and glass. Behind Forster, floor-to-ceiling windows overlooked the crowded chessboard of the New York skyline, including the Empire State Building rising over the smaller buildings like the king. On the other wall of the office, he noted memorabilia from Forster's long media career, including photographs with a variety of public figures—some Jason knew, some he didn't—and framed copies of front-page *Times* articles that included stories written by Forster.

The man himself was small and thin, sixty years old, with wavy black-gray hair and a snow-white goatee. He had a head that narrowed to a sharp V at his chin and eyes that were like slits under perfectly straight brows. His skin was blotchy, with an oddly artificial tan. Rather than a suit like Bourne was wearing, Forster had chosen the casual CEO's outfit, with a knit blue sweater and khakis. The key to looking like a millionaire these days was not to look like a millionaire at all.

"I understand you've been talking to members of my team," Forster told him. "Asking questions about me and my agency. Kenna Martin called you a spy, in fact. She was very upset."

Bourne shrugged. "I'm just an investigator."

"Well, no offense, Mr. Griggs, but if you want information about my agency, I'd rather you talk to me. I don't like seeing my junior staff put in an uncomfortable position."

"I find that chief executives tend to be more forthcoming if they know I've done my homework."

"Fair enough. Well, here I am." Forster leaned forward and steepled his fingers on the desk. "Payton Griggs. You told Kenna that you work for a committee of Senate Republicans, but strangely, I find no record of you, and none of my contacts in the Senate seem to know who you are. You see, I do my homework, too. Which forces me to ask who you really are and what you're doing here."

Bourne got up from the chair and went to the office windows, where he looked down at the expanse of the city. "You're right. My name isn't Payton Griggs, but that doesn't matter for this conversation. I don't work for the Senate, either. That was a lie for Ms. Martin's sake. I represent certain other clients who want your help."

A little smile creased Forster's face. He was a rich professional and not easily intimidated. "And who might they be?"

"For now, that's my concern, not yours."

"All right. Well, we deal with anonymous requests for proposal all the time. I'm sure you'll find our credentials stack up against any other PR firm you may be considering, particularly if it's media help you want. Are your clients looking for communications advice? Reputation consulting? Crisis management?"

With his back to Forster, Bourne said, "My clients have a problem that needs to be eliminated."

"What kind of problem?"

Bourne came back to the desk and sat down again. "Our understanding is that you can put us in touch with someone who can provide the kind of assistance we require."

For the first time, he saw a hint of anxiety on Forster's face. The man's smirk disappeared behind his goatee. "I'm afraid you'll need to be clearer with me, Mr. Griggs. Exactly what assistance do your clients require?"

"They want to hire someone."

"Who?"

"A man named Lennon."

Forster was cool. His narrow eyes squeezed to the point of closing, but other than that, his face showed no reaction. He didn't say anything right away, but Bourne could see the man calculating his options and gauging the risks of whatever he said next. It had been a gamble to mention Lennon's name, but the gamble had paid off. Bourne's instincts had been correct. Forster was connected to whatever was going on.

"I'm sorry, a man named Lennon?" Forster asked, playing the game he had to play. "I don't know who that is."

Bourne shifted in the chair, moving his suit coat just enough so that Forster could see the grip of his Sig Sauer jutting from the holster. The CEO didn't miss it, and the man's aging skin got a little paler. Forster dealt in death, but he didn't like to get his hands dirty.

Violence is a weapon, but so is the fear of violence.

Treadstone.

"Lennon is a problem solver," Bourne replied, "but let's not pretend, Mr. Forster. You know what he does."

"Actually, you have me at a loss."

"You've done work for 4Bear. Any CEO who accepts a project from 4Bear knows they're dealing with Putin in the shadows. That means with a phone call or two, you can also reach out to Lennon. That's the help we're looking for, Mr. Forster. A simple connection. Obviously, you'll be paid handsomely for serving as an intermediary."

Forster stood up. "I'm sorry, but this meeting is over, Mr. Griggs. Tell your clients we're unable to offer them our services. The work we did for 4Bear was in connection with import sanctions and had nothing to do with the Russian government. I have no idea who this Lennon is, or what he does, or how to reach him."

Bourne stayed in the chair. He played his next card. Either it would be an ace or a joker. "Then let's talk about Varak."

Forster stiffened like a corpse, and Bourne thought: *Ace.*

"What about him?"

"He's the reason we came to *you*, Mr. Forster. Not just because of 4Bear. We know you put Varak in touch with Lennon. The *why* of it doesn't concern us. We're just asking for similar consideration."

Forster breathed heavily, unable to hide the impact of that latest assault. Jason could see him looking for an escape, for a way out. The CEO wanted Bourne out of the office. He needed time to think, to make calls, to broadcast an emergency.

A man is here! He knows! God help us, he knows!

"I chair the fact-finding institute for the Varak Foundation," Forster replied, trying to keep his voice steady. "That's the extent of our relationship."

"We hear otherwise."

"Well, whatever you hear, you're mistaken. And if you won't take my word for it, perhaps there's someone else you'll listen to." Forster leaned forward and tapped a button on his office phone. When his secretary answered, he said, "Would you see if Dr. Kohli can join us right away?"

Not long after that, the office door opened behind them, and an attractive woman in her mid-forties came inside. She was Indian, with coffee-colored skin and brown hair that came down as low as her chin. She had intense dark eyes and a friendly but wary smile. Her frame was medium height and very skinny, almost gaunt, and she wore a striped untucked blouse over black slacks and heels.

"Mr. Griggs, this is Saira Kohli," Forster said, using a forced casualness. "As you probably know, she's one of the world's leading epidemiologists and currently a professor at Georgetown. Last year, she was awarded the UNESCO Peace Prize for her work on global vaccine equity."

Bourne stood up and extended his hand. He did, in fact, know Saira Kohli by reputation, and he was surprised to see her in Forster's company. No doubt that was the CEO's whole point—to let him know who he was challenging.

"Saira, this is Payton Griggs, who's vetting our agency as a fit for his clients," Forster went on. "Unfortunately, he and his colleagues seem to be laboring under a mistaken idea regarding our relationship with Varak. I wonder if you could fill him in about the true work of the commission."

Saira cocked her head with a little bit of confusion. She looked back and forth between Forster and Bourne and obviously sensed an odd subtext in the conversation. "Well, of course. Darrell and I are both members of the media institute that Varak set up last year. Darrell's involvement is because of his journalism and communications experience, and mine is on the medical and scientific side. There are hundreds of other participants in various

industries around the globe. Our goal is to combat misinformation and disinformation."

"With censorship?" Bourne asked.

"No, with facts," she replied in a calm voice. "That's
why we've recruited so many scientists and researchers,
to present the best thinking about complex issues. Then
we work in partnership with the tech industry and the
print and broadcast media to amplify facts over specula-
tion and lies. When questions arise, we put journalists in
touch with professionals who are subject matter experts
in the appropriate field. As a result, we hope that what
the ordinary person sees online or in the media is closer
to the truth and less influenced by rumors and unscien-
tific nonsense."

"And Varak? What's his role in all of this?"

Saira shrugged. "He funds the institute through his
foundation. That's how we pay for everything, including
the services of our members. Other than that, he's really
not an active part of the day-to-day operations."

Forster put a hand on Bourne's shoulder. He looked
more relaxed again, as if convinced that he'd regained the
upper hand. "So you see, Mr. Griggs, I'm afraid that
you've come here on a wild-goose chase. I hope you'll go
back and tell your clients that they need to look elsewhere for whatever it is they want. Now, if you don't
mind, I'll ask you to leave. I have to take Dr. Kohli to the
airport."

"Thank you for your time," Bourne replied. He nodded at Saira. "It was a pleasure to meet you."

She smiled back at him, but she seemed to be looking

for answers in his eyes. Bourne got the impression that whatever Forster was doing with Varak, Saira Kohli wasn't on the inside. She was the public face, the impartial scientist that everyone trusted. The real work went on behind the scenes.

He left the two of them in the office.

He hadn't expected to get the truth from Forster, but he'd accomplished his mission anyway. He'd sent a message, and that message would be passed up the chain. Now they knew there was a crack in the wall. The alarm would be sounded.

This man knows about Varak and Lennon! He must be stopped!

9

SAIRA KOHLI STARED OUT THE REAR WINDOW OF THE LIMOU-
sine as the traffic on 36th Street crawled toward the Mid-
town Tunnel. She checked her watch, impatient about
getting to LaGuardia in time for her flight. There were
always later departures to DC, but she had a speech
scheduled that evening to a pharmaceutical convention
at the Mayflower, and once the airport got backed up,
she could spend hours sitting on the taxiway.

Beside her, Darrell Forster looked agitated. She couldn't
remember a time when she'd seen him like that. His
smile had melted away as soon as the stranger left the
office, and since then, his blue eyes had been lost in concentration. He'd said nothing as the two of them left the
building together.

"So who was that man?" Saira asked.

Her voice had a precise, delicate quality, which mirrored

her fragile appearance. People sometimes made the mistake of thinking she was weak, but Saira had a toughness that was not to be underestimated.

Forster's head swiveled. He stared at her with surprise, as if he'd forgotten she was there. "No one to concern yourself with."

"He was asking about Varak. Why?"

"He was simply fishing for information. He knew nothing."

"Still, if someone is investigating the institute? Perhaps we should find out if others have been contacted."

"He knew *nothing*!" Forster insisted.

"Yes, all right. If you say so."

Saira frowned and returned her attention to the streets as the limo inched forward. She had to come to New York often, but in truth, she disliked cities. The noise, crowds, smells, and crime gave her too many memories of her childhood. She'd grown up in the teeming squalor of Mumbai—far worse than anything in New York—but she'd used her intellect and work ethic to fight her way out of the slums. Eventually, as a scientist, she'd escaped to the rarefied world of American academia. Now, even though her research still took her around the world for months at a time, she preferred the serene grounds of the Georgetown campus. She could be by herself in her office. Read. Think. Listen to classical music. Put the hunger and disease of her childhood far behind her.

Disease.

Her whole life had been about the ravages of disease, from then until now.

A malaria epidemic had taken three of her siblings when she was ten years old. She could remember sitting by their shared bed, watching in horror as they died, their little bodies racked by seizures. That was what had set her on the course to become an epidemiologist, to study how diseases spread among people, and most of all, to promote a world in which the cures for deadly pathogens were available to those living in poor countries, not just rich countries. She'd come a long way in her life and was now wealthy and successful, but in many ways, she was still that starving girl swiping *vada pav* in the Mumbai street markets.

"What do you think he hoped to find out?" Saira asked, because she couldn't shake the handsome stranger from her head. There had been something attractive and yet frightening about him. She'd met violent men in many corners of the world, and she knew the look of them, the way they sized up every situation and every person they met through the lens of potential threats. But this man was different. He had more in his eyes than coldness or cruelty.

"I have no idea," Forster replied dismissively. "Varak is a billionaire. When you have that kind of money, someone is always looking to take you down."

"And the institute?" Saira asked.

"You told him the truth. The institute is about defeating lies with facts. That's our mission. We're fighting the good fight here, Saira, but we can't do that without money. Access. Power. That's what Varak gives us."

"Yes, of course." Saira looked out the car window

again. "But sometimes I wonder if we've gone too far. I've never doubted the ends we're pursuing, but sometimes the means trouble me."

"Our opponents are ruthless," Forster reminded her. "We have to be ruthless, too."

"Even if it means ruining people's lives?"

"We simply uncover the truth. People without secrets have nothing to fear."

"I suppose you're right," Saira agreed. Then after a pause, she added, "And that's all, isn't it, Darrell?"

"What do you mean?"

"It *is* simply the truth we uncover? That's what they do in Frankfurt? There's nothing else?"

His eyes narrowed. "Naturally. Why do you ask?"

Saira hesitated but said nothing more. Because she had a secret, too.

She hadn't told Darrell or anyone else about the German girl who'd accosted her during a World Health Organization meeting in Oslo. That had been in December the previous year. They'd had only thirty seconds together before the girl disappeared, but that was enough time for her to deliver a warning.

My name is Louisa. I work at the institute in Frankfurt. It's not what you think! It's evil! Look into it, I'm begging you! Don't tell anyone you talked to me, or they'll kill us both!

Saira hadn't seen or heard from the young woman again. However, she'd arranged to take a trip to Frankfurt not long after, and she'd toured the institute's facility, hoping to catch a glimpse of the girl. But she hadn't seen her anywhere, and she'd found no evidence of anything happening in the building, other than IT workers sifting 24/7 through endless databases. The director had told her there was no one named Louisa working there. So Saira had written the young woman off as another fringe activist, trying to disrupt the work of the institute.

Until the girl's picture had shown up in the newspaper a few weeks ago under a totally different name.

Deborah Mueller. An innocent tourist. A murder victim. But she was clearly much more than that. Since then, Saira had been replaying that meeting with the young woman over and over in her head.

Don't tell anyone you talked to me. They'll kill us both!

"Saira?" Darrell asked again. "Is something wrong? Why are you asking about Frankfurt?"

She smiled at Forster, but she realized, looking at his face, that she'd made a mistake saying anything at all. "It's nothing. Oh, look, we're finally at the tunnel. Maybe I'll make my flight after all."

"OSKAR!" HIS FRIEND JOCHIM CALLED TO HIM IN A WHISPER from the adjacent stall in the toilet. "Oskar, I have a riddle for you."

Actually, Jochim was not technically Oskar's friend. The rules of the institute were very clear about that. There were to be no out-of-office friendships among the employees. No after-work beers in the Wochenmarkt, no Christmas shopping on the Zeil together, no phone calls, no texting, no contact of any kind. A violation was grounds for immediate termination. So Jochim was just a man who'd worked at the desk next to his for the last three years. Oskar didn't know anything personal about his colleague, not where he lived or what car he drove or whether he was married or what his family was like. Even so, you couldn't be complete strangers after three years. So they took turns trading jokes when no one was around to hear them.

"What riddle?" Oskar called through the toilet wall.

"What noise does a parachutist make when his chute doesn't open?"

"I don't know, what?"

"This!"

From the accompanying stall came an enormous splurt as Jochim emptied a full load from his loose bowels into the toilet. This was followed by the man's raucous laughter.

"Oh, that's bad," Oskar told him, but he found himself laughing, too. Jochim was obese, bald, and crude, but he was also very funny.

Oskar finished his own necessities in the bathroom, and then he washed his hands and returned to the office before Jochim did. The layout of the eighth-floor space lacked any imaginative design. It was just a long, large rectangle, with private offices on one wall and dozens of rows of desks stretching from one end of the long building to the other. However, the top floor was high enough to give a view toward the Main River and the redbrick spire of the old Nikolaikirche.

This was the research headquarters of the Varak Institute, where Oskar had worked for three years. Their employment rules were strict, but if you were willing to put up with it, they paid three times what Oskar could make anywhere else in the city, and Oskar had the IT credentials to make a lot of money. As far as he was concerned, the quirks of the institute were worth it for the amazing salary. And given the sensitive work he did, he understood their obsession with security.

His small desk, next to Jochim's, was located near the windows. From there, he could see the south bank of the river, where his apartment was. He liked living close by; he could walk to and from work simply by crossing the Alte Brücke and heading through the plaza toward Berliner Straße. The institute wasn't fussy about hours. They had rules for everything else, but if you wanted to work thirty hours in a row at your desk without sleeping, that was fine. For a hacker like Oskar, it was paradise.

Oskar Vogel was a handsome man, thirty years old and just under six feet tall. He walked with an easy, athletic gait, and he played soccer on most weekends, which kept him in shape. His wavy blond hair was cut short, and he had very pale white skin and light blue eyes. His mouth was small, his jawline bony and square, and his ears jutted out a little too far from his head. He wore a crew-neck gray T-shirt and jeans.

He sat down at his desk, which had nothing on it except a keyboard, mouse, computer, and monitor. Personal items weren't allowed. He tried to get back to work, but he found his gaze drifting to the empty private office thirty feet away. That had been Louisa's office. Normally he would see her there, that intense face, those penetrating eyes, which softened when she stole a glance back at him. But she hadn't been to the office in weeks. He was used to her mysterious trips; she'd come and go for days at a time, and she would tell him nothing about where she went or what she did. But this trip was different.

He knew better than to ask anyone in the institute about her. The last thing he wanted to do was admit that they'd been sleeping together for more than a year. If she ever did come back, she'd lose her job, and so would he.

But she wasn't coming back. Oskar knew that.

Louisa was dead.

He'd only found out about it by accident. He'd been having a beer at an outdoor table in the Römerplatz, and an American businessman had left behind a copy of the *New York Times* that Oskar had grabbed. He'd glanced through it and then felt his heart stop when he saw a small article on page A14 about a woman tourist killed by a homeless man in Washington, DC. The passport photo printed in the paper was of a woman named Deborah Mueller, but with one glance, Oskar knew that it was Louisa Bell. His lover. His soon-to-be fiancée. She was dead, killed on a trip he knew nothing about, identified under an alias he'd never heard of.

He'd thought about nothing else since then. However, he also knew he had to be careful about looking for answers. The eyes of the institute were everywhere. They monitored his searches and outgoing messages. Louisa had hinted that the homes of the eighth-floor employees were all bugged, too. If you stepped out of line even once, they knew it.

Oskar forced himself to concentrate on his project again. Today it was a deepfake video. There was a far-right member of the Polish senate who'd been stirring up violent anti-immigration sentiment in the country and was beginning to poll at alarming numbers in the presidential race. Someone—Oskar didn't know who, and he didn't need to know—had filmed a homosexual interlude with a man who closely resembled the Polish politician. It was Oskar's job to manipulate the video pixel by pixel until there was no way to discover that it had been faked. He was very good at it.

The politician would scream and protest, of course. He'd claim that he was being set up. They all did. But it didn't matter. The distinction between reality and fiction was nothing but a blur these days, and the public had short attention spans. Even if the truth came out a few days later, half the people would still believe the lie, and the other half would have moved on to other things. Perhaps it was wrong, but Oskar had no problems taking down a pig who trafficked in hatred. If you played with fire, expect the fire to come for you, too.

He'd been working on the video for an hour when he heard someone call his name. "Oskar?"

When he looked up, he saw his boss, Heinrich Kessler, standing in the doorway of his office. Kessler gestured for Oskar to join him, and when he did, his boss shut the office door behind them.

Like the other workers, Kessler had no personal displays in his office. No photographs on the walls or the desk, nothing that would identify who he was outside the building. Kessler was a medium-height man in his fifties, who always wore a suit and tie. He had a round head, thinning brown hair parted on the side, and wore black glasses. Oskar couldn't ever remember seeing the man smile, but that was common here. His boss wasn't unfriendly, but there was typically no small talk in the institute.

"Tell me something, Oskar," Kessler said, sitting down at his desk. "Do you like it here? You like the work?"

Oskar was surprised by the question. "I do."

"It's important work, yes? We amplify the facts, we suppress the lies."

"Yes, we do," Oskar replied, ignoring the irony of the fact that most of his daily work was spent on creating lies himself.

"The institute makes the world a better place."

"I agree, sir."

"Good." Kessler pursed his lips, as if satisfied by Oskar's answers. "I have a new project for you."

"Okay. Well, the Polish job should only take another day or two, and then I'll be free."

"No, this one takes precedence. I want you to begin right now. It's top priority and must be done immediately."

"As you wish."

"There is a journalist in Washington who is trying to

take down the institute. I think you'll agree we can't allow that."

"Of course," Oskar said.

"You're my best man, which is why I'm giving you this assignment."

"Thank you, Herr Kessler."

"Also, I would not normally tell you this, but you have a right to know why this particular project is so significant. This journalist is not what she seems. Her media credentials are a cover. She is working for others. She is part of a fascist organization that wishes to stop us at all costs. In fact, we believe she is responsible for the death of one of our colleagues."

Oskar held his breath to avoid a hiss of shock. He had to restrain himself from glancing through the glass wall at the office next door.

"She lured our colleague to the United States," Kessler went on, confirming all of Oskar's worst fears. "She set up a meeting with her. The pretext was to threaten us with damaging information. Instead, it was a trap. Our colleague was murdered. The crime was covered up, false identities established."

Oskar felt his hands squeezing into fists. "May I ask, Herr Kessler, which colleague are you referring to?"

Kessler nodded his head at the office next door. "You know Louisa?"

He struggled to keep his emotions off his face. "Only to pass her in the office. Are you saying she's dead? And this journalist is responsible?"

"That's right. So you see, Oskar, we must know who

this woman is working for, and to do that, we need to discredit her. Isolate her. Destroy her. There can be no mercy on this one. She must be a pariah. Only then will she give up the others in the network."

Oskar shoved down his grief and rage, and he kept his voice flat, almost disinterested. "Fine. I will handle it."

"Good. I've sent you the woman's information."

"Do we have in-person resources in DC we can use for backup? And is our voice actress available?"

"At your disposal, as always."

"Thank you, Herr Kessler. I won't disappoint you."

"I know you won't."

Oskar returned to his desk, his mind a blur of grief and rage. Louisa! This woman *killed* Louisa! Even after seeing the article in the newspaper, he'd prayed that it was a mistake, that this was a false story, like so many he'd planted himself. But no. It was real. His lover was dead, and the woman responsible had to *pay*!

Then he wondered with a flash of panic: Why did Kessler tell him that? It was so out of character for any kind of personal information to be shared.

Did they know?

Had they found out about the two of them? If they did, why did Oskar even still have a job?

But none of that mattered.

What mattered now was revenge for Louisa's death.

He sat down at his desk in a frenzy and opened the file that Kessler had sent him, which was a one-page profile of the journalist, including a photograph. She was pretty, with messy cherry-red hair, smart dark eyes, and a sexy smile. But Oskar had learned working at the institute that evil could hide behind the prettiest of faces.

The journalist's name was Abbey Laurent. *Destroy her! No mercy!*

Oskar began to type.

10

ABBEY SLEPT LATE AFTER GOING TO BED AT NEARLY THREE IN the morning, as she usually did. It was after eleven o'clock when she woke up in her top-floor apartment. She blinked, trying to drag her mind from groggy sleep. She was many things, but she was definitely not a morning person. When she finally hauled herself out of bed, she went first to the kitchenette to start a fresh pot of coffee, and then she stripped off her T-shirt and underwear to take a shower. But on her way to the bathroom, she stopped.

Standing naked in the middle of her apartment, she heard a disruption outside the building. It was close and loud. Drums beating. People chanting and shouting. It sounded like a large protest of some kind. This was DC, where someone was always protesting something, but it was unusual to find them in the Mount Pleasant neighborhood, which was mostly residential.

Abbey stole closer to the window to take a look. When she glanced down, she spotted a crowd of what looked like two hundred or more people squeezed into the tree-lined parkland and spilling out into the nearby street. They were all looking up at *her* building and shouting something in a singsong chant. It took her a moment to decipher what they were saying, and then she gasped and jumped back out of sight.

The crowd was singing: *"Wake up, Abbey."*

She slapped her hands against her face and shook herself, trying to understand what was going on. She wondered if the crowd had spotted her at the window, and the people in the park confirmed that they had, because suddenly she heard an incessant hammering of debris pelting the glass. Rocks. Eggs.

People were throwing things. *At her!*

What the hell was happening?

Abbey glanced at the nightstand and spotted her phone, which she typically turned off when she slept. Still naked, she ran and turned it on and waited impatiently for the phone to grab a signal.

When it did, she stared in confused horror at the impossible numbers on the screen.

She had 1,672 unread emails and 891 unread texts. She had 112 missed phone calls and 89 voice mail messages.

With her stomach squeezed by nausea, she opened the

text app and rifled through the messages. Nearly all were from unknown callers—strangers who'd somehow found her phone number—and the messages they'd sent scared the hell out of her. There were bizarre accusations. Explicit photos and memes. Vile names and insults. Dozens of rape threats and death threats.

Jesus!

Abbey clicked over to her voice mail. She turned on the speaker to listen to the first of the multiple phone messages. The woman's voice had a British accent, and the message itself made no sense to her at all.

"Abbey Laurent, this is Marjorie Steele with the BBC in London. That tweet you made last night is blowing up around the world, and I was hoping you could join us for a radio interview."

The reporter left her number, and Abbey deleted the message.

Tweet?

The sickening feeling in the pit of her stomach intensified, because she'd sent no tweets last night. What was going on? She opened the Twitter app on her phone, and the first thing she noticed with horror was the list of trending hashtag topics. The very first was:

#isabbeyawakeyet

Oh, my God, they were talking about *her*! Then she noticed that her Twitter account had more than *twenty thousand* notifications. Comments. Tags. Retweets. It took her only a few seconds to locate the tweet to which seemingly everyone in the entire world was replying. When she read it, her mouth fell open in shock.

> @abbeylaurent_ 2:47 am
> FIFTH time my car has been broken into in the past month. AYFKM! Shit, I'm so sick of this city. When are the cops going to get a clue? We know who's doing this! Little tip: it ain't people who look like me. GOOD NIGHT, I'm going to bed.

Abbey's whole body trembled, and she sank to the floor. She curled up into a ball and began mumbling, "Holy shit, holy shit, holy shit."

This could not be real. This could not be happening to her.

"I didn't post that!" she screamed to the empty apartment. At two forty-seven a.m., she'd been reading a Jeffery Deaver novel in bed, with her phone off. But that didn't matter. It was *her* account. It even sounded like her—not the wildly racist message, but the slightly drunk tone and the casual syntax. Whoever hacked her account had mimicked her style perfectly. This was an Abbey Laurent tweet.

But it *wasn't*.

Unable even to get up from the floor, Abbey reached for the remote control to turn on the television set. She tuned to MSNBC, and she wasn't surprised to see her face staring back from behind the anchor desk. *Her* photo, the one they usually ran with her freelance articles. Red hair. Smiling, like nothing in the world was wrong. Looking incredibly white.

The chyron headline was: DC WRITER'S RACIST TWEET ERUPTS.

"Fuck!" Abbey shouted.

And then it got worse. She listened to what the anchor was saying.

"Now, as most of you know, tweeting out this racist garbage wasn't enough for Laurent. Around the same time, she called in to the overnight talk radio show on WMAL, and she let loose a rant that wasn't limited to 280 Twitter characters. Most of this has to be bleeped out for profanity, but you'll get the drift."

Then they played a staticky recording of a phone call, interrupted occasionally by a talk show host trying to break in with his own comments, and Abbey recognized *her voice*. In between the bleeped-out racist slurs and swear words, it was definitely her. Anyone listening, anyone who knew her, would confirm it.

And yet it was *not* her.

She'd been asleep at the time.

But who would believe that? If she said the woman on that phone call wasn't her, if she said that her Twitter account had been hacked, they'd laugh. That was every guilty person's lame defense.

Abbey pushed herself off the floor and went to the shower. She left the water on cold, and she sat on the white tile, letting the spray pour over her shivering body, mixing with the tears on her face. Her mind was a blur, a blank. All she could think was: Her career was dead. Her life was over. In a few hours, while she slept, she'd become the Most Hated Woman in America. Maybe the world.

How?

Why?

But she already knew the answer. What had Iris called them? *The Pyramid.* These were people who could make a witness video disappear from the internet. These were people who could invent an alias for a dead woman and wipe her off the customs records. These were people who could post fake statements from nonexistent people in Germany and keep news of a murder out of the European press.

Abbey had asked too many questions.

Whoever killed Deborah Mueller, whoever covered it up, had decided that Abbey was getting too close to the truth. Now they'd come to shut her down.

Abbey shut off the shower, but she stayed where she was. Panic wouldn't help her. She had to think. She had to make a plan. But she didn't know how to get answers in the middle of a firestorm.

"Think," she said to herself. Step by step. What to do. Where to go.

First, a hotel. She couldn't stay here. Her apartment was now ground zero for protests, and as soon as she showed her face outside, she'd be mobbed. She had to get away unseen, and then she could rent a room somewhere else in the city for a few days.

Second, a car. The mob had probably surrounded her car. She'd need to find another.

Third, money. She needed everything she could get her hands on to tide her over for a few days. Cash. She'd have to find a branch of her bank and withdraw everything she could. The less she used her credit cards, the better. Every time she handed over her card, they had a way to track her.

Fourth, a disguise. Definitely a disguise.

Abbey left the bathroom and quickly got dressed. She didn't know how much time she had to get away. It was a security building, but sooner or later, the impatient mob would find a way inside and swarm the place until they found her door. She packed a few things in a travel bag, then stuffed her red hair under a tweed newsboy hat and covered her eyes with large sunglasses. She'd color her hair later when she had time, to make herself less noticeable when she was out on the DC streets.

When she was ready to go, she switched off her phone again—she didn't know if they had a way to track her—and checked the apartment hallway. It was still empty. She took the stairs to the second floor, then made her way to the apartment of a retired woman she sometimes met for tea and chess. Mrs. Lovell answered the door, and it was obvious from the reaction on her face that she'd been watching the news.

"Abbey, oh, my God—" the woman began.

"It's a mistake. It wasn't me."

"Well, I couldn't believe that it was."

"I need your help. Actually, I need your balcony."

Mrs. Lovell understood immediately. She waved Abbey toward the back of her apartment, which faced the rear of the building. Her second-floor balcony was just a few feet above the alley. Abbey gave her a smile and a hug, and then she ran to the apartment's patio doors and slid them open. The angry shouts of the protesters could still be heard on the other side of the building, but back here, she was alone.

Abbey climbed over the balcony and dropped to the alley below her, twisting her ankle as she landed. Not letting that slow her down, she limped past rows of garbage bins and garage stalls. When she got to the opposite end of the street, she stopped, tucked her head down, and shot a quick glance toward the crowd a hundred yards away. No one saw her. Turning her back on the mob, she hurried down 19th Street and lost herself in the DC neighborhoods.

Getting away was one thing, but she was on her own, hunted by an angry mob, with no way to prove that she was innocent. She had no allies. No one on her side.

God, she missed Jason.

She would have done anything to have him with her right now. If there was one man who could help her through this nightmare, it was Jason Bourne. But he was out of her life. She had no way to reach him and no idea where he was.

11

JASON WAS IN NEW YORK IN HIS ROOM AT THE CARLYLE HOTEL.
He was watching Kenna Martin on the video camera
he'd hidden inside her apartment, and he could see that
the girl was falling apart. He'd listened to her call in sick
that morning, but it was obvious that she wasn't sick.
Instead, she was frozen with fear of what came next. She
hadn't showered, and her blond hair was greasy and limp.
Rather than sit on the sofa, she'd curled up on the floor
in a corner of the living room, with her arms wrapped
around her stuffed koala. He could zoom in on her eyes
and see that she was crying.

As the afternoon wore on, Kenna barely moved. She
didn't eat anything. Once, she got up and made coffee,
but she left it on the counter to get cold, and then she sat
back down in the corner with her back against the wall.

Her phone was on the carpet next to her. Several times, the phone rang, but when she checked the screen, she ignored the calls. Her text tone sounded several times throughout the afternoon, but she didn't read any of the messages. Her expression was empty and lost.

Jason felt bad, as if he were torturing this girl. That was a feeling of regret he never got over. He knew it wasn't him; it was others. It was Darrell Forster. It was Lennon. But Jason was the conduit who'd blown up her life, as he'd done with so many others in the past.

At five o'clock, Kenna's phone rang again.

This time she clicked the speakerphone and took the call, and Jason listened as a Chinese man spoke quickly.

"Yeah, this Miss Becky?"

"No, it's not."

"You order food? This is Wok Fun on Third. Your delivery address all wrong. Nobody there."

"I didn't order any food. You've got the wrong number."

The man swore and hung up. Kenna started crying again. Jason knew this was the call. This was the signal. Another drop. The young woman drew her arm back as if to hurl her phone across the room, but then she simply pounded her fist against her forehead in frustration. She closed her eyes, and her breathing was fast and ragged. She got to her feet and disappeared toward her bedroom.

Bourne wondered if she'd dial the number he'd given her. He'd told her to make contact as soon as she got another call. But she didn't. His phone stayed silent. She was still more afraid of the people she was working for than she was of Bourne.

He didn't wait for Kenna to leave the apartment. *Wok Fun on Third.* He ran a search on his phone and found that there was a Pop'n Drop mailbox store only three doors down from the Chinese restaurant. That's where Kenna would be going. The location was a fifteen-minute walk up Madison from the Carlyle. Bourne grabbed his leather jacket and immediately headed downstairs.

Outside, he went north, dashing across the intersections between the lights. It was rush hour, and the street was a parking lot of cars, yellow cabs, and buses. A drizzle fell, and the evening was gray, lit by a sea of red brake lights. When he got to 88th, he turned east. Trees in the sidewalk plots hung over the dark street. He hurried down the long blocks past Park and Lexington, and when he got to Third, he found the Chinese restaurant around the corner. He didn't think it had anything to do with Kenna or the drop; the call itself was fake. He bought himself a takeaway pint of fried rice and took it to the opposite side of the street, where he ate it as he leaned against the wall of a bank.

From there, he had a vantage on the Pop'n Drop store. The after-work crowd kept the place busy, customers going in and out to check their mailboxes. There was no sign of Kenna yet. When the light at 89th turned red, traffic backed up, and an oversized moving truck temporarily blocked his view. After the truck finally moved, he

spotted a bicycle messenger emerging through the doors
of the mailbox store and climbing onto his Schwinn. The
twentysomething kid wore a helmet and backpack, but
what caught Bourne's eye was the T-shirt under his nylon
vest.

It was a caricature of a beast taken from a Lon Chaney,
Jr. movie. A wolf man.

Wolf Man Travel.

Kenna had told him about the mistake the messenger
had made during one of the drops, when she'd found an
envelope from Wolf Man Travel stuck to the package she
was supposed to pass along. Once was a coincidence. Not
twice. Bourne came off the wall to go after the kid, but
he didn't have time. The messenger was already back in
traffic, flying northward on Third through the rain.

By the time Jason finished his fried rice, he saw Kenna
coming around the corner on 88th. She had no umbrella,
and her blond hair glistened with dampness. She wore an
untucked man's dress shirt over jeans, with a large zip-
pered purse over her shoulder. As she got closer, Bourne
studied the crowd. Kenna was on her own; no one was
following her. He also didn't see anyone staking out the
shipping store and waiting for her to arrive.

Letting Kenna stay ahead of him, he crossed the street
and fell in behind her. When she got to the Pop'n Drop,
she went inside, but Bourne stayed on the street, watching through the store window. She headed directly to
Box 156, opened it with her key, and withdrew a large
manila envelope. Something was scrawled in marker on

the back, and Kenna took note of what it said, then stashed the envelope inside her purse and re-zipped it. She checked her watch and headed for the exit.

Bourne turned away as Kenna came back outside. She headed south again, retracing her steps, passing Jason without noticing him. He followed, then matched her pace and came up beside her in the crowd.

"You didn't call me, Kenna."

The girl slapped a hand over her mouth to stifle her scream. "Fuck! How did you find me?"

"I told you I'd be watching."

"I was going to call you. I swear. I was waiting until after the pickup."

"Don't lie. You're scared. I get it. But I need to be with you at that drop."

THEY REACHED THE INTERSECTION AT 88TH, WHERE A MASS of people waited to cross at the light. Bourne wanted to get out of the crowd, so when the light changed, he steered Kenna across the street to a small concrete park. It was located behind a barred fence, but the gate was open. He led her to a wooden bench at the back, and they sat down. The trees overhead blocked most of the rain.

"Really, I was going to call you," Kenna repeated. She pressed her knees together, her legs twitching.

"I said, don't lie. But from now on, you need to listen to me and do exactly what I tell you."

"You're going to get me killed!"

"I only care about who you're meeting. For you, everything's going to go down like it always does. Nothing changes. You'll pass along the envelope to your contact, and then I'll follow whoever that is. After that, you'll never see me again. You can go back to your life."

Kenna shook her head. "I am so fucked."

"Not if you do what I tell you. Now let me see the envelope."

She didn't seem able to move, so Bourne reached over and unzipped her purse. He withdrew the manila envelope she'd collected at the mailbox store. The flap and edges were sealed over with tamper-evident tape. Kenna was right; if she opened it, they'd know. He felt the ridges of the contents and could feel a sheaf of papers inside.

Then he read the handwritten note scrawled on the back.

The High Line. 30th and 11th. 9:30 p.m.

"Is that a typical location?" Bourne asked.

She shrugged. "There's no pattern. It changes every time."

"Is there any kind of code you use at the drop?"

"He makes me show him the pyramid tattoo. Or she. Sometimes it's a woman. The whole thing is done in a few seconds. I hand off the envelope, they leave, and I go in the opposite direction. That's it."

"Do they run any kind of check to see if you're wired?"

"They never have before."

"Okay."

Bourne replaced the envelope in her purse. Then he dug in his inside pocket and removed a plastic bag with a tiny earpiece inside. He handed it to Kenna. "Fit this in your ear. No one will see it, but it will let us communicate. I'll be able to hear you, and you'll be able to hear me."

"Why do we need that?" she asked.

"Plans always change. We need to be prepared."

"I don't like this. What if they find it?"

"They won't."

She frowned, then slid the earpiece into her left ear and let her blond hair fall across it. Her lower lip trembled. He could see that she was barely holding it together.

"That's good. You're doing great, Kenna. From this point forward, do everything you'd normally do. Go to dinner. Walk around. Whatever. Then head to the meeting point and be there at the specified time. Proceed with the drop the way you typically would."

"What about you?"

"I'll already be there, but you won't see me. Neither will the person you're meeting. When the drop is done, go home. Throw away the earpiece, and forget about me."

"Gladly," she said.

She shrugged her purse tightly over her shoulder, and then she got up and walked away from him into the mist. As she did, Bourne spoke softly into the microphone secured under his collar. "Can you hear me, Kenna?"

At the gate leading out of the park, her body stiffened at the unexpected voice in her ear. Without looking back at him, she nodded.

"Good. Now say something back to me quietly. Just a whisper."

"Fuck you. I hate you. How's that?"

Bourne heard her loud and clear.

12

THE HIGH LINE.

It was New York's elevated park, garden, and arts trail, built atop an old freight railroad line, stretching almost a mile and a half through Chelsea from the Whitney Museum to the Javits Center. Bourne arrived an hour before the drop was scheduled. At street level, he surveilled the intersection of 30th and Eleventh in every direction, checking routes in and out of the area. Above him, the elevated park trail followed 30th toward the Hudson, which was one long block away. On the east side of Eleventh were the city's newest glass spires reaching toward the sky, and on the west side were hundreds of train cars lined up on the tracks of the rail yard.

He climbed the stairs, which rose above the trail to an elevated observation platform, then came down via a second set of steps. The trail wasn't wide, only about thirty feet from railing to railing, and about twenty feet above street level. It narrowed even further beyond the stairs, heading west, where he could see remnants of the rusted old freight tracks. At night, bright lights illuminated the city towers, and hidden white lights marked the walking path and glowed in the shrubbery and low trees. The rain continued falling in gauzy streams. He could see the black ribbon of the river not far away.

He tried to anticipate how it would go down.

A meeting on an elevated walkway. That was an odd choice. He found himself concerned about *why* they'd picked this location. On the street, there were limitless routes for arrival and escape. Up here, there were only three—taking the stairs the way he had done and the way Kenna would do, or coming and going on the High Line itself from the west or east. This was an easy place to get trapped, and he didn't like that. Either the people behind this were overly confident, or they had some other plan in mind.

Regardless, whoever showed up to meet Kenna was a link in the chain that would lead him to Lennon. Bourne would follow him. Or her.

Nine o'clock. Half an hour to go.

He chose his location, selecting a dark stretch of railing above the train yard, about fifty feet west of the stairs from the street. There, he was mostly invisible, but still close enough to see Kenna arrive and watch the meeting occur. When he was in place, he studied the area for other surveillance. Even in the darkness and rain, there were plenty of people coming and going, and that was an environment in which it was easy to hide weapons. He knew they'd have backup in place for the drop. In Iceland, Lennon had brought his security team with him in the cars, but he'd also had people waiting on both ends of the road and positioned near the black church and outside the hotel. That was simply smart tradecraft. Things could always go wrong, and you had to be ready.

And yet as far as he could tell, he was alone. That made no sense. His instincts screamed at him. *Something was wrong.*

They should have been watching Kenna outside the shipping store. They should have been staking out the High Line. He would have expected at least four observers in both locations, maybe more.

But there was no one.

The time ticked away, and he was still on his own.

Nine twenty-five. There she was. Kenna arrived five minutes early for the drop. In the soft glow, she climbed the steps from the street and then paused on the observation platform above the trail. She admired the view and swept away her damp blond hair, but the more she tried to look casual, the more he recognized the tension gripping her body. When her face caught the light, he could see how pale her skin was. Her fist was clenched around the strap of her purse.

"I'm here," he murmured. He saw her flinch at the voice in her ear. "The area is secure. You're fine."

"Where are you?"

"I'm at the north railing just west of you."

"I don't see you."

"That's okay."

"Where should I wait?" she asked quietly.

"Go to the railing across from the steps. There's a bench, but don't sit down. I can't see you if you sit down."

"Okay."

Kenna took the handful of steps from the platform down to the High Line. She crossed the walkway and stood at the railing over the train yard. In the darkness, she wasn't much more than a shadow, but her blond hair caught the light. He watched her turn around and lean with her back against the railing, and he could see her head bobbing as her eyes followed the people around her.

"Relax," he told her. "You've done this before. Handle it the same way you always do."

She said nothing.

Bourne checked his watch. It was nine thirty. Go time. He kept his focus on the steps, guessing that the contact would arrive there, rather than from either end of the High Line. He watched a couple of tourists head down to the street. As they did, a thirtysomething man in a track suit jogged past them, climbing the stairs. He was tall and lean, with a chiseled face. Bourne watched the man pause on the elevated platform the way Kenna had done, and then the man descended to the walkway.

"This could be him," Bourne said.

He waited for the man to approach Kenna. First a check of the tattoo to confirm who she was, next the passing of the envelope. But it didn't happen. Instead, the man checked his Apple Watch, then turned eastward and began jogging along the trail.

It wasn't him. He wasn't the contact.

Two more minutes passed. Then five. Then ten.

"Has the contact ever been late before?" Bourne murmured.

"Never. I've never had to wait."

He didn't like it. He felt that same sensation in his brain even louder than before. *Something was wrong.*

At nine fifty, when the drop was twenty minutes overdue, Kenna whispered in a plaintive voice, "What do I do?"

Bourne frowned and made a decision. "Open the envelope."

"What?"

"Open it. Tell me what's inside."

"I can't! The rules say I *never* open it. Never!"

"They've broken the rules. They haven't shown up."

"No!"

"Kenna, do it. Open it. Open it right now."

He heard the loud rasp of her breathing. Bourne pushed himself off the railing and began walking down the trail toward her, step by step. His eyes moved constantly. He studied the walkway, the buildings, the street. He examined the faces of the people who passed him, talking, laughing.

What was happening?

Where were they?

"Are you sure?" Kenna asked. He heard the rustle of paper in her hands. "I don't like this."

"Open it. Do it!"

"Fuck! Okay!"

The next sound in his ear was the tearing of paper. He took another slow, careful step. Then another. He saw Kenna thirty feet away, standing by herself at the railing. The envelope was in her hands, and he could see her digging inside to extract the contents.

"Oh, my God. Oh, my God!"

"What is it?"

"It's blank!"

"What? What are you talking about?"

"The pages inside, they're all blank! There's nothing on them!"

Bourne felt the chill of horror wash over him. Suddenly, he understood. Yes, this was an easy place to get trapped, and *they were the ones who were trapped*.

"Kenna, walk toward me right now," he hissed into the microphone. "Stay calm, but come this way."

"What?"

"Put the pages back in the envelope, and walk my way. Act natural."

"I can't! I'm getting out of here!"

"No!" he shouted, ignoring the microphone. He saw the girl sprint toward the steps, and he called to her again, desperately now. "No, this way, Kenna! Don't run! Get away from the stairs!"

But she didn't listen. Bourne ran after her, but he was too late.

Kenna took the steps two at a time. As she reached the top of the observation platform, her head suddenly snapped back, engulfed in a cloud of red against the white lights, and a sharp crack rolled across the High

Line. Jason swore. A sniper's bullet had been delivered with laser precision. Kenna dropped to the platform, not moving. She was already dead; he knew she was dead. Bourne dove to the ground and rolled away as another shot ricocheted off the railing inches from where he'd been standing a second earlier.

Chaos and screams engulfed the park. People ducked, ran, and shoved, moving in both directions, with no idea where the gunfire was coming from. Another shot landed near Bourne, and it would have hit him if a panicked stranger hadn't flown past him at the same moment, taking a shot that spilled the man off his feet. In the next second, Bourne rose and headed for the steps, timing the reloading of the sniper's rifle. He threw himself down just as the next bullet whistled over his head, and then again he got up and ran. From the angle, he guessed that the shooter was on the roof of a brick building half a block away. He skidded to a stop below the metal beams of the elevated platform, where he was sheltered from the next assault.

Kenna Martin was immediately above him.

She'd landed against the fence, her damp face and blond hair pressed against the mesh, lifeless eyes still open. Blood from the bullet wound in the center of her forehead dripped onto the leather of Bourne's jacket. He felt a surge of anger that this girl had lost her life, a girl who liked to dance in clubs, a girl who still slept with a stuffed bear. She'd been manipulated and blackmailed and thrust into a no-win scenario for which she wasn't remotely prepared. She was expendable.

But he shared the blame himself. He was one of the people who'd manipulated her. He'd put her in a no-win scenario, too. Because of Lennon. Because of his obsession with his own past. Because of Treadstone. She was dead because of him. Like so many who'd come before her.

Another minute passed. Then two. There were no more shots.

He could hear the wail of police sirens getting closer.

Bourne guessed that the sniper was already shutting down his lair and making his escape. He took the chance of climbing the steps to the platform above the High Rise, where he was exposed, a target. But no bullets came for him. He knelt, put one hand on Kenna's face, then continued down to the street. At a run, he crossed toward the redbrick building on the next corner, and as he did, the metal street door burst open.

The assassin emerged, pistol in one hand, rifle case slung over the opposite shoulder. Not a man. Not Lennon. This was a woman. He had only a second to memorize her face as she came out of the shadows. Deep brown hair tied tightly in a ponytail. A bony, jutting chin. Hispanic features, golden skin, dark eyes. Her mouth was an angry slash. She was small and lithe, dressed entirely in black Lycra that clung to her narrow frame.

She saw him just as he saw her. He aimed his Sig; she aimed her gun. They both fired multiple shots, but they were too far away from each other to hit their targets. The wild gunfire froze him where he was, and that gave her the time she needed. He heard the roar of an engine. A white panel van sped southward on Eleventh, its side door already wide open. The van screeched to a stop outside the brick building, and the woman took two steps across the sidewalk and flung herself inside. The van accelerated; the door slid shut. Bourne ran after it, taking several more shots at the back of the van, but the vehicle swerved around the next corner, two wheels lifting off the ground, and then disappeared.

The killer was gone.

13

THE RAIN STOPPED, AND THE NIGHT TURNED STICKY AND warm. Jason didn't go back to his hotel until almost three in the morning. In between, he walked the streets of New York, tormented by one of those stretches of blackness that periodically descended on his mind. When he thought about his missing past, he didn't typically obsess about memories that were gone. He could live with that emptiness. He knew about the things he'd done, the places he'd gone. His skills were still there, like motor instincts that never went away. What he'd lost more than anything else was a sense of *who he was*.

His real identity.

Two years ago, on the boardwalk in Quebec City, Abbey Laurent had asked him that same question. *Who do you think you are?*

He'd answered her without hesitation. *A killer.*

This was one of those nights when he had to face that truth about himself all over again. He was what Tread-stone had made him, and Kenna Martin had paid the price for it.

But he couldn't change, and he couldn't stop.

When Jason finally returned to the Carlyle, he revived himself with a couple hours of sleep. Long before dawn, he slung his backpack over his shoulder and went back out onto the streets. He caught a cab and gave the driver an address near Roosevelt Park in the Bowery. He found the storefront he was looking for, with its door protected behind steel mesh and its windows protected by a roll-down metal panel painted over with garish graffiti. With a quick look up and down the street, Bourne removed a prybar from his pack and twisted away the lock that held the steel mesh in place. After sliding it up, he forced the door inward with a hard shove from his shoulder.

This was Wolf Man Travel.

He spent an hour searching the agency's files, but they'd covered their tracks well. He found nothing to suggest that it was anything but an aboveboard travel business catering to an elite corporate clientele. But it wasn't. He knew that. The documents that Kenna Martin had passed along at her drops had come via a bicycle messenger from this agency. And among the agency's largest clients, based on what Jason found in their files, was Darrell Forster and the Forster Group. That wasn't a coincidence.

Afterward, Bourne waited in the owner's office at the

back of the agency. He took a chair in the corner and sat in the darkness with his Sig on his lap. At six thirty, with a gray dawn filtering in from the street windows, he heard the noise of someone arriving. An unhappy voice muttered a curse, finding the broken door. A man's heavy footsteps thudded toward the back of the storefront, and his wide frame appeared in the doorway.

The office light went on. Bourne extended his Sig, pointing it at the man's chest.

"Fuck!" the man said, throwing his hands in the air as he spotted Bourne and the gun. "Who are you? What do you want? If you're looking for cash, there's nothing here."

Bourne sized the man up. He was small, with an overweight build. He was in his fifties, and he did look a little like a wolf man, with a bushy shock of brown hair and a full beard. Jason noticed the bulge of a weapon inside the man's sport coat, and he gestured at it with the barrel of his gun.

"Take your gun out slowly and put it on the floor. Kick it toward me."

The man scowled but complied.

"Who are you?" Bourne asked, retrieving the gun.

"Ray Wolfe. This is my agency. I told you, we don't keep any money here. You're wasting your time."

"I don't care about money. Sit down, and keep your hands flat on the top of your desk."

Wolfe did. The man's dark, nervous eyes bounced back and forth from Jason to the Sig, and his face flushed.

His desk was messy with travel brochures stacked in piles around his computer. The walls were crowded with posters and calendars from exotic vacation destinations. The man knew how to keep up appearances, but Jason knew the truth. Wolfe was more than an ordinary travel agent.

"You gonna tell me what you want?" the man asked.

"Kenna Martin is dead," Bourne said.

"What? Who? I don't know anybody by that name."

"You sent her on a drop last night, Ray, but the drop was fake. A setup. They shot her. I want to know how it went down and *who* you sent there to do the job. I know it was a woman, and I want to know how to find her."

"Shit, man, I don't have a clue what you're talking about. Drops? Setups? People getting shot? You got the wrong guy."

Bourne shook his head. "Stop wasting my time, Wolf Man. I know about the bicycle messenger. I know about Darrell Forster. I know about *Lennon*. Do I look like I'm with the police? Do you think I'm here to arrest you? There are only two ways this ends. You alive, or you dead. Take your pick."

Sweat gathered on the man's forehead. "I swear—"

"The papers you gave to Kenna were *blank*!" Bourne said angrily. "You knew that, and that means you knew they were going to kill her."

Jason bolted out of the chair and pinned the middle of the man's right hand against the desk with the Sig. His other hand squeezed the man's jaw like a vise. "People think the knee is the most painful place to get shot.

Trust me, the hands are worse. All those nerve endings? A lot worse. You feel like your entire body is on fire."

"Fuck!" Wolfe said, trying to spit out the words. "You're crazy, man!"

"I'm going to count to three."

"Jesus, I'm telling you, all I do for Darrell Forster is book his fucking plane trips!"

"One."

"I don't know who this Kenna Martin is! I don't! I run a fucking travel agency!"

"Two." Bourne pushed down hard with the barrel, crushing bones and veins.

"Come on, man, don't do this! Fuck, please, please, you got it wrong!"

Jason's finger slid around the trigger. "Three—"

"*All right! All right!* Shit, man, okay! I didn't know they were going to kill her! You have to believe me, I didn't know!"

Bourne removed the gun from Wolfe's hand. He pointed it into the man's forehead, between his furry eyebrows. "Talk. Tell me about the drops. What's in them?"

"It's travel documents, mostly. I swear. Plane tickets. Cars. Hotels. But the identities are all fake. Fake driver's licenses, fake passports. I've been in the business for years, so I've got contacts. It's what I do."

"And Forster?"

"I've never met him. Never talked to him. I can't give you anything on him, man."

"How did you get involved?"

"A couple of years ago, a guy came in here. A lot like you, you know? The sort of guy who means business. He knew all about my work with fake IDs, and he said he had a deal for me. A lot of new jobs, a lot of money. And along with it, some big corporate accounts for my agency, too. All legit, easy to launder the money I get from the other shit. That was the carrot. Stick was, if I didn't play ball, the feds would find out about me and I'd go away for years. So I played ball. You bet I did. And they held up their end. A week later, the Forster Group started sending me a lot of their agency travel biz. You think they'd look twice at a Bowery shop like mine otherwise? Yeah, I knew they were connected somehow, but I wasn't going to ask any questions."

Bourne gestured at the man's arm. "Roll up your sleeve."

Wolfe's eyes widened. "You know about that? Yeah, okay, they made me get some fucking tattoo. A pyramid."

"What does it mean?"

"It's an ID. It means you're in. Beyond that, I don't have a clue."

"How do you know what arrangements to make before the drops? IDs, travel, whatever. Who tells you what they need?"

"Phone call. I don't know who it is. They give me the specs, I set up all the docs, and when it's ready, I put the envelope together. Then I get another call with a time and location to write on the envelope, and they tell me which shipping store to send my messenger to. I don't even know who picks it up. One time my guy came back, said he saw a woman there. That's all. I swear, I didn't know what was going to happen last night."

Bourne's finger slid onto the trigger again. "You're lying. The papers in the envelope were blank. There were no documents. You knew it was a trap."

Wolfe squeezed his eyes shut. His breath was sour. "I didn't! I didn't know!"

"You said *you* put together the packages."

"Not last night! Last night was different, man!"

"What happened?"

"I did travel docs, same as always. I had it all ready to go, I did. But instead of a phone call with info about the drop, they said there was a change of plans. Somebody was going to come to the office in person, and I was supposed to do whatever they asked. I didn't like it, but you think I was going to say no? So an hour later, this scary bitch shows up in my office. I don't know who she was! It's not like she gave me a name."

"What did she look like?" Bourne asked.

"Small, skinny, but really in shape, you know? Hispanic, long brown hair."

Jason nodded. It was her. The killer. Then he remembered words spoken by Lennon in a cottage in Iceland. *The new Yoko. A fiery little girl I found in Barcelona.*

Lennon had sent his #2 to do the job.

"Then what?"

"She asked for the envelope, and I gave it to her. Then she gave me a second envelope and said to proceed with the drop. The time and location were already written on there. Somewhere on the High Line last night. That's all. I didn't ask questions. And shit, man, I had no idea the thing was a setup. None! I swear! I didn't know they were going to kill this woman. I'm telling you, I don't even know who she was."

Bourne still had the gun against Wolfe's forehead. He was ready to fire.

The man was telling him the truth. He was sure of that. And it made sense. The switching of envelopes. The trap. It didn't smell of an arrangement made by Darrell Forster or whatever organization Forster controlled. This one was Lennon. It was the assassin sending in one of his operatives to tie up loose ends. And that told him that Lennon knew that Cain was still on the hunt.

Jason stared at the fleshy face of the travel agent in the chair. Wolfe was a low-level cog in a chain of death. He felt a desire to squeeze the trigger, to blow the man's head open, to get some kind of payback for what had been done to Kenna Martin. But it wouldn't solve anything. If Wolfe died, Forster and Lennon would both know that the operation had been blown. They'd be on their guard, watching for Bourne.

He needed them to think they'd gotten away clean.

"If you tell anyone about me or this meeting, either they'll kill you, or I will," Bourne told him. "That's a guarantee. The only way you stay alive is to stay quiet. Understand, Wolf Man?"

"Yes! Yes, I understand!"

"The envelope you gave the woman. The real one. What was in it? Travel documents?"

"Yes, yes, a plane ticket and hotel reservations. The plane was booked for this morning, check-in to the hotel this afternoon."

"Where?" Bourne asked. "Where was she going?"

"Washington," the man replied. "The Melrose Hotel."

14

ON HER SECOND DAY AS AN OUTCAST, ABBEY DROVE HER rental car back to the small town of Hyattsville, Maryland, where she'd first met the girl known as Iris. She'd already tried to reach Iris by phone for more than twenty-four hours, but the girl's voice mailbox was full. So Abbey had only one other way to reach out to the online conspiracy group that had first introduced her to the mystery surrounding the murder of Deborah Mueller.

One of our people, Jerry, works at the post office. He's seen you in there several times.

Abbey had changed her appearance the previous day. Her lush mahogany hair was now jet black, and she'd had it cut short. She'd purchased silver sunglasses that she never took off in public. Her clothes were new and cheap—thanks to a stop at Target—and she'd put on no makeup or lipstick. So far, the disguise had worked. No one had recognized her when she was out in the city.

But the uproar hadn't died down. She was still everywhere in the news. She'd decided that the only way to weather the storm was not to engage, so other than a few emails to close friends to proclaim her innocence, she'd steered clear of her phone and social media accounts. She'd given no interviews and offered no explanations. The calls and texts kept coming in, but she ignored them and, most of the time, she kept her phone turned off to make sure that no one could track her.

Her focus now was on finding the people who'd destroyed her.

The Pyramid.

Abbey parked on the opposite side of the Hyattsville town center from where she'd parked before. She walked down an alley to the post office, and as she reached Gallatin Street, she noticed the coffee shop where Iris had first met her. She took a detour inside the shop, but when she asked the baristas about Iris and described the girl, no one knew her. So she retraced her steps and went into the post office.

First she checked her mailbox, praying for a letter from Jason. But the box was empty, as it had been for months. She didn't really expect a reply, not now, not after she'd sent him a postcard that said *Fuck you, Jason*. She could just as easily have said *I love you*, and it would have meant the same thing. But the result was the same. She'd pushed him away, and she was never going to hear from him again.

Then Abbey went to the postal counter. There was no line. The name tag on the clerk's blue shirt said Paul, not Jerry, and Paul looked immune to her flirty smile. "Is Jerry around?" she asked.

Paul looked uninterested in a customer who wasn't buying stamps or sending packages. "He's in back. Why?"

"I'd like to talk to him."

"Why?"

Abbey shrugged. "We have a mutual friend."

"He's not on break yet."

"Well, would you mind seeing if he could come out here? It'll only take a minute." Abbey glanced pointedly over her shoulder, a little reminder for Paul that the rest of the post office lobby was empty. She smiled again. "Pretty please?"

Paul sighed, then disappeared. A couple of minutes later, Abbey saw a tall twentysomething kid in a baggy USPS outfit appear from the back of the building. Jerry was Asian, with wavy dark hair and soft, almost feminine features. He wore a curious smile as he neared the postal counter, but then his eyes met Abbey's. Almost immediately, he saw through her new look and realized who she was. His smile vanished, and he turned and bolted.

"Shit," Abbey hissed.

She ran, too. She crashed through the doors leading outside, jumped down the steps, and sprinted into the alley that took her behind the postal building. A barbed-wire fence bordered the parking lot, and Abbey saw that Jerry was already outside, climbing behind the wheel of a Corolla. She continued around the corner at a run and got to the gate in the fence at the same moment that Jerry was heading out.

She blocked it with her body and hoped he'd hit the brakes. He did. The Corolla squealed to a stop inches away from hitting her, and Abbey stayed where she was until Jerry turned off the engine. Then she approached the driver's window.

"Stay away from me!" Jerry barked at her. "You need to stay the hell away from me!"

She held up her hands. "You know who I am, right? Look, I just want to find Iris, okay? I need to talk to her. Tell me where she is, or how I can get hold of her. She's not answering her phone."

"Iris is dead," Jerry snapped.

Abbey's eyes widened in shock. "*Dead*? How? When?"

"Hit-and-run. Two days ago. The cops said it was an accident, but that's bullshit. They came after her."

"The Pyramid?" Abbey asked.

"Yeah. Exactly. Because of *you*. Iris approached you, and that's why they killed her. You're part of them, aren't you?"

"Me? No way, I'm not. I didn't know anything about this until Iris approached me. You guys came to me, not the other way around, remember?"

"Then you told someone about her. They found her, and they *killed* her. None of us are safe now. They're going to track all of us down. I've got my family to think about. My parents. My sisters."

"Who *are* they?"

Jerry shook his head. "I don't know. I don't want to know anymore. When I heard about Iris, I shut down my social media accounts. I'm done with this. Go away, and don't come looking for me again."

He turned the ignition key to fire the engine again, but Abbey reached into the car and grabbed his other hand and pulled it off the steering wheel. "Jerry, wait. Listen to me. You know what they did to me, right? You've seen the stories online?"

The kid nodded. "Yeah. They canceled you. So what? I can't do anything about that."

"At least tell me what you've heard. Rumors. Gossip. Theories. What is the Pyramid all about? Who are these people?"

"I'm telling you, *I don't know*. All we know is what they do. They control the narrative. They make sure people only believe what they want them to believe. And if you get in the way, they destroy you any way they can. Look at you. You're a liability, so they cancel you. They change how people think about you, what they know about you. That's who you are now. A racist. It doesn't matter what's true and what's a lie. You're living their reality now. We all are."

Jerry pulled away and shoved the gearshift down. The Corolla lurched forward, dragging Abbey as she clung to his postal shirt.

"Hang on, hang on, wait a minute," Abbey persisted.

The kid tapped the brakes impatiently. "What?"

"Iris said there are others in your group. Young people. How do I find them? Talk to them?"

"You can't."

"Jerry, give me *something*. You people got me into this, and now it's blown up in my face. You owe me. You owe Iris, too."

The postal worker squeezed the wheel tightly with both hands. He stared straight ahead through the windshield. "We think she was meeting someone."

"Who? Deborah Mueller?"

"Yeah. She was there for a meeting, but the Pyramid found out about it and killed her."

"Who was she meeting?" Abbey asked.

Jerry shook his head. "I have no idea. But whoever it is may know something. You should try to find him."

"How do you know about any of this?"

The kid looked over his shoulder, as if he were sure that they were being watched. "You saw the video, right? The homeless woman who saw the murder? The one that's being suppressed?"

"Yes."

Jerry sighed. "I took it."

"*You* did? Why?"

"Because that's what we do. When we think a story's being manipulated, we try to get the facts out before the media and the tech companies can stifle them. So I went down there to poke around and see what I could find. I'm the one who found this woman and interviewed her. Don't you get it? That's why I'm at risk. If they figure out it was me, they'll kill me, just like they killed Iris."

"Okay. I get it. Tell me about the meeting, and then we're done."

The kid looked as if he wanted to punch the accelerator again. He spoke quickly. "After I shut down the video, I told this woman I'd buy her some soup and a sandwich, okay? We started walking out of the park together. When we got near the parking lot, we saw a guy near a car on the far side. The woman pointed at him, said he was there that night. She said she saw him standing by the body a few minutes after Deborah Mueller was killed. The guy must have noticed us looking at him, because he got in the car and drove away."

"Did you recognize him?" Abbey asked.

"No, he was too far away. Plus, he had sunglasses on. He was old, though."

"How old?"

"I don't know. Gray hair, wrinkled. He looked ancient to me. He moved that way, too. And his car was old. Vintage. Silver. I ran to get a better look and see if I could get the plates, but he was already gone. I think it was an out-of-state plate, though. Colors didn't look right for anyplace around here. Not Virginia, Maryland, DC."

"Is there anything else you remember?"

"That's all."

"But you don't think this man killed Deborah Mueller?" Abbey asked.

"Nah. Definitely not. The woman said the killer was young, blond hair."

"Okay. Thank you, Jerry." She backed up from the car. "Stay safe."

"Yeah. You, too. Watch your back."

*   *   *

THAT NIGHT, ABBEY LEFT HER CAR AT THE HOTEL. SHE WALKED twenty minutes to a beer hall on Wisconsin Avenue in Georgetown. It was noisy and crowded, but she figured there was safety in numbers. Nobody was likely to recognize her there. She found an empty seat on one of the long benches, at a table filled by a group of twentysomething college girls. She didn't have to worry about trying to be sociable. She brought along her Deaver novel to read, although she couldn't concentrate on anything. She ordered a veggie burger and fried cauliflower, which she barely touched, and she drank an Oktoberfest-sized beer way too quickly. When she finished that one, she ordered a second, which drew a raised eyebrow of surprise from the waitress.

Halfway into the second beer, Abbey was drunk and feeling sorry for herself. Her plan had ground to a halt, and she didn't know what to do next. Iris was dead. She had no clues that would lead her forward, and her life was in ruins. She tried reaching out to several editors for whom she'd done freelance work, and in every case, she was met with deafening silence. She texted Tom Blomberg at the *Sentinel*, but he didn't answer, and the text didn't show as read. When she dialed his number, the call went to voice mail.

Abbey kept drinking, and the beer hall began to spin. When she checked her watch, she saw that it was nearly midnight. Several hours had already passed as she sat in a numb stupor, feeling more and more depressed. She paid her bill, but she didn't leave. She felt the need to talk to *someone*, to have a chance to explain, to tell anybody who knew her that she was innocent.

But nobody wanted her. Nobody called her back.

"Hey," she said to one of the college students sitting next to her on the bench. "My phone died. Mind if I make a call with yours?"

The girl gave Abbey a once-over, as if she must know her from somewhere, and then she unlocked her phone and handed it to her.

Abbey dialed Tom Blomberg again. This time, with a call coming in from an unknown number, he answered.

"Hello?"

"Tom, it's Abbey Laurent. Don't hang up."

There was a long pause. "What did you do, borrow a phone? Very smart."

"You weren't taking my other calls."

"And I'm not taking this one," Tom said. "Goodbye, Abigail."

"Wait! Wait, just hear me out. Jesus, Tom, you have to know that this is all fake. I've been set up. This Twitter shit wasn't me. Somebody hacked my account."

"And then they called into a radio station pretending to be you?" Tom asked. "That was fake, too?"

"I know it sounds wild, but yes."

"Why would someone do that to you?"

"My guess? Because of Deborah Mueller."

She heard a sad chuckle on the phone.

"What did I tell you about chasing zebras? To me,

those hoofbeats sound like horses. They sound like they're from a reporter who got drunk and made a big, big mistake, and now rather than own up to it, she's concocting a fantastic conspiracy story to cover her ass. And by the way, I can hear in your voice that you're still drinking, so maybe it's time to admit that you have a problem."

Abbey tried to say something, to protest, but she was too angry and humiliated to say anything at all.

"I'm sorry, Abigail," Tom went on. "You're smart, and you're good, but you're toxic right now, and you will be for the foreseeable future. I can't help you, and I can't give you any more work. We're done here."

He hung up.

"Fuck!" Abbey swore. Even in the noisy beer hall, her voice was loud.

The college girl on the bench gave her a concerned look. "You okay?"

"Yeah. Great. Thanks for the phone."

She handed it back to the girl, and she swayed to her feet. Seeing her unsteadiness, the girl took her arm. "Hey, you're not driving or anything, right?"

"No. I'm not."

Abbey did her best not to fall down as she exited the beer hall onto the quiet after-midnight street. She walked—staggered—half a block toward the waterfront park at the Potomac, then realized she'd never make it back to her hotel without having to pee or throw up. Or both. When she saw the lighted sign of an empty cab in the cross street, she flagged it down, and then she poured herself into the back.

"Where to?" the cabbie asked her.

She leaned back against the seat, her head spinning. She closed her eyes and told him where to go. "The Melrose Hotel."

15

MIDNIGHT CAME AND WENT, AND JASON STILL HADN'T SPOT-
ted the assassin anywhere near the Melrose. He sat in a
cobblestoned park on the other side of Pennsylvania Avenue, hidden by the darkness and the trees. For hours,
he'd watched people come and go under the black aw-
ning of the eight-story hotel. She hadn't emerged; she
hadn't arrived. And yet, if the man from Wolf Man Travel
had been telling him the truth, Lennon's handpicked
killer was somewhere nearby.

Where?

And *who* was she targeting?

Bourne checked his watch again. He glanced up and
down the street, where the traffic had thinned as it grew
later. It was time to end his vigil for the night; he could
begin again in the early morning. He'd already checked
in to his own room at the Melrose, and he'd made a

master keycard for himself. As soon as he located the assassin, he could follow her, trap her, and extract the information that would lead him back to Lennon.

But for now, there was no sign of her inside or outside.

On the street, Bourne watched a taxi pull up to the curb. In the warm nighttime glow of the hotel lights, a woman got out of the back. He saw her for only an instant as she turned toward the doors. His mind made an instant calculation, watching the shape of her face and the frame of her body. It wasn't her. This woman wasn't the killer he'd seen near the High Line in New York.

Then, as she disappeared inside with a drunken wobble in her gait, Jason froze. He tried to focus on her again, but she was already gone.

His brain caught up with his eyes. All day, he'd made quick judgments on the people coming and going from the hotel, ruling them out as the woman he was looking for. Beyond that, he didn't care who they were. But now he felt sweat on his body, and his heartbeat sped up in his chest. He closed his eyes, recapturing that momentary glimpse from his memory, seeing that face again.

It couldn't be *her*!

It couldn't!

The hair was all wrong. Black, short, not long, lush, and red. The clothes, downscale and not trendy, didn't look like her style at all. And *why* would she be here, now, in this place, at the exact moment when Bourne was tracking a killer? It made no sense!

But he leaped to his feet, because he knew he was right.
Abbey!

The woman at the hotel was Abbey Laurent.

Jason marched through the park and across the four lanes of Pennsylvania Avenue. The emotion he'd forced out of his soul for months—for *two years!*—roared back. Abbey. The Canadian journalist he'd kidnapped and interrogated and then let go, only to have her come back to him. The fearless woman who'd traveled across the country with him as he hunted the Medusa group. The confident lover who'd slipped naked into his arms in a hot, humid motel room near Amarillo, Texas. The quirky, smart, funny, sexy girl he'd said goodbye to forever outside the Château Frontenac in Quebec City.

Abbey. He'd cut her out of his life to keep her safe, but there she was, back again. His attraction to her returned in a rush of desire. It was as if none of the time apart between them had happened at all.

But what was she doing here?

When Bourne walked into the lobby of the Melrose, he saw that the woman—*was* it really Abbey, or was his mind playing tricks on him?—had already disappeared. He looked left and right, but didn't see her anywhere. Abbey was a nighttime girl; he knew that. She stayed up until all hours. Was she meeting someone for a late drink? Had she already gone up in the elevators?

He crossed the hotel's striped marble floor to his left, past cool dark columns, where the lobby was decorated with cushioned rose-colored chairs, leather sofas, and dozens of rows of well-stocked bookshelves. The bar was already closed, and no one was sitting in the lounge. There was no sign of her.

Then Jason glanced to the far side of the lobby again, and his heart stopped.

Up a handful of steps, a woman waited outside the hotel's two elevators. Not Abbey. She wore a trim navy suit, and if anyone looked quickly, they might think she was part of the hotel staff. But she wasn't. Her body was small, strong, wiry. Long, full brown hair made a waterfall around her shoulders. He spotted her face in profile and noted the golden skin and prominent chin.

The assassin. It was her. She was here. *Yoko.* He also knew with dread clutching his stomach that it was no coincidence that Yoko had appeared at the same moment as Abbey Laurent.

Bourne headed across the lobby. He couldn't run or attract attention to himself; he couldn't let her *see* him. Then a quiet bell sounded as one of the elevators arrived, and Yoko vanished inside the car without a look in his direction. He ran now, but he was too late; the doors closed, and she was already gone. He shot up the handful of steps, watching the numbers above the elevator as the car climbed toward the top of the hotel.

Six. It stopped on the sixth floor.

He jammed the button, urging the other elevator to *hurry.*

Yoko was in the hotel. A killer was on the sixth floor. And so, he knew, was Abbey Laurent.

THE TAXI RIDE FROM THE BEER HALL HAD SOBERED ABBEY A little, but she was still unsteady on her feet. She felt sick and knew she should have drunk less and eaten more. When she got to her hotel room, she didn't turn on the lights immediately, because the brightness would hurt her eyes. She used the bathroom, then crossed to the windows, which looked out toward the dark ribbon of the Potomac and the towers of the Watergate complex. For more than a year, this city had felt like home. She'd felt as if she'd found a place here. But now that home had cast her away.

Abbey fell backward on the king-sized bed. She didn't bother getting undressed. She closed her eyes and tried to sleep, but instead, her eyes flew open again as she heard a rapping on the hotel door only seconds later.

"Shit," she muttered.

They'd found her. The media or the protesters or any of the others who'd been hounding her for two days. She'd been recognized. Someone had seen through her disguise and followed her into the hotel. Abbey thought about pretending to be asleep or in the shower, but whoever was there knocked again, and she realized she was being stupid. It was after midnight. No one would be confronting her now.

She got off the bed and went to the door, and when she looked through the peephole, she saw a small woman in a navy blue suit. She had long brown hair, and her mouth was creased into a polite smile.

"Yes?" Abbey called through the door.

"Ms. Laurent? This is Maja from the front desk. I'm sorry to bother you, but we saw you come back in, and I'm afraid there's a problem with your credit card."

"Shit," Abbey muttered again. Then she called through the door. "Can this wait until morning?"

"I'm afraid not. It's hotel policy. This will only take a moment. I can process a new card from here."

She sighed. "Yeah, all right."

Abbey opened the door.

BOURNE STARED DOWN THE SIXTH-FLOOR HALLWAY. IT WAS empty and quiet. He had his gun in the pocket of his coat, finger already around the trigger. He walked quickly, focusing all his concentration on what he could hear behind the hotel doors. Most of them were dead silent at this late hour. He heard a few people snoring. One couple was having loud sex. But he heard nothing to tell him where Abbey was.

She needed him. He knew that. Somewhere on this floor, a killer was with her, and Jason was running out of time. Yoko was a pro. She'd be in and out in a few minutes, and Abbey would be dead.

But he reached the hotel's rear wall, and still he heard *nothing*. Urgently, he retraced his steps from door to door, running now. Sweat poured down his face. His heart pounded, and all his muscles tensed with fear and panic. There had to be *something*! Some noise! Some clue to where she was!

There.

What was that? He stopped at a door and listened. Barely audible on the other side, he heard a low, erratic thump, like a foot jarring against a heavy door. That was all. Then, a second later, someone gasped, and he recognized the smothered noise of a struggle. Jason shoved the Treadstone key quietly into the lock, and as he launched his shoulder against the door and charged into the room, he already had his Sig out of his pocket.

The lights were off. All he saw was the dark glow from the city through the windows. In the next instant, his eyes adjusted and painted the terrible scene. Abbey dangled on a thin rope jammed through a hook at the top of the bathroom door. The rope was wound tightly around her neck, choking her, and her feet were inches off the floor. She couldn't breathe and couldn't make a sound, but she fought wildly, struggling and kicking to dislodge Yoko, who held her tightly as Abbey's oxygen bled away.

The noise of the door alerted Yoko now, and she let go. As Jason swung up his gun, the killer planted one leg on the carpet and spun, kicking the Sig out of Bourne's grasp, where it landed in shadows somewhere on the far side of the room. She charged, drawing her gun from her belt, but Jason grabbed her wrist as she raised the barrel. He twisted hard until Yoko screamed and the gun dropped. With a surge of adrenaline, he swung her entire body like a hammer throw, launching her off the ground and hurling her into the hotel room wall.

Yoko hit hard, crumpled, but then shrugged off the impact and was instantly back on her feet. As Jason bent for her gun, she took two steps and kicked, her foot landing under his chin and snapping his head back. He staggered, dizzied by the blow, and fell against the hotel bed. As he righted himself, he saw Abbey frantically clutching at the cord wound around her neck, but she couldn't free herself. She twisted and shunted, trying to dislodge the hook hammered into the top of the door, but it wouldn't budge. Her eyes bulged; the color of her face deepened into purple.

She had no air. She had only seconds.

Yoko charged again. She drove Jason backward onto the bed, her body on top of his. She was small but ferociously strong. As he tried to throw her, she clung to him and held on, her forearm crushing his throat. He head-butted her face, breaking her nose with a sickening crack, but the spray of blood over both of them didn't slow her at all. His left arm snaked free, and he hammered the side of her head, then wrenched her head back, far back, until he could sense the bones of her neck ready to break. She let go at the last second and sprang away, but he hooked a foot around her ankle, tripping her. She toppled onto the carpet, and he pushed off the bed, stripping a knife from its scabbard on his ankle. He landed on her, slashing with the blade, but she deflected the blow, which cut deeply through her shoulder.

Her knee hammered his groin. Her teeth bared. She hissed.

On the wall, Abbey's arms and legs twitched, then grew still.

Bourne drove a fist into Yoko's chest so hard that it nearly stopped her heart, and the killer was paralyzed for an instant. That was long enough. His arm free, he drove the point of the knife straight up into her chin, through her jaw and mouth, into the center of her head. Blood spurted between her locked teeth and out her nostrils. She squealed in agony but didn't die, and with a silent roar, he drew out the knife and struck again, a brutal blow down through her throat and windpipe, severing her spine and burying the blade so deeply it stuck in the floor under her body.

She was done now, flailing and gurgling.

Jason yanked the knife free. He flew to his feet and jumped for Abbey, who was now motionless and unconscious. He grabbed the cord that held her off the ground—it was not nylon rope, as he'd thought, but the silk belt of a bathrobe—and sliced cleanly through it with the blade. Her body dropped. He unwound the belt from her neck and pushed down heavily on her chest with both hands. Kneeling over her, Jason prepared to do CPR and force air into her lungs, but with a croaking gasp, Abbey's chest swelled. Her eyes flew open. She coughed and choked, dragging oxygen back into her body, and in the next seconds, the pink color began to return to her face.

She was alive.

On the floor a few feet away, Yoko was dead.

Abbey stared at him as if she couldn't believe he was real. She shook herself, then threw her arms around his neck, and her raspy voice whispered in his ear. "Oh, my God, it's you. You're here. You're really here. *Jason.*"

PART TWO

PART TWO

16

"WE CAN'T STAY HERE," JASON TOLD HER. "GATHER EVERY-
thing you've got. Quickly."

In a daze, Abbey got to her feet, then collapsed into
his arms, her knees buckling. He held her steady. She
reached out to touch the blood that was all over his face,
and then she stared at the dead woman sprawled on the
floor of the hotel room. Her voice fluttered, rising and
falling. "That woman. She was going to kill me. Who
was she?"

"As soon as we're safe, we'll talk, but we have to go
now. I need to wash up, and you need to pack."

"But who *was* she?" Abbey repeated, her mind con-
vulsed by shock.

Jason guided her to the bed and sat her down. He
took her by the shoulders and spoke softly. "Abbey, it's
okay. It's over. You're alive, and I'm going to keep you

safe, but we can't stay in this hotel. The man who sent this woman here will be expecting a report soon, and when he doesn't get it, he'll know something went wrong. That means there will be more killers arriving in a few minutes."

"But the woman—the body—"

"I don't think they'll want anyone to find her. They'll take care of the scene themselves. But if not, I have a contact in DC. A cleaner. I'll send him over here in the morning, and if necessary, he'll make sure the body is taken care of. No one will have any idea what happened here."

Abbey just shook her head over and over. Her eyes were glazed.

"Sit here," Jason told her. "For now, don't move. I'll take care of everything."

Bourne found her travel bag, and he checked the dresser and closets in the hotel room and repacked her clothes. She hadn't brought much, which was good. He found a few toiletries in the bathroom and shoved those in a pocket of her case, and then he washed his face and hair in the sink until the blood from his fight with Yoko was mostly gone. Unless someone looked closely, they wouldn't see anything amiss in his appearance.

Back in the main part of the hotel room, he checked Yoko's pockets. She had a fake ID, which he took with him; otherwise, there was nothing to tell him who she really was or to point him back to Lennon. He could wait and watch for the killers who would follow her, but he knew they would be no more than hired drones, knowing nothing. The trail to the assassin had gone cold again.

But for the moment, he didn't care about that. He had Abbey with him. She was back in his life.

When he had everything ready, he took her hand and guided her to her feet. "We need to get out of here. Can you do this?"

She stared at him blankly. "Yes. Yes, okay."

He led her to the door, put on the DO NOT DISTURB sign to keep the maid out, and guided her down the hallway with a hand around her waist. He had his gun in his other hand, coat slung over his arm to hide it. He didn't think that reinforcements would be on their way yet, but he was taking no chances. They stopped at his room, where he grabbed his daypack; it was always ready to go. Quickly, he shoved Abbey's things into his pack, then broke the zipper on her case and left it by the trash. A maid who found it wouldn't think twice about a damaged suitcase left behind.

They returned to the elevator, but he took them off one floor above the hotel entrance. He found the stairs and guided her down to the ground floor, then checked to make sure the lobby was empty before they emerged.

"Try to smile," he told her. "Act natural. Nothing's wrong."

She wasn't able to smile, but she did manage to walk on her own. He could feel her body trembling, and he was afraid she might collapse again. Jason held her hand tightly, squeezing her fingers for reassurance. They headed through the lobby, and he nodded at the desk

clerk, who didn't seem to find it unusual that two lovers
were heading out in the middle of the night. His daypack
attracted no attention. When they got to the street,
Bourne steered her past the church next door. Traffic was
light, but he kept an eye on the nearby cars and on the
park where he'd maintained his surveillance. At the corner, he took her arm and steered her diagonally across
the street and led her northward on 25th.

"I have a car in a garage a couple blocks away," Bourne
said. "It's not far."

Abbey said nothing. She just clutched his arm more
tightly.

They walked past rows of upscale Georgetown condo
buildings, with Jason forcing Abbey to go faster. Parked
cars lined the street, and he stayed alert, his gun ready
under his coat. When they reached the garage, they
found his rented black Jeep Wrangler, and he threw his
bag in the back. Abbey stood next to the car, her arms
wrapped around herself. Even when he opened the door
for her, she didn't get inside.

"Do you need help?" he asked.

"No." Her voice was stripped of emotion.

"Are you okay? Should I get you to a doctor?"

"No."

"Are you in pain?"

She touched her neck and grimaced. "A little, but it's
not that."

"Then what is it?"

Her lovely dark eyes found his in the shadows. They

were wide open, in shock, as her brain began to grasp the reality of what had just happened. When he looked at her, there was something in her face now that he'd seen in others many times. Fear. Fear of *him*. He'd seen it in Abbey's eyes before, but he'd hoped she was past that. But he didn't blame her for feeling that way.

"What you did—" she said. "That woman—"

Jason nodded. "I didn't have a choice."

He understood the images that were replaying in her mind. When they'd been together two years ago, she'd known what he was. He'd *told* her what he was. A killer. But she'd never seen it happen; she'd never actually witnessed the things he had to do. Now she had. She'd seen it up close, right in front of her. She'd seen a knife jutting out of a woman's throat, her dead eyes open in agony. That was his life.

"You saved me," she murmured. "It was just so— brutal."

"I know. I'm sorry."

She shook her head. "Don't be sorry. Fuck, don't ever be sorry, not with me."

"We need to go," he told her again.

"Yeah. Hang on."

Abbey wet her lips and swallowed hard. She inhaled loudly and took a couple of steps from the Jeep down the row of parked cars. She braced herself with one arm against a concrete support pillar in the garage. Then she bent over at the waist and vomited across the hood of a gold Mercedes.

* * *

THE ONLY LIGHT IN ROCK CREEK PARK CAME FROM THE GLOW
of the Jeep's headlights. It was still dark, and the park
was closed. The densely forested refuge felt a million
miles away from DC, although they were barely twenty
minutes north of the Melrose. He found a picnic area
on the road that paralleled the creek, and then he bumped
the Jeep over the curb onto the grass and parked inside the trees. Bourne turned off the engine and shut
down the headlights. They were only inches away from
each other, but they were largely invisible.

"Seems like you've done this before," Abbey said.

"I have."

Always know where to run. Always know where to hide.
Treadstone.

"We'll be safe here until sunrise," he went on. "You
can sleep if you want."

"I'll never sleep." She added a moment later, "I'm not
sure I'll ever sleep again."

They were quiet for a while. Feeling her next to him,
he remembered things about her from the brief time
they'd spent together. Her perfume. The way she
breathed. The softness of her skin. She'd changed her
hair and her look, but in the darkness, that didn't matter.
She felt intimately familiar to him, even after two years
apart.

"How, Jason?" she asked him finally. "How did you
find me? How did you know I needed you?"

"I didn't," he admitted. "I had no idea you were in-volved in any of this until I saw you get out of the cab at the hotel."

"But why were you even there?" Then, in the next instant, she put it together. "Her. That woman, that killer. You were following *her*."

"Yes."

"Who was she?"

"She worked for an assassin I've been tracking around the world. He calls himself Lennon. This woman was his latest number two. Yoko."

He heard a sour laugh in the car. "Lennon and Yoko? Seriously?"

"He thinks it's funny."

"And this Lennon. Are you after him for your bosses? For Treadstone?" He heard the part of her question that she didn't say out loud: *Are you still working for them? Are you still part of that world?*

"Partly. I've put distance between me and Treadstone, but Nash Rollins knows how to keep me from escaping the web entirely. You remember Nash, don't you? But this chase is also personal. Lennon claims to be a part of my past."

Abbey's voice was hushed. "The past you can't re-member."

"That's right."

"Why does that matter now, Jason?"

"Honestly? I don't know. I don't even know if what Lennon says is true. But there's something in my past that's still a threat, and I'm pretty sure Lennon knows what it is. Until I find it, I don't think I'll ever be able to move on."

"So you were following Yoko, hoping that she would lead you to Lennon," Abbey concluded. "Except now she's dead, and she can't help you."

Jason smiled. Abbey was always smart. "Pretty much. But I do have one lead that I didn't have before."

"What's that?"

"You. The people Lennon is working for obviously sent him after you. I don't know why, but they want you dead, Abbey."

"I know why," she replied bitterly. "Or at least, I think I do. You obviously haven't spent any time online recently, have you? I'm a nonperson now. They made up vicious lies about me, and that was enough to destroy my career. I'm sure they figured no one would question that I'd hung myself. If you hadn't been there, the story would have been Disgraced Journalist Commits Suicide."

Jason reached for her. "Jesus, Abbey."

Then he thought about the short black hair. The downscale clothes. The lack of makeup.

"You're in hiding, aren't you?" he asked. "You've been trying to disguise yourself."

"Yeah, but they found me anyway."

"Do you know who they are? Or what made them come after you?"

Abbey sighed, and she told him everything. About the girl named Iris—now dead—and her conspiracy theories. About the murder victim called Deborah Mueller who didn't seem to exist at all. About a group operating in the shadows that goes by the name the Pyramid. Jason listened to the whole story, and his mind worked feverishly to connect what had happened to her with what he knew of Kenna Martin, Darrell Forster, and Varak. And Lennon.

"The tattoo," he murmured. "This tattoo on Deborah Mueller that they tried to hide in the media photographs. I've come across people who have it, too. It's obviously some kind of brand for people working for the Pyramid."

"So the Pyramid is what ties this all together," Abbey said. "We've been working the same story from opposite sides."

"I think so."

"Well, where do we go from here?"

Jason heard the way she phrased it. *We.* The two of them together. Just like two years ago, Abbey wanted to stay with him. The risks didn't matter to her, and this time, he didn't object, because she was right. If she had any hope of getting her life back, it lay in exposing the Pyramid.

"The kid in Hyattsville told you that Deborah Mueller was meeting someone," Jason said. "Older man, vintage car. We need to find him."

"How?"

Bourne thought about it. "He came back to the park two days after the murder. Even if the Pyramid was able to eliminate video evidence from the night that Deborah

Mueller was killed, they probably didn't think to erase security camera footage from later on. Maybe we can find him that way."

"Security there is handled by the park police, right?" Abbey asked. "Will they let you see the footage?"

"Nash has contacts. Treadstone has its fingers everywhere. I'll call him in the morning, and he'll find a source for us. Until then, you really need to get some sleep. Even if you don't think you can."

"Because sleep is a weapon?" she asked with a smirk in her voice.

He smiled, hearing her throw his Treadstone rules back in his face. "Yes, it is."

Jason eased Abbey down across the seats into his lap. He couldn't see her face in the darkness, but he stroked her hair and ran the back of his hand along her cheek. It felt natural to do so. Too natural. Too easy. He was already breaking the first of the rules again. The one Lennon had used to mock him. *Never get involved.*

"Hey, Jason?" Abbey murmured. Her voice already sounded thick with exhaustion.

"What is it?"

"I'm sorry about my note. You got it, right?"

"I did."

"Well, I'm sorry for what I said. I was pissed that you were cutting me off. Not staying in touch."

"I was trying to keep you safe."

"By keeping me away from you?"

"Yes."

She was quiet for a long time, long enough that he

wondered if she'd already drifted into sleep. Her breathing grew steady under his hands. Then her fingers curled tightly around his, and she whispered to him.

"Don't do that again. Don't shut me out. I'm a big girl, Jason. I know what it means to be with someone like you. And I'm all in."

17

"LENNON TOOK NO CHANCES," BOURNE SAID AS THEY AP-
proached the area near the Tidal Basin where Deborah
Mueller had been murdered. The bone-white monu-
ments to Washington and Jefferson glistened under the
morning sunshine on the other side of the water. "See
the camera on the light post? It was disabled. Shot out.
He wanted to make sure there was no record of what
happened."

"You think it was Lennon himself?" Abbey asked.
"He did the actual killing?"

"The description of him was tall and blond. That fits,
although he changes his appearance a lot. I'm beginning
to think that the payoff in Iceland was for Mueller's murder. Which means the Pyramid was taking no chances
with her. If they brought in Lennon, she must have been

a high-value target, and they've worked hard to keep the truth behind her death under the radar."

"But who *was* she? My source at ICE couldn't find her at all. It's like her photo had been erased from the system."

"Lennon has moles in most of the government agencies. Plus the airlines, too, I'm sure. He could have eliminated any record of her arrival, made sure she got wiped off the books. That's why people pay for Lennon's services. It's not just a question of assassinations. There are a lot of killers for hire if you don't care how it's done. But Lennon can handle things quietly in a way that others can't."

They continued past the cherry trees to the water, where the sidewalk was crowded with tourists. Abbey pointed out the area where the killing had taken place, and she played him the video from her phone of the homeless woman who'd witnessed the murder. Then she showed him the second video of the taxi line outside Reagan National, where the woman named Deborah Mueller had skipped to the third taxi in the queue.

Bourne played it twice more, and then he froze the video in place. His finger tapped the screen. "She was already being followed."

Abbey leaned in to see where Jason was pointing. "Where? How do you know?"

"This man here. The middle-aged guy in the turtleneck. He's checking his phone whenever Mueller looks his way, but as soon as she focuses somewhere else, he's watching her. They knew she was coming. Hell, this guy was probably on the same plane with her."

"He doesn't look like a killer."

"He's not. Just surveillance. The video cuts off as Mueller leaves, but I'm sure he passed along her cab number to somebody outside the airport. Then they took over the tail as the cab headed out."

"So the whole meeting was a trap?" Abbey asked.

"No, I don't think so. Not the meeting itself. If it was, the guy she was planning to meet wouldn't have come back a couple of days later. In fact, he wouldn't have shown up at all. He would have left the whole thing to Lennon. That's what makes him worth finding. Whatever this meeting was, it was worth killing Deborah Mueller to stop it from taking place."

They continued along the Tidal Basin. Ten minutes later, after crossing the channel over the Potomac on Ohio Drive, they arrived outside the Jefferson Memorial. They sought out the wide grassy area behind the colonnade, where the imposing statue of Jefferson was just visible between the white columns. Bourne spotted a park police officer in the middle of the grass. She was only in her mid-twenties, Black, with rigid posture. Her hair was tucked under her cap, and her uniform fit snugly on her muscular physique.

"Is that our contact?" Abbey asked quietly.

"Yes."

"Do you want me to hang back?"

"No, you should hear this, too."

Bourne approached the police officer in the grass. She

had no smile, and her eyes watched him warily, which told him that she knew he was the man she was supposed to meet. He came up beside her and made a show of pointing at the memorial, as if he were nothing but a tourist asking a question.

"Who's your favorite president?" Bourne asked.

"How about Chester A. Arthur? I'm a sucker for muttonchops."

Jason smiled. "Nash says hi."

"Yeah, right. Tell Nash I do this, and we're even."

"I will."

The police officer eyed Abbey. "Who's this? Nash didn't say anything about a third party."

"She's with me," Bourne replied.

The woman shrugged, then gestured at the building, as if answering Jason's history questions. "First of all, you're right about the night of the Mueller murder. Somebody took out the security camera in that area. So we don't have any footage that shows what actually happened. Although I don't know what you're looking for, because the whole thing sounded pretty cut-and-dried."

"And what about two days later? The parking area?"

She frowned. "Nash said you were looking to ID an old man driving a vintage silver car with out-of-state plates. That doesn't exactly narrow it down around here. Every retiree in the country shows up in DC sooner or later, and silver or gray is a pretty common color. Plus, it was cherry blossom season. Everybody has to see the cherry blossoms."

"What did you find?" Bourne asked.

"Ten possibles. I captured the best shots I could get from the feeds."

She dug into her pocket and slid out her phone. With a few taps, she opened the photos app and slipped the device to Bourne. Still pretending to converse about the memorial, he began to examine the pictures, which all showed old men in or near gray and silver cars in the parking area near the FDR memorial. Abbey sidled close to him, and together they swiped through the photographs.

A couple of the pictures were too blurred to make out the faces properly. There was also one silver SUV from DC, not out of state. Two of the men looked way too young, their hair too dark, to match the description that Abbey had gotten from the postal worker in Hyattsville.

Bourne glanced at Abbey. "What do you think?"

"I'm not sure how to tell which one it could be. Or whether it's any of them."

"Look again," Jason said.

With his thumb, he scrolled slowly through the pictures a second time, and this time, he enlarged the faces as much as he could with each photograph. He wished that the park police officer had downloaded actual video clips, rather than stills, because the behavior of each person would have helped rule them in or out. With just a picture of a face, it was hard to isolate whether one of these men was something more than a tourist.

Then Abbey said, "Wait. Look at that one."

Bourne stopped. He examined the picture that had

drawn Abbey's attention. The man in the photograph was old, possibly in his eighties. He wore stylish sunglasses that wouldn't have been out of place on a much younger man, and his clothes were casual but definitely expensive. Age had worn deep wrinkles into his skin, but he had a notably angular face, the bones looking as if they could have been sculpted by an artist working in stone. He was tall, with shoulders slightly hunched, as if worn down by time.

The silver car he stood beside definitely qualified as vintage. A collector's car. It was a Lincoln Continental Mark IV that must have dated back to the 1970s. And the plates were partially cut off in the photograph, but the coloring suggested that the car was registered in Pennsylvania.

"He fits the profile," Bourne agreed, "but so do a couple of the others."

Abbey shook her head. "It's more than that."

"What do you mean?"

"I feel like I *know* him. I mean, I'm sure we've never met, but I know who he is."

"Who?"

She frowned. "That's the thing, I'm trying to place him. I've seen the face, but younger, and only in a photograph. A formal portrait. No sunglasses. He's got amazing blue eyes. I can *see* his blue eyes, so I know I've seen his photo somewhere. Damn it, *where?* The picture was close-up, like on the—"

Abbey stopped. Jason watched her squeeze her eyes

shut, trying to think, trying to *remember*. He knew only too well that memory didn't work that way. But then Abbey's eyes flew open.

"*Serpent!*" she whispered.

"What?"

"The novel that came out last year. The one that was obviously about the Medusa operation. I wrote to you about it, don't you remember? There were characters in it that seemed to be based on you and me. They were too close to both of us to be a coincidence. I think I even asked you if you'd talked to him."

"I didn't," Bourne replied, "but I remember you mentioning the book in one of your letters."

Abbey jabbed a finger at the photograph. "It's *him*. He wrote it. He wrote *Serpent!* He's been writing conspiracy thrillers like that for years—Jesus, for decades. I found one of his books in the library when I was a teenager. It was supposedly just a novel, but the premise was that J. Edgar Hoover had actually been murdered. I remember thinking that he knew something, like it really could have happened that way. There's no way this is a coincidence, Jason. Deborah Mueller was in DC to meet *him*. His name is Peter Chancellor."

BY NIGHTFALL, AFTER NEARLY SIX HOURS OF DRIVING, JASON and Abbey were near the town of Clarendon, Pennsylvania, population three hundred and seventy. Their route took them deep into the heart of the Allegheny National Forest. Dense trees closed in on both sides, but every few miles, they passed a lonely house or trailer carved out of the wilderness. The road was dark, with a railroad track and overhead power lines running parallel to the highway. Somewhere nearby—they didn't know exactly where—was the wooded hideaway belonging to Peter Chancellor. According to magazine articles they'd found, Chancellor lived like one of the characters in his conspiracy novels, in a reclusive, high-security estate.

Clarendon itself was only a few blocks long, tucked in a valley between the ridge lines of hills on both sides. Bourne's rented Jeep was the only vehicle on the road. The small population lived in modest country homes, and the people and their children were mostly inside for the night. There were no fences separating neighbors. It was the kind of locals-only area where everyone knew everyone else, and Bourne was counting on the fact that a millionaire celebrity author couldn't hope for privacy in a place like this.

The town included one stoplight on the main road, which was one more than it really seemed to need. A small tavern with a weathered wooden exterior was located at the intersection, and it seemed to be the only business that was still open in Clarendon when they arrived late in the evening. There were several other vehicles in the gravel lot adjacent to the building.

Bourne parked there, and he and Abbey got out. It was a cool night, and the sky was bright with stars. Inside, half a dozen people clustered near the counter of the bar, and others played darts and hung out in small groups. Alan Jackson sang on the jukebox. There was a

loud, drunken vibe in the place, but it came to a dead
halt—other than the chorus of "Chattahoochee"—as
soon as they walked in. Strangers were obviously a rare
sight here, and nobody hid their curiosity. Bourne ignored the stares as he led Abbey to two empty stools at
the far end of the bar.

The bartender was a woman in her thirties, with
bushy blond hair, who wore a Phillies T-shirt and old
blue jeans. She was pleasant enough and obviously figured a customer was a customer, even if they were
out-of-towners. "What'll you two have?"

"Rolling Rock," Bourne said. That was his own rule.
Always order what the locals were drinking.

Abbey nodded, taking a cue from Jason. "Same."

The woman popped open two green bottles and put
them in front of them. "So what brings you two in here?"

"We're just passing through on our way to James-
town," Bourne said.

"You want some food?"

"Sure."

They both ordered burgers. While they waited,
Bourne spun around on the stool and checked out the
other people in the tavern. He and Abbey were still the
center of attention. The crowd stole glances at them and
conversed under their breath, no doubt speculating
about who they were. Most of the people appeared to be
harmless, but Bourne spotted four men at a table in the
corner who didn't hide their suspicion of the newcomers.
All four were in their thirties, burly and tall, and one
seemed to be the leader of the pack. He was bald, wear-

ing a camouflage jacket and drinking whiskey rather than beer. His rolled-up sleeves revealed muscular arms and multiple military tattoos. Unlike the others, who shot sideways glances at Bourne and Abbey, this man held Jason's stare without flinching.

Their burgers came. They ate in silence and nursed their beers. About ten minutes later, the man in camouflage pushed back his chair with a screech and came up to the bar. He stood next to Bourne, flagging the bartender's attention. He didn't look at Jason, or say anything, but the man stood close enough that his arm bumped Bourne and caused him to spill some of his Rolling Rock.

The man didn't apologize. Bourne said nothing, but as the bartender headed their way, he nudged Abbey. He wanted the man to overhear their question.

Abbey smiled at the blond woman behind the bar. "Hey, I'm curious. I read that Peter Chancellor lives near here. Do you know where?"

The bartender glanced at the man in camouflage, then back at Abbey. "Who?"

"Peter Chancellor. You know, the writer."

"Sorry. Don't know him."

The pained look on her face made it clear that she was lying. Next to Bourne, the bald man slowly clenched his fists together. Instead of ordering more beers, he waved the bartender away and then returned to the table in the corner. Not long after, all four men got up and left the bar.

Bourne and Abbey took their time finishing their meals. He didn't drink most of his beer, and neither did she. Half an hour later, he paid cash, and they got off the stool and headed for the door, with the eyes of the crowd still following them. They exited to the quiet main street, then turned left to the gravel lot where he'd parked the Jeep. He had his hands in his pockets, fingers around the butt of his Sig.

The bald man in camouflage was waiting for them. He leaned against Bourne's Jeep, one hand holding a phone, the other holding a Smith & Wesson revolver. Next to him, one of the other men stood with a Ruger 10/22 rifle pointed across the lot at Bourne's chest. Jason stopped, then glanced over his shoulder to see another man emerge from around the far side of the tavern, an AR-15 propped against his shoulder. The last man walked their way down the sidewalk north of the bar. He carried a shotgun.

Their escape routes were closed off.

"Jason," Abbey murmured.

"Don't worry. It's okay."

Bourne stayed where he was. He took his hands slowly out of his jacket pockets and spread his fingers wide. "Evening. We're not looking for any trouble here. What can we do for you gentlemen?"

"Why are you looking for Peter Chancellor?" the man in camouflage asked.

"I'm a fan," Abbey blurted out, before Jason could stop her. "I've read a lot of his books."

The man was smart enough to recognize the lie. "Bullshit. What's the real reason?"

"All right, we want to talk to him," Bourne said.

"Why?"

"We think he has information that can help us."

"What kind of information?"

"About a woman named Deborah Mueller," Bourne replied. "She was murdered in Washington. We think Mr. Chancellor knows why."

"And who are you?" the man asked.

Jason nodded for Abbey to talk first.

"My name is Abbey Laurent," she said. "I'm a journalist. Although I suspect Mr. Chancellor already knows that, because he based a character in his book *Serpent!* on me."

The man in camouflage waited, but Bourne said nothing more.

"What about you?" he demanded when he could see that he wasn't getting a reply.

"I'm with her," Bourne said simply.

There was a long silence. Then the man held up the phone to his ear and said, "You get all that? What do you want us to do?"

The man listened, then hung up the phone and shoved it back in his pocket. He holstered his pistol and nodded at the other three men, who lowered their weapons. He took a few steps away from the Jeep, clearing a path for Bourne and Abbey.

"Follow us," the man in camouflage told them. "He's waiting for you."

18

THE BALD MAN AND ONE OF HIS FRIENDS LED THE WAY NORTH-
ward out of Clarendon in a white F-150, with Bourne's
Jeep keeping pace behind it. The other two men brought
up the rear in an olive green Ford Explorer. The parade
on the highway lasted for about two miles, and then Jason saw the F-150 turn onto an unmarked dirt road that
led upward into the trees. He followed, noticing that the
third vehicle stayed behind, blocking access to the road.
They climbed in sharp switchbacks, following the slope
of a wooded hill rising above the valley. In the glow of
his headlights, he spotted security cameras mounted in
the trees.

As they reached the summit of the hill, the road
opened into a wide clearing. In the middle of a lush lawn,
landscaped with fruit trees and flower gardens, was a
sprawling log home with several steep gables. The front

porch was illuminated by lights, and Bourne saw an old man standing at the top of the steps, awaiting their arrival. He recognized him from the photo they'd seen. It was Peter Chancellor.

The F-150 pulled to a stop in front of the porch, and Bourne parked the Jeep behind it. The man in camouflage got out, and Chancellor came down the steps and greeted him by shaking his hand. Bourne and Abbey got out, too.

"Thank you, Timothy," the writer told the man. "I appreciate the help from you and your friends, as always. I think you can go now. We'll be fine here."

"Yes, sir." The man nodded at Bourne. "I'm sure that one's armed."

Chancellor smiled. "I'd expect nothing less."

The bald man nodded, shot a wary look at Bourne, then got into the F-150 and drove off down the hillside, leaving Bourne and Abbey alone with Chancellor. The writer approached Abbey first.

"Ms. Laurent, I'm so pleased to meet you. I've followed what they've done to you online this week. How terrible."

"It's all a lie," she told him.

"Well, of course it is." He turned to Bourne. "And I assume you are the one they call Cain?"

Jason had to suppress the look of surprise on his face. He hadn't expected this man to know who he was, but there was no point in pretending that Chancellor was wrong. "That's an identity I've used, yes."

A little smile broke across the writer's face. "I have

good sources, you see. That's one advantage of being around as long as I have. Plus, as Abbey correctly surmised, I became familiar with the two of you when I did my research for *Serpent!* Well, please, won't you come inside? We have a lot to talk about."

The interior of the log home was expensively decorated, but in an antique style that matched their country surroundings, lush with aged wood and leather. There was nothing modern about it—except for the discreet high-tech security devices in every room—and there was also nothing modern about the man who lived here. Peter Chancellor was as tall as Bourne, and dressed in dark khakis, with a thick yellow wool sweater over his torso that looked hand-knitted. His hair was wavy and gray, but still full. He was an old man, at least eighty, and he walked with a slight limp, but otherwise, his entire attitude was alert and full of energy. His face was sharply angled, which Bourne remembered from the photograph, and Abbey had been right about the power of his eyes. They were light blue, friendly when they looked at the two of them, but also constantly moving and missing nothing. Even in the secure surroundings of his home, Chancellor seemed to be always on alert.

He led them to a large high-ceilinged library at the back of the house. The ceiling and frame, like the house's exterior, were constructed of logs hewn from light oak. One wall was made up entirely of windows that obviously looked out across the hills of the national forest during the daylight hours. Another wall included an enormous fieldstone fireplace. Around the fireplace, and taking up the other walls, were built-in bookshelves lined with hundreds of hardcover volumes. Bourne noticed that all the books appeared to be written by Chancellor, some in English, but many others in translated editions reflecting dozens of foreign languages. The titles all had the same unusual style, a single word followed by an exclamation point.

Reichstag!
Sarajevo!
Counterstrike!
Genesis!
Serpent!

And many more. It was a library dedicated to nearly five decades of novel-writing.

"This is amazing," Abbey said.

"Vain is probably a better word," Chancellor replied with a smirk. "Or so my wife tells me. But when you get nearer to the end of your life, you like to be reminded of the things you've done. All around you, these books are my legacy. Other people can find other meanings for themselves."

"Well, the entire house is beautiful," Abbey went on.

"And secure," Bourne added pointedly.

Chancellor shot him a stare that was equal parts pride and self-awareness. "Alison does the decorating, so if it's beautiful, that's her work. The security is my doing. As is the remote location and the 'friends' you met in town. The people of Clarendon look out for me and my wife. They're very protective of us. I suppose you think I'm paranoid, that I confuse my fiction with real life."

"I don't think that at all," Bourne replied.

"Well, good. Believe me, my life has been threatened more than once. My books have dealt with sensitive issues, outrageous conspiracies. Things that powerful people would prefer to keep concealed. I wrap them up as novels, but more often than not, the truth is even worse."

"All right, Peter, get off your soapbox," said a teasing voice from the doorway.

A woman joined them, carrying a wooden tray that had the makings of an elegant tea service. She was as old as Chancellor, but regardless of age, Jason could see that she was an elegant, beautiful woman. Her hair was colored light brown and fell easily about her shoulders. Her face had a delicate, china-like bone structure, her makeup carefully applied. Her motions were precise, as if every step, every turn, every expression, had to be thought out in advance. Looking at Bourne and Abbey, her smile was polite, but still maintained a distance that seemed almost aloof. But that reticence disappeared when she looked at Chancellor. It was clear that they were deeply in love.

"This is my wife, Alison," Chancellor introduced her. "We met when I was working on *Genesis!* I can't believe that was nearly fifty years ago."

"That was your Hoover book, wasn't it?" Abbey asked.

"Yes, exactly."

"I have to tell you, it didn't read like fiction. I was convinced that was how it happened. That Hoover was murdered."

Chancellor and Alison shared a look between them, and both just smiled.

"Tea?" Alison asked.

They all took seats in comfortable chairs near the fireplace, and for a few minutes, the four of them talked about books, authors, and writing. The tea was hot and sweetened with honey and lemon. A Doberman joined them and curled up near Chancellor's feet—a friendly dog, but Bourne had no doubt that it would defend its owners to the death if called upon. Chancellor and Alison shared stories about life in Pennsylvania, as well as their travels, which had taken them around the world for research on his novels.

Bourne found Chancellor himself to be an interesting enigma. The old man still showed flashes of a young man railing against the system, exposing violence and corruption. He paged through a couple of the man's novels that lay on an end table near him, and even just a glimpse of Chancellor's prose showed the raw dramatic power of an author wielding his pen like a sword. But then the man would look at his wife, and his face would soften, and he'd be reminded of his age.

An hour later, when the tea was done, Alison announced that she was heading to bed. She got up and offered Bourne and Abbey both a delicate handshake, and then she kissed the top of her husband's head. She left them alone, and Chancellor's eyes followed her until she was gone.

"Does she know?" Bourne asked.

The writer's eyes shifted to Jason. "Know what?"

"That you still take risks. Like you did in DC."

Chancellor gave them a weary, secret smile. "I pretend to be careful, and she pretends to believe me. I could retire, but then what would I do? Writing is in my blood. But all the security here? I do that for her. I don't care what happens to me, but Alison saw too much violence growing up. When I married her, I swore to keep her safe."

Abbey leaned forward, her hands on her knees. "It *was* you, wasn't it? You came to DC to meet the woman named Deborah Mueller. The woman who was murdered in West Potomac Park. You were there that night."

Chancellor frowned. "Yes. I was. Although I admit, I'm curious how you found me."

"You were seen near her body. And then you came back a couple of days later, and a witness spotted you again. That's how we tracked you. Someone remembered you and your car."

"The Silver Mark IV," he reflected. "I suppose it's a pretty obvious vehicle. I've had a new engine put inside it more than once. More vanity, I guess. Alison says it's foolish. I almost died in a car like that a long time ago, but I keep it as a reminder of the past. Of a time when I was an angry young man. Anyway, yes, I went there to meet Deborah Mueller. That's not her name, of course. That's just an identity they created for her."

Then Chancellor eyed Bourne with a glimmer in his pale blue eyes. "You know a little bit about that sort of thing yourself, don't you?"

Again Bourne felt unnerved by how much the writer knew about him. "I do."

"So who *was* she?" Abbey asked. "If she wasn't Deborah Mueller, who was she really?"

"I only knew her as Louisa," Chancellor replied. "Beyond that, I don't know her full name."

"And why the meeting? Was it your idea? Or hers?"

Chancellor pushed himself out of the chair and clicked on the gas fireplace, which came to life in flames. His reflective face was in shadows. "If I tell you, what do you plan to do with the information?"

"Find the people who killed her," Bourne replied.

"And then will you kill them?" Chancellor asked.

Jason didn't answer, but the look on the writer's face said he already knew the truth.

"I'm not saying I have a problem with that, but I do have one condition for our conversation," he went on.

"What is it?" Abbey asked.

Chancellor returned to the chair and sat down again. "Very simply, Ms. Laurent, the condition is you."

"I don't understand."

"When you're done with whatever you're doing here, I want you to come back and tell me everything. Hold nothing back. The truth, the secrets. And then I'd like you and me to work together and write it all down as a novel. Because like I told you, fiction is my reality. The rest of the world can decide for themselves what to believe."

"Why do you need me?" Abbey asked. "You've written dozens of novels."

"Because I'm old." Chancellor smiled, and his eyes

drifted to the many books on the bookshelves. "And because I'm dying. Cancer. Please, please, no sympathy, it is what it is. I've led an amazing life, and I've had the love of an amazing woman. I'm a lucky man. But death has a way of focusing your thoughts on what you leave behind. I'd like my work to continue. I know a lot about you, Abbey Laurent. I researched you extensively when I was writing *Serpent!* Back then, I remember thinking you were the kind of writer who could do what I do. Write books that let you channel your outrage, fight back against the system."

Jason watched Abbey's face fill with surprise. She hadn't expected this at all. Even so, he also realized that her mind was working furiously. Yes, she was flattered, but this was something more than that. He saw a hunger there. A sense of purpose and possibility. When he'd left her in Quebec City, she'd been unsure of her future, and now her future was up in the air again. She'd been flying in circles, looking for a place to land. But Peter Chancellor had just offered her an opportunity that clicked in both her heart and head.

She glanced at Jason, as if needing his approval, which she didn't. But he nodded anyway.

"All right," Abbey said. "All right, I agree. It would be an honor to work with you."

"Excellent."

"But now back to the reason we're here," Bourne interrupted them. He stared at Chancellor until the writer turned his attention back to him. "Deborah Mueller. *Louisa.* Tell us what happened in DC."

"I will, but first you need a little history lesson." Chancellor eased back in his chair and steepled his fingers together. "Fifty years ago, I discovered the existence of a group of men who called themselves *Inver Brass*. They were powerful, accomplished people. Academics. Judges. Bankers. Philanthropists. The group went back for decades, men—nearly all men—who wielded incredible amounts of money to solve critical problems around the world when they felt that political leaders had failed to do so. They stepped in behind the scenes, shaping policy, influencing decisions, stemming the sources of violence and unrest wherever they could. Their tactics were often ruthless. People were killed. Ultimately, they became the very evil they were trying to destroy, so they had to be destroyed themselves."

Abbey shook her head. "I don't understand. You said this was fifty years ago. What does this have to do with a murder in Washington? Why does it matter now?"

"It matters," Chancellor told them, "because Inver Brass is back."

19

"TODAY THEY CALL THEMSELVES THE PYRAMID," CHANCELLOR
went on. "But make no mistake. Their goals are the
same, to take control where they see a failure of political
leadership. They have the same hubris as the original
members of Inver Brass—the hubris of powerful people
everywhere—that they know better than everyone else.
They think they can save democracy—ironically, by dic-
tating what they want people to believe. And they are
every bit as ruthless about the ends justifying their
means. Obviously, you can attest to that, Abbey. You got
in their way, and their response was to destroy you."

Bourne got up and paced, trying to wrap his head
around what Chancellor was telling them. "How do you
know about all this? I haven't even heard about this
from—"

He stopped.

"From Treadstone?" Chancellor replied with a smile. "Oh, yes, I know about them, too. Which is why I know about you. The thing is, my books are designed to do exactly what Abbey said earlier. To make people wonder if certain conspiracies could be possible, to ask if this is how it really happened. Because of this, over the years, I've been contacted by many people who know things that others wish to hide. Secrets. Crimes. Failures and mistakes by governments and businesses. These are the stories that I expose, in my way, as fiction. But the people who reach out to me often can't go anywhere else. They don't trust the government or the legal system to get to the truth or to protect them. And more and more, they don't trust the media, either. Sadly, with good reason. But they trust *me*, because my only agenda is telling the truth. Which is ironic, of course, given my profession."

Bourne went to the rows and rows of bookshelves, and he ran his hand over some of the spines. He liked Chancellor, and he knew the man was sincere in his outrage. He also knew, looking at Abbey's face, that she was drawn to the old writer's idealism and fire. She was much the same way herself. But Bourne didn't have the luxury of that brand of naivete. Words on a page only masked the hard choices that needed to be made. In the end, there wasn't really a lot of difference between Inver Brass and Treadstone.

"Did Louisa tell you about the Pyramid?" he asked Chancellor. "Did she reach out to you?"

"Actually, no, I went looking for her. Or someone like her. I've heard rumors about the Pyramid for years. In fact, I've been expecting some version of Inver Brass to be resurrected for a while now. Mostly because of who's behind it."

"You know who that is?"

"I have my suspicions. You see, the man who led Inver Brass in the 1970s—when they were manipulating me and Alison—went by the code name Genesis. Hence the name of my book. Genesis started out as a good man, but ultimately, power did to him what it always does. It corrupted him. Made him blind to the evils of what they were doing. There was a Czech immigrant who worked with Genesis back then. He did much of the dirty work for Inver Brass. He was a ruthless, talented operative—brilliant, in his own twisted way. Ultimately, he was killed, as was Genesis, when Inver Brass eventually fell. But this operative left a legacy behind for others to exploit. A son."

"Who was this man?" Abbey asked.

Chancellor frowned. "His name was Varak."

"Varak?" Bourne hissed from the other side of the room.

"Yes. Exactly. I'm sure you know the name. After the father's death, his son was brought up by a rural couple in a small town in Iceland—ostensibly an ordinary life, but with hidden advantages that made sure he would be successful. I knew about him. I watched his rise. And I suspected that one day, Varak the son would follow in the footsteps of his father. He would lead the return of Inver Brass. Only this time, *he* would be Genesis."

"The Pyramid," Abbey said.

"That's right."

"What exactly is the Pyramid? What does it do?"

"Well, it's all cloaked in respectability, of course. The Varak Institute is the public face, funded by billions funneled through his 'foundation.' And who could argue with the premise? Combat the rampant misinformation and disinformation propagated through social media. Focus on facts. Create panels of subject matter experts in science, economics, energy, whatever—and then work with the media and technology companies to emphasize those responsible voices instead of uninformed rumormongers. I'm sure you remember that Varak was treated as a hero when the institute was announced."

"The savior of democracy," Abbey said.

Chancellor chuckled. "Yes, because democracy is far too important to be left to the actual people."

"So are the institute and the Pyramid the same thing?" Bourne asked.

"No, no, as I said, the institute is the cover. The Pyramid *is* Inver Brass—a small group of leaders, with Varak as Genesis. Some of the others are media, but I assume there are more. Politicians, scientists, academics, maybe military, too. They decide on the message and do whatever it takes to control it, because they know that whoever controls the message controls what people believe. You only know what you're told, after all. If you don't read about it online, or in the newspaper, or on television, then it might as well not exist. It started with suppression. Strategic censorship. Stories that didn't advance the desired narrative simply vanished from public view. A few thousand people heard about something? So what? As long as *millions* knew nothing about it, the story didn't exist."

"I assume it hasn't stopped there," Bourne said.

"No. It hasn't." Chancellor got up and went to the heavy library door and closed it. "This is the part I'd rather Alison not hear."

"Does Varak know about you?" Bourne asked. "Are people trying to kill *you*?"

"Well, Varak is ruthless, just like his father was. Fortunately, up until now, I think he and his colleagues have seen me as harmless. A novelist, someone who makes things up. But I'm worried Louisa may have changed that. That's why I've been taking extra precautions, including the men you met at the tavern."

"Those men won't be much good against the kind of people Varak employs," Bourne warned him. "I got involved with this because I'm chasing an assassin. One of the best in the world. Treadstone thinks he's working for someone new, and I'm pretty sure that means Varak and the Pyramid. If they want you dead, he'll find you, and he'll kill you. Your security measures won't be good enough to stop him."

"I'm aware of the risks," Chancellor assured him.

Abbey shivered and got up, too. Talk of Lennon obviously reminded her of what she'd been through in the hotel room in DC. How Lennon's Yoko had nearly killed *her*. She came up to Bourne, and in a gesture that felt very natural, she slung her arm around his waist. He liked it. He liked it far too much.

"Tell us about Louisa," she said.

Chancellor's face darkened. He shoved his hands in his pockets and wandered to the windows, where he stared out at the darkness. "I feel very guilty about Louisa. She's dead because of me."

"How did you connect with her?"

The writer turned back to face them. "Abbey, I believe you met a young woman who first told you about the murder in DC."

"Iris? You know about her?"

Chancellor nodded. "She made contact with you at my suggestion. As I told you, I've been quite interested in you ever since I wrote *Serpent!*"

"Iris is dead, too," Abbey told him. "Killed. Did you know that?"

"Yes. I was devastated to hear it. The walls of the Pyramid are closing in, you see. That's what makes this so urgent. And so dangerous. Iris was part of an online group that I use from time to time as my eyes and ears when I need research for my books. I don't leave my estate here very often anymore. I don't want to leave Alison alone, and frankly, I'm an old man now. Traveling is a burden. So the young people online go where I can't go. Much of what I know about the Pyramid is because of work they did. Of course, none of them know it's me or who I am. I stay in the shadows, just one more anonymous account. It's all done on the dark web, and I thought that was keeping us safe, but I was wrong. Someone inside the Pyramid found the group. Found *me*. As it happened, I was lucky, because it was someone who'd grown disillusioned with the things she was forced to do. She reached out and told me she wanted to meet."

"Louisa," Abbey concluded.

"Yes."

"What did she tell you?"

"Not a lot. She was concerned about our messages being intercepted. She said she worked at something called the bot farm. I don't know where it's located, but I gather it's a technology center for the Pyramid. She hinted at the things they do there. Deepfakes, hacked social media accounts, artificial identities. The things that happened to you, Abbey? I'm sure they originated at this bot farm."

"Jesus," Abbey murmured.

"But Louisa indicated there was much more. She was one of their most trusted people, which meant traveling around the world to implement complex operations in the field. *Lies*. She manufactured lies, amplified all over the media, used to do everything from shape legislation to sway elections. According to Louisa, those lies included murder. She didn't give me details, but she said she would when we met in person. She swore that she had no idea how far it had all gone, and when she discovered the truth, that's what convinced her to betray them. To tell me everything and get my help in exposing the Pyramid."

"So the two of you agreed to meet in DC," Bourne said.

"Yes. She flew in that night."

"From where?"

Chancellor shook his head. "That I don't know. I gave her detailed instructions on how to shake a tail—I've learned some tricks of the trade over the years from people like you—and we arranged a meeting in West Potomac Park. However, for all the precautions, the Pyramid obviously discovered what she was planning to do. They killed her. I would have been killed, too, if I'd been there on time. But I was fifteen minutes late. I planned to walk from my hotel, but of all things, my knee went out halfway there. I've been putting off having it replaced, and it stiffened up on me. By the time I got there, I was horrified to find that Louisa was dead."

"You didn't talk to the police?" Abbey asked.

The writer shrugged. "And tell them what? I had no evidence of anything. By the next morning, it was clear that the Pyramid had already erased who Louisa was. She'd become a fictional creation, like one of my own characters."

"What did you do next?"

"I hinted in my online group that there was more to this murder than the media and police were saying. They took it from there, and they came up with quite a lot of evidence to challenge the official story. But the Pyramid suppressed everything they found. It was like none of it ever existed. Videos, witnesses, airline manifests, customs info. All gone. That's when I sent an anonymous message to Iris and suggested that she reach out to you for help. I even mentioned that I'd 'heard' that a character in a Peter Chancellor novel was based on you. It may sound vain, but that upped your credibility with her."

"But why not contact me directly?" Abbey asked.

Chancellor hesitated. "To be honest, I didn't know whether I could trust *you*. The Pyramid has people everywhere, especially in the media. It wasn't safe for you to know about me until I was sure you weren't part of them. Also, I wanted to see how far you were willing to go, how much you could discover on your own. Call it a test. Of course, I should have foreseen that pursuing this story might put you in grave jeopardy. And Iris, too. I'm very sorry."

Bourne joined Chancellor at the windows. "So you think Varak is the head of the Pyramid. That he's *Genesis*."

"I believe so."

"The problem is that Varak is largely untouchable," Bourne said. "He walls himself off in his estate in the Hamptons, and he's built a public reputation as a great philanthropist, doling out millions around the world. We won't bring him down without a lot more evidence than we have. Do you know anyone else in the group?"

Chancellor shook his head. "I'm afraid not, but as I told you, they have fingers throughout the media. Most probably don't even know they're being manipulated. However, the inner circle itself is bound to be very small. Half a dozen, ten people at most. But even if we knew who they were, we have no leverage to turn them. We need to know more about what they've done. Things that can be exposed, proven, things that can't be suppressed or ignored. That was what Louisa promised to bring me. But she paid the price for her bravery. So I'm not sure where we're going to find someone else who's willing to betray the Pyramid."

20

OSKAR VOGEL WAS BEING FOLLOWED. HE KNEW IT.

There was nothing particularly memorable about the woman who was sitting at a table outside the Chinese restaurant, across from the grim beige building where Oskar worked. He only noticed her because the Beth-mannstraße streetcar passed between them at that moment, and when it was gone, there she was staring right at him. She was in her forties, smoking, wearing a white blouse and jeans. Her sandy hair was tied in a ponytail. She looked at him, saw him looking back, and immediately went back to the copy of *Die Aktuelle* she was reading. That was that.

He forgot all about her until an hour later. After leaving the office, Oskar did what he usually did on his walk home. He stopped in the Römerplatz for a hefeweizen. He typically went to the same place near the red-and-white steeple of the Nikolaikirche, on the fringe of the cobblestoned square. He nursed his beer, played games on his phone, and watched the tourists snapping photos of what they thought were medieval German buildings, most of which had actually been built after the war.

Then came the collision. A little Japanese boy who'd been separated from his parents saw his mother near the steps of the church. He went running to her, bumping against the legs of a police officer and starting a chain reaction of people tumbling to the ground. The accident drew Oskar's attention, but what he spotted more than anything was that same woman in the blouse and jeans, who was one of the people caught up in the collision. And as she got up, she was looking right at him again.

Strange.

Not long after that, Oskar finished his beer and headed for home, but he was curious whether the woman would show up behind him. He made his way casually through the narrow alleys leading out of the square and reached the Mainkai by the river. He didn't look back or give any indication that he thought someone was on his trail. He continued along the water past the canal boats, until he reached the Alte Brücke, which took him to the south side where his apartment was located. This time, however, he crossed two-thirds of the bridge and then spun around with a tap on his head, as if he'd stupidly forgotten something. He started back across the bridge, and he spotted her immediately.

The woman, flustered and not expecting him to turn around, took a picture of the river like a tourist, which she clearly was not. Then she walked quickly in the opposite direction, back toward the city. Oskar followed her, but she made a pretense of tying her shoe and obviously saw him getting closer behind her. At that point, she flagged the first taxi that passed her, then climbed inside and disappeared.

Who *was* she?

But Oskar knew. The institute was spying on him. He'd worked there for three years, but suddenly they didn't trust him to keep their secrets. It didn't take a genius to figure out why. He'd been sleeping with Louisa, and now Louisa was dead.

He retraced his steps across the bridge and went home. His apartment was on the top floor of a four-story building, and although the flat wasn't large, the windows faced the river, giving him an amazing view across the city. Inside, he went to the small kitchen and opened another bottle of beer. He sat down heavily on his leather sofa, put his feet up on the coffee table, and reached for the TV remote.

That was when he realized something else. His apartment felt *off*. Wrong. Not the way he'd left it. It started out as just a feeling—was there a different smell in the place?—but then he began to look around the flat in detail. Next to the television was a set of bookshelves, which included two shelves lined with various coding books and a few titles dedicated to graphic art and anime. He remembered that he'd been looking at the first book in the Naruto manga series the previous day.

Had he replaced it on the bookshelf? He didn't think

so. He thought he'd left it on top of the other books, because he'd been interrupted by the ding of the microwave while he was reading it. Then he'd never gone back to it. But there it was, neatly back on the bookshelf. In fact, all the books were neat, their spines aligned, none jutting out farther than the others. Oskar was fussy about some things, but not about that.

He got off the sofa and went into his bedroom. His furnishings were sparse. He really wasn't home that much. His bed was made, which was normal, but as he stared at it, the bed almost seemed to be made too well. The folds were crisper than he usually made them. And when he glanced at the carpeted floor, he spotted a dent where the caster had been moved. The bed had been shifted.

Had he done it himself when he changed the sheets? But that was days ago.

His dresser, too, didn't seem right. He had two drawers of underwear, and he was the kind of man who overstuffed one drawer to the point where he could barely close it, while leaving the other drawer half-empty. But not now. Now the top drawer opened and closed easily, because his shorts were balanced between them.

There was only one conclusion to draw. Someone had been here while he'd been at work. They'd searched his apartment.

He remembered what Louisa had told him once. *Be careful what you say at home. Your place is probably bugged.* He'd laughed, because she had to be joking, but her face had been dead serious. She'd never wanted them to get together at their apartments; they always met elsewhere in the city, and when they wanted to sleep together, they did so in hotels or on weekend getaways.

Because the institute was watching.

Oskar went to the windows that overlooked the river. Down on the quai, he saw a man leaning against the railing. Was the man looking up at *him*? When he spotted Oskar, the man turned away and walked westward along the water. But there was no doubt in Oskar's mind. The man had taken the woman's place. He was a spy.

This was too much.

Oskar took the stairs back to the ground floor of the building. When he got to the front entrance, he glanced toward the river and noted that the man hadn't returned to his post yet. Oskar quickly turned in the opposite direction and crossed the street past an Afghani restaurant. He spotted a VGF streetcar arriving with a clang of bells on Dreieichstraße, and he waited until it was ready to leave, then dashed across the street and jumped aboard. Glancing through the tram's window, he didn't see anyone running from the river to catch it or barking orders into a phone.

Nobody had seen him.

He settled back into the seat. Truly, he had no idea where he was going, but he'd felt suffocated in his apartment. The tram rattled southward, and he simply watched the city go by. It was still light outside. He was hungry, because he hadn't eaten, but none of the restaurants the train passed appealed to him. Then, a few minutes later, as the train stopped near Hedderichstraße, he knew where he had to go. He got up at the last second before the doors closed and hurried out to the sidewalk. Across the street, on the other side of a small park, was a German restaurant on the corner.

This was where he and Louisa had first met. Well, that wasn't technically true; they'd worked together for months before that. But their real meeting, outside the office, had been here, by accident. He'd gone to the restaurant by chance, and so had she, and they'd been seated at adjacent tables. Even though socializing together violated the institute's rules, they'd chatted, then sat together, and they'd both known there was a spark between them that couldn't be ignored.

That was how their affair had begun.

And, strangely, that was where it had ended, too. They'd met here again on the day before Louisa left. For old times, she'd said when she suggested it. Then she'd headed off on her latest mysterious trip. The trip from which she'd never returned. The trip that he knew nothing about, only that it had killed her.

Oskar went into the restaurant, feeling an incredible wave of sadness. It wasn't a big place, with blond wood on the walls and tables, and chambered windows looking out on the street in two directions. Tiffany-style lamps hung over the tables like yellow roses. Standing near the entrance, he saw the two tables where he and Louisa had been seated when they'd first begun to talk to each other. The memory was so vivid that he wasn't even sure he could stay here. He turned to leave, but before he could do so, one of the waitresses spotted him at the door and came over and took him by the arm. He knew that waitress; Louisa had known her, too. She'd said they were friends.

"You," the waitress said with an odd intensity. "Oskar. Come, sit, it's good that you're here."

He was puzzled by her reaction, but he let her lead him to a table by the bar.

"You want a drink?" the girl asked. She had short black hair and a plump face. He remembered her smiling a lot the last time they'd been here, but this time, she had a darkness in her eyes.

"Beer, sure."

"I'll get it for you. And a menu."

She disappeared for a couple of minutes. Oskar sat by himself, overwhelmed by Louisa's presence, feeling the loss of her. He saw the other diners eating their dinners, and although the food looked good, he found his appetite had vanished. The waitress returned with a tall beer and handed him the menu. He was about to decline it when she opened the menu for him, and he saw that she'd clipped a small note inside.

Oskar read the note. *Die Toilette. Fünf minuten.*

She wanted to meet him. Why?

But the request was odd enough—this whole day, this whole week was odd enough—that he needed to hear what she had to say. As instructed, he waited five minutes, sipping his beer and studying the menu, and then he got up and pushed through the doors that led to the toilets. The first door was open, and when he went inside, the waitress was waiting for him. She pushed a cell phone into his hand.

"She said you'd come again sooner or later, but she didn't know when. Here. I've queued the video for you, so watch it. Then leave the phone on the counter, and I'll get it when you go back to your table."

Oskar shook his head. "I don't understand."

But the waitress bustled through the door and was gone. Oskar locked the door behind her; he didn't want to be disturbed. Then he held up the phone and saw that the photos app was open, frozen in place at the beginning of a video. His heart stopped; he couldn't breathe. The face he saw on the video was Louisa.

How?

He pushed the play button, desperate to hear her voice, but as it began to play, he stopped it again. He saw the background and realized that Louisa had filmed it here. She'd been right here in this toilet. What was she wearing? A pretty yellow dress. That was what she'd been wearing when they were last here.

She'd made this video while they were at the restaurant!

Why? Why not just tell him what she wanted to say? Why leave it with the waitress and hope Oskar would come back someday? It was crazy!

He played the video. God, her voice! Her *face*! It killed him to hear and see her again, because he was still crazy in love with her.

"Oskar," Louisa began, practically whispering quickly to the camera. "Oskar, my love, if you are watching this, then it means I never came back. I'm dead. The institute killed me. They are killers, Oskar!"

He paused the video again and shut his eyes. A searing pain stabbed him behind his forehead. *The institute!* What was she talking about? He knew how Louisa had died. There was a woman, a journalist in Washington who'd betrayed her. His boss had told him what had happened. *She is part of a fascist organization that wishes to stop us at all costs. We believe she is responsible for the death of one of our colleagues.*

Oskar had taken revenge against that woman! Destroyed her as she *deserved* to be destroyed!

He wanted to turn off the video, but he had no choice but to hear more.

"It's my fault as much as anyone's," Louisa went on. "I'm part of the lies. I've helped spread those lies. But no more. I can't stand by and let it happen, never again. I'm going to America. To Washington. I'm going to meet a man who can help me expose the truth. But the institute may know. We're all being followed! Bugged! They're everywhere. I'm sorry, Oskar. I wanted us to have that future you talked about, but it's too late. I'm sorry, sorry, sorry, my love."

In the video, tears rolled down Louisa's face. He remembered now! She'd gone to the toilet, and when she'd returned, she looked upset. He'd asked her if anything was wrong, and she'd pretended that she was fine. But she wasn't.

Lies!

He watched the video, wondering if she was done. She reached out with a hand as if to stop the camera, but then she spoke again.

"The fire," she said. "That was what changed every-thing for me. Children died! Children, Oskar! They swore to me no one would be hurt! Don't you see? They must be stopped. I have to stop them. Please be careful. You're watching this, so please, God, you have to be careful. If the Pyramid knows about me, then they may know about *us*, too. They will be watching you. You're in danger, my love."

21

ABBEY ROLLED OVER IN BED AND WONDERED WHAT TIME IT was. Without even opening her eyes, she sensed the brightness of the room and knew it had to be deep into the morning hours. They'd stayed up very late talking to Peter Chancellor, and the writer had invited them to stay overnight. He'd offered them two bedrooms, but Abbey had interrupted to say that they only needed one. She wanted Jason with her. She wasn't going to sleep alone after what they'd done to her.

Lying there now, sensations of the night with him came back to her mind. She remembered the complete darkness of the house, not a light anywhere outside. The feel of Jason in bed beside her. His strength as he held her. Their bodies molded together, skin on skin. But they hadn't had sex. She'd made it clear that if he wanted her, she was his, but two years hadn't changed him. He was an enigma, a riddle, still desperate to keep his distance. She'd felt desire from him, maybe even love, but there was also that infuriating reluctance he'd had with her from the very beginning. As if his first instinct was always to push her away.

But they were together again. That was what mattered. When she opened her eyes, she saw him by one of the windows that looked out on the Allegheny forest. He was already dressed.

"Good morning," he said.

She softened at the sight of his smile. "Hi. What time is it?"

"It's after ten."

"You should have woken me up," Abbey chided him. "When did you get up?"

"Six. It doesn't matter when I go to bed, I'm up at six."

"Hardass," she told him. "Is there coffee?"

He pointed to an urn on a silver tray, which was placed on a table near the bed.

"Thank God," Abbey said.

She got out of bed. She wore nothing but skimpy cotton panties, and she was pleased to see the look that Jason stole at her body as she dug in his backpack and found a T-shirt she could wear. She poured herself coffee, then joined him at the window. The green trees of the forest, underneath a cloudy sky, stretched over the hills without any visible break. Peter Chancellor had chosen a remote location for himself and Alison.

"Do you like my hair this way?" she asked. "Black, not red. Short, not long."

"I think you'd look good no matter what you did with it."

"Yeah, yeah," she murmured as she sipped her coffee, but she had to suppress a smile, because she was extremely pleased with that response. "I mean, it *was* my hair you were looking at just now. Right? Nothing else?"

She smirked at the flush on Jason's face.

"Sorry," she went on. "I'm a bitch when I first get up."

"Only then?"

Abbey punched him in the arm, then got on tiptoes and kissed his cheek. They were quiet for a while, standing close to each other by the window, her hips brushing against his. It was a little respite from everything they'd faced, but she knew it wouldn't last.

Gently, he touched her face under her chin, where the skin was still bruised and discolored. "How's your neck? Are you in pain?"

"It stings a bit, but that's all."

"We should get you a scarf or turtleneck to cover it up. It'll attract attention wherever we go next. People will remember."

She cupped her coffee mug in her hands and frowned. "So where *do* we go next? What's the plan? We know more about the Pyramid now, and we know Varak is this so-called Genesis. We know that Deborah Mueller was actually someone named Louisa, but we don't know where she came from. As a journalist, I'd say we still know almost nothing."

Jason nodded. "I agree."

"You saw Saira Kohli with Darrell Forster, but you

said you didn't think she was involved. Could we talk to her? She has credibility. If people hear from her, maybe they'll listen."

"Maybe, but what would we tell her? There's no reason for her to believe us right now. We need to get *inside* the Pyramid. Find out how they work. Find a weakness. If we do that, then there may be a way to expose them and tear them down."

"I've been thinking about that," Abbey said.

"And?"

"Well, the Pyramid is basically about *media*, regardless of whether it's traditional or online. That's what Varak is trying to influence. And that's my world. There's somebody I think we should talk to. I don't know if he can help, but if there's anybody who would have heard something about the Pyramid, I think it's him."

"Who is it?"

"Walden Thatcher."

Jason shook his head. "I don't know him."

"Walden was one of my journalism professors at Mc-Gill. Actually, he was a visiting professor on loan from Columbia that semester, so I was lucky to get him. He's one of the legends of the business. His textbook *Principles of Journalism* is sort of like the bible for media grad students. He's taught an insane percentage of the leading editors in newspapers around the world. I can't believe something hasn't bubbled up to him about the Pyramid. He might be able to give us names. Or some insights on how it may work."

Jason nodded. "Is he still at Columbia?"

"No, no, he's long since retired. But I'm sure he keeps his fingers in the business. He's got a place in New York State outside Bedford. I was there once for a reunion of Walden's students. I know it's a long way to go, but I want to see what he has to say about all this."

"Okay. Let's go."

"Just like that?" Abbey said.

"Like you say, this is your world. And the road back to Lennon leads through the Pyramid, so that's the road we need to follow."

Abbey liked hearing him say *we*. She didn't know if it would last, but she wasn't about to let go of it. Meanwhile, a ray of sunshine broke through the clouds and lit up the green hills. She stared at it as she sipped her coffee.

"Or we could stay here for a while," she said. "I think Peter Chancellor would let us. Take a little break from reality."

Bourne shook his head. "It sounds nice, but that doesn't work, believe me. You can't hide. Sooner or later, reality always finds you."

SAIRA KOHLI READ THE ARTICLE IN THE *NEW YORK TIMES* FOR the third time.

The headline was shocking enough—DEATH, CHAOS IN HIGH LINE SHOOTING—but the details of the incident alarmed her. The woman who'd been killed was identified as Kenna Martin, a publicist with the Forster Group. *Darrell's agency!* The police believed that Martin had been lured to the High Line and targeted, but they offered no hints of a possible motive. However, they described a person of interest, wanted for questioning, who bore a striking resemblance to the man Saira had met in Darrell Forster's office only two days before the shooting.

Saira didn't believe in coincidences.

Her first instinct was to pick up the phone and call Darrell and demand an explanation. What was going on? Who was Kenna Martin, and what was her role in his agency, and why would anyone have wanted to kill her? And who *was* the man in his office? But she remembered Darrell's odd behavior in the taxi to LaGuardia and his defensiveness about the stranger and about the institute's office in Frankfurt. She didn't think her questions would get any answers from him.

She got up from her desk. She went to the window of her fourth-floor faculty office in Regents Hall at Georgetown, which looked out on Cooper Field, where the lacrosse team was currently practicing. In fifteen minutes, she had to give a lecture in her class on global patterns of disease, but she was having trouble concentrating on her work. Lately, all she could think about was the girl she'd met in Oslo who called herself Louisa. The girl who'd delivered a warning to her and then wound up dead in West Potomac Park under another name.

I work at the institute in Frankfurt. It's not what you think! It's evil!

Could that really be true?

Saira looked around her office at some of the personal items she kept there. There was a leather drum made for her as a gift by an Ethiopian tribesman after her work to eradicate HIV in his village. A fountain pen that had once belonged to her scientific hero, Albert Sabin. A wooden *lattu*, a spinning top with a coiled string around it, that had belonged to her youngest sister before the malaria took her away. These were the little things that defined who she was, more than her academic credentials and degrees, more than the honors and awards. They were tangible reminders that science wasn't about research in a laboratory. It was about bettering the daily lives of real people.

But Saira was beginning to fear that she'd betrayed those people.

Two years ago, she'd been approached by Darrell Forster to join the Varak Institute, to lend her name and reputation to an effort to put science ahead of politics and facts ahead of misinformation. The pandemic had been raging, and she'd signed on gladly. But ever since, her uneasiness had grown. It had started a year ago. A chemist in France she'd once respected—a friend—had published a paper that raised doubts about one of the important new treatments for the disease. Stupid! Irresponsible! His conclusions had been *wrong*! But to the deniers, he became a hero. Saira had criticized his study and spoken out against his findings, but that was like holding back the ocean with nothing but her hand.

Then a front-page story broke, accusing her friend of academic fraud, of falsifying his research in return for a huge payout from a competitor of the company that had developed the new treatment. Other, uglier rumors piled on, too. A former grad student accused him of sexual assault. Her friend had called Saira, delirious with despair, to deny everything, to beg for her help in salvaging his reputation. She'd turned him down. She'd said he was getting what he deserved for selling his soul.

A week later, he shot himself in the head.

Not long after that, Saira discovered that the grad student who'd made the accusation of assault had drowned in a strange accident while on vacation near Palermo. A forensic accountant looking into the alleged bribe determined that there were irregularities in the handling of the money and that there was no actual evidence that her chemist friend had ever even known about the account that was opened in his name. But none of that information got more than a one-sentence mention in the newspapers that had blared his guilt around the world.

That was when Saira had begun to wonder. To doubt. When she met the woman who called herself Louisa, those doubts grew.

What had she done by signing on with the institute?

What was really going on in Frankfurt?

Saira went back to her desk. She checked her watch and saw that she had only five minutes before her lecture was scheduled to begin. Even so, she grabbed her phone and dialed a number from memory.

"Reese Security," a familiar voice answered. She'd used Evan Reese to install and monitor security systems at her home, and she'd often used his guards to supplement her personal security when she traveled overseas. The profile of her position was such that she had to be cautious. She often received death threats, and although most were frivolous, she couldn't afford to take chances.

"Evan, it's Saira Kohli."

"Dr. Kohli, how are you?" the man replied in a voice like steel wool. He was in his forties, with a cold, analytical mind when it came to risk. He was former military and still tough as nails.

"I'm good, thank you. I was wondering if you'd had a chance to make inquiries about that matter I mentioned."

"The Deborah Mueller murder? I'm still looking into it. I talked to one of my contacts in the park police, and they claimed that the matter was straightforward. There was nothing that raised any red flags with them. However, I've unearthed a couple of anomalies that I'd like to investigate further."

"Anomalies?" Saira asked. "Like what?"

"Well, there are rumors about a witness who claimed that three men were involved in the murder. She made it sound more like an assassination than a drug-related homicide. I've heard that there was a video of her accusations, but I haven't been able to locate it online."

"Who was this woman?"

"I've only got her first name. Retha. She was homeless. She used to hang out in West Potomac Park when she wasn't at a shelter, but she disappeared from the area shortly after the murder of Deborah Mueller. Nobody saw her after that, and I just found out why. Retha turned up dead a week ago inside a closed storefront in Anacostia. Her body had been there for a while. No word yet on homicide, overdose, natural causes, whatever. But if you ask me, it's kind of an odd coincidence."

Saira frowned, and her stomach lurched. "Yes, it is. Please keep at it, Evan, and let me know if you find anything else."

"I will. Oh, there's one other thing. It sounds like you're not the only person looking into this case."

"What do you mean?"

"Seems like everywhere I ask questions, somebody else has been there ahead of me," Evan told her. "A freelance journalist. You probably know who she is, because she's been in the headlines the last couple of days over a racist post she supposedly made on Twitter. Her name's Abbey Laurent."

22

"PROFESSOR THATCHER IS IN THE GARDEN," THE MAID TOLD Bourne and Abbey when they arrived at his home outside Bedford, New York. "He said to show you out there when you arrived."

She led them through a dimly lit Cape Cod–style house, with dark wood floors and antique furniture filling rooms that were decorated with heavy Victorian wallpaper. There were hardcover books everywhere, on shelves, on tables, and balanced precariously in piles on the floor. Most were decades old, and all appeared to be nonfiction. Copies of at least a dozen different daily newspapers, from the *New York Times* to the *Chicago Tribune* to the *Washington Sentinel*, were archived in yellowing stacks. There were photos on the walls of Thatcher with five decades of print and broadcast journalists like David Brinkley, Helen Thomas, and Mike Royko. Jason didn't see any electronic devices in the house, not a computer or phone, not even a television.

"Walden's sort of a Luddite," Abbey commented with a smile.

They headed outside into the gardens. It was seven o'clock, almost sunset, and long shadows stretched across the green grass. The trees and neat square hedges made for a kind of maze through the acreage. The house itself was on a small country lane, lined with stone walls, not far from the Cross River Reservoir.

"Just follow the smell of pipe tobacco," the maid told them.

The garden sprawled across several acres, with dead ends that went nowhere and ended in Grecian-style sculptures. The grass was wet under their feet. They did smell tobacco nearby, but it wasn't enough to guide them to Walden Thatcher. After getting lost for almost fifteen minutes among the hedges, Abbey finally called out loudly to her old professor, and a hoarse but cheerful voice called back and led them to where he was.

They found him sitting in a small white gazebo, shadowed by a large oak tree, with a gurgling moat running completely around it and sculpted cherubs spitting fountains of water at each other. A footbridge led across the creek to the steps. There were several other chairs inside the gazebo. Bourne and Abbey joined the professor, but before they could sit down, he sprang to his feet with considerable energy and embraced Abbey in a warm hug.

Abbey was about to introduce Jason when he interrupted her.

"Alan Longworth," Bourne said, plucking out a name he'd spotted in one of Peter Chancellor's books. He extended a hand, which the professor shook. "I'm a friend of Abbey's, and I help her with research from time to time."

"A pleasure, Mr. Longworth," Thatcher said, his voice scratchy in the cool evening air. "If you're a friend of Abbey's, then you're also a friend of mine. She's one of my very favorite people."

They all sat down in the gazebo. Thatcher was in his seventies, and he looked as if he hadn't left his university life behind him, wearing a tweed sport coat, tan pleated slacks, and burgundy penny loafers. He was a small, skinny man, but spry when he moved, despite his age. He had wiry gray hair that looked as if it had been blown back in a windstorm, a thin pale mouth, and deeply lined skin. Reading glasses dangled on a chain around his neck, and he had intense, dark eyes that didn't appear to miss much. Although he was focused on Abbey, he kept glancing over at Bourne with an appraising gaze that suggested he didn't trust the cover identity that Jason had given him.

"How long has it been, Abbey?" Thatcher asked. "Two years?"

"More like four, I think. It was the last of your alumni parties."

"Oh, yes, I need to get another gathering scheduled. People keep asking about it. However, these days, I don't worry much about seeing anyone else. It's easier just to get lost in my books. And in the newspapers, of course.

I'm becoming a bit agoraphobic, but I find I can keep up to date without setting foot outside the gardens."

"If you're up-to-date," Abbey said, "then you probably know—"

Her voice trailed off, and Thatcher gave her a sharp look. "About this nonsense regarding you? Of course. Naturally, I didn't believe a word of it when I read it. It's hard to imagine anyone would."

"I appreciate that, Walden."

"However, what I believe or don't believe isn't worth a hill of beans, is it?" the professor went on. "I can't change anything, not at my age, which I'm sure you know. So the question is, why are you here?"

Bourne suspected that Thatcher was being modest about his influence. According to Abbey, he'd taught some of the biggest names in media, and he could probably reach any of them in moments by picking up the phone. It was also obvious to Bourne that, old or not, retired or not, Thatcher hadn't lost a step. His intelligence seemed as sharp as ever.

Abbey leaned forward, studying her professor in the shadows of the gazebo. "Have you heard about a group that calls itself the Pyramid?"

Thatcher didn't answer immediately. He sat back in the chair and tapped a finger thoughtfully on his lips. "An upside-down pyramid?" he said eventually. "Perhaps with an eye in the center?"

"You've seen it!" Abbey exclaimed. "You know about it."

"I've heard rumors about the group, yes. Of course,

you know as well as anyone the significance of the upside-down pyramid, Abbey. It's the most fundamental principle in all of journalism. The key facts of a story go at the top, the least important toward the bottom. That's the message, isn't it? Get back to facts. Fight against the plague of misinformation. That seems to be the driving philosophy behind this group. If it exists at all, that is. If it's not just one more online conspiracy."

"You don't seem to think so," Bourne said.

Thatcher's sharp eyes focused on him again. "You're right, Mr. *Longworth*. I don't think it's a conspiracy. The Pyramid exists. I've talked to enough people who think so that I'm convinced of it, as well."

"Who have you talked to?" Abbey asked.

"You know me. Just about everyone. Here I am in my garden, so what is there to do but talk? Fortunately, my name carries enough weight that people still take my calls. Columnists. Reporters. News anchors. Bureaucrats. They speak of the Pyramid in hushed tones. They're afraid."

"Of what?" Bourne asked.

"Of the things that happened to Abbey happening to them," Thatcher replied. "Of careers being ruined. Reputations destroyed. Marriages broken up, prison terms for newly exposed crimes, take your pick. Most people have secrets they'd rather not come into the public eye. So they remain silent."

"I had no secrets," Abbey replied. "What they did to me was a lie."

"Well, do you think that matters to them? When your cause is just, you can justify any sacrifice. *You* are their sacrifice, Abbey. Anyone who gets in the way of the higher order must be neutralized. Even the innocent."

"Do you know how it started?" Bourne asked.

"With good intentions, like most things of this nature," Thatcher replied. "Most journalists I talk to have been horrified by the events of the past few years. Not just the politics of the country, but of course, that's part of it. They look at social media and see a sewer of lies and errors being amplified to the detriment of society. They see no unity of purpose anymore, no agreement on fundamental principles and facts. They perceive a threat to our way of life—even an existential crisis for the earth itself—as a real, tangible prospect. In the face of that, what do you do? Do you stay unbiased? Or do you figure you need to put a thumb on the scale? If a house is burning down in front of you, do you write a story about it, or do you go running for a bucket of water? I'm not saying the choice is easy or clear, but that's the choice."

Abbey frowned. "And that's the Pyramid?"

"No, no, I'm merely saying that's the climate in which the Pyramid came to be. Don't you see? If you're literally trying to save the world, what options are off the table? I'm saying that something like the Pyramid was probably inevitable. Powerful people have always taken it upon themselves to do what they think is right."

"What powerful people?" Bourne asked. "Who's behind it?"

"Their names? I have no idea. As I say, most people don't talk about it openly. It's in the shadows. Partly because of fear and partly because they have a certain amount of sympathy with the *goals* of the Pyramid. So they turn a blind eye to some of its methods."

"Varak," Bourne said. "Do you know that name?"

"Of course."

"We hear he's the driving force behind it. *Genesis* of the Pyramid."

Thatcher stroked his chin as he stared at Bourne. Then he turned his attention back to Abbey. "Mr. Longworth here seems like more than a friend and a researcher. Perhaps you'd like to tell me who he really is."

"I'd like to, Walden," Abbey replied. "I would, really. But I can't. It's not safe. Not for him, not for you."

"I see. Well, Mr. Longworth, whoever you are, I hope you will be careful with this young woman. She's very important to me. I don't want to see anything bad happen to her, any more than has already happened."

"She's very important to me, too," Jason replied.

"Good. All right, yes, I've heard what you've heard. Varak is the man behind the Pyramid. But I'm not sure what good it does to know that. The two of you aren't going to take down someone like him."

"Who else is part of it?" Bourne asked. "Varak has the money, but he needs more than that."

"I told you. I don't know."

Bourne shook his head. "I think you're holding back, Professor. You know more than you're telling us. Is it out of some kind of loyalty to your former students? Or are you afraid, too?"

Thatcher shrugged. "At my age, I have very little to fear."

"Then tell us."

Abbey leaned forward in her chair and put a hand on the old man's knee. "Walden, please. We need your help."

Thatcher exhaled a long, reluctant sigh. "It's not so much what I know. I only have suspicions. There are people who normally take my calls, but don't anymore. Or who feign ignorance about things they can't possibly be ignorant of."

"Like Darrell Forster?" Bourne suggested.

The old man's eyebrow arched. "You think Darrell is involved?"

"I do. He chairs the Varak Institute, after all. Plus, I have other reasons to believe he's part of the Pyramid."

Thatcher nodded. "Darrell is a brilliant journalist, one of my best students ever. But he was always arrogant. The danger for the brightest student in class is assuming you know better than everyone else. Darrell had a way of letting success and power go to his head. So you could be right about him."

"Is there anyone else?" Bourne demanded.

The professor hesitated, saying nothing. Darkness stretched over the garden and the gazebo. Jason knew there was more, and so did Abbey.

"Walden, who else?" she asked. "Give us the names. If you know about Darrell, you must suspect others."

"I do, but you may not want to hear it."

Abbey cocked her head. "Why not?"

"Because in a world like this, you can't even trust the people you respect the most," Thatcher replied.

"Who?" Abbey repeated.

"Another of my former students is one of Darrell's closest friends," Thatcher told her. "They go way back. Darrell helped launch his career, and they've been allies ever since. If Darrell is part of the Pyramid, then it's inconceivable to me that he's not involved, too. But I also know that this man has been instrumental in *your* career. In fact, I was the one who introduced him to you."

Abbey closed her eyes in the dense shadows. "Tom. Tom Blomberg."

"I'm afraid so. And if it's true, you know what that means."

She nodded. "Tom's the one who destroyed me."

23

THE PARKING GARAGE ON K STREET HUMMED WITH A QUIET
throb of machinery. Utility pipes ran along the low concrete ceiling. The walls and support columns were all
painted white, but the paint had flaked off in multiple
places, dinged by cars backing in and out of the parking
spots. The floor was stained with grease. It was after
seven o'clock in the evening, but cars still lined the garage, and there were only a few empty spaces. This was
Washington, populated by eager young bureaucrats
working crazy hours.

"Tom's still here," Abbey said, pointing at a black
Lexus parked in a monthly space halfway down the aisle.
"I recognize his car."

Bourne used binoculars to study the Lexus from inside their Jeep, which was parked in the last spot by the
wall, its nose facing outward. He noted a Mercedes SUV

and a red BMW parked on either side of Tom Blomberg's Lexus. Both were empty.

"I'll plant the tracker."

He got out of the Jeep. Staying close to the cars, he walked casually toward the bank of elevators. His eyes moved constantly, watching for anyone in the shadows. He listened, too, but heard nothing, no footstep on concrete, no metallic click from a gun being cocked. Even so, a trap was always possible.

Bourne kept his head down. He wore a baseball cap and sunglasses. There was one camera monitoring this aisle of the garage, mounted on the ceiling not far from the Lexus. Usually, whoever was watching the surveillance feed in a place like this was a bored security guard reading a book and paying no attention to the people coming and going, at least until a panic button was pushed. Still, Bourne didn't want to take the chance of someone noticing what he was doing.

When he was near the Lexus, he shoved a hand into his pocket, as if reaching for his keys. He pulled out a handful of change and let the coins spill to the concrete. With an annoyed shake of his head, he began picking them up, and then he walked over to the front wheel of the Lexus. Again he bent down, as if grabbing a loose coin, and quickly shoved a GPS tracker under the car's wheel well.

He continued to the elevators, then reversed his steps, this time with a phone pressed to his ear, as if taking a call. If anyone was watching, he was just a businessman who'd had a change of plans. He returned to the Jeep and climbed in behind the wheel next to Abbey.

"All set."

She nodded. Her face was pale and tense.

"Are you ready for this?" Bourne asked. "The approach will be better coming from you. You need to rattle him. Scare him. The point is to get him to make contact with someone else at the Pyramid, and then we can start following the chain."

"I remember the rules, Jason," Abbey said. "*Once a target is off-balance, keep him that way.* Isn't that what Treadstone taught you?"

Bourne smiled. "That's right."

"We did it with that lawyer in New York two years ago, remember?"

"I remember."

"Believe me, I'm ready to rattle this piece of shit," Abbey said.

Jason put a hand over hers. "I know you're angry about what he did to you. Anger is good, but you have to channel it. Let it drive you, but don't let it get in your head. You still need to think clearly. If you let your emotions win, you'll make mistakes."

Abbey nodded, her voice clipped. "I know."

"I'll be watching and listening the whole time." Bourne held up the Smith & Wesson with the laser sight that he'd purchased in Baltimore as they drove south. "If he tries anything, if he threatens you, I'll be there in seconds."

"Tom won't try anything with me."

"Maybe not, but don't take any risks. If something feels off, get out of there. You showing up is going to rattle him regardless of what else you say."

"I get it. Now what?"

"Now we wait."

They sat next to each other in silence. He felt anxiety radiating from her, however much she pretended she was fine. It had gotten worse as they'd gotten closer to DC. They'd stayed overnight at a motel outside the city and then headed down the coast through New York and New Jersey. Bourne used back roads rather than the inter-states; it was easier to see if they were being followed. He also made a couple of stops to restock with cash and lo-cate an additional gun. Then he'd found a range and spent two hours with Abbey, giving her training on how to use his Sig. She didn't like it. She didn't like guns. But if the time came, he wanted her to be prepared to use it.

An hour passed. Then two. He began to wonder if Tom Blomberg wasn't returning to his car that night.

Then Abbey murmured, "There he is."

Bourne used his binoculars again. He zeroed in on Tom Blomberg shuffling toward his Lexus from the ele-vators. The oversized newspaperman looked as if he'd had a few drinks, based on the wobble in his walk. He wore an ill-fitting suit, the tie loose. A briefcase swung in one hand.

"You better go," he told Abbey.

He watched her clench her fists before she got out of the car.

* * *

ABBEY WALKED DOWN THE MIDDLE OF THE AISLE IN THE PARK-ing garage. She made no attempt to hide from Tom, and she wasn't wearing a disguise. Her emotions spilled over her in waves as she approached him. Fury at what he'd done to her. Regret for the man he once was, for the man she'd thought she knew. Shame that she'd allowed herself to be fooled.

When they'd reconnected after she moved to DC two years earlier, she remembered thinking how much he'd let himself go to pot. The drinking. The weight gain. The black half-moons of sleepless nights under his eyes. Maybe drugs, too. She hadn't realized it was because he'd sold his soul.

Thinking back, she also recalled an evening with him in a bar in the Hay-Adams. He'd been in a strange, angry mood, spouting off a laundry list of frustrations with the impotent Washington status quo. How bipartisanship was dead. How the simplest things in Congress didn't get done without a fight. How people couldn't agree anymore on whether two plus two was really four. He talked about how they—journalists, the media, the people who communicated with Americans—ought to do something about that. That it was their responsibility to make a difference.

He'd asked her a question after their third martini. *Would you change the world if you could?*

She'd been sober enough to tell him that changing the world wasn't her job. She was a reporter, and the only way she knew to do that was to squeeze her own biases out of whatever she wrote. Somehow, that answer had disappointed him. And now she understood why.

That had been the pitch. The drunken, awkward, failed attempt to bring her on board. Tom Blomberg had been trying to recruit her as a foot soldier for the Pyramid.

Barely ten yards away, Tom stopped near his Lexus. He finally heard the approaching footsteps and looked her way. When he saw her, his eyes widened, just for a moment. He couldn't hide his reaction. Shock. Fear. Shame. That look was as close to a confession as she'd ever get. He was the one. He'd fed her to the wolves, regardless of their history together, regardless of their friendship. She'd come to him to do a story about Deborah Mueller, and that was something the Pyramid couldn't allow.

Just as quickly, he covered by pasting a smile on his face.

"Abbey," he said, and she could hear whiskey in his voice. She kept walking, until she was close enough to smell it, too. She was right in his face. "Abbey, I'm sorry, but I already told you, I can't help. I feel bad, but what's done is done."

Abbey just stared at him silently, making him uncomfortable. She sent a message with her eyes. *I know.*

"What do you want?" Tom said awkwardly. "Money?"

"Her name was Louisa," Abbey hissed.

She and Jason had talked about what to say. How to scare him, throw him off his game. And they'd been right. This was a body blow. Tom's face twitched at the sound of the name. "What?"

"Her name was Louisa. Did you know that? Of course you did."

"Abbey, I don't—"

"Don't even try to lie to me anymore. I know all about the Pyramid, Tom. I know you're part of it. Pass along the message. I'm going to destroy it, starting with *you*. That's fair, don't you think? After what you did to me?"

She'd said it. She'd said the word.

The Pyramid.

"First I deal with you," she went on. "Then Darrell Forster. Then Varak. You're all going down."

"Abbey, I have no idea what you're talking about," he protested, but she could see a sheen of sweat on his face.

"Did you think it was just the cancellation, Tom? Did you think that was all they were going to do to me? I'm curious. I really want to know." She yanked down the collar of her turtleneck so he could see the purplish line of bruises on her neck. "Or did you realize they were going to kill me, too? Did you know they were going to send a woman to string me up in my hotel room and make it look like I'd hung myself?"

Tom's eyes widened. "Holy fucking shit."

"Oh, so you didn't know. You have one fragment of a soul left. That's good. Let's start there."

"Abbey, I swear to God," he murmured.

"Tell me *why*, Tom. You're good. You're one of the very best. How could you let it happen? How could you become the very thing that you hated and investigated and wrote about for your whole fucking career?"

She heard Bourne in the receiver in her ear. He was trying to pull her back.

"Easy, Abbey. You've done enough. He's scared. Let it go, and get out of there."

But she couldn't let it go. Her voice rose.

"They tried to kill me, Tom. Do you understand that?"

He reached for her shoulder, but she slapped his hand away.

"It wasn't supposed to happen that way," he pleaded with her. "Nobody said anything about murder. For God's sake, you think I'd let anyone harm you if I knew?"

"Louisa was murdered. And you knew about that."

Tom's eyes closed. His whole body stiffened. "Choices had to be made. *Sacrifices.* Louisa didn't understand that. What were we supposed to do? Allow another far-right fascist in the Senate? The country is coming apart at the seams, Abbey! You know it, I know it, everybody knows it! Are we supposed to stand by like observers and do nothing? Is that the answer?"

Bourne spoke again. *"Abbey, walk away."*

She breathed in and out, trying to calm herself. The man in front of her had been a mentor, but now she saw him only as pathetic, as evil. She was done with him. "I'm coming for you," she said again, her voice level. "Spread the word, Tom. I'm coming for all of you."

Abbey turned on her heel and marched away.

Behind her, she heard Tom call her name, but then he

gave up, letting her go. His footsteps scraped on the concrete floor of the parking garage. She heard the whistle of his car door unlocking as he got inside the Lexus. Ahead of her, Jason emerged from the darkness, the gun still in his hand as he drew near. There was a rumble behind her as the engine of the Lexus fired.

And then, strangely, she saw Jason running. Sprinting. Diving for her.

She heard him shouting, the words echoing from his lips and in the receiver in her ear. *"Get down, get down!"*

He was right there, crashing into her, pulling her to the hard floor and covering her with his body.

In the next instant, an explosion shattered her ears, metal twisting in a tortured scream, glass landing on them like rain. A shock wave slammed across her body, then a second wave almost immediately after, simultaneous with another explosion. Her brain made somersaults. The garage went silent; she couldn't hear anything, just a dull buzz. She felt a hot wind of fire, as if the oxygen had been sucked from the air.

Then she was in Jason's arms.

He was on his feet above her. He picked her up like she was weightless, carrying her through the strange airless silence, taking her quickly away from the burning hulk that had once been Tom Blomberg's Lexus.

24

THE MAN ON THE FLYBRIDGE OF THE AZIMUT SIXTY-FOOT
yacht cut off the engine, silencing the noisy whine. The
gusty wind created swells that made the boat rise and
fall, and he pushed a button to lower the anchor, holding
them in place. There were no other crafts nearby, and the
ribbon of Montauk and the Long Island coast was just a
smudge on the horizon two miles away. A seagull had
followed the boat out on the water and screeched noisily
at him as it perched on the railing of the upper deck. The
man removed a small plastic bag from his pocket and
held up a piece of hard cheese, which the gull snatched
out of his hand.

"That's all for now," he told the bird. "But I'll have a
treat for you later."

The man was in his mid-fifties, but his exercise regimen kept him in top shape. He ran four miles each morn-

ing, lifted weights, and swam and played tennis multiple times a week at a club in East Hampton during the nicer months. During the winters, he relocated to an estate in Costa Rica, but his athletic routine didn't change. His six-foot frame was toned and muscular, and he had a natural grace as he moved. The ocean air across the deck was cold, but he wore a formfitting dark blue short-sleeve shirt with the top four buttons undone, plus tan shorts. His feet were bare, and his pale skin was flushed pink by the sun.

In appearance, he looked younger than he was, his face unwrinkled except for a few parallel lines across his forehead. He had high cheekbones and a mostly square face, which signified his Slavic heritage. Based on photographs, he closely resembled his father, Stefan, a man he'd met only briefly as a child and didn't remember at all. He had short, choppy hair, still blond with no gray at all, a small, rounded nose, and prominent ears. The skin around his blue eyes had a puffy quality, which sometimes made him look bored or sleepy, but that was deceiving. He had a cold, calculating mind.

With the boat anchored, he joined his guest on the lower deck. Darrell Forster was drinking Stoli on a white sofa near the bow.

"Talk to me, Darrell," Varak said, taking a spot near the railing, with his hands on his hips. "What's the report from Washington?"

"Tom Blomberg is dead," Forster replied, his mouth tight. He finished his vodka in one swallow and refilled the glass from the bottle beside him.

"It had to be done," Varak said. "I know you disagreed."

"Tom and I went back a long way. It was my call to bring him into the Pyramid."

"Yes, it was. It should also be obvious to you now that he was a weak link."

Forster said nothing. He kept drinking.

"And the woman?" Varak went on. "The journalist, Laurent? She escaped the blast."

"Yes."

"Unfortunate. Cain is with her, yes?"

"We assume so," Forster replied. "Lennon's operative was killed while attempting to execute Laurent. We think Cain was responsible."

"Cain knows about you," Varak pointed out. "He came to your office. He turned your cutout, this Kenna Martin. You've been careless, Darrell."

"He knows about you, too," Forster said with a note of irritation in his voice. "But so what? There's nothing he can do with that information. Plus, he's chasing the assassin. His focus is on Lennon, not us."

"Don't be so sure. Even if Cain is after Lennon, he's a threat to the Pyramid. As is this journalist. We need to deal with both of them promptly."

Varak sat down in a leather chair across from Forster. He studied the older man, who had a nervous, shifty look today. Forster's fingers tapped the sofa, an impatient tic. He was drinking more than usual. His eyes kept examining the wide-open, empty ocean, as if worried about surveillance. Worry was counterproductive, the first sign of weakness. A worried man was a man prone to making mistakes, to dithering instead of acting decisively.

He'd known Forster for years. He'd been a quiet investor when the man started his public relations agency, because debts like that were useful. When the right time came, Varak had recruited Forster, mainly for his wide-ranging contacts in media, business, and government. The Pyramid needed people who could be bought, persuaded, tricked, and influenced, and Forster had been a valuable resource. But all resources, like tapped-out silver mines, eventually went dry.

The impatient seagull landed near Varak with a screech. The billionaire shook his head. "No, no more treats yet. You have to wait."

The bird flapped its wings and took flight, circling the yacht.

Varak opened a small compartment next to his seat, from which he removed a bottle of Barbadillo Reliquia sherry. He filled a crystal tumbler, then replaced the bottle in the compartment. He lit a dark Parisian cigarette, blowing out acrid smoke that the wind quickly carried away. He studied the amenities around him. The smooth leather of the seats. The electronics and satellite hook-ups. The boat was new, and he was still deciding whether he liked it. This was to be his personal yacht, the dayboat he operated himself, when he wished to avoid the prying eyes of the crew. Not that any of them would dare say a word about what they saw. But still.

He savored the cold ocean air on his bare arms and legs. Poor Forster looked like he was freezing in his heavy sweater. Varak didn't respect men who couldn't abide the cold. That was part of the toughness of his upbringing in rural Iceland, where you learned to love the winters even when your house had almost no heat. Back then, he'd thought he was no more than an impoverished child with no future ahead of him, and so he'd learned to rely on himself. Later, he realized that was part of the plan. Inver Brass and his father had wanted him brought up with no advantages, to know that nothing in life came without hard work and an educated mind. They'd been right. That was the kind of man who could work for the *new* Inver Brass, the way his father had done before him.

"I'm also worried about Saira Kohli," Varak said.

Forster shrugged. "She's useful to us. No one doubts her credentials or objectivity. Having her associated with the institute enhances our credibility. Plus, it tends to blunt any objections that our group is just another billionaire plaything bought and paid for by a Bezos, Soros, or Musk."

"So you said when you recruited her. You'll recall others of us were against it. *Genesis* was against it."

"Saira can't be corrupted, it's true. But that's what makes her valuable."

"She's asking questions," Varak said.

"It's of no consequence. She suspects nothing. She expressed some curiosity about Frankfurt recently, and I put her mind at ease. That was the end of it."

Varak sighed at the man's foolishness.

He opened the compartment again and removed a small recording device, which he placed next to his glass of sherry. Forster looked at it curiously. When Varak pushed a button, a recorded conversation boomed across the deck, not from the device itself, but from speakers built into the boat around them.

Two voices. The first voice belonged to Saira Kohli and the second to a man with a hard-edged, military manner.

"I was wondering if you'd had a chance to make inquiries about that matter I mentioned."

"The Deborah Mueller murder? I'm still looking into it."

Varak let the entire conversation play out on the speakers, and he watched Darrell Forster's unusually tanned face grow paler as it went on. When it was done, Varak shut off the device and replaced it neatly out of sight.

"I had Dr. Kohli's Georgetown office phone tapped," he said. "You see, I didn't share your confidence that her suspicions were so easily put to rest. As it is, her inquiries are proving dangerous."

"I had—I had no idea," Forster blustered. "Still, there's nothing she can learn about Louisa."

"Isn't there? I'm not convinced."

"What would you like me to do? How would you like me to deal with it?"

Varak waved his hand dismissively. "It's no longer your concern, Darrell. I'll take the appropriate steps. The bigger issue now is the lapses in judgment you've demonstrated. First Iceland was exposed, leaving us vulnerable to this operative *Cain*. And now your recruits are proving to be serious liabilities, putting the entire Pyramid operation at risk."

"I don't think that's fair. None of this was my fault."

"Leaders take responsibility, Darrell."

Forster nodded. He was sweating, and he swigged his vodka again. "Yes. Yes, of course, you're right. Ultimately, I'm to blame. This is on me. What can I do to regain your confidence?"

"I've been thinking about that," Varak replied.

He opened the compartment next to him again and reached inside.

"Unfortunately, Darrell, I'm afraid that confidence, once lost, is impossible to restore. Even improved performance comes with doubts, and in our operation, we can't tolerate even the slightest doubt. I'm sure you understand that."

Varak removed his hand from the compartment. He now held a compact Ruger EC9s semiautomatic pistol. He extended his arm across the short space in front of him, and before Darrell Forster even had a chance to open his mouth in horror, Varak fired a single shot perfectly into the middle of the man's forehead. The bullet went into Forster's brain without exiting the back of his skull and causing a mess on the rich white leather.

Dead, Forster slid off the sofa onto the varnished deck of the yacht.

Varak casually flipped the gun into the ocean water, where it sank under the whitecaps. Then he removed a phone from the pocket of his shorts and dialed.

"It's me. Forster has been dealt with. But given the reports from Washington, I'm afraid that things are getting out of control. We need to move swiftly to remove the others, so I suggest you involve our friend once again. He should be receptive, given that it's an opportunity to deal with Cain once and for all."

He hung up the phone, which he also tossed into the choppy waves surrounding the boat. Then he snapped his fingers, and the seagull landed near him on the railing, screeching wildly and flapping its wings.

"As promised," he told the bird. "Another treat."

The gull swooped down on the body of Darrell Forster, and with the sharp end of its beak, the bird began plucking out the dead man's eyes.

25

IT WAS MIDNIGHT. JASON AND ABBEY LAY IN DARKNESS IN A budget motel two hours south of Washington. He'd ditched the Jeep—it was too easy for the police and others to trace it from cameras in the parking garage—and he'd stolen a dented Ford Bronco and swapped out its license plates. Over Abbey's objections, he'd taken her to see a discreet doctor he'd used on missions in the past. The doctor had checked her out for any serious effects of the shock waves rippling from the car bomb, and then he'd given her an all-clear.

But Abbey was still fragile. Jason knew that. The shock waves she felt now were more than just physical. She lay naked on her back beside him, although her body was nearly invisible in the lightless room. They'd purchased new clothes for both of them at a Walmart in Fredericksburg, and after changing in an I-95 gas station, they'd discarded their old clothes, which smelled of char and gasoline. At the motel, he'd helped her in the shower to remove shards of glass from her hair, and then he'd rebandaged the cuts and abrasions she'd received.

During all that time with him, she'd said almost nothing. Now he listened to her breathing in bed, but he knew she wasn't asleep.

"How did you know?" she finally murmured. "I mean, about the bomb. How did you know?"

"As the engine started, I saw a red light go on under the car. I guessed it was wired."

"Tom was part of them. He was part of the Pyramid. Why did they kill him?"

"Loose ends," Bourne said. "They must have realized you'd make a connection to Tom, and you'd figure out a way to leverage him. They couldn't let that happen."

She was quiet again for a while, but still she didn't sleep.

"You heard what he said, didn't you?" she went on a couple of minutes later. "About taking sides in a Senate race? I think he meant last year's special election in Georgia. A conservative candidate had to drop out, and Sadie Adamson won. It makes me wonder. Did the Pyramid do to him what they did to me? Make up lies?"

"Maybe," Bourne said. "If we could prove that, it might help us."

"I have a friend in Atlanta. A reporter, Canadian like me. We both went to McGill, and he worked with me at *The Fort* for a couple of years. He covers Georgia politics now. We should talk to him."

Jason hesitated. "I think it would be better to take you somewhere where you can hide out for a while. I want you safe."

"Is anywhere safe for me right now?" she asked.

He frowned. "No. Not really."

"Then why even suggest it, Jason? After what they did to me, I'm not walking away."

"I'm not saying walk away, but you've seen what these people are willing to do. This isn't just about your reputation or career. This is your life. I can go after them, but if you're with me, you're in danger every moment. Plus, in order to stop them, I may have to do things you don't want to see. You said the media was your world, not mine. Well, *this* is my world. I don't want you to be a part of that. You're better off without me."

"Without you, I'd be dead," Abbey insisted.

"Without me, you'd probably be in Quebec City living a happier life."

She reached out and took his hand. "I don't regret any of it. Not two years ago. Not now. I already told you not to try to put me off." She hesitated, then spoke out of the darkness again. "Mistake or not, I have to say this, Jason. I'm in love with you. You understand that, don't you? It was true back then, and it's still true. Nothing's changed for me. Seeing you again, it's only gotten stronger."

"Abbey—"

"You don't have to say it back. I doubt you can even admit it to yourself. But that doesn't matter. I haven't stopped thinking about you for two years. I couldn't let go of you, even after you let go of me. And yes, I know what you said and why you walked away. I know the risks. I know the man you think you are."

"I *am* that man," Bourne said. "I'm a killer. You've seen it."

"I also saw you save my life. I saw you go into a frenzy because someone was trying to kill *me*."

"That was instinct," he lied.

"Fuck that. I don't believe that. You don't have to say it out loud, Jason, but I know you love me, too."

He wanted to deny it. He wanted to tell her she was wrong. His feelings for Abbey were radioactive for both of them. Having her in his life could end only one way, with her dead because of him. With her killed because he couldn't let her go again. But he also couldn't lie to her. He could only hide the truth.

"You haven't seen me in two years," he said. "Two *years*! You don't even know me anymore."

"Don't I?" He heard the rustle of sheets on the bed and felt her body shifting. In the shadows, Abbey propped herself up on an elbow beside him. "Then tell me what happened during those two years."

"What do you mean?"

"Tell me what you went through. I know you can't tell me everything, but you can tell me some things. I know you live in Paris. Do you think I didn't wonder every day about flying over there and trying to find you? About tracking you down somehow and forcing you to deal with me? So tell me about your life." She stopped, as if trying to find the words for a new thought that had come into her head. "Was there someone else? *Is* there someone else? Is that why you're hesitating?"

Jason pulled her naked body into his arms, and she settled against him. Her head rested in the crook of his neck and shoulder, and he smelled her hair, which was floral and familiar, the way it had been in the past. He tried to decide what to say, what was *safe* to say.

His instincts screamed: Say *nothing*! Anything you tell her will put her at risk.

But Jason was a loner by necessity, not by choice. His first love, Marie, had known that about him. Being with Abbey made him want to unburden himself and tell her everything. There was something about her that made him trust her, and there was no one else in his life—no one, not a soul—that made him feel the same way.

Nothing gets you killed faster than trust.

Treadstone.

"Do you remember me telling you about Nova?" he asked.

"Of course. You worked with her at Treadstone. You were in love with her. It was obvious in how you talked about her. I could see that. But she was killed in that mass shooting in Las Vegas."

Jason hesitated. "Nova is alive."

"What?" Abbey's head lifted off his shoulder. "How is that possible?"

"The details aren't important. I found out last year. I *saw* her last year."

Abbey slid away from him to the other side of the bed, and her voice cooled with embarrassment. "Oh. Okay. You two are together again. Sure, naturally, of course you are. Holy shit, I feel stupid."

Jason followed her across the bed. He reached to turn on the light, which made them both squint. He needed to see the expression on her face, which was what he expected. She was hurt, regretful, and jealous. Her lower lip trembled as she held back tears. She reacted stiffly when he slid an arm under her shoulders, but he didn't let her pull away.

"You're wrong," he said. "Nova and I aren't together. I only told you she's alive because you deserve the truth, not because I was trying to push you away."

"Come on, Jason. I already told you, I'm a big girl. You were head over heels for this woman. Why would I expect anything to be different when you found out she was alive? I'm happy for you. Really."

He shook his head. "It wasn't the same between us. Yes, we became involved again. Very briefly, and in circumstances I can't tell you about. But Nova knew I didn't love her anymore. We aren't together, and we never will be."

"Why not?"

Jason took a breath and crossed a line that he'd sworn he would never cross again. He knew it would end badly, but he did it anyway. "Why do you think, Abbey? Because of you."

Her eyes widened. "What?"

"Nova said everyone I love, I push away. And that's

what I was doing with you." He ran his hands through her hair. "She was right."

"What does that mean?" Abbey asked softly.

"It means I'm a fool. It means you should be anywhere else but where you are right now."

"I am *exactly* where I want to be right now," she told him.

"Abbey, I'm taking chances with your life that I have no right to take."

"It's my life. I'm the one taking the chance, and I don't care."

She put her hands on his face, and she brought her mouth to his, and they kissed. It had been two years since they kissed. That was on the boardwalk in Quebec City, that last night when they'd said goodbye. And nothing had changed. It felt soft and wet and erotic and perfect. They kissed until they were breathless and both wildly aroused.

"Turn off the light," Abbey murmured when they finally broke apart. "Quickly, quickly, turn it off."

"Why?"

"Because I like to make love in the dark, and I need you inside me right now."

THE FIRE! CHILDREN DIED!

Oskar kept hearing Louisa's words in his head. He'd been in a daze ever since he saw the video she made for him, because she'd ripped out the props holding up his whole life. Could it really be true?

The institute killed me! They are killers, Oskar!

Louisa. She'd confessed to him from the grave. How could she have been part of something evil like that? What lies had she told? And what had *he* done? He'd spent the past three years creating the most ingenious of lies himself, because they'd sworn that it was in service of a good cause. But God in heaven, was that the worst lie of all?

Oskar leaned against the wall of a convenience store, located across from the concrete monstrosity that was the institute building. He could hardly bring himself to cross the street and go to work. He chewed gum with his jaw pumping until it lost all flavor in his mouth. Commuters passed in front of him, going both ways on the sidewalk, and he glanced at their faces to see if anyone was paying special attention to him.

Were they still following him?

Was someone watching him right now?

Act natural. Don't let them know you suspect anything.

He swallowed his gum and crossed to the building entrance. They checked his ID badge, and he joined the others heading to work. Most of the people around him went to the other floors, where they dealt with normal things like grant proposals and press releases, but Oskar had a special access card for the eighth floor. That was the part of the building where the secret work got done.

Jochim was already at the desk next to his. He looked as if he'd been at work for several hours. The fat, bald programmer gave Oskar a wink, but he made no small talk. That wasn't allowed, other than the occasional conversation through the walls of the toilet stalls. Jochim whistled under his breath to music coming through his earbuds, and he tapped on his keyboard at lightning speed with his thick fingers. He wore an untucked red shirt, and his jutting stomach looked ready to shoot off the buttons like missiles.

As Oskar logged in to his computer, he heard a whisper. "Hey."

He glanced at Jochim with concern, because he couldn't remember the man ever speaking to him out loud where others could hear them. His nerves were on edge, and everything made him suspicious now. Rather than saying anything, Oskar simply cocked his head at his coworker to see what he wanted.

"Hey, you want a slice of *stollen*?" Jochim asked. "I'm starved. There's a new bakery a couple of blocks away. Thought I'd try it out."

Oskar sighed in relief. *"Danke, nein."*

The other programmer shrugged. Jochim hoisted his bulk out of his chair and shouldered his way to the elevators. Oskar had no appetite for food, but he did need caffeine, so he went to the coffee counter near the toilets and poured himself a cup. He sipped it for a minute before returning to his desk, and he kept thinking about Louisa.

I'm part of the lies. I've helped spread those lies.

What did she mean?

He had to know what Louisa had done, but he didn't think it was safe exploring the institute's computers. If they were watching him, following him on his way home, then they would probably be watching his institute account, too. They'd track his keystrokes, monitor any searches or downloads he made, and they'd know immediately that he was poking around in areas he shouldn't be.

Then a thought occurred to him.

Jochim's desk sat empty right next to his. If the new bakery was a couple of blocks away, it would be at least fifteen minutes, maybe more, before the other man got back.

The institute might be watching *him*, but they had no reason to watch Jochim.

His breathing heavy, Oskar headed through the warren of eighth-floor desks. Maybe two-thirds were occupied, but no one made eye contact with him or watched what he was doing. The door to Heinrich Kessler's office was closed, so his boss couldn't see him. As he neared Jochim's desk, Oskar simply sat down and sipped his coffee, as if he were right where he should be. He didn't look around; he didn't act suspicious.

Instead, he moved the man's mouse to wake up the screen and noted with satisfaction that Jochim had failed to log out of his account before making his bakery run. Oskar typed quickly. He didn't know exactly what he was looking for, but he knew where to find it. He didn't bother attempting to access Louisa's account directly, because he was certain the institute had already disabled it and deleted its contents both from her local computer and the main server. However, one of Oskar's tasks in his own work was to locate and recover deleted files from targeted organizations all over the world. The institute's security was no less vulnerable to his efforts than any other private business or government agency.

But it proved harder than he thought. Accessing the raw server data was no problem, but he knew none of the file names, and he had no idea what to search for among the millions of records. The time ticked by, and he nervously checked his watch over and over and kept glancing at the elevator doors. If they opened, if Jochim reappeared, the man would see immediately that Oskar was using his computer. There would be no way to explain it. But Oskar stayed. He had no idea when or if he'd get another chance.

Ticktock.

He imagined Jochim wandering through the institute lobby as he chewed on his piece of *stollen*.

Help me, Louisa, he thought. *What am I looking for?*

Then he remembered. The fire. *Tod von Kindern*. The death of children.

He narrowed his search, but even looking for references to *fire* and *children* produced an absurd number of documents. His fingers scrolled; his eyes scanned the words. Then he came upon a single sentence written by Louisa as part of a trove of travel documents filed with Heinrich Kessler for reimbursement.

The fire in Atlanta is having the desired effect.

Atlanta.

Oskar narrowed his search even further. This time he found his screen flooded with American newspaper articles. He chose one and, with another quick glance at the elevators, he began to read. As he did, the blood drained from his pale face, and he slapped a hand over his mouth, feeling a wave of nausea.

"Gott im Himmel, nein." God in heaven, no.

26

THE NEXT NIGHT, BOURNE PARKED THE STOLEN FORD BRONCO at a neighborhood bar in the downscale West End district of Atlanta. There was no urban feel to the area, just wide-open lots and old houses tucked among the trees and telephone wires. Across the street was a car wash, and next door was a discount warehouse. The bar was busy. Live music played from inside, and outside a food truck served up meat pies to a long line of customers. He and Abbey found a picnic bench along the side of the bar and ordered beers.

Abbey kept an eye on the people arriving.

"Sloane said ten o'clock," she commented. "If he shows up, that is. He didn't sound excited about the idea of getting together. Not that I blame him. I'm toxic at this point. Plus, it's not like we were really friends. We took a few classes together at McGill, and we both worked for *The Fort*, but we didn't really hang out together."

"How did he end up in Atlanta?" Bourne asked.

"He got married. His wife's from here, and she had a good job with Delta. It was easier for him to move than her. I think he's had a rough go, though. The *Journal-Constitution* wasn't hiring, and he ended up taking a job at a weekly business newspaper. It's not much money and not much of a profile for a top-notch reporter. But if I know Sloane, he's still clued in on the political scene. He was always a wizard at finding sources."

She waved at a man near the food truck, and Jason saw a tall, thin Black man acknowledge them and head their way. Sloane Jenks carried a meat pie in one hand and a half-pint of dark ale in the other. He wore a button-down blue shirt and jeans with cuffs upturned at his ankles. He had only a thinning crown of hair left on his head, but his beard was full and neatly trimmed. The black frames of his glasses gave him an austere look, and he didn't smile as he greeted Abbey. The look he shot Bourne was equally cold as Abbey introduced them, using Jason's cover as Alan Longworth.

"It's good to see you, Sloane," Abbey said when they were all sitting down again. "Thanks for meeting me."

"You said it was important, but I'm not sure what you want." He took a sip of beer and eyed both of them. "You're in the big bad Black city, Abbey. Aren't you afraid someone is going to steal your car?"

Abbey made a little hiss through her teeth. "Fuck, Sloane. Do I really need to tell you that the story was bullshit? I was set up. It wasn't me."

"Sure sounded like you."

"Well, it wasn't."

"Uh-huh." Sloane didn't look convinced. He used a plastic fork to take a bite of his meat pie, and he chewed slowly. "Steak, mushroom, and ale. Best in Atlanta. You should try it."

"I'm serious," Abbey went on. "That post wasn't me. The woman calling into the radio station wasn't me, either."

"And why would anybody go through that kind of trouble to set you up?"

"Because of a story I'm pursuing."

"Uh-huh," Sloane said again. He focused on Bourne. "And who are you? Her lawyer?"

"Let's just say I'm after the people who targeted Abbey," Bourne replied.

He watched Sloane take his measure from the other side of the bench. Abbey was right that the man had good instincts, because the reporter's eyes narrowed with a new curiosity, sizing up Bourne as someone who didn't fit easily into any of the usual equations. Sloane took note of the jacket that Bourne was wearing on a warm Georgia night, and he frowned, probably guessing correctly that the coat hid a gun.

"Well, I'm here," Sloane said, digging into the meat pie again. "You might as well tell me what you want."

Abbey leaned forward. "Have you heard of a group called the Pyramid?"

Sloane froze with the fork halfway to his mouth. He shoved the fork back into the meat pie and pushed it away, as if he'd lost his appetite. "Nope. Never heard of it."

"It looks to me like you have," Bourne said.

"I don't care what it looks like. I've never heard of the Pyramid."

"We just saw Walden Thatcher," Abbey told him. "He says a group called the Pyramid is manipulating stories. Censoring them. And shutting down anyone who gets in their way. Like me."

Sloane picked up his glass of beer, then put it down without drinking. He took a slow look at the other tables on the patio, then turned his attention back to the two of them. When he spoke again, his voice was light, as if he wanted to switch their conversation to safer ground. "Walden, huh? How's the old man doing these days?"

"Still as sharp as ever," Abbey said.

"I remember his lectures in that class we took at Mc-Gill. That commanding voice of his, broaching no disagreement. 'The greatest sin for any reporter is to become part of the story. Self-referential journalism isn't journalism at all. It's nothing more than mental masturbation. The word that you should avoid in your stories at all costs, like rats scurrying from the plague, is the word *I*.'"

Abbey smiled. "I remember that, too."

"Of course, Walden lost that battle long ago, didn't he? It's all self-indulgent bullshit these days."

"Not your work," Abbey replied. "And not mine."

Sloane shrugged. "We're fighting a losing battle."

She reached across the table and took his wrist. "Talk to us, Sloane. We think the Pyramid was involved in the Georgia Senate race last year. The contest that Sadie Adamson won. If they were, then you must have come face-to-face with them somehow. I know you. If there were rumors floating around the state, you would have heard them."

There was an immediate change in Sloane's demeanor at the mention of the Senate election. Bourne watched the reporter's fingers tighten around his beer glass. The man's face flinched, surveying the patio again, worried that they were being watched. Then he shifted his attention back to Bourne. "So was this *your* idea, coming here? Is this some kind of test? Who the fuck are you?"

"Sloane, *I'm* the one who wanted to talk to you," Abbey told him.

"Leave me alone. Both of you. Leave my *family* alone. I did what you wanted. Isn't that enough?"

He swung around on the bench, then pushed himself up and marched toward the parking lot. Abbey looked stunned by Sloane's response, and Bourne took her quickly by the arm, and the two of them followed. They rushed to catch up with him, and Bourne spoke softly, but loud enough for the reporter to hear.

"I don't know what threats they made against you, but we're not part of them. We're trying to stop them."

"You're lying. Get away from me."

"He's not lying, Sloane," Abbey insisted. "Don't you get it? They came after me, too."

Sloane said nothing. He continued toward a white Kia parked near the street, but as he opened the driver's door, Bourne slammed it closed again. "Yesterday they killed an editor named Tom Blomberg in Washington. Did you read about that? They blew up his car. Abbey and I were there when it happened. They were targeting *her*, too. They're shutting down everyone that might expose what they did. If you know something, then you're next on the list. How long do you think it's going to be before they come after you?"

The reporter squeezed his eyes shut. "I don't care about me. They can do what they want to me. But they threatened my wife and my little girl, too. Somebody got close enough to my wife to slip a garrote into her purse. I told her it was probably some gangbanger ditching evidence, but I knew what it really was. When I picked up my daughter at school the next day, there was a guy watching us from across the street. Just watching, not doing anything, but making sure I spotted him. It was a message. Drop the story, and shut the fuck up. You think I'm going to take any chances with shit like that?"

"Talk to us," Bourne said. "Right now, we're your best hope."

"No way."

Abbey took his shoulder. "No one will know the information came from you."

"*They'll* know," Sloane replied, "because I'm the only one who has it. They'll know I gave it to you."

"Gave us what?"

He breathed hard, his nostrils flaring. "A video I took."

"A video?" Abbey asked. "Of what?"

"The fire."

"Sloane, please. Tell us what happened."

The reporter glanced around the parking lot. A gravel road led to the back of the bar, and there was a band of tall trees behind the road, separating the building from a residential neighborhood behind it. Sloane gestured that way with his head, and the three of them headed for the trees. The darkness swallowed them up at the back of the parking lot, but Sloane still kept a nervous eye on their surroundings.

"You know the race, right? Sadie Adamson was the left-wing candidate. No one figured she had a chance down here. Marshall Gage was an Atlanta cop, well liked, moderate, or at least that was the image he put out there. Then stories started showing up. Most of them were national, not local, which is strange to begin with. We know this area, they don't. But interviews began to run with people claiming that Gage had a long history of pulling over Blacks on pretext stops, roughing up suspects, some real racist shit. There was talk of bodycam footage being covered up by the department. Now, I'm the first to tell you, you don't have to search hard to find cops like that down here. But this is my beat, and I never heard any of that shit about Gage. Maybe I missed it, but I figured it was worth a second look to see whether this was all legit. I started digging into the stories, and nothing added up. Hell, most of the people being interviewed on the morning shows, I couldn't even *find* them. It was like they didn't exist. I started writing about it, but my stories disappeared. Nobody picked them up. Nobody listened. Anybody who shared them on social media had their accounts disabled. It was fucking weird. And by the time the riots started, demanding Gage quit the race, believe me, the narrative was done. There was no changing it."

"And the fire?" Bourne asked.

"It was a downtown building. Closed because of the pandemic and supposedly empty. It got torched during the riots. Except the building wasn't empty at all. Several homeless families had been squatting there, and nine people died, including three children. The outrage was overwhelming, and it only got hotter when two white supremacists were arrested for setting the blaze. Newspapers and politicians all over the country called for Gage to get out of the race. He kept denying everything, but to the party, he was damaged goods. He dropped out a few weeks before the election, and Adamson won easily."

Abbey shook her head. "So what did you get on video?"

"The guy who really started the fire," Sloane replied.

"It wasn't the two they arrested?"

"I don't think so. I was downtown filming the unrest that night. There were plenty of bad actors around, but most of the shit was petty fights, looting, broken windows, that kind of thing. The fire was on a whole different level. I'd been shooting video with my phone right around that area, but I didn't even know what I had until I reviewed the footage later. As soon as I saw it, I tried to get the news out there. Posted it. Wrote about it. But the same weird shit happened. The story and the video both fell down a hole. Nobody would touch it. The social media platforms shut it down. I started to make noise and reach out to some of my national contacts, and that's when the threats started. I'm used to the usual anonymous crap I get on email, racist messages on my phone, whatever. I can deal with that. But this was different. This was organized and serious, and I didn't doubt for a second that they meant business. If I kept pushing to get the story out there, they'd kill me and kill my family."

"Who really started the fire?" Bourne asked.

Sloane heard something in the trees, and he shot a look over his shoulder. He hesitated, then kept going. "You've heard rumors about this guy they call Umbrella Man? He shows up at riots, but nobody knows who he is? I caught him on video coming out of the building. A minute later, there's an explosion—a *series* of explosions— and the whole place goes up. He did it. He fucking did it. But he's masked, and the umbrella hides him most of the time. I don't know who he is, but somebody really didn't want him getting the blame."

Abbey put a hand on his shoulder. "Give us a copy of the video."

"And have them go after my wife and daughter? No."

"At least let us *see* it," she said.

Sloane frowned. His body twitched with anxiety, but then he reached into a pocket and brought out his phone. With a few taps, he queued up the video, and Bourne and Abbey leaned together to watch it. It was hard to make out anything on the small screen. The video had been filmed at night in the middle of chaos, with hundreds of people running back and forth on the streets and sirens blaring in the background. Clouds of tear gas descended like a cloud, and the video jittered as Sloane gagged while doing the filming. For a while, everything went out of focus, and then as the camera steadied, they saw a three-story redbrick building on the other side of the downtown street.

"He shows up now," Sloane said.

They watched closely. Very clearly, they saw a tall man emerging through a broken window in the building and dropping gracefully to the ground. He was masked and too far away to make out any details about him, even when Sloane paused the video and enlarged the frame. As the playback continued, they watched the man pop an umbrella that covered his face and torso. Then he headed for the street.

Bourne froze. He asked Sloane to replay the footage and then replay it again. *The walk!* He knew that walk. He'd seen that odd floating gait before, and it was always a precursor to murder.

Lennon.

Lennon had been in Atlanta. Lennon had started the fire.

"Do you see something?" Sloane asked. "Do you know who that man is?"

Jason's voice was clipped. "No. I thought I saw something, but I was wrong. What does he do next?"

"I lose him pretty fast," Sloane said. "The explosions are coming soon."

"Keep going anyway."

The video continued as Umbrella Man walked away from the building, heading down the Atlanta streets at an unhurried pace. He even twirled his umbrella in his hand for show. But just before he walked out of the video frame, he stopped, passing a woman on the sidewalk. It wasn't obvious whether they knew each other, or whether the meeting was a coincidence, but Bourne thought a message had passed between them.

The woman's profile was to the camera, but then she turned, showing her face.

"Stop!" Abbey hissed. "Back up, enlarge it, let me see her again."

Sloane did. He zoomed in on the woman on the street, and even at that distance, there was no mistaking the face.

"That's Deborah Mueller," Abbey murmured. "That's *Louisa*."

27

"THE PYRAMID DIDN'T JUST MANIPULATE THE STORY," BOURNE said as they drove northeastward toward the Georgia state line on I-85. "They *created* it. They used Lennon to start the fire, and they must have known there were people in that building. Murder was the point all along. That was the key to getting Gage out of the race and swinging the election. And this woman Louisa knew all about it. If she was planning to tell the story to Peter Chancellor, it's no wonder they had to get rid of her."

"But who *was* she?" Abbey asked. "We still don't know anything about her. Chancellor said she came from Varak's bot farm, whatever that is. But he didn't know anything more than that."

Bourne was quiet as he considered the problem. He kept his eyes on the mirrors, making sure they hadn't picked up a tail outside Atlanta. It was late, and there were only a few other cars sharing the interstate with them. He stayed close to the speed limit, not wanting to draw any attention from the highway patrols. Ahead of him, he saw a glint of water under the starlight as they crossed the bridge at Lake Hartwell. A highway sign welcomed them to South Carolina, and he took the first exit past the bridge. He bypassed the welcome center, which would be routinely checked by police, and instead used the next overpass to head for a state recreation area that bordered the water. He drove deep into the park until he found an empty campsite near one of the lake's inlets.

"Do you want to spend the night here?" Abbey asked.

"Yes. We should rest, even for a couple of hours. But I've also got an idea about how we can find out more about Louisa."

"What is it?"

"We don't know her name, but we do have her picture. So it's possible we can find her online that way."

"You mean a photo-matching search?"

"Yes, but it has to run deeper than that. This isn't just about Google results. We need a hacker who can access databases we can't get to."

"Do you have someone in mind?"

"I do, but you won't like it," Jason said. "Do you remember Aaron Haberman? We used him when we were in New York together two years ago. He worked for Carillon Technology, but of course, they went belly-up after the Medusa operation. I've kept track of him since then, just in case I ever needed him again."

"Haberman?" Abbey remarked with a disgusted curl

of her lip. "Wasn't he the prick who dredged up nude photos I sent to a college boyfriend? You want to call *him*?"

"He's a sleazebag, but he's good."

She rolled her eyes. "Well, don't tell him I'm with you. You're the only one who gets to see me naked these days."

Jason smiled. He opened a video call and punched in a number from memory on his burner phone. He wasn't surprised that Haberman answered immediately. Like most hackers, he kept odd hours. He could only see the man's head and shoulders, but he saw enough to know that Haberman was shirtless, with a bony chest and matchstick limbs. The two-tone frames of his glasses were purple and red, and his oversized mop of curly hair had streaks in the same colors. His eyes shot with annoyance to the portion of his computer screen where he'd answered the incoming call, and he didn't immediately recognize Bourne's shadowy face in the darkness of the Bronco.

"Who the fuck are you?"

"You don't remember me, Aaron?" Bourne said. "I'm crushed. We're old friends."

The twentysomething tech's eyes narrowed as he stared at the screen, and Jason could hear him typing furiously in the background. Haberman had the odd ability to type one-handed, because with his other hand, he lifted a middle finger at the screen.

"You," he muttered. "How'd you get this number? Nobody has this number."

"We have mutual friends."

He clucked his tongue in disgust. "CIA?"

"You sold your soul to the government after Carillon," Bourne said. "The government likes to keep track of the souls it owns."

"What do you want?" The hacker continued to type at a frenzied pace. "And what the fuck are you doing in South Carolina, Bourne? Oh, and you can tell the Canadian bitch I know she's with you, so she doesn't have to pretend. By the way, tell her she'd love to see the photo I just transferred to my screen saver."

Haberman snickered.

In the SUV next to Jason, Abbey's mouth fell open in shock. She was about to scream a profanity back at the hacker, but he held up a hand to silence her.

"Let me guess, photo recognition on the highway traffic cams?" Jason asked. "I'm clued in to your magic tricks, Aaron."

The hacker shrugged. "That, plus cell phone towers. And just so you know, the plates on that Bronco you're driving don't match the vehicle they're registered to. So tell your girlfriend to keep her tongue in her mouth this time, or maybe I'll call the South Carolina cops and tell them where they can find a stolen car."

"And maybe I won't tell the IRS about the corporate accounts you skimmed and transferred to crypto when you were helping the FBI shut down Carillon," Bourne told him.

Haberman's face flushed. He pushed his glasses up his nose. "Tell me what you want. I'm busy."

"Busy jerking off," Abbey muttered. "No wonder the little perv types one-handed."

"I heard that! I fucking heard that! What did I say? Tell her to shut up!"

"Zip it, Aaron," Bourne told him. "We're looking for someone. A woman. The photo's on my phone, but I assume you already hacked my photo library while we've been talking."

Haberman shrugged. "Yeah, sure I did. Pretty boring stuff. I thought maybe you'd been taking some new naked pics of your girlfriend. She still keep the lawn mowed down south?"

Jason reached out and put a hand over Abbey's mouth, because she was about to erupt. "Don't piss me off, Aaron. You really wouldn't like the consequences. Just find the woman. I need to know who she is."

"She's dead," the hacker replied with another shrug, because he was already running the search. "She was murdered in DC."

"I know she's dead, but her name's not Deborah Mueller. Her name's Louisa, but that's all we know about her. I want to know who she really is and where else she's been and who she's been hanging out with in the last year or so."

"All right, give me a sec."

Haberman blacked out his screen so they couldn't see him anymore, but they could still hear the tapping of keys. A few seconds later, they heard swear words mumbled under his breath, then another flurry of keystrokes. Five minutes passed, then ten, which was an unusual amount of time for the hacker to be stumped. Finally, his annoyed face reappeared on the screen of Bourne's phone.

"Well, you always give me the cute ones, Bourne. This is fucking weird, I'll tell you that."

"What is?"

Haberman shook his head. "First of all, I don't find a Louisa anywhere in the world who matches her face. No way she hasn't had public records somewhere along the line, but they're all gone, or they've been tampered with."

"Tampered with? What does that mean?"

"That's the other thing that's pretty wild. I've only found a handful of photo hits of her in various databases—literally not even ten—but I also found those same exact photos with different faces in them. I.e., not her anymore. She's been replaced. In one pic, there's this Louisa, but in every other version I find, it's somebody completely different. And not the same person each time, which makes it even harder to track."

"How is that possible?" Bourne asked.

"They're deepfakes. Really good ones. Somebody has been meticulously calling up online images of this woman and erasing her out of existence. They've been thorough. Only a few of the originals made it back to me, mostly because the search recognition is marginal. I'm pretty sure it's her, but there's only a sixty-odd-percentage match. The one thing I'll tell you is that it seems like she's been a bad girl."

"Meaning what?"

"The places I've found her seem to be mostly where shit's happened," Haberman said. "Since you're not far from Atlanta, I'm guessing you know about her and the fire. She was there when that building went up last year. But I've also got her in Budapest where those dissidents were jailed a few months ago. And in Minnesota when there was some kind of pipeline explosion that killed a couple of protesters. Also in Wuhan in late 2019, which, shall we say, is *really* interesting."

"But nothing about her identity? Who she was, where she worked?"

"Not a thing."

Bourne frowned. "Okay, send me what you found."

"Pics are on the way. And with that, we're done. All debts are paid. Right?"

"Almost," Jason said. "If you've got any pictures of Abbey, delete them. Hard delete, Aaron, gone from the internet. Got it?"

The hacker scowled. "Got it."

Bourne hung up the phone. Abbey leaned over and kissed him. "Thank you for that."

"He won't do it."

"I know, but you tried."

Jason opened the photo library on his burner phone, and he saw that several new images had arrived there. With Abbey leaning in close to him, they went through each of the pictures carefully, enlarging the images as far as they could without completely losing the resolution. But most told them nothing. In several, Louisa's face was blurry, barely recognizable, and she was part of a crowd where she didn't seem to be interacting with anyone else. In others, she was alone, in settings neither of them could identify. None of the pictures gave them a clue as to who she really was.

Then Bourne stopped.

He swiped back to an earlier picture, and this time, he focused not on Louisa, but on another woman half-cropped out of the shot. He could only make out part of her profile. She was talking to someone else who was out of the camera frame, and she was nowhere near Louisa, who stood in the shadows behind her. But Louisa's eyes were clearly trained on the other woman in the picture.

"Do you see it?" Bourne asked Abbey. "Do you recognize her?"

"I don't think so," she replied with a frown. "Can you zoom in?"

Jason enlarged the photo again, and Abbey whistled under her breath.

"Saira Kohli."

28

YOUR BIGGEST ADVANTAGE IS SURPRISE.

Treadstone.

Bourne wanted Saira Kohli off-balance, unable to plan, only able to react to the information they put in front of her. Her response had to be raw and unfiltered. He needed to know if he'd been right in his original assessment that she *wasn't* part of the inner circle of the Pyramid. If she really was an outsider, then they could find a way to make her an ally. But they couldn't give her time to formulate a lie. There was no room to make a mistake.

"Is there any sign of her?" Bourne murmured.

He heard Abbey's voice in his earpiece. "Not yet."

Bourne made another loop around the sidewalks of the Georgetown campus. He walked with purpose, a faculty member heading to a late meeting. If you looked like you were going somewhere, no one challenged you. It was early evening, the shadows lengthening, the sky dark with clouds. He passed the rough gray stone of the Hariri Building, and the windows of Regents Hall loomed in front of him. Saira Kohli had a fourth-floor corner office, and he'd already identified her location in the building. Her window was still illuminated. She hadn't left for the night yet.

A groundskeeper approached him in a golf cart. Bourne stepped to the side to let the man pass, and he used that opportunity to check his surroundings again. Up the steps near the plaza of the Hariri Building, he spotted a tall, slightly stooped professor in conversation with a blond graduate student. The professor leaned on a cane, and the girl laughed at something he said. Closer to Bourne, a jogger came from behind him and took a side trail leading toward the red façade of Harbin Hall. From where he was, he saw Abbey sitting on a blanket on the green slope to his left. She was pretending to read a biology textbook they'd purchased in the Georgetown bookstore, but she had a view down the hill to the main entrance of Saira Kohli's building.

Bourne felt uneasy.

Nothing looked out of place in the campus environment, but his brain saw things before his eyes did, and his mind told him that something was wrong. He checked the area again, trying to pinpoint the source of his alarm, but he ran out of time. On the fourth floor of Regents Hall, he watched the light go off in the scientist's office.

"She's coming," he said.

Jason followed the path toward the dormitory, beside the fence separating him from the athletic field. He didn't want Saira to see him. Not yet. She'd met him once in Darrell Forster's office, and he was sure she'd remember. She'd be instantly on her guard. But Abbey was a stranger—a stranger ready to shock her and turn her world upside down.

As he crossed to the residence hall, he spotted a campus police vehicle parked at the curb. That was a problem. Any kind of disturbance outside the science building—and Bourne *wanted* a disturbance—would bring a security guard running. He took a casual glance toward the vehicle's windshield, and there was just enough light to see that the man behind the wheel was asleep. Jason ignored him for now. Loud voices might wake him up, but it couldn't be helped.

He continued to the stone wall near the entrance to the dormitory, where he took his phone and zoomed in on the entrance to Regents Hall. Any moment now, Saira Kohli would come through that door.

His instincts sent him another warning like a siren. The scene wasn't secure. Something about the quiet campus wasn't what it seemed to be. His gaze went from face to face among the people around him, from window to window in every building. He looked for surveillance. A watcher. A gun. A rifle.

But there was nothing.

What was wrong?

He was tempted to tell Abbey to break it off, to come

his way right now before Saira saw her. He didn't want her walking into a trap.

But across the street, the glass door to Regents Hall opened.

Abbey was already on her feet, marching down the slope.

THAT WAS HER.

Abbey recognized the thin, almost fragile-looking woman she'd seen many times on CNN and in press conferences from the World Health Organization and the United Nations. The wind blew Saira's brown hair across her face, and the woman delicately put it right. She was dressed in a red blouse, trim black slacks, and black sneakers. A purse dangled from her shoulder. Outside the building, she hesitated, then turned right along the sidewalk. She didn't glance up the slope. She seemed to be in her own world, an absentminded scientist.

Abbey hurried to the sidewalk and accelerated to come up behind her. When she was just a few steps away, she spat out her words just loud enough for Saira to hear.

"Who was Louisa?"

The reaction was instantaneous. Saira froze, then spun around, her eyes wide. The scientist glanced both ways, then closed the distance between them and whispered, "What? What did you say?"

"You heard me. Who was Louisa? Why was she killed?"

"How do you—" Then Saira stopped. She cocked her

head, peeling back Abbey's disguise as if she were look-ing through a microscope. "*You*. Oh, my God, it's you. I know your face. I know what was done to you. You're Abbey Laurent, aren't you?"

Abbey had wanted to throw Saira off-balance, but now she was off-balance herself. This woman *recognized* her! She knew who she was!

Saira took Abbey's wrists and spoke urgently, her voice low. "What are you doing here? How do you know about me?"

Abbey stuttered. "I could ask you the same question."

"You've been investigating Louisa, just like me. I know you have. *Why?*"

"Because of the Pyramid," Abbey snapped.

"The Pyramid? I don't know what that is."

Abbey remembered Jason's advice. *Watch her eyes. Look for the lie.* But she saw no lie in the woman's face, only confusion and fear. If Saira Kohli was really part of the Pyramid, she was a magnificent actress.

She heard Jason's voice in her ear. *"Press her again. Press her hard."*

"Don't play games with me, Dr. Kohli. We know about the Pyramid. We know you're part of it. So is Dar-rell Forster. So is Varak."

"Darrell? What do you know about Darrell? I've been trying to reach him, and I can't. He's *missing*."

Again Abbey felt herself thrown off-balance. Darrell Forster was missing? What was going on?

Jason spoke to her, his voice adding to the chaos in

Abbey's mind. *"If Forster's missing, then he's dead. The Pyramid must have killed him. They're shutting down every path that leads to Varak. Tell her!"*

"If Forster is missing, that means he's dead," Abbey told Saira, feeling like a robot. "The Pyramid killed him. Like they killed Louisa."

"Oh, my God! I'm telling you, I don't know what that is!"

"Then tell me about *Louisa*," Abbey went on. "Who *was* she?"

Saira shook her head. "I don't know anything about her. She came up to me at a conference last year. She said she worked for the institute in Frankfurt. She said it was evil, that it needed to be stopped. I didn't know whether to believe her."

"Frankfurt," Abbey murmured.

They had a location. They had *something*.

"Ever since then, I've been looking for Louisa, too," Saira told her. "When I saw the story in the paper, I knew she'd been murdered. I've been asking questions, trying to find out what she knew about the institute. And the man I had digging into it, he told me you'd been asking questions, too. I was going to reach out to *you*, but here you are."

Relief flooded Abbey. Saira wasn't lying. For just a moment, Abbey didn't feel that they were alone anymore, that it wasn't just her and Jason against the entire world. They had someone who could help them.

"Where can we go?" Abbey asked. "We need to talk,

but we can't stay here. We shouldn't be anywhere that we can be seen together. It's not safe."

"There's a garden near the observatory," Saira suggested. "It's close, and it's quiet. There are benches where we can sit."

Abbey nodded. "I have a lot to tell you. I have a lot of questions for you, too. And there's someone with me. You need to meet him. Actually, you met him once before, in Darrell Forster's office."

"*Him*? That man? Do you trust him?"

"I trust him with my life," Abbey said. "He's *saved* my life more than once."

"Who is he?"

"His name's Jason Bourne."

JASON WATCHED THE TWO WOMEN WALK TOGETHER DOWN THE sidewalk away from him. He checked a paper map of the Georgetown campus and noted the location of the Heyden Garden near the college's observatory. It was only a five-minute walk from where they were. As a precaution, he waited, making sure they weren't being followed. The only people he saw were the elderly professor and the blond grad student, who were slowly making their way down the steps of the Hariri Building, still engaged in animated conversation.

No one else took any notice of the two women. When Abbey and Saira disappeared from view, blocked by the bushes near Cooper Field, Bourne finally pushed off the wall and headed across the street again. In his ear, he heard the noise of Abbey's breathing, but otherwise, she and Saira Kohli didn't talk.

He passed near the campus police SUV as he reached the opposite sidewalk. With a quick glance, he noticed that the guard behind the wheel was still asleep. The man hadn't moved at all in the time that Jason had been monitoring Abbey's meeting.

Not at all.

Coldness flowed through Bourne's veins. He stopped in the grass, then changed course and approached the security vehicle where it was parked at the curb. As he neared the door, he saw what he feared. Below the level of the window, the guard's white shirt was soaked red with blood, his organs bulging from inside where a knife had cut him open. The man's head was back, his eyes closed.

He wasn't asleep. He was dead. Murdered.

"Abbey, where are you?" he hissed into the microphone. "Tell me exactly where you are right now."

He tensed, waiting for her reply, which came through the receiver a moment later. *"We're crossing the parking lot to the garden. The observatory's just ahead of us."* Then, obviously hearing the tension in his voice, she went on. *"Why? What's going on?"*

"There's a security guard here. Dead."

He heard a quick intake of breath. *"What do we do?"*

Bourne checked the campus map again and isolated their location. "Don't stop in the garden. Keep going. Walk quickly, but don't run. Don't let anyone realize you know they're onto you. There's a trail on the other side of the garden that leads down into a park. Find a place in the trees where you can both hide, and stay there. Don't move. Don't make a sound until you hear from me."

"*Jason, oh my God.*"

"I'm on my way. Do you have the gun I gave you?"

"*Yes, it's in my purse, but I don't think—*"

Bourne didn't let her protest. "Listen to me, Abbey. Open your purse, keep your hand around the gun. Make sure it's racked the way I showed you, so you're ready to fire. Trust no one. No one. If someone approaches you, if *anyone* approaches you, pull out the gun. You have to be ready to use it."

29

JASON SPRINTED PAST THE HARIRI BUILDING AND UP A SET OF concrete steps that led to a small parking lot. From this height, he could look down on the athletic field below him and across at the university's redbrick buildings. On the other side of the parking lot, he saw the white dome of the observatory telescope.

Abbey and Saira were nowhere to be seen. In his ear, he heard the rustle of leaves. They were already in the trees beyond the garden.

He walked slowly, alert for threats. He reviewed each car in the lot, looking for movement, but saw none. The fenced roof of the field house loomed just above him, but he saw no one hiding there. There were a handful of people coming and going around him, and automatically, his mind evaluated each one, but he concluded they weren't threats. There were no killers here.

And yet there *were*! A man was *dead*!

His instincts screamed at him that he'd missed something. Something should have been there, but wasn't. *What?*

Then he remembered. The elderly professor! The blond grad student! They'd come down the steps and headed in the same direction as Abbey and Saira. The professor was slow, walking with a cane. Where was he? Where were *they*? By now, Bourne should have caught up with them; he should have passed them. But instead, the professor and the blond girl with him had both vanished.

Bourne looked in every direction. From this height, he could see each alternate route they could have taken. They were gone. The professor who limped with a cane had suddenly been able to move as quickly as a panther. Because he was not old. Because he was not the faculty member he'd pretended to be. Because his awkward gait with a cane masked the odd grace that he used whenever he walked.

Lennon. Lennon was here.

And he had a new Yoko with him.

They'd been watching for Saira Kohli just as Bourne and Abbey had been, waiting for the scientist to leave the building. That told him that Saira was a target now. She'd been marked for death by the Pyramid, and they were taking no chances. They'd brought in the team from the master assassin to take her out.

And now Abbey was in the crosshairs, too.

"Abbey, where are you?" he murmured into the microphone. "Keep your voice down, but give me your location. There are two killers on the campus close by. At least two. One is pretending to be an older professor, tall, with a cane; the other is a young blond woman in a T-shirt and shorts. They're both lethal and dangerous. Don't let them see you."

Jason waited. There was no response.

"Abbey? Where are you?"

Nothing.

"Abbey!"

He cursed out loud, and adrenaline surged through him.

Again Bourne ran, plunging into the garden that led past the observatory. The spring flowers were in bloom, and a few trees created shadowy groves. There were several benches, mostly empty, but he spotted a twenty-something man stretched out on one bench near a large stone urn with a fountain gurgling out of the top. Bourne slowed. The man had his head balanced on several textbooks, earbuds in, and he wore shorts, a T-shirt, and had bare feet. He looked like a student. But the kid was faced away from him, his hands invisible.

Bourne took no chances. He slid his gun from his pocket. He gave the bench a wide berth, but he didn't take his eyes off the man as he continued toward the west end of the garden. He began to jog again, but at the same moment, a muffled pop sounded from above him, and pain sliced in a hot gash across the back of his shoulder.

Another shooter!

He dove, rolled in a somersault, and scrambled to his

feet again at a dead run. The new assassin was to his right, firing down from the roof of the field house, using a suppressed semiautomatic through the rungs of the fence. With Bourne on the move, the man's aim was wild, and Jason threw himself sideways and rolled until the field house wall blocked him from view. But at the same moment, more spits hissed around him, much closer and more deadly. The kid on the bench had spun backward and was shooting awkwardly as he repositioned himself, his gun held sideways. Grass and dirt exploded in Bourne's face, nearly blinding him, but he swung his gun up and trained fire at the kid on the bench. The first shot missed left, thudding into the white observatory wall. The next seared through the kid's throat.

He had to get to *Abbey*!

Firing toward the field house to keep the man on the roof at bay, Bourne covered the remaining distance to the end of the garden and launched himself down the grassy slope. More bullets chased him but landed harmlessly in the trees. At the bottom of the slope, he hopped a low fence and saw a gravel trail leading into the valley of Foundry Park. The trail took him into dense woods, and soon the campus buildings were invisible behind him.

He stopped, listening. Trees and brush made thick walls on either side of the path. He wasn't alone. Somewhere in the forest, a branch snapped, caused by a footstep. He crouched, just as another pop blew from the trees and another bullet whistled above him. He fired back, deliberately high, not taking the risk of his shots getting anywhere near Abbey and Saira. But the return fire had its effect, because he heard the trampling of brush as the shooter changed locations at high speed.

Where were they?

"Abbey," he whispered again into the microphone.

She didn't answer.

On the trail, Bourne was an easy target. He plunged off the path into the woods. He couldn't move silently, but he was more protected here. The park itself was a narrow ribbon that stretched through much of downtown DC. If he turned north, he headed through the city; if he turned south, the park ended barely a quarter mile away at the Potomac. Which way would Abbey go?

Jason turned south. He stayed close enough to the trail that he could see it through the trees, but his progress was slow, picking through a web of branches and brush. Every few feet, he stopped to get his bearings and listen for any sounds that Abbey and Saira might make. They weren't pros; they wouldn't be able to keep silent for long. But he heard nothing. When he called softly, he got no answer.

The black thought occurred to him that they might already be dead.

But no. They weren't. He knew, because he spotted a tall man slipping from the woods onto the trail fifty yards away. Gun in hand. The figure looked like an old man, but he moved like someone decades younger.

Lennon. He was still hunting them. They were still *alive*!

Bourne raised his gun, but he didn't have a shot at

that distance. In the next instant, the assassin was gone, moving southward toward the river. Jason followed. He returned to the path, where he could close the distance between them with stealth. His footsteps were hushed, but he couldn't move fast, and he couldn't see beyond the curve of the trail. He didn't have to go far. As he came around the curve, the path opened into a grassy clearing, and a rusted trestle bridge spanned the narrow valley between the treetops.

Lennon was in the middle of the clearing.

He wore a tweed sport coat—like a college teacher's uniform—plus khakis and Top-Siders. Thinning gray hair sprouted in tufts from his mostly bald head. And yet it was *him*. Wasn't it? The walk was the same—that strange gliding walk that gave him away. He'd ditched the cane that he'd used when he limped past the campus buildings. This was Lennon. This was the killer he'd hunted for a year. The killer who claimed to be a crucial link in the chain of Jason's missing past.

Or was he making a mistake?

Was this really just an old man out for a hike?

If he was Lennon, where was his *gun*? Jason was sure he'd seen a gun through the trees, but the man's hands were empty. It could be in his belt. Or under the coat. For the first time, Bourne found himself gripped by hesitation. Doubt. Unable to act.

Never hesitate. Hesitation kills.

Treadstone.

He stopped where he was and raised his gun. He took aim across the field at the old man's back. There was no time to wait. Lennon—it *was* Lennon, it *had* to be Lennon—kept walking, getting farther away, making the shot more difficult with each step. If Bourne missed, he wouldn't get a second chance.

Shoot!

Then a scream pierced the woods behind him. The opposite direction, to the north. It was a woman's cry, muffled but not far away. His heart lurched.

Was it *Abbey*?

The unmistakable crack of a gunshot followed the scream.

In the field, the old man—the *young* man—lurched leftward and spun, drawing the gun from where it had been holstered in his coat. But Bourne was already gone, leaving Lennon behind, letting him go. A hail of bullets chased Jason down the path as he plunged toward the source of the scream.

"SHIT," ABBEY HISSED AS SHE DRAGGED SAIRA KOHLI TO A stop on the trail. She whispered to Jason over and over without getting a response, and when she checked her ear, she found it empty. "I lost the receiver. It must have fallen out as we ran. I don't have any way to tell him where we are."

They were heading north, deeper into the park that led through the city, but they hadn't gone far. Now she felt the weight of the silence, knowing Jason couldn't find her. He'd told them to hide, but Saira had suggested they put as much distance between themselves and the

Georgetown campus as they could. If there were really killers hunting them, then the best thing they could do was get far away. Abbey had agreed, but now, with the two of them on their own, she began to hesitate.

"We should go back," she said. "Turn around. We can find a place in the woods to take shelter until Jason finds us."

Saira shook her head. "And march into a trap? Abbey, we need to keep going."

"But what if there are more of them coming down from the north? We'll run right into them if we stay on the trail. We need to get to Jason."

"*No.* He'll find us later. Come on, let's go, *hurry.*"

Saira headed north, and Abbey reluctantly followed. But they hadn't gone more than a few yards when she took hold of Saira's wrist. "Wait. Listen!"

From behind them, they heard the pounding of footsteps. Someone was getting closer, running toward them from the campus. Abbey's gaze shot to the woods, but there was nowhere to hide, and they didn't have time to get off the trail unseen. With nausea gripping her, she remembered Jason's advice, and she unlatched her purse and shoved her hand inside. She felt the cool metal of the gun, and she pulled the slide back, preparing a cartridge. Her thumb undid the safety. Her index finger curled around the trigger, not along the barrel.

Be ready to use it.

Abbey tensed, her eyes glued to the trail. She didn't see what she expected. Through the shadows, she spotted a woman jogging their way. She couldn't have been more than her mid-twenties. Her hair was blond, tied in a ponytail behind her, and she wore a Georgetown T-shirt and satin blue running shorts. Her feet were in neon yellow sneakers. Her eyes didn't look alert or cautious; instead, she ran with her head bopping to whatever music was coming through her wired earbuds.

Next to her, Saira relaxed. "It's okay. That's just Tara. She's in one of my classes."

Seeing them, the girl made a little start, then stopped on the path. Her face broke into an easy grin, and she slipped one of the earbuds—just one—out of her ear. "Oh, hey, Dr. Kohli."

"Hello, Tara," the scientist said.

"Out for a hike? Great day for it."

"Yes, it is. Did you pass anyone? Did you see anything unusual as you were heading this way?"

The girl shrugged. "Didn't see a soul."

"Or hear anything?"

She lifted up the coil of her earbuds. "Just Billie Eilish."

Abbey still had her hand wrapped around the gun. She hadn't loosened her grip yet. Jason's words echoed in her head. *If someone approaches you, if* anyone *approaches you, pull out the gun.* But Tara didn't look like a threat. Saira knew her. She was a Georgetown grad student out for a run.

Tara shifted her gaze and smiled at Abbey, inviting her to introduce herself. The girl gave her a curious look when Abbey said nothing. But Abbey kept staring back at her, her mind racing. She was trying to see everything, absorb everything, trying to remember the things Jason had told her about the life he led.

Nothing is a coincidence.

Force your brain to ask questions.

Why was this girl jogging out here in the park now, at this exact moment?

Why was she acting out of breath when she wasn't sweating at all?

Why did she leave one of her earbuds *in her ear*, and why could Abbey not hear any music from the earbud that dangled at the girl's side?

"Everything okay, Dr. Kohli?" Tara asked casually. "Your friend here looks kinda tense."

Saira noticed it, too. "Abbey?"

Abbey tried to control the trembling she felt. She wanted to panic and give in to the fear. If only she could pretend what was happening was *not* happening.

But it was.

"I'm Tara," the girl said lightly to Abbey, taking a step forward and extending her hand. "Tara Dean."

Abbey held up her hand to stop her. "Back away. Take two steps back."

A confused grin crossed the girl's face, but she didn't back up. "Huh?"

"Abbey, it's okay," Saira reiterated. "I told you, I know Tara."

But Abbey ignored the scientist and kept all her focus on the girl in front of her. "Turn around. Let me see what's behind your back."

"Behind my back? What are you talking about?" Tara's blue eyes darkened. "I don't like this. Dr. Kohli, you want me to call the cops or something? Is this woman causing problems for you?"

Abbey gripped the gun tighter. Her breathing came faster in her chest, and she felt light-headed. Bending her elbow, she drew the Sig out of her purse and straightened her arm, pointing the barrel across the short space between her and Tara.

Beside her, Saira gasped. "A gun? For God's sake, Abbey, put that away now!"

Tara held up her hands, but she didn't move. "Whoa, what the fuck? Are you crazy? Chill out, okay?"

"How many are there?" Abbey asked.

"What?"

"How many? Where are they coming from? Just the south, or do you have more men coming from the north?"

"Lady, I don't know what you're talking about. Put down that gun, okay? Seriously, you don't want to hurt anybody."

"She's right, Abbey, put away the gun," Saira said, reaching for her arm. "Tara's right. You're going to hurt someone with that thing."

Abbey's arm stayed rigid, and she shrugged Saira off. Her eyes burned into Tara's blue eyes, but the girl gave nothing away. "Turn around. Slowly. Do it right now. I think you've got something hidden in your belt. If I'm wrong, I'll lower the gun. But first you have to turn around."

"Hey, sure, no problem, whatever you say."

Tara spread her arms wide, and she began to rotate at the hips. Her next movement happened so quickly that Abbey barely had an instant to react. Tara drew a bloody knife from behind her back, and she leaped across the space between them, slashing the blade toward Abbey's throat.

Saira screamed, and Abbey fired. She didn't think, she just *fired*. A bullet tore into Tara's shoulder, making the girl stumble backward in disbelief, as if she couldn't believe Abbey had really done it. Tara shook herself and looked down, watching the blood spread on the gray T-shirt, the stain getting larger. The girl actually laughed. She dipped a finger into the blood, and she laughed. Her eyes went from Abbey to the bullet wound and back to Abbey again.

"Fuck you, you *bitch*! You shot me!"

Tara hoisted the knife and charged.

Abbey fired a second time, and again a bullet seared through Tara's body, breaking her collarbone with this shot, making her howl with pain. Her knees buckled. Her head tilted, and her face grimaced into twisted agony.

Abbey grabbed Saira, and the two of them backed away from the girl. A roar growled from Tara's throat, and she came at them again. This time Abbey's arm shook as the terror caught up with her, and she missed. The bullet soared high into the trees. She didn't have time to shoot again.

The knife came flying for her throat.

Then another gunshot erupted with a crack. Tara bent backward stiffly, her whole body stretching, like a runner at the finish line. The knife fell from her hand. She stood there, swaying, a tree deciding which way to fall. Her mouth went slack, and blood dripped from her lips. Then she crashed sideways to the trail, dead.

Behind her, gun at the end of his outstretched arms, was Jason.

PART THREE

PART THREE

30

BOURNE KEYED IN SIX DIGITS TO UNDO THE COMBINATION lock on the heavy metal door of the warehouse. Then he led Abbey and Saira to the upper floor of the building. Halfway down the hallway was a second door, unmarked, also with a combination lock that he disarmed. When they were inside, he went to the single narrow window and stared out at the darkness. Seeing no movement outside, he shut the blackout curtains, then switched on the light, revealing the bare-bones furnishings of a studio apartment.

They'd driven for nearly two hours south of Washington to reach the industrial park near Fredericksburg, Virginia. He'd switched vehicles along the way, trading the Bronco for a stolen Toyota Camry, and he'd parked the sedan in the green field behind the warehouse. The apartment inside the building was a Treadstone safe house, one of dozens located near metropolitan areas around the country, used by agents who needed to stay undercover or who were on the run.

"We can stay here for the night," Bourne told them. "Are you hungry? There's no refrigerator, but there should be food in the cabinets. Power bars, that sort of thing. You both should eat something."

He watched Abbey sit down on one of the two twin beds in the apartment. She'd said very little as they escaped from Washington, and she kept stretching out her arms and staring at the spatters of blood on her sleeves. He understood, and he was worried about her. The deeper she dove into his world, the more her sanity rebelled against the things she'd seen him do—and now the things she'd had to do herself, too.

"When do you think I can go home?" Saira Kohli asked. The scientist, always practical, took Bourne's advice and found a high-protein snack bar in a cabinet over the apartment's kitchenette. She unwrapped it and ate it quickly. "Because I can't run forever."

"I wish I could answer that, Dr. Kohli," Bourne said. "These people were targeting you tonight, not Abbey. They were waiting for you, and they came very close to killing you. One of the most dangerous assassins in the world was in that park. If you'd turned south when you were running instead of north, if you'd met *him* instead of his colleague, odds are you'd both be dead right now. As it is, he's still out there looking for you."

"All right. I accept that. I find it impossible to imagine, but I accept it. Given that an ordinary grad student in one of my classes tried to cut my throat tonight, I guess I can't argue with you."

"She wasn't an ordinary grad student," Bourne said. "I'm sure she was in your class specifically to watch you. They've been spying on you for months. Probably since you became part of Varak's institute."

"And you think this *Pyramid* group that Abbey mentioned is behind all of this?"

"Yes."

"Then we should go to the police. These people are killers. Surely they can be arrested."

"We have no proof of anything that would implicate the people who are actually part of the Pyramid. We don't even know who they are, other than Varak, and we have no evidence against him. If anyone's arrested, it won't be the ones in charge. Plus, as soon as you put yourself in the spotlight, they'll ruin you, discredit you, and take away your platform. Then they'll kill you anyway. That's what they tried to do to Abbey."

"All right, all right, but what if the reverse is true? What if the police start looking for *us*?"

"For the time being, it doesn't look like you or Abbey have been linked to what happened in the park tonight," he told her. "There's nothing to tie you to the violence. Your names haven't come up. That may not last, but we need to keep it that way as long as we can."

"So back to my original question. How long do we have to run?"

"Tonight we run," Bourne said. "Tomorrow we fight back."

Saira didn't ask him anything more for the moment. She examined the small, sterile space, studying it like a researcher, as if the drab furniture could tell stories about the spies who'd been here. When she went to the window and began to pull aside the curtain to look outside, Bourne intervened to stop her.

"Better not to let anyone see that we're here," he said.

"Do you think we were followed?"

"No. I know we weren't followed. But the assassin I mentioned—he calls himself Lennon—has moles inside most of the intelligence agencies. I can't rule out that he has access to the locations of safe houses we use. He might think to surveil the ones near DC on the chance that we'd go there."

"Ah." She took careful note of his face, still using her scientist's curiosity for a phenomenon she didn't understand. "Who exactly are you, Mr. Bourne? Abbey said she trusted you with her life, and you obviously saved both of our lives tonight. I'm very grateful. But you have me wondering about you. Given your tactical skills, I assume you're some kind of government operative. Black budget work, that sort of thing?"

"I was."

"And now?"

"Now let's just say I have an arm's-length relationship with the people who trained me. Sometimes our interests overlap, sometimes they don't. In this case, the overlap is Lennon's work for the Pyramid."

Saira left the window and sat down next to Abbey on the bed. "You've talked about Darrell Forster and Varak.

I assume the institute is somehow connected to all of this, too."

"The institute appears to be the public face," Bourne explained. "The Pyramid acts behind the scenes. A handful of powerful people setting the agenda, deciding on the narratives, the *lies*. With Varak as the leader. The one they call Genesis."

"Genesis," Saira mused. "Interesting choice. And what do they want? What's their goal?"

"To control what people think by controlling what they know."

Saira pursed her lips in thought. Then she focused on Abbey. "Do you mind if I ask you a question? The things they said about you, were they all lies?"

Abbey looked up, her eyes fierce. "Yes."

"None of it was true?"

"No."

Saira got up from the bed, her arms wrapped tightly around her chest. "Well, those are my worst fears realized. I've been manipulated. Used as a pawn."

"How did you become involved with the institute?" Bourne asked.

"Through Darrell," she replied. "He approached me. He was chairing the project for the foundation, and he made the whole thing sound so sensible. So practical. We were coming off several years in which trust in science and facts had disintegrated. Wild misinformation was spreading everywhere. The institute was a way to combat that scourge. To provide resources for journalists and tech companies to make sure they could separate fact from fiction and then provide that information to their readers. Except—"

She hesitated.

"Except what?" Bourne asked.

"I had to make excuses for things that made me very uncomfortable," Saira went on. "Darrell insisted—and he wasn't wrong—that there were bad actors on the other side, people who were deliberately stirring up chaos for their own ends. Part of the job of the institute was to expose those people. Hold up their sins to the light. Conflicts of interest, bribes, crimes, anything that showed the world who they really were. I didn't like it, but Darrell said we were simply exposing their secrets. But now I see they were *creating* lies, as they did with Abbey. Destroying people simply because they got in their way."

"It's more than that," Abbey said. "It's worse."

"What do you mean?"

"Do you remember the Georgia Senate race last year? The fire?"

"Of course."

Bourne showed her a screenshot that Sloane Jenks had given them from his video of the riots that night. "Lennon was the one who set the fire. And Louisa—well, you can see in the photograph that Louisa was there, too. The Pyramid was responsible for those deaths."

Saira's hand flew to her mouth. "Oh, my God. You're talking about murder. The murder of *children*."

"That's what persuaded Louisa to try to expose them," Abbey said. "You said Louisa sought you out at a conference to warn you that the institute was evil. When was this?"

"Last December. In Oslo, at a World Health Organization meeting."

"That was only a few weeks after the fire," Abbey pointed out.

Saira shook her head in dismay. "That must have been what she was talking about. She wanted my help. She wanted me to stop it. I tried to find out who she was, but I hit a dead end. I don't know, maybe on some level, I didn't even *want* to know the truth. But then, when I saw that she'd been killed—"

"Louisa came to the U.S. to expose the Pyramid," Bourne said. "If she was at the scene of the fire, then she was deeply involved in their operations. Obviously, she had access to enough data on them that they needed to eliminate her—erase her whole identity. Since then, they've been shutting down every trail that leads back to her. We need to find out what she knew, what information she had. That's how we fight back."

"I'm not sure how we do that," Saira replied.

"You said she worked at the institute in Frankfurt," Abbey said.

"That's what she told me. I arranged to visit the institute offices in Frankfurt on a European trip a few weeks later. I asked about her, but they said no one named Louisa worked in the building."

"You mentioned her by name?" Bourne asked, frowning.

"Yes. I was hoping to talk to her. I didn't tell them

why, of course. I made up some story." Then Saira's eyes widened with dismay. "You don't mean— Oh, God, was it me? Did I accidentally expose her?"

"If she was one of their field operatives, there's no way you should have had her name," Bourne acknowledged reluctantly. "You asking about her must have set off red flags. After that, they probably started watching her. They discovered that she was planning to betray them. When she flew to Washington, she was flying into a trap."

"*I* killed her."

"No, you didn't. The Pyramid did. Varak did."

Abbey got off the bed and went to her. "Saira, what's in Frankfurt? What do they do there?"

She shrugged. "My understanding has always been that it's the institute's primary research operation. They facilitate fact-based responses to stories trending in the mainstream media or on social media platforms. If something significant happens—for example, some kind of notable weather event or catastrophe—they monitor the reporting and posts about it, and they loop in subject matter experts to counter false or unsubstantiated information."

"According to our source, Louisa claimed it was much more than that," Abbey said. "They have teams of hackers building deepfake videos, artificial online identities, anything to swarm and shape the narrative on a story. She called it a bot farm."

Saira closed her eyes. "I can't believe this. I can't believe I was a part of this."

"When you were there, did you see the entire operation?"

"All but the eighth floor," she replied.

"What was up there?"

"The director said it was sensitive material. Secure access only. I was a board member of the institute, but even I wasn't allowed in that area. You needed a special elevator pass, special security ID, et cetera. I thought it would look odd for me to push it, so I said that was fine. But I had no idea that any of the things you're talking about could be going on."

Bourne began to see a plan take shape in his mind. He did what he always did, build a flow chart of actions and reactions, maneuvers and countermaneuvers. The first step was basic. Transport. Get from Point A to Point B.

"Do you have contacts without any connection to the institute?" he asked Saira. "Someone who could arrange discreet access to a private jet for a trip that's entirely off the books? I don't want to use any of my usual sources. There's too much chance of a leak, given that Lennon's involved."

"I think so. Why?"

"Because we need to get to Frankfurt," Bourne replied. "We need to get into that building."

AT THREE IN THE MORNING, JASON AWOKE. HIS INSTINCTS HAD jarred him from sleep. He lay stretched out on the floor in the safe house apartment, but automatically, as his eyes opened, he was alert. When he got to his feet, he saw immediately that the twin bed where Abbey had been sleeping was empty.

She was gone.

Saira Kohli was still in the other bed. Bourne did a quick check through the apartment window—the lights inside were off, giving nothing away—and he saw no indication of any cars or people in the industrial park. He grabbed his gun, then slipped through the apartment door and took the metal steps downstairs.

The back door of the building led to the grassy field where he'd parked the Camry. Beyond the open field was a grove of evergreens. In the starlight, he saw Abbey standing by herself near the trees. She wore a T-shirt and shorts, her legs and feet bare. He came up silently behind her, and when he touched her shoulder, he had to cover her mouth with his hand to keep her from screaming.

"What are you doing out here?" he asked when she'd adjusted to his presence. "It's not safe. You shouldn't go off on your own."

"I know, but you were asleep. I wanted some air."

"How were you going to get back inside?"

Abbey shrugged. "I watched the combinations when you keyed them into the locks. You trained me well."

He couldn't help but smile. "I appreciate that, but I don't want you taking chances."

"You're right. I'm sorry."

He pulled her close to him and kissed her. She was stiff in his arms. "Tell me what's wrong."

Actually, he knew what was wrong. He knew what memory was playing over and over in her head. But he needed her to face the line she'd crossed. That was the only way to get past the shock.

"I *shot* someone, Jason," she replied. "I pointed a gun at that girl, and I shot her."

"You didn't kill her. That was me."

"Does it matter? If I'd had better aim, it would have been me."

"She was trying to kill *you*. Shooting that girl when you did saved both of you. You realized she was a threat, and you did what you needed to do."

"The blood," she murmured. "There was so much blood."

"I know."

Abbey shook her head. "How do you live with it?"

"Badly," Jason admitted. "The truth is, I don't live with it well at all. That's why I pushed you away after Quebec. That's why I didn't want you anywhere near my world. Because it eats away at you from the inside."

"Well, it's too late for that. I'm in it now. I can't go back."

"Yes, you can," he insisted. "We're going to Frankfurt, and we'll find what you need to get your life back. To prove that what they did to you was a lie. After that, you can just be Abbey Laurent, reporter, all over again. Nothing's changed."

Abbey kissed him back, but her face was full of shadows. "That's sweet, Jason, but don't lie to me. You know that's not true. Once I pulled that trigger, I became an entirely different person. I'll never be who I was. That Abbey is gone for good."

31

OSKAR HAD A PLAN.

He stood under the hot water of the shower in his apartment, and he wondered if he had the courage to do it. He was risking his job—no, not true, he was walking away from his job, and his apartment, and everyone he knew in Frankfurt. That was a given. What he was *risking* was his life. They'd killed Louisa, and as soon as they discovered what he'd done, they'd try to kill him, too.

They will be watching you. You're in danger, my love.

The smart thing, the safe thing, was to do nothing at all. Keep his head down. Forget Louisa, cash his paychecks, and eventually, when enough time had passed to ease their suspicions, he could take a new job far away. Under a different name, maybe. He would help no one by getting himself killed.

But, my God, the things he'd discovered in Louisa's

account. The files, the emails, the photos, the videos, all retrieved from the stream of deleted documents. The evidence of deception. Lies. And murder, too.

The things she'd *done*! The things the institute had made her do.

How could he forget that?

Oskar turned off the shower and stood there until he was cold. It was early morning, barely past dawn, but he'd been unable to sleep. Finally, he got out of the shower and dressed, and made coffee in his kitchen. He turned on the television to a morning show, but uneasiness trailed after him. He remembered that they'd searched his apartment. *They will be watching you.* He went to the window that looked out on the Main River, and he studied the grassy riverbank to see if there were strangers watching his window.

Then he thought: That was a foolish thing for him to do.

What if they'd planted cameras inside his apartment? Were they looking at him right now? Watching everything he did? He couldn't afford to do anything that would arouse suspicion. He couldn't let them know that he was aware of their surveillance. That was an admission of guilt.

By the window, Oskar yawned and sipped coffee, as if he were simply admiring the sunrise. Then he turned around with feigned casualness and went back to the kitchen to pour cereal for his breakfast. He ate it, watched TV, drank more coffee, and pretended that this was an ordinary day.

Not a day that would change his whole life.

The plan!

His gaze flicked to a small paper bag on the table by the door. On an evening walk the previous day, he'd avoided being followed, and then he'd made his way to an electronics supply store on the Zeil. It was a quick stop, in and out in less than five minutes. The bag had fit in his pocket, so if the watchers had picked him up again later, they wouldn't have seen it. He tried to remember: Had he emptied the bag when he got home? He'd been in a hurry at the store, barely noticing what he'd plucked from the shelf. Had he taken out the device, examined it, confirmed its size and shape?

If they were watching, could they have seen it in his hand?

He didn't think so.

Oskar checked his watch and saw that it was time. He had to go to work. His heart was racing, and he'd already sweated through his clean clothes. He wanted to procrastinate, but he couldn't. Everything had to look normal. Nothing about his behavior could attract any attention, not until the thing was done.

He got ready to go. He whistled, a normal man on a normal day. At the door, he picked up the paper bag, and he slipped its contents into his hand. One item was a packet of chewing gum he'd found at the checkout counter of the electronics store. He made a show of unwrapping a stick of gum and putting it in his mouth. Then he slipped the rest of the pack into his pocket, along with the other item he'd taken from the bag.

A two-terabyte thumb drive.

Large enough to download the entire contents of the deleted files that had been stored in Louisa's account. Everything. But that kind of transfer would attract attention. It wouldn't take long to be found out.

Oskar crumpled the paper bag and threw it away, and then he left the apartment to take his walk to work. He wasn't sure when or if he'd be able to return to his apartment again. As soon as the download was done, he needed to run. They'd know about it in minutes. The alarm would sound. He didn't even know if he'd have time to leave the building before they found out.

What would happen then?

But he couldn't think about that. Louisa was right. *They must be stopped.*

Outside, he strolled by the river and crossed the Alte Brücke to the other side of town. He walked without hurry. He made a point of stopping to buy a newspaper near the Römerplatz, and then a chocolate croissant at a *Bäckerei*. There could be nothing suspicious in his behavior. But as he took a bite of the pastry when he was back on the street, he glanced at the people around him and spotted a woman in a red raincoat turning away to glance in a shop window. He'd already noticed that red raincoat twice before on his walk from his apartment. The watchers were definitely back.

Oskar reached the gloomy edifice where the institute was housed. He felt a twinge of worry when he handed over his ID card, wondering if this time there would be a flag on his record. They'd smile at him, but they'd nod at the security guards, who would show up on either side and usher him away.

But no. The bored attendant returned his ID card and waved him through. Oskar exhaled with relief, then headed for the elevators. There, too, his ID still worked. The light for the eighth floor went on. He traveled upstairs with one other privileged hacker like himself, a woman around forty, but they didn't know each other's names, and they didn't speak or make eye contact.

On the ride to the top of the building, his mind kept going back to the plan. His boss, Heinrich Kessler, was a man of routines. Unlike so many of his hackers, he kept a rigid schedule. He arrived at the same time, left at the same time. And he went to lunch at the same time, too, every day at exactly one thirty in the afternoon. That was the moment. When Kessler was gone, Oskar would plug the thumb drive into his computer and reaccess the deleted files from Louisa's account. In a few minutes, he'd have them copied over to the thumb drive, and then he'd immediately exit the building—hopefully before anyone realized what he'd done and alerted Heinrich Kessler.

He'd leave with Louisa's entire account in his pocket. All the evidence. The truths to combat the lies.

And then he would go—where? He still hadn't made up his mind. Not Frankfurt. Maybe not even Germany. The information could only be delivered by hand to people he could trust, people who would *act*. But who? The highest authorities, the European police, they were the ones. That meant a long journey. He had to make his way to the headquarters of Interpol in Lyon, France. And stay alive as he did so.

That was the plan.

The elevator doors opened, and Oskar got out. As he did, his heart skipped with fear, and acid rose into his mouth. His entire plan fell apart.

The security protocol for the eighth floor had completely changed overnight. A plexiglass wall now separated the bank of elevators from the cubicles where everyone worked. There were only two accesses through the wall, a way in and a way out. A guard waved Oskar and the woman through the entrance, but Oskar noticed that the way out was now being carefully monitored. They'd installed an AIT scanner, and anyone wanting to leave had to empty their pockets and put their possessions through an X-ray machine and then proceed through the body scanner as if they were entering an airport.

By instinct, he slipped a hand into his pocket, and his fingers closed around the thumb drive. There was no way he could get it out of the building now. They'd find it when he tried to leave.

Scheiße!

Oskar went to his desk in a daze. He passed Jochim's desk, but his friend—who was not officially a friend—wasn't in the office yet. As he sat down, he traced the outline of the thumb drive again. What to do? He couldn't access Louisa's account; he couldn't download the files now, when his pockets and body would both be searched as he tried to leave. *Oh, my God,* he had to get rid of the thumb drive, too! Even blank, it would give him away. But how? He couldn't carry it out, and if he threw it away somewhere on the floor, they would find it. And then what? They'd know a traitor was in their midst. They'd be watching. They might even swap out the institute server entirely to make sure there was no electronic footprint of any of their past activities. A clean slate. Louisa would be gone, and so would any hope he had of avenging her murder.

He booted up his terminal. He pretended to type; he pretended to do his work. No one could know that his mind was in chaos. He was so focused on the ruins of his plan that he barely even noticed Jochim arriving at the desk next to his. A few minutes passed before he became aware of the person next to him, and he glanced that way.

Except it was not Jochim.

It was a stranger. A skinny twentysomething man with bushy black hair, a pimply face, and a thin mustache sat in the chair. He wore a gray T-shirt and jeans, and he tapped away at the computer as if he'd been working there for months.

"Wo ist Jochim?" Oskar asked, although he knew he was breaking the rules. Never ask personal questions.

The young man glanced back at him with a shrug. *"Wer? Ich kenne ihn nicht."*

Jochim, Oskar wanted to say. You don't know him? You're sitting at his desk! He's been in that same place every day for the past three years!

But he said nothing.

Oskar glanced at Heinrich Kessler's office. His boss was working, the way he always was, his head down. The man's door was open. Oskar needed a lie, something that wouldn't be noticed, but he had to know. Where was Jochim? He got up and strolled over to Kessler's office, and the man greeted him in his typical perfunctory way. Oskar took five minutes to discuss the project he was working on—ordinary questions on an ordinary day—and then, as he was leaving, he threw out one last query. His body language said it was a matter of no particular importance.

"Say, where is Jochim?"

Kessler looked at him. "Who?"

Oskar nodded toward his desk. "The man who worked next to me. He's not there anymore."

"Why do you care?"

"He borrowed fifty euro from me the other day. Said he left his wallet at home."

Kessler shrugged. "You're out the money, I'm afraid."

"Oh? He left the institute?"

"He died."

Oskar stared at his boss and tried not to let the shock creep onto his face. He kept his voice low and casual. "Died? How terrible. What happened?"

"Heart attack. You saw him, always ate enough for four people. All that fat finally caught up with him."

"I see," Oskar replied. "Well, thank you for letting me know."

Cold sweat returned to his body as he went back to his

desk. He tried working again, but he found himself typing random characters, because he couldn't concentrate on anything else now. The walls were closing in. *Jochim!*

Oskar didn't believe in coincidences, not after the things Louisa had told him. There had been no heart attack. It was *him*! This was his fault. He'd used the man's computer. He'd used Jochim's account to access private areas of the server.

And now Jochim was dead.

32

FRANKFURT WAS A CITY WITHOUT MUCH OF THE CHARM OF other places in Germany. There was no Brandenburg Gate as in Berlin, no Neuschwanstein Castle or Nymphenburg Palace as in Munich, no cathedral as in Cologne. The business of Frankfurt was business. It was a place for bankers and lawyers doing international deals, not tourists looking for Oktoberfest beer halls or Danube river cruises. That drab, modern practicality was evident in the massive research headquarters of the Varak Institute, which took up an entire city block near the Main River. The building showed no architectural flourishes, just flat walls built of soot-stained concrete and dozens of rectangular windows. Most of the building was five stories high, but there was a taller perpendicular wing attached at the east end, and that section rose three stories higher.

The eighth floor was the top level. That was where Louisa had worked.

Bourne and Abbey walked along Bethmannstraße beside the building's south wall. A streetcar rattled past them, heading toward the giant open square of the Römerplatz. There were no access doors on this side of the institute building, not even an emergency exit, just ground-floor windows that offered no view inside. But he noted cameras aimed at the sidewalk in both directions.

"Keep your head down," Jason told her. "Pull your hat a little lower. I don't want to take any chances on them recognizing you."

"In Germany? I've never been here before."

"If this is where the hackers work, then someone in there may know your face."

Abbey nodded. She tugged her beige beret down her forehead and kept her eyes on the sidewalk as they passed the building.

They both wore clothes they'd purchased at an Oxfam shop upon arriving in the city the previous day. Jason didn't want them standing out, and in dull earth tones and old shoes, they weren't immediately recognizable as Americans. German was also one of the languages he spoke fluently, with no accent, and that helped them pass as natives. Learning German was part of his missing past. He didn't remember studying the language or recall any time he'd spent in the country growing up. Even so, parts of the city were familiar to him, even places he'd never visited during his work for Treadstone. He had a history here. He had a history in many cities that he didn't remember.

For now, they were like ghosts in Germany. No one— almost no one—knew they were here. Saira had arranged transport on a Gulfstream jet owned by one of her corporate contacts in the pharmaceutical industry, and they'd flown nonstop from Reagan National to the Frankfurt airport. There, Bourne had used his contacts to bypass passport control and find them a safe house near the Palmengarten. His contacts were trustworthy, but they were also longtime Treadstone assets, and that meant they'd probably delivered an update to Nash Rollins about Bourne's location.

It couldn't be helped. If anyone would keep this particular secret, it was Nash.

When they reached the end of the building, he led them several more blocks to Willy-Brandt-Platz, where they found seats on a bench in the plaza. Gleaming silver skyscrapers rose above them. He kept an eye on the crowds, making sure they hadn't been spotted during their surveillance and that no one was following them.

"We'll give it half an hour," he told Abbey. "Then we'll check out the front of the building. If they keep a close eye on their cameras—and I suspect they do—I don't want them to notice us coming back the other way too soon."

Thirty minutes later, they retraced their steps out of the plaza. This time, they turned north to approach the institute building on Berliner Straße. There, he spotted two separate entrances, one to the lower building, one to the higher perpendicular building that included the eighth floor. They stayed on the sidewalk on the other side of the street, but he noted that there were cameras positioned to observe anyone who came near the building. He also noted two security guards in suits outside both entrances.

"Those guards at the doors are armed," Bourne murmured. He assessed their skills with a quick glance. "They're pros, not just window dressing. I suspect that's what we'll find inside, too."

"That's a lot of security for a nonprofit fact-finding organization," Abbey replied.

"Yes, it is."

"So what do we do?"

"Well, we're not breaking in," Bourne told her. "We need another approach. That means using Saira."

They continued past the building and found a Thai restaurant with outdoor seating. The two of them sat down, and Jason took a chair that gave him a vantage on the building. They got menus and ordered a late lunch. Across the street, Bourne noticed a steady stream of workers coming and going from both entrances. Several of the departing workers headed their way, and as they passed the café, he took note of the electronic ID cards clipped to their belts. The IDs included photographs, but no employee names and no mention of the institute or the Varak Foundation. He also noted that none of the employees talked to each other or walked together after leaving the building.

Abbey noticed, too. "Not a very social place."

"No."

Then Bourne's gaze landed on a man wearing blue maintenance scrubs who emerged through the front door of the eight-story building. The man was in his fifties, six feet tall, with a shock of gray hair, a salt-and-pepper goatee, and a dour face smudged with grease. He crossed Berliner Straße at a jog between traffic and paused long enough to light a cigarette. As he neared the restaurant where Bourne and Abbey were sitting, Jason took out his phone.

"Pose," he told her. "Give me a smile. Act like I'm taking your picture."

Abbey held up her half-pint of beer in a toast and summoned a smile as Jason focused the camera. He zoomed in over her shoulder and snapped several pictures of the maintenance man as he passed them.

When he was gone, Bourne gestured for the waitress. Most of their lunch was still on their plates, but he paid the bill in cash, and the two of them returned to the sidewalk. The man in the blue uniform was more than a block away, but Bourne kept him in sight as they followed.

"Who is he?" Abbey asked.

"Hopefully, he's our way in," Bourne said.

"You're not going to hurt him," she said, not making it a question.

"No." Then Jason glanced her way. "But remember what the Pyramid does, Abbey. They're not innocent. Neither is anyone who works in that world. There are times when we have to make trade-offs."

"You do, Jason, but not me. We don't hurt him."

He didn't argue with her. The maintenance man walked for several more blocks, then hopped a bus. Bourne and Abbey got on, too, and sat a few rows behind him. The man stayed on the bus to the far northern part of the city, then exited near a block-long row of attached three-story apartment houses. He climbed the steps of one of the buildings and let himself into a ground-floor apartment. Abbey stayed on the sidewalk, and Bourne followed, digging a backup wallet from his pocket.

He knocked on the man's door. The man answered a few seconds later, and Jason held up the wallet.

"Entschuldigen. Haben Sie das verloren?"

The man tapped his pockets, confirming that his wallet was still where it should be. *"Nein, nicht mein."*

Jason smiled. *"Ja, okay. Ich habe es im Bus gefunden."*

He waved and trotted down the steps, and the man closed the door behind him. Jason rejoined Abbey at the sidewalk, and they crossed the street to catch another bus southward back to the heart of the city.

"Well?" she asked.

"Looks like he lives alone."

"I take it that's a good thing."

Bourne nodded. "Yes, it is."

AN HOUR LATER, THEY MADE THEIR WAY BACK TO THE SAFE house near the Palmengarten, where Saira Kohli was waiting for them. The top-floor flat looked out across the crowns of trees at the glass roof of the garden's conservatory. Bourne, as was his usual practice, checked the street below to make sure the apartment wasn't being watched, but Siesmayerstraße was empty for the moment.

"What did you find?" Saira asked.

"Well, I have a plan," Bourne replied, "but I'm going to need your help. I need someone who can provide details about the security setup, locations of the guards, computer terminals, elevators, entrances, exits, et cetera. The more I see of the interior, the more options I have for a strategy once I get in. You're the best person to do that, Saira. I can wire you to transmit sound and video, so I'll be watching the whole time you're there."

"Except I'll be inside, and you'll be outside," Saira pointed out.

"Yes."

"And they're trying to kill me," she added.

"Yes. This is definitely a risk. If you're not willing to try it, I understand, but right now, I think it's the only way."

Saira thought about the problem from all sides. "If I get into trouble, I'm on my own."

"Pretty much. I'll know if there's a problem, and I'll do what I can to help, but I have no guarantees that I can get you out in time."

The scientist gave a low chuckle. "At least you're honest, Bourne. I appreciate that you don't sugarcoat things."

"What if I go in with her?" Abbey asked. "I could be her research assistant or something. At least then she's not alone."

Bourne shook his head. "No, you could be recognized. If anyone realizes who you are, neither one of you walks out of that building alive. I could go inside with you myself, Saira, but if we're together, that will make it harder for me to go in later and find a way to access their server."

"And how do you propose to do that?" she asked.

"I don't know the details yet. That's why I need intel from you."

Saira frowned. "They may not recognize Abbey, but they *will* definitely recognize me. They know who I am. I've been there before."

"Actually, I'm counting on that," Bourne told her.

"I don't find that reassuring."

"My point is, people know you're a big fish. They know you're connected to the institute. You're respected, famous. It's natural that you'd have a reason to be there, and no lower-level employee is going to risk insulting you by refusing to take you on a tour. Which also takes *me* on a tour through the video feed."

"Unless the word has already gone out that I'm a threat," Saira said.

"Agreed. That's the risk. But I don't think that's the kind of news that would be spread widely around the institute. The more people who know, the more questions get asked. If anyone has been told, it's likely the director, but hopefully nobody else."

"Hopefully."

"Yes. Like I said, it's a risk. Who's the director?"

"His name is Heinrich Kessler," Saira replied.

"You know him?"

"I do."

Bourne nodded. "Okay. Tomorrow we keep an eye on the building, and as soon as we see Kessler leave, we send you in."

"Except if Saira goes in, won't they just call Kessler and tell him she's there?" Abbey asked. "He'll come back."

"I'll take care of Kessler," Bourne said. "I can keep him out of touch for a while, but you won't have much time, Saira. Don't stay in there more than half an hour. At that point, you can invent an excuse for why you have to leave."

"But they'll know she's been there," Abbey pointed out. "Kessler will find out, and they'll be looking for some kind of trap. They'll be on alert, Jason. That puts *you* at risk whenever you go in."

"That can't be helped," he said, "but I don't see another way."

Saira went to the window and stared out at the Palmengarten below them. "You know, as a scientist, Bourne, I weigh risks all the time. When you're trying to stamp out a virus, there's always risk. But I have to tell you, I think your strategy is more likely to kill *us* than kill the disease."

"You may be right," Bourne agreed. "In the end, it's up to you. Are you ready for this?"

Saira leaned against the glass and folded her arms. "Varak has been playing me for two years. I'd like to play him right back."

33

"*THERE,*" SAIRA SAID, HER VOICE CLIPPED AND PRECISE through the receiver in Bourne's ear. *"That's Kessler. Thinning black hair, black glasses. Dark suit and red tie. Do you have him?"*

"We've got him," Bourne murmured.

Heinrich Kessler headed away from the institute building on his lunch break. It was just after one thirty in the afternoon. The stocky, fussy-looking director carried a slim black briefcase clenched tightly in his right hand. His round face was expressionless as he threaded through the bustling lunch crowds on Berliner Straße, using a wide, open-toed walk. Bourne waited until the man had passed them, and then he and Abbey followed on the sidewalk.

"You have his phone number?" Jason asked.

"Yes," Saira replied.

"Make the call, but be sure he doesn't recognize your voice."

A few seconds later, Bourne saw Kessler stop on the sidewalk as other pedestrians flowed around him. Jason watched as the man switched the briefcase to his left hand and dug a mobile phone from the inner pocket of his suit coat. In his ear, he heard Saira Kohli, who sounded nothing like herself as she spoke to Kessler on the phone.

"Annalise? Annalise, wo bist du? Du bist spät!"

On the busy street not far away, he heard Kessler bark into the phone in an irritated voice. *"Nein, nein, bin nicht Annalise."*

Saira hung up. Bourne watched Kessler slide the phone back into the same pocket in his coat.

They stayed a few steps back as Kessler reached the cobblestoned square of the Römerplatz. The director joined the dense lunch crowd, and Jason whispered to Abbey to stay back as he accelerated his pace and came up on the man from behind. The volume of people forced Kessler to walk awkwardly, dodging back and forth through the square. As the man shifted to avoid a running child right in front of him, Bourne nimbly hooked a foot around his ankle.

Kessler tripped with a shout. He began crashing to the ground, but Jason caught him and kept him from falling. As he helped Kessler right himself, he gave the man a quick, concerned smile. He also made sure there was no hint of recognition in the man's eyes. Bourne wore sunglasses and a fedora, and he didn't think any photographs of himself would have made their way to Kessler. The director showed no indication that he knew who Bourne was.

"Sind Sie verletzt?" Jason commented politely, asking if the man was hurt.

"Nein, danke."

The director brushed his coat with an annoyed gesture and continued into the square, checking to make sure the locks on his briefcase were secure. Bourne headed in the opposite direction to rejoin Abbey, who was standing on the street near the entrance door of a pharmacy. They watched Kessler proceed to an open-air restaurant forty yards away, where he took a seat under a blue umbrella. He kept his briefcase on the table in front of him.

"Did you get his phone?" Abbey asked.

"I did," Jason replied, handing her the Samsung Galaxy device he'd taken from the man's pocket. "Let me know if he gets any texts or messages."

"I will."

"Keep an eye on Kessler from here. Give me a heads-up if anything changes on this end, or if he starts heading back to the institute. But don't let him see you. I'm sure he knows who you are, Abbey."

She nodded. "Be careful, Jason."

Bourne retraced his steps toward Berliner Straße and the institute building. As he walked quickly, he murmured into the microphone. "I'm on my way back, Saira. I'll be watching the video feed on my phone. Go."

*   *   *

SAIRA SWEPT THROUGH THE DOORS OF THE INSTITUTE BUILD-ing as if she owned the place. Bourne had told her: *You're imperious, you're on the board. Anyone challenging you should fear for their job.*

She was dressed to intimidate in a black business suit, her hair carefully styled, her makeup perfect. Her feet balanced atop sky-high stiletto heels. She had a tablet computer in a leather case under one arm. On the lapel of her coat, she wore a jeweled pin that looked expensive—and it was, but not because of the ruby paste in the center of it. Bourne had acquired the wireless device through one of his contacts, and the pin transmitted a wireless video feed. Saira also wore an earpiece out of sight that allowed her to communicate with Bourne.

It was strange, being part of a world like that.

She listened as he spoke to her from outside the building.

"Stop in the middle. Turn around. Let me see the whole lobby."

She followed Bourne's instructions. With her hands on her hips, she paused near the security desk, then slowly pivoted in a circle, a disapproving frown on her face. She noted—so that Bourne could note—the secu-rity checkpoint, the man processing IDs, the location of the elevator banks, and the faces and locations of the guards. Some were in suits; some were in uniforms. She imagined they were all armed.

"Kann ich Sie helfen?" called a guard from the desk.

Saira walked over to the man, her heels tapping sharply on the marble floor. She spoke in English. "Yes, you may help me. You may tell Mr. Kessler to join me downstairs, and inform him that *Dr.* Kohli is waiting."

Hesitation spread across the man's face. Guards didn't like the unexpected. He replied in English slowed by a heavy accent. "I'm sorry, ma'am, but Herr Kessler is at lunch."

"Then his assistant will have to do. Who is his assistant?"

"Frau Liebler, ma'am."

"You can call me Dr. Kohli. Now get Frau Liebler down here." Saira checked her watch and made a point of giving an exaggerated sigh. "And be quick about it. I have to head to the airport shortly, so I have very little time."

"Yes, of course—Dr. Kohli."

The guard made a call and spoke in German in a hushed, impatient voice. Then he hung up and addressed Saira again. "She'll be down in one minute. Perhaps if you would care to take a seat—"

"I'll stand," Saira replied.

She checked her watch again, then folded her arms together and tapped a toe on the marble. In less than a minute, she saw one of the elevators open, and a blond woman in her forties bustled through the security gate. She was short, with a heavyset physique and a face flushed with anxiety.

"Dr. Kohli!" the woman exclaimed with nervous surprise. "We weren't expecting you. Did you and Herr Kessler have a meeting scheduled?"

"You've got her off-balance," Bourne said. *"Keep her that way."*

"There was no need for an appointment," Saira told the woman. "I wasn't sure I'd be able to get here before my flight, but as it turned out, I did."

"I'm afraid Herr Kessler is at lunch. He only left a few minutes ago, so it could be an hour or so before he returns."

"I don't have an hour," Saira snapped.

"Oh, I see, well, let me call him. I'm sure he can rush back for you."

Frau Liebler punched a speed dial number on her phone, and Saira waited. She heard the voice of Abbey Laurent in her ear.

"His phone's ringing."

The fact that Kessler didn't answer increased his assistant's stress. She tried texting—which prompted another report from Abbey—and again there was no answer. Frau Liebler looked stricken.

"It seems I can't reach him," she told Saira. "That's very unusual. Herr Kessler makes a point of *never* being out of touch."

Saira shrugged with a dismissive little hiss between her lips. "It doesn't matter. I don't need to consult with him. When I was last here, I didn't have time for a full tour of the facility. Since I'm in the city, I wanted to correct that. You may accompany me."

"Me? I'm sorry, but I'm not authorized."

"Not authorized? To show the facility to a member of the institute's board of directors?"

"Well, Herr Kessler—"

"Mr. Kessler is unavailable, as you say. So we'll proceed in his absence."

"I don't think—"

But Saira ignored Frau Liebler and proceeded through the security gate, which beeped an alarm because she didn't present an ID. In the same moment, a guard appeared and blocked her way before she could reach the elevator banks. The man was in his thirties and tall, with buzzed blond hair and a muscular physique. His face was handsome but unyielding.

Saira made a point of looking the guard up and down, so Bourne could assess him.

"He's armed," Jason said in her ear. *"And watch out, this one's smart and dangerous."*

"Dr. Kohli," the man announced in an oily voice. "It's a pleasure to have you here again. I couldn't help but overhear your conversation. We're all aware, of course, of who you are, but as Frau Liebler indicates, visitors are not authorized to tour the facility except in Herr Kessler's presence and accompanied by security."

"And who are you?" Saira asked.

"Herr Haber," the man replied. "I'm the deputy head of security."

"Then I don't see what Mr. Kessler can offer that you can't. In fact, you're probably more familiar with the things I want to see than he is."

"And what are those things?" Haber asked. "You've

been here before, haven't you, Dr. Kohli? Earlier this year? Surely you saw everything then."

"I received an overview, yes, but discussions were raised at the last board meeting about physical and technological infrastructure issues at all the institute's facilities. Not just here, but around the world. We concluded that we needed to conduct personal inspections over the course of the coming year. Since I was going to be in Frankfurt, I offered to represent the board for our visit to this location. We need to gather data in order to prepare a report and make recommendations for upgrades. Obviously, this will include significant budget increases for security services where appropriate."

"Smooth," Bourne said.

"Well, I suppose I can help in Herr Kessler's absence," the security man replied. "Which areas do you wish to inspect?"

"Don't mention the eighth floor," Bourne said. *"You'll raise a red flag if you start with that."*

"The physical plant in particular," Saira replied. "This is an older building. I'd like to review maintenance operations. Conditions. And then your server room, too, of course. The physical security of our technology resources—as well as our firewalls and other backups— are naturally among our primary concerns."

"Naturally."

"And I'm afraid my time is short, so can we get started?"

Haber smiled at her, but it wasn't a pleasant smile. He didn't trust her, and she didn't trust him. Bourne hadn't needed to tell her the obvious. Herr Haber, deputy head of security, was a dangerous man.

"By all means, follow me," Haber told her. Then he called over her shoulder. "Frau Liebler, please do keep trying to reach Herr Kessler. I'd hate to have him miss the opportunity to see Dr. Kohli."

ABBEY BOUGHT HERSELF A *WEISSWURST* AND A PRETZEL, which she ate while she kept an eye on Heinrich Kessler on the other side of the plaza. The director of the institute building nursed a stein of beer and ate a large plate of what looked like pork schnitzel. It was a warm, sunny day in the Römerplatz, and he didn't look in any hurry to finish his lunch. That was good, because Saira had already been inside the institute for nearly half an hour. Frau Liebler was getting impatient, because every couple of minutes, Abbey felt a buzz as a new text or call arrived on the stolen phone in her pocket.

She listened to the conversation between Saira and the security man as Haber took her around the building. In the process, he was unknowingly taking Jason around the building, showing him the routes to the corridors and offices, the stairwells, the emergency exits, the checkpoints for IDs, and the locations of the critical infrastructure. The video was all being recorded on Jason's phone.

The plan might work. So far, it *was* working. Even so, Abbey felt anxious. She heard Jason in her earpiece urging Saira to wrap up her visit and head for the exit. They had enough; they had what they needed. But Saira hadn't broached the idea of seeing the eighth floor yet, and Abbey knew that she wanted to see it for herself.

"Haber won't let you up there," Jason warned her. *"I can read him, and this one won't be intimidated. All you'll do is raise his suspicions. If I can get to the server room overnight, we won't need access to the top floor."*

Still Saira stalled, asking Haber whether she'd seen everything, hinting that she knew there was more.

"Time to go," Bourne reiterated.

But Saira ignored Jason and asked the question directly. Her voice was cool through the receiver, demanding that the security man give her a straight answer. *"And the eighth floor? We need to talk about the eighth floor."*

On the other side of the plaza, Abbey saw Heinrich Kessler flag his waitress. His plate was empty, and he drained a few last drops from his beer stein. He was done with lunch.

"Kessler just called for his bill," she warned them through the microphone. "As soon as he pays, he'll be on his way. Saira, you need to be out of the building before he gets back. Come on, let it go, and get out of there."

Then, watching Kessler, Abbey swore under her breath.

The waitress brought the man his lunch bill, and he reached not for a wallet in his pants, but for a money clip inside the pocket of his suit coat. He peeled off a bill and put it on the table and then replaced the clip in his pocket. But at that point, his face changed, screwing up with surprise and concern. He reached back into the same pocket. When he found nothing there, he began to pat his other pockets.

"Shit," she told them. "Kessler just realized his phone is gone."

"What's he doing?" Jason asked.

"He's searching for it. He looks puzzled. I can't tell if he thinks he left it at the office, or lost it, or whether he knows someone stole it."

"Saira," Bourne said urgently. *"Get out of there right now."*

Abbey watched Kessler as his fingers worked the two combination locks on his briefcase. He clicked the briefcase open and lifted the leather top, and he dug through the papers inside. When he still found nothing, he undid a flap on one of the briefcase pockets.

She saw something in his hand.

"Fuck, oh, fuck," Abbey hissed. "Jason, Saira, *he's got another phone.*"

"THE EIGHTH FLOOR?" HABER SAID PLEASANTLY, WITH A shrug of his muscular shoulders. "It's mostly storage."

Saira gave him a withering stare, and her voice went down to a whisper. "Storage? Really? How strange. On my last visit, Mr. Kessler indicated that the eighth floor was a special security zone. So spare me the excuses, Herr Haber. I think we both know what goes on up there."

Haber examined the people around them. They were on the building's third floor, amid a sea of workers typ-

ing on computer terminals, but no one was within ear-
shot. That was why Saira had chosen that moment for her
query, but the head of security didn't look pleased. His
thick lips squeezed into a frown.

"If you're aware of the activities on the eighth floor,
then you'll understand why it's off-limits."

"And you'll understand why it's a matter of concern to
the board," Saira retorted.

At the same moment, she heard Abbey's warning in
her ear. *"He's got another phone."*

Bourne chimed in immediately. *"Kessler will call the
office. You have less than a minute before you're blown."*

Saira tried to keep her face calm and to swallow her
fear. She checked her watch and then made a show of
changing her mind. "Well, never mind with that for this
trip. As it turns out, I've run out of time. Someone else
from the board will have to follow up. Please give my
regrets to Mr. Kessler when he returns, but I need to get
to the airport."

She started across the long length of the building toward the bank of elevators. Her legs wobbled on her
heels, and she steadied herself as she lost a step. Haber
kept pace beside her, but she saw his eyes narrowing with
curiosity as he studied the change in her demeanor. "Is
everything all right, Dr. Kohli?"

"Oh, yes, fine. I just lost track of time. I'm quite late."

She accelerated her pace. Mentally, she counted the
steps, watching the elevators get closer. And then she
heard a terrifying buzz nearby, like the whine of mosqui-
toes flying around her. Haber was getting a phone call.

Saira fought the urge to run. Barely holding herself upright, she walked even faster toward the elevators. Behind her, she heard the head of security take the call, and his voice was sharp.

"Ah, Herr Kessler."

Then she heard words in quick German that included her name.

Saira stabbed the button for an elevator. She punched it over and over, as if that would make it go faster. Footsteps thumped behind her, heavy and quick. A bell announced the arrival of the car, and the doors began to open, but way too slowly. She stumbled inside, directing the elevator to the ground floor.

If she could just get there. If she could just get outside.

The doors began to close.

Then a hand slid between them, and the doors reversed direction and opened again. Herr Haber stood there, the oily, cruel smile back on his face. His hand took her wrist. Firmly. He pulled her out of the elevator.

"Dr. Kohli. I'm afraid you'll have to take the next flight. That was Herr Kessler. He's on his way back. He's most anxious to talk to you."

34

"*EINE BOMBE*," BOURNE TOLD THE EMERGENCY OPERATOR IN harsh German. "I've placed a bomb in the offices of the Varak Institute on Berliner Straße. For too long, billionaires have wielded the power in this world, and we must fight back. You have exactly fifteen minutes to evacuate the building before the bomb explodes. At that point, his enablers will face the consequences. You have been warned."

Then he placed the same call to Deutsche Welle television.

And to the offices of the Frankfurt mayor.

In an emergency, use panic as a diversion.

Treadstone.

The police would come soon. He'd hear sirens wailing, heading their way in less than a minute. The fire department, too. And ambulances. Word would spread just as fast on television, on radio, on social media, by text, by telephone. There were hundreds of employees inside the Varak Institute buildings, and friends and family would begin reaching out to them with the urgent alert.

Get out! A bomb!

Bourne needed chaos; he needed security to make a move, to get Saira out of the building.

"Where is Kessler?" Bourne asked Abbey through the microphone. He stood near a concrete pillar at a building directly across the street, where he had a vantage on both of the primary doors leading in and out of the institute facility.

"He's almost there," she responded through the receiver. *"He's two minutes away."*

Jason swore. While Kessler was out of the building, the security men would hold Saira, but they would do nothing to her. Once Kessler was back, that would all change. If the director was in the loop, or if he'd reached out to the Pyramid for guidance, he would know that they wanted Saira Kohli dead. They'd interrogate her, torture her, and kill her.

He checked the video feed on his phone.

"Where are you?" he murmured to Saira. "Look around. Let me see."

She did. Bourne saw that they were still on the third floor. They were surrounded by dozens of institute employees at their desks. Herr Haber stood at Saira's side, and two other guards had joined him, but they'd made no effort to relocate her. They were talking pleasantly, deflecting Saira's insistence that she needed to catch her flight. Kessler's instructions had obviously been to detain her, but not to take any other steps yet. Not until he returned.

Then Bourne saw him. The heavyset director walked quickly westward on Berliner Straße, and he'd almost reached the building entrance. The man was on his backup phone. His *Pyramid* phone. Jason was sure he was getting instructions about exactly what to do with Saira Kohli. He couldn't let Heinrich Kessler back into the building, even though Kessler would recognize Bourne as the stranger who'd bumped into him in the plaza. The man would put two and two together and realize that had been when his phone disappeared.

Stopping him, or killing him, blew up their plans. They'd never get inside the institute after that. But that was also the only way to give Saira a chance to get out.

Jason dashed across the street, dodging traffic. Kessler looked distracted, pushing around pedestrians who were heading the opposite way. He'd almost reached the wall of the building, and Bourne closed the gap between them, wondering when Kessler would look up, when their eyes would meet. In that one glance, he'd have to strike.

Then it happened.

An eruption of screams flooded through the receiver in his ear. The bomb threat had made its way inside the building. He glanced at the video feed on his phone, and as Saira turned to watch what was happening, employees bolted from their desks, shouting to each other in panic. Fear shot from person to person like lightning.

"Eine Bombe! Hier!"

"Fünfzehn Minuten!"

"Wir müssen gehen! Jetzt! Jetzt!"

The stampede began.

Institute employees formed a wild crowd sprinting between the desks and out of private offices toward the building stairs. They bore down on Saira, and he saw her instinctively back out of their way, clearing a path. Next to her, Haber and the other guards reacted with the confusion that Bourne wanted. They didn't know what was going on, and their uncertainty paralyzed them. But that wouldn't last long.

"Now, Saira," he hissed into the microphone. "Push into the crowd. Follow them outside."

Bourne looked at the sidewalk. Kessler was close, but the chaos had spilled out of the building and begun to envelop him. On the street level, dozens of people poured through both sets of doors, streaming through the parking lot and running to get clear of the building. There were more screams, more shouts. Others joined the melee. The tide surged around the institute director like a rogue wave, pushing him backward.

Not far away, speeding closer, Jason heard the wail of sirens. The first emergency vehicles drew near, weaving around streetcars as other vehicles skidded to a stop with nowhere to go and no chance to get out of the way. Berliner Straße became a circus of cars and people, of blaring horns and police loudspeakers. Bourne swam upstream. He needed to get to Saira as soon as she left the building and guide her safely away, but first he had to stop Kessler. He couldn't let the director get back inside.

Jason caught a glimpse of the man, struggling sideways with his back to the building wall, no more than twenty feet away. Men and woman ran between them, shouting, shoving, and falling. There were *hundreds* of them. Bourne weaved through the crowd, snaking behind Kessler, elbowing past the people who collided with him. Then he was right behind him. Kessler shouted angrily and tried to shove against the wave pushing the opposite way. Bourne crept closer and timed his assault. Just as a woman bumped into Kessler's shoulder, Jason reached out and slammed the man's head hard into the building wall.

Bone cracked. Blood sprayed.

The director slumped to the ground, unconscious. The stampede continued, some people stepping over and around him, some simply trampling his fleshy body beneath their feet. Jason jumped the body and fought his way forward. Around the corner of the building wall, he found breathing room from the frantic escape, and he checked the video feed on his phone. But the screen was black.

The camera had stopped transmitting. Through his receiver, all he heard was the thunder of footsteps and overlapping voices. The pin had obviously been stripped from Saira's coat and crushed in the confusion.

"Saira!" he called into his microphone. "Where are you?"

*　*　*

AS HE WALKED BACK FROM LUNCH, OSKAR STARED IN DISBE-
lief at the scene unfolding outside the institute buildings.
It was bedlam! Madness! People were everywhere, flood-
ing down side streets in every direction. Restaurants
were empty, food still on the tables where diners had left
their meals behind. He saw drivers getting out of their
vehicles and running away, abandoning their cars with
the doors wide open. Mothers and fathers carried children in their arms.

Insanity!

He tried to stop a man to ask what was going on, but
the stranger shoved him aside, and Oskar lost his bal-
ance, stumbling into a building wall. When he spotted a
policeman in riot gear, he grabbed at the man's shoulder
and refused to let go.

"Was ist los? Bitte, was ist los?"

The man lurched away and pointed toward the east
end of the city. *"Eine Bombe! Laufen Sie weg! Schnell!"*

A bomb.

Everyone was running from a bomb. It had to be *inside* the institute. Oskar froze, deciding what to do. Was
the threat real? And did it have something to do with
Louisa? The timing couldn't be a coincidence! He cursed
his luck, because if he'd been inside when the alert
sounded, he could have found a way to get the thumb
drive outside. Surely they wouldn't force people to go
through a security scanner when they were escaping a
bomb!

"*Nur fünf Minuten!*" someone screamed.

Only five minutes left. Was that when the bomb was going to explode?

Oskar was paralyzed with indecision. Think! What to do? Should he use this opportunity to run? Leave the country? What was going on?

The rats continued to swim away from the sinking ship. He joined them, putting as much distance between himself and the institute as he could. If there really was a bomb, how far would the blast zone go? How many buildings would fall? Oskar ran, but he hadn't gone half a block when he stopped dead in his tracks. People shoved into his back, nearly bringing him down, so he threw himself sideways into the shelter of a doorway. He stared in shock at a lone woman in front of him who was fighting against the crowd, heading toward the building that everyone else was trying to escape.

Mein Gott! It was *her*! It was *impossible*!

The hair was different, black not red. Her eyes were hidden by sunglasses. She was in *disguise*. But Oskar had spent too many hours staring at that face on his computer screen not to recognize her.

How? How could she be here?

But she was. There was no mistake.

The woman pushing toward him was Abbey Laurent.

THERE!

Bourne saw Saira Kohli emerge through the doors on the other side of the parking lot, but she wasn't alone.

The guards accompanied her, all three of them. They hustled her down the steps, one on either side of her, holding on to her arms. Haber led the way. They didn't run like the other people around them; instead, they walked quickly, heading for the street.

Jason hugged the building wall, dodging the people who were still trying to escape. Finally, the flow of panicked employees had begun to thin. Most of them had already made their way out of the building, and police were closing in from both sides. The guards couldn't take any action with police nearby, but neither could Bourne. He closed the gap, drawing nearer to them as they crossed into stalled traffic on the street. They headed for an alley that was now almost deserted, and Jason knew that was where they would do it.

A street crime. A mugging. A murder. A thief taking advantage of the panic to assault a woman running away.

They were still in front of him, and they didn't hear him coming, thanks to the clamor of sirens and shouts. Haber led the way impatiently, six feet ahead of the others who walked abreast, Saira in the middle. She struggled, knowing what was coming. She shouted for help. For him. For anyone. *"Hilfe!"*

But they hit her so hard she crumpled in their arms, and they had to hold her up. That was his chance.

Bourne slid his gun from inside his jacket. He'd added a suppressor to dull the noise, and he didn't think anyone outside the alley would hear the shot, not with the noisy chaos of the bomb threat roaring from the street. He aimed at the guard on the left.

He squeezed the trigger and fired. The man fell.

The other guard was momentarily stunned, watching his comrade let go of Saira and pitch to the ground. As he looked down the alley, Bourne fired again. Adrenaline made his aim perfect, and the other man fell with a bullet in the middle of his forehead. But Haber had heard the shots. The head of security spun, gun in hand, already firing. Haber's first shot missed Jason's head by inches, and the second burned across the flesh of his arm. Jason threw himself toward the wall, but the bullets continued, raining down the alley toward him.

He fired back. Missed. Fired again. Missed.

Haber unleashed another volley of shots, and as Jason took cover from the hail of bullets, he saw the head of security take two steps and redirect his gun toward the woman on the ground. He was aiming at Saira. The man was barely six feet away, standing over her body.

One shot, one bullet in the head.

Bourne had less than a second to fire back. If he missed again, Saira was dead. He didn't even have time to aim as he squeezed the trigger.

Halfway down the alley, Haber collapsed.

ABBEY HEARD THE EXPLOSIONS OF GUNFIRE, WHICH WERE deafening in her ear. She stopped on the pavement, tears filling her eyes. *"Jason!"* she screamed into the microphone, her voice shrill. "Jason, talk to me, are you okay? What's going on? Saira? Are you there?"

There was no answer.

She covered her mouth with her hands. "Jason, my God. *Jason!*"

The chaos dizzied her. People rushed by. She knew it was all in vain. There was no bomb in the building. But somewhere close by, there had been real bullets. A storm of gunfire back and forth, with Jason and Saira in the middle of it. She wanted to rip the receiver out of her ear, it had been so loud and terrifying.

And now silence. Horrible silence.

"Jason," she murmured again, not expecting a reply.

Then something crackled in her ear. She heard heavy breathing, and her heart seized with relief.

"I'm okay, Abbey," Jason told her. *"So is Saira."*

"Thank God! Where are you?"

"It's an alley a few blocks away. Keep going straight, and you'll find us. I've got cleanup to do here. I need you to come this way and take Saira back to the safe house. They hit her, and she was unconscious, but she's coming around now. I want both of you away from here as quickly as possible."

"I'm on my way."

Abbey started to run, to fight her way against the tide. She was scared, and their plan was in ruins, but nothing mattered now as long as Jason was alive. Tonight he would be in her arms again.

She was hardly able to focus on the scene in front of her. The faces were a blur. The screams and sirens filled her ears. She saw police officers in the street, still wildly telling people to run, to get away, that there was no time and they had to escape the bomb. Some of them reached out to grab her and told her to go back, to go the other way, but she ignored them and avoided their grasp as she ran.

Then Abbey stopped. She had no choice.

A man stepped out of a doorway directly in front of her to block her way. He was young, blond, and good-looking in a sturdy, German sort of way. His eyes looked weary, and there was something strange in his expression. He looked at her as if she were a ghost that no one else could see.

He held up a hand. "Abbey, wait."

"You *know* me?" Abbey said, suddenly scared of this stranger. "Who are you? Get out of my way!"

"We need to talk. Please, I think we can help each other."

"Who *are* you?" she asked again.

"My name is Oskar," the blond man replied. "I'm the one who destroyed your life."

35

IN THE SAFE HOUSE NEAR THE PALMENGARTEN, ABBEY
tended to the wound on Jason's arm. The bullet had
grazed him, tearing a long gash in the flesh and leaving
him bloody. He winced silently as she cleaned and disinfected the cut, then covered the laceration over with
gauze. She worked calmly and quickly, her emotions
numb. In her earlier life, she wouldn't have been able to
handle this, but now she simply washed away the blood
and did what she had to do.

Three men were dead in an alley. He'd killed them.
She'd seen their bodies. But Jason was alive. That was the
only thing that mattered.

"You should see a doctor," she murmured. "Don't
you have someone you can call? A Treadstone contact?"

"I could find someone, but we don't have time. I'll be
okay."

Abbey shrugged, because that was the answer she'd expected. She didn't argue with him. She handed Jason a new shirt and helped him put it on and button it. Then she went to Saira, who was still in shock. The scientist stared out the window, her face strained and dark. Abbey poured brandy and gave her the glass, and Saira sipped it, but she said nothing. Abbey didn't push her to open up. She poured brandy for herself, drank it all, and poured more.

Finally, she went to the small table in the apartment and sat across from Oskar Vogel.

The young German looked at her, then glanced away with guilt in his blue eyes. It was one thing to cancel a stranger; it was another to be face-to-face with her. There had been no opportunity for them to talk since he'd approached her on the street. She ought to have been angry at him—this was the hacker who'd created the *lies*!—but she'd already directed her anger elsewhere, to the men in shadows. Oskar was a victim, like her. He'd been deceived and manipulated.

"Here we are," Abbey said. "Tell us what you know."

Oskar's stare went back and forth from Abbey to Bourne. She'd kept him away from the alley and the bodies, but this man was no fool. He'd seen the blood, and he knew he was in the middle of something violent.

"Who are you people?" he asked.

"We're trying to take down the Pyramid," Abbey said. "Do you know what that is?"

He frowned. "Louisa mentioned the Pyramid. She warned me about it. She had a pyramid tattoo on her arm, too. An upside-down pyramid with an eye in the middle. I asked her what it meant, but she wouldn't tell me anything."

Saira spoke from the window. "*Louisa*? You knew Louisa?"

"We were lovers. I wanted to marry her. But she was killed. Killed and erased, like she didn't even exist. Herr Kessler told me that you were involved in her death, Abbey. That you were the one who'd lured her into a trap. That's why they had me do what they did to you. I'm sorry for that, because now I believe the institute was behind it. Louisa left a video for me. She said she'd done terrible things, that she was trying to make amends by betraying them. Exposing them. But she said she was afraid the Pyramid knew about her and me. I assume the Pyramid and the institute are linked somehow?"

"We think so," Abbey said. "And no, I had nothing to do with Louisa's death. I didn't know about it until after it happened. I was trying to find out the truth, and that's when they sent you to ruin my life."

Oskar shook his head. "Again, I'm terribly sorry. You have to understand, I thought I was doing the right thing. Herr Kessler always said there was no other way, that we were in a war with people who were threatening our very way of life. That the lies I created were for a greater good. I had no idea that the institute was lying to *me*."

Bourne came and sat down at the table. He flexed his arm, and Abbey could see a flinch of pain on his face. "This video that Louisa made for you. Do you still have it?"

"No. She said I should delete it, that I was in danger

if anyone found it. It wasn't even on my phone. She left it with a waitress at a restaurant we often visited." Oskar briefly closed his eyes. "But I did some research. I used someone else's computer at the institute. They deleted Louisa's account, but I was able to extract and reconstruct most of the information anyway. It was horrifying. She'd been involved in lies around the world. And even murder, too. A terrible fire in America."

"In Georgia," Abbey said.

"Yes. I understood why Louisa had risked everything to expose the truth. But the man whose computer I used—they *killed* him. They thought *he* was the one infiltrating the system. That's when I realized how dangerous this all is."

"Can you still access this information?" Bourne asked.

"Yes, it's all still there for now, but I doubt it will be for long. If they suspect the data was breached, they'll swap out the server and destroy the old one. I was planning to download the information and go to Interpol, but they changed their security protocols. Everyone who leaves the eighth floor gets searched and put through a scanner. There's no way I could get anything out of there on a physical drive, and there's no way I could export the data past the firewall."

Bourne didn't look discouraged. "But you could get the information onto a drive?"

"It would take me a few minutes, but yes," Oskar replied. "There's a huge amount of data. The trouble is, once I start the download, they're likely to become aware of it down in the server room. I won't have much time before they track it to me. And what difference does it make if I can't get the drive out of the building?"

"Leave that to me," Jason said.

Saira joined them from the other side of the apartment. Her glass of brandy was empty. "My God, Bourne, you're not still thinking about going inside that building, are you? After today? They know I was there, and word will have made its way back to Varak and the rest. The entire complex will be on alert."

"You heard Oskar," Bourne said. "The longer we wait, the greater the chance the data will be gone forever. Plus, now is exactly the right time. Haber is dead. Kessler is in the hospital. They are *off-balance* inside the institute. They don't know what's real and what's not. Soon Varak will get someone there to reassert control, but for the moment, we can take advantage of the confusion."

"Or you'll get yourself killed," Abbey said. "I think Saira's right. Oskar is with us now. Why can't we go public? Use him to tell the story?"

Bourne stared at her. "If you were running a newspaper or a news show, and we came to you with this story, would you print it? Would you say we had enough evidence to back up everything we're claiming?"

Abbey frowned. "No."

"Then we need more." Bourne turned to Oskar again. "We need your help. You're the only one who can get the information for us. I won't kid you about the risks. If they catch you before you pass off the drive to me, you'll end up like your friend whose computer you used. And even if we both make it out, they'll stop at nothing to find you and kill you before we have a chance to go public."

The hacker didn't hesitate. "I owe it to Louisa."

"All right. We need to move fast. First thing tomorrow morning."

"But how do you expect to get inside?" Oskar asked. "You won't have an ID, not for the building and definitely not for the eighth floor."

Bourne unlocked his phone and found a photo that he'd taken outside the institute offices. He showed Oskar the screen. "Do you know this man?"

Oskar's brow furrowed. "I know who he is. His name is Horst, but I don't know his last name. He does maintenance work in the building."

"Does he come up to the eighth floor?"

"Sure, sometimes. The toilets are terrible. They're constantly overflowing. Shit everywhere. Horst is the poor guy with the snake."

Bourne nodded. "Then that's how we do it. Tomorrow morning, there's going to be a flood."

AT FOUR O'CLOCK, BEFORE SUNRISE, THE STREET IN THE northern part of Frankfurt was mostly deserted. Only a handful of early risers drove through the darkness. Jason parked a tan Renault on an inlet off Friedberger Landstraße, near the row of three-story apartment houses. The Renault was stolen, but the car would be back in the place where Bourne had found it before the owner had awakened for the day.

He got out of the car and crossed to one of the apartment buildings. A handful of steps led to the ground-floor doors. The one on the left led inside Horst's flat. With a quick glance at the street to confirm that he wasn't being watched, Bourne knelt in the shadows and picked the locks for the doorknob and the dead bolt. He let himself inside and silently clicked the door shut behind him.

The flat was dark and quiet, but he could hear snoring in another room. Horst was out cold. Jason smelled the spices of takeaway Indian food, and he noticed several empty bottles of Carlsberg on the sink of the apartment's kitchenette. He slid a daypack off his shoulders and retrieved his supplies. Two lengths of nylon rope. A clean white T-shirt. Duct tape. He carried those with his left arm, which burned whenever he moved from the flesh wound he'd received. His Smith & Wesson was in his right hand.

Bourne moved to the bedroom. There was a window facing the back of the building, but the blind was pulled down. He let his eyes adjust, noting the man on the bed, his leg half out of the blanket, his mouth hanging open as he slept. For the moment, Horst was in no danger of waking up. Bourne put the supplies on the bed. He checked the nightstand and found what he was looking for—the man's wallet, his security ID for the institute, and his mobile phone. Jason pocketed all of them. In the small closet, he found maintenance scrubs on a hanger, plus the man's work boots. He moved those back to the other room.

Then he returned to the bedroom and stood over Horst on the bed. With his gun pointed at the man's face, he switched on the lamp on the nightstand. The brightness stirred Horst, who blinked groggily. His eyes were nothing but half slits, but when he became aware of Bourne standing over him and saw the gun aimed at his head, his eyes flew wide open.

"*Wer sind—*" he began to shout, but Jason shoved the barrel against his forehead and put a finger over his lips, which shut him up.

"*Sag nichts,*" Bourne whispered. "*Ich würde Sie nicht erschießen.*"

"*Was wollen Sie von mir?*" the man whispered back. Then he took note of Bourne's face and remembered the stranger at his door, asking about a dropped wallet. His confusion deepened. "*Sie waren im Bus? Versteh nicht.*"

"*Stille,*" Bourne said harshly, cutting off his words. He added, "I don't want to hurt you, but I need to make sure you don't go anywhere this morning. I'm sorry."

He flipped his hand, indicating for the man to turn over on the bed. Horst did, and in a few moments, Bourne tied his wrists tightly with the nylon rope. He did the same with the man's ankles. With the maintenance man secure, he turned him over on the bed again and shoved the white T-shirt deep in his mouth and taped it over to gag him. Then he took the second length of rope and tied one end to the metal leg of the bed frame. He looped the rope around Horst's neck and tied the other end of the rope to the bed frame on the other side.

"The more you struggle," Bourne told him in German, "the more the chance you'll choke yourself. Got it? Don't try to get free. The best thing to do is lie here quietly. In a few hours, when I've done what I need to do, I'll make a call, and someone will come by and let you go. Until then, don't make a sound, and you'll stay alive."

The man, who'd begun to struggle, settled back on the bed, his eyes filled with terror.

Jason turned to leave, but then he remembered one more thing.

He checked both of the man's arms, confirming that neither one was inked with a pyramid tattoo. He'd promised Abbey that he wouldn't harm the man, but if Horst was part of the Pyramid, all promises were off.

But there were no tattoos. This man was just a pawn, like so many others.

Bourne headed toward the door. A few seconds later, he was back in the cool morning darkness outside.

36

OSKAR TOOK A DEEP BREATH. THE DOOR OF THE INSTITUTE building loomed in front of him. He'd gone through that door thousands of times, but this time he felt as if he were heading through a portal that led to a battlefield. He didn't know if he could do it. Once he was inside, he was on his own. There would be no communication, electronic or otherwise. No receiver in his ear, not for someone going through security on the eighth floor. There was too much risk that any devices might be discovered. But that meant he had no way to seek help if things went wrong.

He glanced across the street. The man who called himself Jason Bourne leaned against the opposite building, drinking coffee and seemingly waiting for his shift to begin. Oskar felt the man watching him without appearing to watch him at all. A disguise had transformed

Bourne, who was now dressed as an ordinary maintenance man in a blue, slightly oversized uniform. The
man's shoulders slumped, and he'd made himself up to
look older than he was. His hair was shot through with
gray. His expression was bored, uninterested in the
world, a man with a dead-end job.

Who was this man? This stranger. This *killer*.

Bourne had told Oskar almost nothing about his
background, and yet he was someone who inspired both
fear and trust. Oskar was putting his life in his hands,
which made no sense at all, but he had the impression
that Bourne would be willing to die if it meant keeping
Oskar and his information safe.

Even so, the man was not a robot. He was human.
That was obvious whenever he looked at the woman Oskar had destroyed. This man, Bourne, was clearly in love
with Abbey Laurent, and she was in love with him.

Oskar pasted an expression of calm on his face. To
everyone else in the building, this had to look like an
ordinary day. He climbed the steps and went inside,
along with a dozen or so other workers arriving at the
same time. No one talked to each other, but there was a
cloud of nervousness in the air. Yesterday there had been
a bomb scare. What did that mean? Was it safe to go
back?

He saw it among the guards, too. The two men who
ran the show here, Heinrich Kessler and Fritz Haber,
were both gone. In their absence, confusion reigned. But
Bourne had warned him that if the remaining guards

were scared, they might be overzealous in their desire to make sure nothing else went wrong. They might intensify their searches and screenings. They might ask him things they never had before.

Don't panic. Stick to the plan.

That was easier when he wasn't staring at an armed, uniformed guard watching every employee go inside. In the line ahead of him, a worker from another floor asked about the chaos of the previous day. *"Was gibt's mit dieser Bombe?"*

The man checking IDs didn't answer, but the guard next to him did. *"Es war ein Streich."*

That was the story they were going with. It was a prank. A false alarm. No reason to be concerned. But Oskar could tell in the faces of the people around him that many of the others were not convinced.

He walked up to the checkpoint and handed over his ID. He worked hard to keep a bland, uninterested expression on his face, but he could feel the guard giving him a thorough look from head to toe, the way the man had done to everyone in line this morning. Oskar kept repeating the mantra in his head: *It's an ordinary day. Nothing is different.*

The computer beeped. He knew his name had popped up on the screen. Oskar Vogel. Eighth floor.

Was there also an alert? *Detain this man!*

But the clerk simply handed him back his ID, and Oskar headed for the elevator banks as usual. He used his access ID to select the eighth floor, and again, his badge worked without difficulty. When he got off at the top of the building, he repeated the process of showing his ID to people who had known him and watched him come and go for three years. But they treated him like a stranger. Scanned his card. Confirmed his name and face. Cleared him to go to his desk.

Nearby, he saw the X-rays and full-body scanners that were in place to search everyone who wanted to leave the floor. Soon he would do just that. He would leave the building and never come back, but he wondered if the guards would stop him before he got out.

Oskar wandered to the far end of the building, where the windows looked toward the river. The pimply kid who'd taken over Jochim's desk hadn't arrived yet. He noted that Herr Kessler's door was shut and locked; the office was empty. He booted up his terminal and pretended to work, but his eyes were on the clock. It was almost eight thirty in the morning. At nine o'clock— precisely at nine o'clock—he'd begin the download. If all went well, Bourne would be in position downstairs, waiting. If all didn't go well, Oskar knew he was unlikely to make it out of the building alive. They'd be coming for him.

He got out of his chair and went to the kitchenette area to get himself a cup of coffee. But coffee wasn't what he wanted. He poured himself a cup, then cursed as he spilled it while reaching for a packet of sugar. Hot brown liquid poured over the counter, and Oskar bent down to grab a roll of paper towels from under the sink. As he did, he reached farther back to retrieve the thumb drive that he'd wedged into a hiding place behind the pipes. The last thing he'd wanted was to leave the thing at his desk, because he suspected that every desk got searched overnight after they left.

As he straightened up with the towels in hand, he slipped the drive into his pocket. He completed the cleanup of the counter, then returned to his desk.

A normal day. *Nothing was different.*

But Oskar felt sweat under his arms and on the back of his neck. The reality of what he had to do stared him in the face. At nine o'clock, he had to plug the drive into his computer—*My God, if anyone walks by, they'll see it!*—and then begin downloading the files from Louisa's deleted account. It was a sea of data and would take several minutes to complete, and every second the download was in process, he was at risk. The guards might spot what he was doing. The other workers might see the drive in the USB slot and report him. The tech in the downstairs server room would get an alert, and if Bourne wasn't there to stop him, then a phone call would be made upstairs.

Oskar Vogel. Take him to security. He is a spy!

He could still walk away. He could quit, and no one would be the wiser. But in his mind, he saw Louisa's face. Her face in that video had been full of pain and despair. She'd given up everything to make amends for her lies, and now she was dead. Murdered. He couldn't fail her.

Nine o'clock. He'd begin the download.

But first things first. It was almost eight forty-five, and Bourne would be entering the building. Oskar needed to clear the way for him, which meant taking the first risk in their plan. He glanced around the eighth floor to make sure that no one was watching him. Then he logged out of his account and used one of his dummy accounts to hack into the institute's personnel files. It wasn't hard; it didn't take him long. This was what he did to other businesses day in, day out. He was leaving fingerprints of his work behind, and sooner or later, they'd track the unauthorized access back to this terminal.

Hopefully, by then, he'd be long gone.

Oskar called up the record for Horst Grauman and saw the personnel record, photo, clearance, and contact information for the maintenance man. Quickly, eyes on the clock, Oskar changed the man's name: *Hans Dugan.*

Then he deleted the man's photograph with a new picture that he'd planted in the cloud overnight. This photo showed a bored older man with graying hair. Underneath the disguise, the picture was of Jason Bourne.

EIGHT FORTY-FIVE.

Bourne entered the building. With no way to communicate with Oskar, timing was everything. And if things went wrong, he had no gun. He couldn't risk it being discovered during a security search.

As he headed through the lobby, he walked with a slight limp. The hunch of his body made him look smaller than he was. His face was devoid of expression, nothing but an older man counting off the days until he

could retire. But behind dead eyes, he stayed alert to the
two men at the checkpoint—the man running IDs
through the scanner and the armed uniformed guard
beside him.

When he got to the front of the line, he dug in his
pocket with an annoyed expression, as if he couldn't remember where he'd left his ID card. Then he found it
clipped to his pocket and handed it over to the man at
the computer terminal. Without giving anything away,
Bourne tensed as the card went through the scanner. He
wondered if Oskar had successfully hacked the database,
because if not, the photo of Horst Grauman would not
match the man standing in front of them.

Just for an instant, the clerk at the computer terminal
cocked his head in surprise. Bourne wondered if one
cached entry had appeared for an instant, only to be replaced by new information and a new photo. The man
looked at the screen, looked at Bourne, and then back at
the screen.

Noticing the delay, the guard with the gun grew alert.

"Name?" the man asked.

"Dugan," Bourne replied in a lazy voice. "Hans Dugan."

"Sind Sie neu?"

Jason shook his head in mock disgust, as if the idea of
being a new employee was ridiculous. *"Drei Jahre."*

The man checked the screen again, comparing employee dates on the record, and confirming that the system agreed that Hans Dugan had worked for the institute

for three years. The face was unfamiliar to him, but the man saw hundreds of faces every day. He shrugged, as if some people were simply forgettable, and waved Bourne into the building. Jason felt the armed guard's eyes following him as he headed for the stairwell, but he made a point of not looking back.

Time: Eight fifty-two. The entry had taken longer than he'd wanted.

Bourne took the stairs to the building's underground level. He'd watched and rewatched the video taken by Saira when she was inside the facility, and he'd used it to build a map in his head. He followed the corridors to the location of the physical plant, where the maintenance area was located. Outside, he hesitated, not wanting to confront anyone who would recognize that he didn't belong there. Watching the area, he saw only one man, obviously the boss, behind the glass door of an office. The man was on the phone and was facing the other way, so Bourne quickly found the locker belonging to Horst Grauman. He took the man's tool belt and strapped it around his waist, then grabbed a six-foot ladder under his arm and headed out again before the boss turned around.

Time: Eight fifty-five.

His next stop was the server room. Bourne entered, listening to the hum of the mainframes, feeling cool air from the vents overhead. No one challenged him. Watching Saira's video, Oskar had pinpointed the office where a senior tech monitored data activity around the building. Jason carried the ladder there and rapped his knuckles sharply on the closed door. Someone on the other side shouted for him to enter.

He opened the door, dragging the ladder with him. A man sat at a long counter with half a dozen computer monitors in front of him. He was in his thirties, with long blond hair tied in a ponytail behind his back. He wore a wool sweater, because the room was cold, and he had music from a German rock band playing from speakers. The noise was loud, but Bourne hadn't heard it outside the office, which meant the place was soundproofed. That was good.

Jason shut the door.

The man in front of the monitors glanced at him, but seeing the maintenance uniform, he looked away again. *"Was wollen Sie?"* he asked in a bored voice.

"There's an issue with the vent," Bourne replied in German. "Somebody called it in."

"I haven't noticed anything."

"Must have been the overnight man. Shouldn't take me long to fix."

The tech shrugged. His gaze returned to the monitors, which included rotating camera feeds from throughout the building, as well as two monitors that streamed data—a raw tracking list, Oskar had reported, of keyboard commands and information going in and out of the building. Emails. Search requests. Data transfers. As soon as he began the download, the volume of data being transferred would quickly trigger an alert for follow-up with the on-duty tech.

Time: Exactly nine o'clock.

If they were on schedule, Oskar was plugging the thumb drive into his terminal on the eighth floor and launching the download.

Bourne set up the ladder not far from where the man was sitting, which drew an annoyed look. He climbed several steps until he could reach the ceiling panels, and then he removed one and continued climbing until he could shine a flashlight inside. Then he waited. Every minute or so, he grabbed a tool from the utility belt and pretended to be working on machinery in the ceiling.

More minutes ticked by.

Five. Ten. It was taking longer than Bourne expected. Maybe the download wasn't triggering an alarm. Or maybe Oskar had already been grabbed by the guards. Then he heard a shrill whistle from one of the computers, and the tech hissed from the desk below him.

"Was gibt's?" the man murmured to himself.

Bourne glanced down from atop the ladder. He watched the tech lean forward and squint at an area of the data feed. The man backed up the stream and watched the information transfer, and a low curse growled from his throat.

"Scheiße!"

The man reached for a phone.

As he did, Bourne lashed out with his boot. His kick caught the tech under his jaw and lifted him off the chair. The man flew, his body hitting the tiled floor, the wheeled chair rolling away. Jason dropped down heavily from the ladder. The tech was groggy but still conscious. Bourne took a fistful of the man's blond hair and knocked his skull hard against the floor. The man's eyes rolled and closed, and he was out.

Bourne grabbed for the phone. He dialed Oskar's extension. "We're clear. How long up there?"

"Ten more minutes, maybe fifteen. The transfer is going slowly."

"You have to be heading out of the building at nine thirty," Bourne reminded him. "That's when they need to call maintenance."

"I understand."

"Remember, when it's done, get out right away. Don't wait for anything. Head for the train station. Abbey and Saira will meet you there."

OSKAR HUNG UP THE PHONE. HE WATCHED THE FILES DOWN-loading on the screen, one after another, hundreds of them. It was as if Louisa's whole life were streaming in front of his eyes. Her secret life.

He scribbled nonsense on a yellow pad as if he were working, and all the while, he surveyed the morning activity on the eighth floor. The kid next to him had shown up and was tapping on his keyboard. Two additional guards had suddenly appeared—both of them armed—and were waiting next to the exit scanner and X-ray. Why were they there? What did they think was going to happen?

Then he understood.

Someone exited the elevator, wearing a suit. He was in his thirties, tall and muscular, with an air of authority.

Seeing him, the two guards snapped to attention, and Oskar heard one of them call, "Herr Gerlitz."

The new man snapped his fingers. He marched between the desks with long strides, and the two guards followed on his heels. They headed straight for Heinrich Kessler's office, and Gerlitz used a key to unlock the door. He signaled the guards inside, and Oskar could see the men beginning to unload papers from Kessler's file cabinets. As they did, Gerlitz stood in the office doorway, his arms folded over his chest, and his gaze went from worker to worker on the eighth floor.

Oskar looked down, not wanting to meet his eyes, not wanting to show any fear or concern. But he felt a wave of both.

Mein Gott, *do they know?*

He stared at the screen, willing the transfer to go faster. It was too late to stop now, too late to do anything but see it through.

Time: Nine twenty-five.

Too slow! He wasn't going to be done! And what would happen to Bourne if the call didn't come on time?

Then, finally, finally, the streaming of files on his screen stopped, and the cursor blinked at him. The download was complete. Oskar silently withdrew the thumb drive from the computer, making sure he wasn't being watched, then slid it into his pocket. Not waiting, he stood up and headed for the men's toilet. The route took him past Kessler's office, and he had to go right by Herr Gerlitz, who was still in the doorway, his face icy.

It would be strange not to acknowledge him, so Oskar nodded at the man, and the man nodded back, saying nothing.

Time: Nine twenty-six.

He went into the bathroom. With a curse, he realized there was someone in one of the stalls! He couldn't follow the plan unless it was empty. Killing time, Oskar turned on water at one of the sinks and began to wash his face. Whoever was in the stall had a lot to do, or he was busy playing games on his phone, because Oskar heard humming and no indication that the man was getting ready to leave.

Two minutes passed.

At last he heard a flush, and one of the other hackers emerged, giving a loud sigh. The man didn't acknowledge Oskar and didn't wash his hands. As soon as he was gone, Oskar yanked a small spool of duct tape from his pocket, along with the thumb drive, and he taped the device under the first sink. Then, hurrying, he went into the farthest stall from the door and kicked off his shoes. He was wearing multiple pairs of socks, and he peeled off the first pair, shoved them into the toilet, and flushed, watching the water go down and then rise back up as the balled-up socks clogged inside the pipe. As water overflowed the toilet, he switched to the next stall and repeated the process. Water spilled from under the stall doors and spread across the toilet floor.

Oskar put his shoes back on over wet socks and returned to the office. He didn't go back to his desk.

Instead, he headed straight for the security checkpoint in front of the elevators. With a smile and a roll of his eyes, he emptied his pockets and then proceeded through the scanner with his arms over his head. On the other side, he reclaimed his wallet, keys, and ID card.

The guard gave him the all-clear, then said, *"Wo gehen Sie?"*

"I need to pick up a prescription at the pharmacy," Oskar replied with a shrug. "I'll be back in ten minutes."

He turned for the elevator, then casually stopped and called over his shoulder. "Oh, and the fucking toilets have flooded again. You better call maintenance."

The guard swore.

Oskar headed for the elevator and noticed the time. Nine thirty-four. His heart sank, and he swallowed a curse as the elevator doors closed with him inside.

He was late.

BOURNE CHECKED TO MAKE SURE THE TECH IN THE SERVER room was still out cold. He grabbed the ladder, closed the door behind him, and retraced his steps to the maintenance facility inside the building. It was nine twenty-nine. If Oskar was on time, then the call about the flooded toilets on the eighth floor should be coming in to the head of maintenance in the next few seconds.

He waited near the lockers, staying out of sight. From where he was, he saw the boss in his office, door open. It was only twenty yards away. When the phone rang, he'd see the man take the call, and as soon as the boss hung up, he'd make his move. But nine twenty-nine clicked to nine thirty, and there was no call. Then nine thirty-one.

Oskar, where are you?

Nine thirty-two.

The physical plant area around him was noisy with the throb of machines, and the overhead lights were dim. He was mostly invisible from where the boss was sitting, but the more time passed, the more the man might take note of one of his staff hanging around near the lockers with nothing to do. But *not* one of his staff. A stranger.

Nine thirty-three.

Bourne kept his eyes locked on the man in the office, and he was so focused on him that he missed the footsteps coming from behind.

"Hey, Horst, wie geht's?" said a booming voice.

Jason couldn't help it. He turned around. As he did, he saw a short, overweight bald man in a matching blue maintenance jumpsuit. The man had a grin on his face, but the grin evaporated as he realized that the man in front of him was not Horst Grauman. Confusion and suspicion filled his eyes.

He knew everyone who worked in maintenance, and Jason was not one of them.

The man shouted, both at Jason and at the boss in the office.

"Hey, wer sind Sie? Hey, Klaus, kommst du hier! Schnell!"

Bourne shot out a fist that caught the man in the throat, cutting off his cry, but it was too late. The alarm had been raised. He spun the heavyset man around and wrapped his neck in a chokehold that cut off the blood to his brain and rendered him unconscious in seconds. The man slumped in his arms, and Jason lowered him to the floor. At the same moment, he heard the thunder of heavy footsteps from the office behind him.

He also heard the phone ringing.

As Bourne turned back, the boss flew at him. The man had a hammer raised high over his head, and he came at Bourne, swinging the tool hard and landing it with a painful crack on Jason's shoulder before he had a chance to dodge the blow. His muscles froze with a shudder of pain. The man drew back and swung the hammer sideways, aiming for Bourne's skull, and Jason ducked as the tool rushed over his head. The missed swing left the man off-balance. Bourne took the man's wrist and bent it sharply, then shoved both wrist and hammer toward the man's head. With a sickening fracture of bone, the man slammed the hammer into his own skull, and he keeled forward.

The phone was still ringing.

Bourne leaped for the office, crossed the distance in a few long strides, and scooped up the receiver. He was out of breath and tried to hide it. *"Ja, ja, was ist los?"*

A guard on the eighth floor told him about the flooded toilets, and Bourne replied, hoping the man didn't recognize that he was talking to a stranger. *"Ja,* okay, I'll send Hans up there now. He'll take care of it."

Jason hung up the phone.

He dragged the two unconscious men into the office and found some twine to quickly tie their hands and feet, but he wasn't sure how well the knots would hold. He closed the door, hoping that if the men woke up, there was enough noise in the physical plant to cover their calls for help.

With a shop vac in tow, Bourne headed for the elevators.

The clock was ticking, but the plan was coming apart.

37

THE ELEVATOR DOORS OPENED, AND BOURNE EXITED, USING a shuffling walk and dragging the shop vac behind him. Tools hung loosely from his utility belt. With a slow glance, he examined the eighth floor, which was laid out the way Oskar had described it. First he checked the area where Oskar's desk should be, and he saw that it was empty. Oskar was gone, and that was good.

Then he noticed the man in the doorway of one of the private offices on the far side of the floor. The sight of that man set Bourne on edge. The man was tall, with short blond hair, a rectangular face, and a honed physique. His suit didn't hide the bulge near his shoulder that marked a weapon. Bourne knew this man was more than an ordinary executive. Like Fritz Haber, he was a professional, with physical skills and cunning eyes that made him dangerous. That man was smart enough to know that looks were deceiving, and he was assessing Bourne with more than casual interest.

Jason made a point of ignoring him. He didn't try to walk straight onto the floor. Instead, he went up to the guards at the security desk. They wouldn't recognize him, and he wanted to defuse their suspicion immediately.

"Hans Dugan," he told them. *"Für die Toiletten."*

But the guards knew they were being watched by the blond man, and they were taking no chances. *"Wer sind Sie? Wo ist Horst?"*

"Krank."

"ID," the man demanded.

Bourne shrugged and snatched the ID clip from his uniform pocket and handed it to the guard, who had the meaty build of a wrestler. As he waited, Jason hummed tunelessly and shifted back and forth on his feet, a worker not caring one way or another whether they let him deal with a flooded bathroom. The heavyset guard scanned the ID, then carefully reviewed the personnel record of Hans Dugan and matched the photograph with the man in front of him. Seconds passed. Then a couple of minutes. Jason knew that every minute provided more time for the men downstairs to be discovered and a building-wide alarm to be sounded.

"Was ist los?" said a new voice with cold curiosity.

The blond man had crossed the office and was now standing next to the guard by the security desk.

"Maintenance sent someone to fix the flooded toilets, Herr Gerlitz," the guard replied. "We don't recognize him, so naturally, we wanted to check before allowing him access to the floor."

"Naturally," Gerlitz agreed. The blond man bent down to review the computer screen, then straightened up and studied Bourne. "Dugan. It says you've been here three years, and yet these men don't know you. Why is that?"

Bourne didn't bother with excuses. An innocent worker didn't offer excuses. He simply shrugged. "Who knows? Maybe they're stupid."

The face of the beefy guard at the desk flushed with anger at being insulted by a man sent to fix clogged toilets. Jason didn't care; he liked it that way.

Angry men make mistakes.

Treadstone.

"You say Horst is sick?" Gerlitz asked.

"That's what they tell me."

"So your boss sent you."

"Yeah."

"Who is your boss? What is his name?"

Jason remembered the name the other man had used to call the man from the basement office. "Klaus. But me, I call him shithead."

The blond man laughed loudly at the joke. He tapped a leather shoe on the floor, and his eyes squinted with another careful assessment, but he decided for the moment that Bourne was not a threat. With a hand on the seated guard's shoulder, he jerked a thumb toward the bathroom.

"Go with him. Make sure he does his work and comes

back, and that's all. Got it? Don't let him out of your sight."

"Yes, Herr Gerlitz."

The guard jumped to his feet, but he didn't look happy with the assignment. He jabbed a finger at Bourne, and Jason followed him across the office with the shop vac in tow. The man walked quickly on his tree trunk legs, and Bourne limped at a slow pace, causing the other man to urge him to go faster. They reached the corridor leading to the toilets, and the guard held open the door, shoving Bourne inside ahead of him with an impatient hand on his back. Then the guard followed, and the door swung shut.

The two of them were alone inside.

The guard looked down at the floor and swore at the toilet water pooling around his shoes. *"Scheiße."*

Bourne struck.

In one seamless move, he spun back, grabbed the guard's head with one hand, and shoved him face-first against the marble counter of the sink. The crack was so sharp and fierce that he heard the man's teeth break, and blood spurted from his mouth. The guard's knees buckled, but he was built like an ox and didn't fall. He shoved Bourne away with an eruption of strength, and then dizzily, he lashed a foot at Bourne's stomach, landing a heavy blow. As Jason recovered, gasping for breath, the guard grabbed for the holster at his belt. He was fast; he already had the gun halfway out.

Bourne couldn't let him get off even a wayward shot. The noise would bring others running. He charged the man, whose face was now a mass of blood. With his shoulder groaning, he punched the man square in the throat with his left fist, choking him. His other hand bent back the man's trigger finger, snapping it. A howl of pain was squelched by the man's collapsed windpipe, and the gun dropped. Bourne kicked it, sending it flying away across the wet floor. The guard landed a thunderous blow on Bourne's chest with his uninjured hand, and the impact made Jason feel as if his lungs were empty. He shook it off, steadied himself, and saw the man plant his foot for another kick.

Bourne feinted backward, then grabbed the man's ankle as the kick came and spilled him off his feet. He was over the man in an instant, but he felt the guard's hand pawing at the utility belt on his waist. Out of the corner of his eye, he saw a screwdriver flying toward his neck. He ducked his head back just in time, then clutched both hands around the man's fist. Tilting the screwdriver blade, he thrust the guard's hand down and impaled the screwdriver deep into his chest, through his ribs and into his heart. He held it there as the man wriggled, with blood spreading from the wound, and he clasped his fingers around the man's throat to choke off any sound.

The guard wasn't dead, but Bourne couldn't wait for the man's last breath. He needed to get out *now*! He glanced at himself in the mirror, seeing the blue shirt of the maintenance uniform stained with the man's blood. His face and hands were smeared with blood, too, giving the fight away. Quickly, frantically, he washed his face, and then he popped the buttons of the shirt and stripped it off. The T-shirt underneath was clean; the blood hadn't soaked through yet. It would have to do.

Bourne felt around under the bathroom sink with his fingers and found the thumb drive that Oskar had left for him. He peeled the duct tape away, then took a heavy metal flashlight from his utility belt and unscrewed the cap. He dumped the batteries out, slipped the thumb drive inside, and reattached the cap and secured the flashlight to his belt again. Breathing hard, he took one last look in the mirror.

No blood.

There was no time to wait any longer. Someone else might come in any second. He stepped over the guard's body and walked out of the toilet. Shaking his hands as if to dry them, and using an awkward gait to emphasize that his pants were soaking wet, he shouldered toward the security desk. Gerlitz was still there. So were three uniformed guards near the checkpoint. As he got closer, Bourne pinched his nose between his fingers and gave them a grin. He aimed directly for the elevators, not the security scanners.

"What a fucking mess," he called. "Shit all over the floor. It's a health hazard. Your buddy's keeping everybody out, but I need to get the snake to unclog the damn things. The plunger isn't working."

He reached for the elevator button, but Gerlitz's voice cut through the silence.

"Halt."

Bourne stopped and turned around, pasting impatience on his face. He took note of the nearest stairwell and calculated his odds of getting past all four men with no weapon. They weren't good.

"You want something?" he asked. "The sooner we get that place cleaned up, the better."

Gerlitz jabbed a finger at Jason and then made a loop, directing him back. "Through the scanners."

"Seriously? I've been up here like two minutes."

"Bitte," Gerlitz said, but there was no *please* on his face. The hands of the other guards drifted to their guns.

Bourne shrugged. He returned to the other side of the security checkpoint, then unhooked his utility belt and fed it through the X-ray machine. He entered the full-body scanner and held his arms over his head, giving them a view of his body through his clothes. That was fine; he had no guns, no knives, anything he would typically carry. Gerlitz was at the X-ray machine, carefully examining the utility belt. The man almost looked disappointed that he didn't see anything out of order. The metal of the flashlight hid what was inside.

"Proceed," Gerlitz told him in a pained voice.

Bourne slung his belt around his waist again and rolled his eyes as he pushed the button for the elevator. He waited, feeling each second pass in slow motion as he willed the car to come faster. The guards were still watching him. Gerlitz's face was still a mask of suspicion. On the other side of the building, Bourne saw a man emerge from behind the closed door of a private office and head toward the corridor that led to the toilets. If he got there, if he opened the bathroom door and found the body of the other guard, the game was up.

The man kept walking.

The elevator didn't come.

Jason began making a plan for the next few seconds—what to do if someone began screaming about a dead man in the toilet. He forced himself to look bored, but he watched the man turn toward the bathroom doors, and he was imagining which of the guards to tackle first as he broke for the stairs.

Then a low bell sounded.

He started breathing again as the elevator doors opened.

But when he stepped toward the elevator car, he found himself face-to-face with Klaus, the head of maintenance, who stood there with ribbons of blood across his forehead and nose. Seeing Bourne, Klaus's eyes widened with shock, and he pointed a finger at him.

"Das ist der Mann! Das ist der Mann!"

The guards were quick. So was Gerlitz. Bourne saw them grabbing for their guns. He took two hands and grabbed Klaus's shirt and threw him bodily out of the elevator. The big man blocked the gunfire and blocked the way of Gerlitz chasing toward him. Jason dove inside, stabbing the button for the lobby and hearing the pounding of boots running for the car. The doors closed slowly, but they closed. He caught a glimpse of Gerlitz outside the elevator as the doors slammed shut. The man's face was twisted with rage, but he fell short as he tried to jump inside, and he had no chance to take a shot.

The elevator rattled downward. It was old and moved at a glacial pace. He didn't dare go all the way to the lobby. Gerlitz would already be on the phone, and when the doors opened on the ground floor, men with guns would be waiting for him. He punched the buttons for each of the intervening floors, and he got out at the first one where the elevator stopped, which was floor five.

There was no security here, but that would change soon. He had two or three minutes, maybe less. Bourne left the elevator, drawing no notice from the workers typing at their computers. He crossed to the row of private offices on the other side, and he checked two or three before he found a man who was reasonably close to his size and build. The man was in his forties, wearing a suit as he sat behind his desk. He looked up in surprise as Bourne walked in and shut the office door behind him.

"Was wollen Sie?" the man asked. *"Gibt's ein Problem?"*

Jason had no time for subtlety. He grabbed a pair of pliers from the utility belt and took the man's jaw between his fingers and clenched it until his mouth opened. "You have one minute to get undressed, or I start removing your teeth. Do it. *Now.*"

The man was naked in forty-five seconds.

As each item of clothing fell away, Jason swapped his maintenance uniform for the man's business suit. The fit was rough, but it would work as long as no one looked too closely. He retrieved the thumb drive from inside the flashlight, then took the maintenance clothes and the utility belt and stuffed them all inside a plastic wastebasket. When he was ready to go, he took the man by the jaw again.

"Hide under your desk. Stay there, and don't say a word. If I see you, if I hear you, you're dead."

"Ja! Ja, okay!"

The naked man scrambled under his desk, and Bourne left the office and closed the door again. Nobody around him had noticed a thing; nobody looked up from their desks. He took the wastebasket to the next empty office and put it inside, and then he headed for the stairwell and headed downstairs.

The guards were coming up the other way. He could hear them.

Bourne ran to meet them like a man fleeing from a mass shooting. He pasted a look of terror across his face. The guards—six of them—had their guns out, and as they pointed them at him, he shot his arms into the air and then gestured frantically to the upper floors of the building. *"Danke Gott! Der sechste Stock!"* he shouted. "Sixth floor! Quickly, he's on the sixth floor! The man is insane!"

The guards swarmed past him.

Jason took the stairs two at a time. When he got to the ground floor, he tightened his tie, then emerged into the crowded lobby of the building. Amid the shouts and chaos, he marched for the doors and headed out into the Frankfurt sunshine.

38

THE TRAIN FOR PARIS WAS DUE TO LEAVE FROM THE FRANK-
furt Hauptbahnhof in thirty-five minutes. The departure
platform hadn't been posted yet, so Bourne and Abbey
sat on the cold ground near the building's huge stone
pillars. The arched metal roof loomed high over their
heads, and warm air blew in with the arrivals and departures of the trains. They both had sections of the *Allge-
meine Zeitung* newspaper that they pretended to read
while they observed the activity inside the station.

Saira and Oskar browsed in a nearby clothing store.
He wanted them out of sight until the last moment when
they could board the train.

There were police everywhere. That wasn't unusual.
But Bourne kept an eye on them, checking their behavior
periodically to see if their alert status suddenly changed.
He'd switched clothes in a bathroom, and he wore a

tweed cap and sunglasses, in case any description of him had been posted. So far, he saw nothing but the ordinary bustle of travelers coming and going. Even so, he'd be happier when they were on the train.

"You look like you're waiting for something to happen," Abbey murmured.

"I am."

"What?"

"I don't know yet, but I don't think the Pyramid will waste any time in striking back."

He looked up to see Saira and Oskar standing over them. Oskar slid down the stone wall and sat next to Jason, but Saira stayed standing, her face taut with concern. She watched the feed from CNN International on a large television screen near the train schedules. Oskar wrapped his arms around his knees and pulled a fedora lower on his forehead.

"I told you to wait in the store," Bourne said.

Oskar nodded. "I know, but we were taking too long in there. The woman at the checkout counter kept staring at us like we were shoplifters or something. I was afraid she would call the police."

"Okay. Smart move." Jason checked the time on the railway board. "Still no platform, but there's no indication of a delay. Hopefully we'll be on the InterCity train in less than fifteen minutes. We've got seats together, and I bought out the rest of the compartment."

"Why Paris?" Oskar asked.

Bourne shrugged. He didn't mention that his selection of Paris as a destination was automatic, that Paris always felt like home to him. "It's as good a place as any. We may not get that far. I chose a route with intermediate stops so we have a chance to get off if anything changes. I don't want us trapped on a long-haul for multiple hours."

They sat for five more minutes. There was still no platform announced on the board. Bourne reminded himself that the platform was usually only posted a few minutes before the train's departure, but the delay made him nervous anyway. He knew they weren't in the clear yet. He wasn't sure what the Pyramid would do, but he could imagine phone calls flying back and forth between Germany and the U.S. Critical information had been stolen—data that could blow the conspiracy wide open. That couldn't be tolerated. Varak would try to defuse the bomb, but Bourne wasn't sure how. Not knowing made him anxious.

Then, above him, Saira hissed sharply.

"What is it?" he asked.

Saira began to point, but then she dropped her arm and turned away, as if she wanted to make sure that no one saw her. Looking up, Bourne understood why. He glanced at the jumbo television screen and saw a picture of Saira's face staring back at him on the international news.

He read the chyron.

LEADING SCIENTIST ACCUSED OF
RESEARCH FRAUD

"They're not wasting any time," he said.

Saira slid down the wall to sit beside Abbey, who took

her hand. The scientist looked hollowed out, staring at the screen. There was no sound, and the subtitles were in German, so Bourne gave Saira a summary of what they were saying.

"They're not talking about any evidence yet, no interviews or documents," he translated. "They must not have had time to manufacture it. It's all 'anonymous sources say,' but they're accusing you of falsifying test results and manipulating studies to draw erroneous conclusions. They claim the fraud goes back for years."

"It's *bullshit*," Abbey interjected, squeezing Saira's hand. "Everyone will know that."

Saira shook her head. "Like they knew with you?"

"You have friends. Colleagues. They know your work."

"So did you. Lies are easier to believe."

"This is a proactive strike," Bourne said. "They know you were involved in the theft of the data. They're laying the groundwork to discredit you, so that no one believes anything you say. If you stand up and talk about the Pyramid and what they've done, the talking heads will say it's all a desperate attempt to change the subject from the allegations against you."

"And it will work," Saira said. "My life. My career. Over, just like that. How could I ever have allowed myself to be taken in by these people?"

She put her head between her legs, her hair falling forward. Abbey draped an arm around her shoulders. Bourne kept watching the television screen, and when the report was done, he checked the schedule board again. With relief, he saw that there was now a platform number for the Paris train. Platform nine, on the far side of the station. They had six minutes to get aboard, and German trains always left on time.

"We need to go," he told them.

Automatically, he did a survey of their surroundings again before he stood up. Then he froze with alarm. From where they were sitting, he could see two German police officers on opposite ends of the station. They'd passed back and forth several times since Bourne had arrived, but up until now, they'd patrolled the area with the typical jaded expressions of cops having a dull day. Now everything had changed. Both men had their radios in their hands. Their faces were hard, and their alert eyes had begun to go from face to face, watching the passengers on the platforms.

"Shit."

"What is it?" Abbey asked with concern.

"Something's wrong. An alert has gone out to the police."

"For you?"

Bourne didn't have a chance to answer. Oskar interrupted with a fierce whisper, and the hacker's stare was glued to the TV screen.

"Oh, fuck. No, not for you, for *me*. They're after *me*."

Above them, on the oversized screen, the local Frankfurt news channel had interrupted the international broadcast with a special report. A manhunt. A photograph of Oskar filled the screen, so large that anyone in the station had to notice it. Below the photograph were three words in huge black type: **Wegen Mordes Gesucht**.

Wanted for murder.

"They're saying I killed a guard in the institute building today," Oskar muttered in disbelief. "Stabbed him with a screwdriver! They're saying I was the one who called in the bomb threat yesterday. Shit, oh my God, now they're claiming there *was* a bomb! They disarmed it before it blew up the whole building! They've got a citywide manhunt underway, and I'm armed and dangerous. A terrorist! Jesus, they're going to *kill* me! They're giving the police an excuse to shoot me down!"

"Oskar." Bourne spat out the man's name in a hushed voice. He took the man's wrist. "Keep it together. Don't draw attention to yourself."

"They're *looking* for me. And the woman in that shop saw me! If she sees my photo on the screen, she'll tell them I'm here."

"I know. We need to get you on that train and get out of here."

Abbey turned to Jason. Her expression was completely calm, and he couldn't help but notice the change in her. Ever since she'd fired that gun in the park near Georgetown, she was someone different. It was as if she'd gone from her world to his world, and she was thinking like him. Like a spy, like a killer, which she was *not*. He hated to see it, and yet she was also learning fast.

"We need a diversion," Abbey said, reading his mind.

"Yes."

"It can't be you," she went on. "Your picture may not be on the news, but the police may have a description of you, too."

"It doesn't matter. The three of you can go on without me."

"No, Jason." Abbey got to her feet immediately, and she spoke in a low voice. "I'll redirect the police. I'll tell them I saw Oskar in that shop, and he was heading toward the first-class lounge. That should bring them all running. As soon as there's a clear path, the three of you get to the train. I'll follow. I'll get there before it goes."

"Not a chance," Bourne told her fiercely. "No way."

But Abbey didn't listen to his protest. She walked away, knowing he didn't dare make a scene. Jason watched her, but he didn't have time for the emotions rolling through him, so he shut them down. He made sure Saira and Oskar stayed undercover, their heads down, as he watched Abbey approach one of the cops near the station entrance. She was acting, and she was good—just the right amount of panic and fear as she pointed to the TV screen, which still showed Oskar's face.

The plan worked. The cop barked something into his radio, and the cop who was closest to the three of them ran toward the other side of the station, not noticing Oskar in the shadows of the stone pillar. As soon as the cop was gone, Bourne helped Saira to her feet, and they started toward platform nine. Oskar had his hat low, staring at the station floor the whole time. Saira was lost in her thoughts. He led them through the crowd, watching eyes, making sure none of the others around them did a double take of recognition. He was also conscious of the station cameras, because he was sure the people in the security booth had received an alert with Oskar's photograph.

"Relax," he murmured to them. "Don't hurry. Act casual."

They reached the slim bullet of the train at platform nine. It was scheduled to depart in two minutes, and most of the passengers had already found their seats. Bourne went to the first car and waited while Saira and Oskar climbed on board. He glanced back toward the heart of the station, looking for Abbey, willing her to *hurry*. But there was no sign of her. Two minutes turned to one, and he knew there would be no reprieve. If she wasn't on board, the train would leave without her.

At the far end, the train attendant began going from car to car, slamming the doors shut.

"Abbey," Bourne hissed to himself under his breath. "Where are you?"

Then she was there. Running. She flew through the station toward him, and she arrived almost at the same moment the conductor reached the car to shoo them aboard the train. Bourne let Abbey go first, and they'd barely cleared the steps when the door clicked shut behind them. The train was already slouching out of the station as they made their way down the corridor, looking for the compartment where Saira and Oskar had taken their seats.

"You're amazing, do you know that?" he murmured to Abbey, who glanced back at him with a flushed grin.

They found the compartment in the third carriage,

and they slid open the door. There were six leather seats inside, with a small table in the middle of the compartment near the large window. Saira and Oskar sat next to each other on the right side, and their faces dissolved with relief as they saw Bourne and Abbey.

Bourne let Abbey sit by the window, and he sat next to her. He didn't like that the sliding glass doors of the compartment offered no privacy, but that couldn't be helped. He kept an eye on the corridor, but for the moment, the other passengers stayed in their seats. As he looked outside, he saw the train clear the station platform, and they passed along the wide spread of railroad tracks as they slowly picked up speed. Rows of apartment towers loomed beyond the tracks.

Then the train jolted.

Their momentum thudded to a halt as the train lurched into an emergency stop. They were just outside the station building, still among the field of parallel tracks that converged from multiple directions like wires tied together.

Bourne jumped to his feet. "We need to get out of here."

But they were too late. Through the window, he saw police officers running along the tracks. They all had guns drawn. When he went to the compartment door, he saw more police taking up positions on the other side of the train. He slid open the door, but he heard the pounding of footsteps on both ends of the train car. They were trapped. Pinned on all sides with nowhere to hide.

He shut the door again and sat down. A look of despair and defeat crossed Abbey's face. "How did they find us so quickly?" she asked.

"They were waiting for us," Jason said. "They knew. They let us go, because they already knew where we were."

"Can we run?"

"Not and stay alive," he told her.

The police were already close. He heard them in one of the nearby compartments, opening doors, closing them; he heard the guttural shout of voices in German. They knew exactly who they were looking for. He slid a hand inside his coat, wrapping his fingers around the barrel of his gun, but they were outnumbered. There wasn't going to be a chance to fight their way free.

He felt the thumb drive in his pocket.

They'd get that, too. All the evidence would be gone.

Bourne looked up and saw a police officer in the corridor, flanked by three other men. The senior man reached for the compartment door, but then, oddly, he stopped. He glanced down the corridor with annoyance, and Jason saw a new man arrive, not in a uniform, but in a suit. The new man was older, with a take-charge attitude that the cops didn't like. He was definitely not police. Bourne knew the look of a spy. The new man barked orders at the senior policeman, who put up a furious argument for a few seconds, then gave up and stormed away, leading the rest of his men with him.

Outside the train, Bourne saw the same thing. The police began to withdraw.

The intelligence man in the corridor stroked his chin

as he studied the four people in the compartment. A little smile crept onto his face, and he tipped his finger to his forehead in a little salute to Bourne.

Then he, too, disappeared.

They were alone again. A few seconds later, the train jerked, and they accelerated again, heading out of the city.

"Jason, what the hell?" Abbey asked.

"I don't know," he replied in genuine confusion. "I have no idea what's going on."

Then as the train rattled along the tracks, he saw a small man with wiry, brushed-back gray hair appear at the doors. The man was almost sixty, and he walked with a cane, stumbling a bit with the side-to-side motion of the train. He slid open the door and came inside, then piled down into one of the two empty seats, sitting across from Bourne and Abbey.

"Hello, Jason," Nash Rollins said. "And Ms. Laurent, what a pleasure to see you again. It's been a while."

39

THEY GOT OFF THE TRAIN IN THE CATHEDRAL TOWN OF CO-
logne, and an hour later, they were on an unmarked
Treadstone jet heading west toward New York. The
thumb drive with Louisa's information was in Nash's
hands, and he spent the first several hours of the flight in
a secure room on the private jet, reviewing the situation
with higher-ups at the CIA. That included a woman
whom Bourne knew well—and didn't trust at all—a
deputy director named Holly Schultz, who had sent him
on questionable missions more than once in the past.

Bourne sat in the back of the jet with Abbey. While
she tried to sleep, he stayed awake, watching the ocean
out the windows. They'd hit a patch of turbulence, giving them a bumpy ride. Oskar played a computer game
on a laptop. Saira had filled two yellow pads with notes,
sketching out details of a press conference to announce

what they'd discovered. Organizing a summary of the lies that had been spread. Highlighting specific missions that Louisa had spearheaded in various countries. Naming names.

He didn't want to tell her that her preparation was a waste of time. There would be no press conference.

They were within two hours of landing when Nash returned. He had a smile on his face, but Bourne had worked with Nash for a long time, and he knew the smile was a cover for things they wouldn't want to hear. He gathered them around a conference table without notes and without a phone. Jason also noticed that Nash hadn't brought the thumb drive back with him. None of them were likely to see it again.

"I've been in touch with senior people throughout the government," Nash told them, "and the first thing I have to say is how grateful we are for everything you did and everything you risked to bring this situation to light. The information that Mr. Vogel downloaded in Frankfurt is profoundly shocking. We take it very seriously, and we will be taking aggressive action in response."

"Yes, it's imperative that we move quickly," Saira interjected. "The longer we wait, the more time they have to mount a PR counteroffensive to undercut our revelations. We can't leave any doubt in people's heads about what's been going on. I've already got a structure prepared for a public announcement. I'm happy to lead and moderate the presentation, but the key question is deciding who else should be part of it. Obviously Oskar, who can describe Louisa's actions and his role in Frankfurt in detail. I assume Jason will need to stay out of it for security reasons, but Abbey should be involved. And we'll need other media and government representatives, too. You can probably offer suggestions on that, Mr. Rollins. There's a lot to organize in a short time, but I think we should aim to go public no later than tomorrow morning."

Nash let her finish her thoughts. Bourne could see him waiting to drop the bomb. Saira was a scientist, and she didn't understand the government.

"While we all appreciate your enthusiasm, Dr. Kohli—and we welcome your help in dealing with this situation going forward—we've concluded that full disclosure of these events wouldn't serve the public well."

Saira leaned forward on the table with disbelief on her face. "Excuse me? What are you talking about? Not serve the public well? The people have been lied to. They've been manipulated. Elections were hijacked. Innocents were murdered."

"That's true," Nash agreed.

"So how can it be in the public interest to keep all of that secret?"

Nash sighed. "In this case, I'm just a messenger, Dr. Kohli. If you want to talk about this further, I can put you in touch with others in the government. Honestly, if you want a sit-down with the president, I can probably arrange that. Trust me, he's in the loop now on what has happened. This is his call, supported by other senior advisors in the intelligence community."

"A *cover-up*? Really? That's your solution?"

"Consider the alternative, Dr. Kohli. The institute

was ostensibly formed to deal with an epidemic of mistrust regarding the mass media and social media platforms. Do you think it will do anything to improve trust if we announce that the very organization that claimed to be battling misinformation was itself a cover for murder and political control? Will that make us *less* divided?"

Saira opened her mouth to protest, but then she shut it in frustration.

Sitting next to Jason, Abbey didn't look surprised. "So what do you intend to do?" she asked.

"As I said, we're taking aggressive action," Nash replied. "There is a lot of data to analyze, and it will probably take months to assess every area where the Pyramid distorted news reports and destroyed lives. In each case, we'll be looking for ways to rectify any injustice we find. I admit, it's going to take time, and there may be situations where there's little we can do. But we'll make every effort, I promise you."

"What do you plan to do, fight lies with lies?" Saira asked bitterly. "Isn't that exactly what the Pyramid was doing?"

"I'm afraid we have to deal with the world as it is," Nash told her. "I wish there were another way, but there's not."

Abbey interjected again. "What about the *fire*? And the Senate election? You can't unring that bell."

"As far as the terrible deaths in Atlanta, you're right. But the president will be having a private conversation with Senator Adamson this evening, and he'll confront her with the evidence we have in hand. She's about to have a personal crisis that will necessitate her resigning her Senate seat. In addition, she'll provide us with details of the inner workings of the Pyramid, particularly the names of those involved. That will give us the tools to dismantle it entirely. The latest incarnation of Inver Brass will be destroyed."

"And if she refuses to play ball?" Saira asked.

"She will. She has no choice."

"But if she doesn't?"

Nash shrugged and didn't answer, but Bourne knew what that meant.

At the other end of the conference table, he spoke for the first time. "What about Abbey? How does she get her life back? And Saira? And Oskar?"

"Well, with regard to Mr. Vogel, the Frankfurt police will issue an apology and a correction tomorrow. Oskar will be cleared of any wrongdoing. We'd like your help over the next several months in working through the information you provided, Mr. Vogel, but after that, if you want to go home, you'll be free to do so. On the other hand, I hope you'll consider staying in the U.S. on a permanent basis. Your skills would be very useful to us."

Oskar said nothing, and his face was impassive, not giving his feelings away. But in the end, Jason knew he'd be forced to do what they wanted. He'd be enlisted, recruited, paid to do the same work he'd been doing before, for a different kind of Pyramid. The one that was on the back of the U.S. dollar. Treadstone always got its way.

Bourne shook his head. Saira was right. They fought lies with other lies.

"As for the rest," Nash went on, "the Justice Department will hold a press conference in the next couple of days. We'll announce the indictment of a hacker based out of Romania. A teenager, nineteen years old. His whereabouts are unknown, but we'll be mounting a global search to locate and arrest him. The attorney general will announce that this individual was responsible for manufacturing false online profiles that were used to smear a number of prominent people, including both Dr. Kohli and Abbey Laurent. He'll confirm that there is absolutely no basis in fact for any of the allegations that were made against them. We expect this will go a long way toward restoring your public reputations."

"Meanwhile, this hacker is another lie," Saira commented. "He doesn't exist. And, of course, he'll never be found."

"Yes, of course," Nash acknowledged. "But the two of you will have your lives back."

"What about the institute?" Saira asked.

"Naturally, you'll resign and suggest that the entire project be disbanded. Your voice will carry a lot of weight. You can say that it seemed like a good idea, but you've concluded that the only way to deal with misinformation is more speech, not less. That every attempt at censorship, however well intentioned, makes the problem worse and only feeds greater distrust. It's messy, but freedom is messy."

No one spoke. Nash put both hands on the table.

"Anyway, I have more calls to make before we land. Jason, could I speak to you privately for a moment?"

Bourne had been expecting that.

He got up from the table, along with Nash, leaving the others behind in silence. Like Oskar, Saira would ultimately do what they asked her to do. She'd protest, but in the end, she'd toe the party line and say what they wanted her to say. And they'd all sign nondisclosure agreements, keeping the secrets that the government wanted them to keep. Even Abbey would go along. She'd hate it, but she'd do it to protect him.

Nash led him to the private room near the front of the jet, which was sound protected and hacker protected, like a SCIF in midair. There was a computer, a phone, and a desk inside, but not much else.

Jason sat down in an upholstered chair, and Nash took a seat behind the desk.

"What about Varak?" Bourne asked. "I assume that's what you want to talk about."

"Yes."

"Do you want me to kill him?"

"No. Actually, I want you to stay away from him. Those are Holly's orders."

Bourne's face creased in confusion. "You're letting him go? Varak is *Genesis*. He controls the money, the assets. Even if you shut down the Pyramid, he'll simply reconfigure it in another form. You won't stop anything."

"Obviously. Varak has to be dealt with."

"Then what am I missing?" Bourne asked.

"Varak is out of the country for a week. He's leading a convention of nonprofits in Lisbon. It's too risky to make any move on him there. Once he's back in the Hamptons, we'll be able to eliminate him."

"How?"

Nash's eyes turned cold. "That's not your concern."

"Not my concern? Why does Holly want me out of the loop? I know she prides herself on playing three-dimensional chess, but I don't see what she's trying to do here."

"Let it go, Jason," Nash repeated.

Bourne shook his head and got out of the chair. He turned for the door, then stopped. Suddenly, he understood. He knew exactly what the CIA was planning. *"Lennon."*

Nash said nothing.

"Lennon," Bourne said again, turning around. "Putin wants Lennon back on his payroll, but he doesn't want any more heat from the U.S. So he makes a deal. Lennon takes out Varak and, in return, he can start working for the Russians again. And what else do we get? What's the other piece of the puzzle? There has to be more to the deal than that. Why is Holly intent on using an outsider?"

"In this case, I don't know any more than you do," Nash replied.

"In one week, Varak will be back at his estate in the Hamptons," Bourne protested. "Lennon will be there, too. This is my chance to get him."

Nash stood up, leaning across the desk. "Let me be very clear, Jason. Stand down. Lennon's not your problem anymore. That search is done. Over. Go back to Paris, and figure out a new life for yourself. Bring Abbey

Laurent with you, if you want. But stay clear of Lennon. If you don't, Holly assures me that she'll have you killed."

THE NEW YORK SKYLINE GLOWED LIKE FIRE THROUGH THE windows of the suite in the Carlyle Hotel. It was almost two in the morning. Jason watched Abbey standing near the glass, the curves of her naked body in shadow. He came up from behind and slid his arms around her, with her breasts resting in his palms. She leaned her head back against his chest, a little purr in her throat. When she turned around, they kissed, and their bodies molded together. Then he picked her up and carried her back to bed.

The week they'd spent in the hotel together had felt like a vacation from reality. They'd gone to Broadway shows and walked through the park. They'd toured the museums and eaten hot dogs at a Yankees game. They'd drunk wine and made love until their bodies were sated. Time had slowed down along the way, but even slow time eventually ticked on to its inevitable end.

Varak would be back at his estate in the Hamptons the following night. Lennon would be there.

So would Jason.

They hadn't talked about the future. All week, that subject had been off-limits. What they would do when he came back. What she would do if he didn't come back. But suddenly, the future was the present, and they didn't have any choice.

"I heard from Peter Chancellor," Abbey murmured as they lay next to each other in bed, both staring at the ceiling. "He's been watching the news all week. Adamson's resignation. Exposing the lies about me and Saira. He knows something big has been going down behind the scenes."

"Does he still want you to work with him on his next book?"

"Yes, he does."

"And you're going to?"

"I am. I mean, I like having my old life back. Not being an outcast anymore. Nash came through on that score. Half the people still think the truth about me is a lie, but I don't care. If I wanted to be a reporter again, I could. I've already gotten job offers. But after what we've been through, I've realized that Chancellor is right. Sometimes there's more truth to be told in fiction. The government left me with a gag order about everything I know, so if I can't tell the real story, I can turn it into a novel. Let people decide for themselves if it really happened that way."

"What's Chancellor going to call the book?" Bourne asked with a smile. "I suppose it will be *Pyramid!*"

Abbey laughed, too. "Probably. I'm okay with that."

Then the laughter between them bled away. She rolled over on top of his body, and she propped herself above him, with her hands on either side of his chest. Her face was very close to his. Her skin was warm all over. "Tell me something. If I asked you not to go after Lennon, what would you do?"

"I'd stay with you."

"Because you know I can't ask you that," she said.

Bourne shrugged. "Yeah."

"Are the answers really worth it? Worth dying for? Worth losing me?"

"I don't know, Abbey. I don't even know the questions. But they're keeping secrets from me. Not just Lennon. Holly Schultz and the CIA. Nash and Treadstone. There's something in my past they will do anything to hide from me. The only way to be free is to find out what it is."

Abbey rolled off him again. "Then I guess you have to go."

"I do."

"I'm not going to wait for you here, Jason. I'm sorry. I'm not going to sit in a hotel and wonder if you're alive or dead. My old professor, Walden Thatcher, called me. He asked me to stop by his place. He wants to congratulate me on recovering my career. And I imagine he wants to know what I found out about the Pyramid, even though I can't really tell him anything. So I'm going to visit him, and after that, I'll go to Peter Chancellor's home in Pennsylvania to start the book."

"Okay."

"If you want to come back to me, that's where I'll be."

"I'll always come back to you," Jason said.

Abbey kissed him. "That's sweet. But don't make promises you can't keep."

40

THE HAMPTONS DID NOT APPRECIATE STRANGERS IN THEIR neighborhood, especially at night. The police were very protective of their wealthy enclave. Bourne couldn't simply drive a stolen car along the Old Montauk Highway and park it on the shoulder of the road, not without being discovered and prompting a house-to-house search. Instead, he'd turned to a New York executive in the defense industry who'd needed his help in the past. So now he drove a Bentley convertible that the police were unlikely to challenge.

It was a clear, fiercely windy night. Gales twisted the woods on both sides of the beach road. He'd left the more populated towns behind him as he neared the far eastern end of the peninsula, and all that was left were unmarked trails leading to uber-rich estates hidden deep inside the trees, with views looking out on the Atlantic waters. He knew where he was going. For the past week, while Abbey slept, Bourne had stayed up, memorizing maps and satellite photos of the East Hamptons, analyzing where each road went, researching the elaborate houses and who owned them.

He'd found an estate half a mile along the ocean bluff from Varak's compound, owned by a pop singer who was on tour in Australia. Its access road was separate from the road that led to Varak's mansion, which meant the billionaire's security wouldn't cover that area. That was his jumping-off point. That was his way in.

Bourne watched the narrow road through his headlights, alert for men and vehicles. If he could analyze the area and come up with that plan, then Lennon could, too. There was at least a small chance that he was walking into Lennon's staging ground, so he needed to be cautious. But he saw no indication that the road was being guarded.

Ahead of him, the singer's estate loomed in the moonlight as he broke from the trees. There were no lights on in the two-story house. It was after midnight, and if there were staff living there, they were asleep. He didn't bother hiding the Bentley. He parked it outside the front door the way any rich person would, and then he got out and went to the trunk of the convertible. He removed the supplies he'd gathered for the mission, and then he shut the trunk with a quiet click.

Bourne headed for the water.

Not far away, the thunder of ocean waves crashed against the base of the bluff. The wind was loud, covering any noises around him. He found a grassy trail through the trees, and the trail led him to the very edge of the cliff, where steep wooden steps led down to the beach. The Atlantic stretched out in front of him, angry and vast, surging with whitecaps. He saw no boats or lights anywhere on the water.

The bright night, under a clear sky and three-quarter moon, left him visible, so he stayed close to the woods as he followed the cliff westward toward Varak's estate. Where the trail ended, he dived back into the trees. The tumult of the wind allowed him to go faster, unconcerned with being heard. He used a penlight pointed at his feet to guide him, despite the risk that it might be seen. He kept an eye out for night vision cameras surveilling the woods, but if they were there, they were well hidden.

He didn't have to go far to reach Varak's estate. The trees led him to a huge stretch of green grass and a sprawling Cape Cod–style home, with two perpendicular wings, several turrets like in a castle, and a back porch stretching from one end of the home to the other to take advantage of the ocean views. He saw an empty helipad at the rear of the lawn, not far from the bluff. There was a pool with its own separate guest house adjacent to it, but both looked closed for the season. Multicolored Adirondack chairs lined the cliffside, but the wind had blown them over.

He saw something. A body lay in the green grass just in front of him.

Bourne took his Sig Sauer in his hand—Abbey had

insisted that she didn't want the gun anymore—and he curled his finger around the trigger. He approached the body, feeling exposed in the moonlight. The man on the ground had a red slash across his throat; he'd been killed silently and professionally. He was dressed all in black and had an empty holster around his shoulder. A guard. One of Varak's guards, monitoring the border of the compound.

The defenses had already been penetrated.

Lennon was here.

Jason hesitated, just for a moment. One part of his brain told him to leave. To walk away. Whatever secrets Lennon was hiding, they were part of Bourne's past, and the past was dead. Nash was right. He could forge a new life for himself with Abbey. She wasn't far away, just on the other side of Long Island Sound, staying the night with Walden Thatcher before she headed west to meet up with Peter Chancellor. Jason could join her. He didn't have to fight old battles.

But he could also hear Lennon's voice in a small cottage in Iceland.

I was Treadstone.

Pistol in hand, Bourne sprinted across the lawn toward the house. With each step, he expected gunfire to chase him. But there was a strange silence about the estate. The only thing he heard was the roar of the ocean gales. If there were other guards from Varak, they were already dead.

He reached the base of the wide wooden porch, where tall steps rose toward the house. Crouching, he slid an

M4 carbine off his shoulder and secreted it under an
overhang at the base of the steps. He didn't know if he'd
need that kind of firepower, but he wanted backup if
things went wrong.

Things always go wrong.

Treadstone.

Bourne continued to the house. He followed the
ground-floor wall, keeping below the level of the picture
windows. He had a heavy backpack slung over his shoulder. That was the second part of his plan, for which he'd
been gathering components for days. Where the perpendicular wing jutted off the main house, he found a stone
patio extending into the grass, with an elaborate brick
kitchen built for parties, including multiple grilling sta-
tions.

A gas line at the wall fed the grills.

He slipped the backpack off his shoulder, unzipped
the pocket, and armed the electronic switch on the IED.
The little red light went on, indicating that the receiver
was active. He left the backpack under the gas line, then
removed a small plastic radio transmitter from his pocket.
It didn't have much range, but it didn't need to go far.
The button inside was covered by an acrylic flap on
hinges.

Lift the flap. Push the button.

That was all it took.

Backup.

Bourne kept the transmitter in one hand and his Sig
in the other. He continued along the edge of the wall,
and as he did, he heard a muffled noise behind him from

the other wing of the house. A crack that he knew had come from a gun. He ran, finding a locked door that led inside the estate, and he kicked it in with two blows from his boot. He rushed into the house, where the air was dusty and cool. There were no lights on, but the outside moonlight lit up his path through the rooms. Everything was decorated and furnished to the tastes of a billionaire, like a European museum.

He found a hallway leading toward the other wing, which faced the ocean. It was papered in heavy red wallpaper, with chandeliers overhead. At the end of the hallway, a shadow appeared, then stopped as the guard spotted him. Bourne threw himself down an instant before a bullet coursed over his head, and he had no choice but to extend his arm and fire from the ground. Even with the suppressor, the noise was loud in the quiet house. The man fell.

But they knew he was here now. Lennon knew.

Above him, he heard the creak of the floors. Someone was upstairs. He continued through the dark mansion until he reached the foyer with its double doors and high ceiling. A staircase with a brass railing wound upward, and he ran up the stairs two at a time, his Sig leading the way. Up here, he smelled the cordite of a gun that had been fired. It led him down another hallway to a sunroom facing the Atlantic. The room was huge, with floor-to-ceiling windows leading out to the wide porch over the lawn. There were modern, colorful paintings on the wall. Bouquets of fresh flowers in vases. Italian marble on the floor.

In the middle of the floor, bleeding all over the stone, was Varak.

Jason knelt over the billionaire. He recognized the face. The man lay on his back, eyes open. His skin was still warm, but he was already dead. But Bourne wasn't alone. A man sat in a wicker chair in the far corner of the room, almost invisible.

"Hello, Cain."

Jason jumped to his feet and pointed his gun at the man. He walked slowly toward him, his eyes making out the image in front of him. The killer sat with his long legs casually crossed. His right hand loosely gripped a semiautomatic, but the gun was angled downward, not pointed at Jason. The shadows made the man's face difficult to distinguish. High cheekbones. Slim, eaglelike nose. Jutting chin. A shock of black hair. This man looked very little like the killer he'd confronted in the cottage in Iceland, but that didn't matter. Disguise was the man's specialty.

It was Lennon.

Jason trained his Sig on the assassin. From this distance, he couldn't miss, but he remained cautious. Something was wrong. If Lennon had wanted him dead, he could have taken a shot when Bourne first entered the room, but he hadn't. The killer's face looked oddly smug. As if he still held all the cards.

"Go ahead," Lennon said. "Shoot. That's what you want, isn't it? That's why you're here."

Bourne held the gun steady in his hand. His finger was on the trigger, but he didn't fire.

Lennon smiled. "No. We both know that's *not* what you want. You've come here for the truth. You've risked everything to find out what I know. But obsessions like that come with a terrible price, Cain. Are you ready for what it will cost you?"

Again Jason hesitated. His eyes flicked around the dark space, illuminated only by the moonlight, but he saw nothing. No threats. It was just the two of them. One of the doors to the patio was open, and cold, ferocious wind whipped inside.

"You told me you were Treadstone," Jason said.

Lennon tilted his head, a dismissive gesture. "And I was. Just like you. We were friends back then, you and me. As much as people like us can be friends. Too bad you don't remember. But they lied to you. They manipulated you. They made you think I'd *turned*, and then they sent you to kill me. Does that sound familiar? You of all people should know how they twist the truth for their own ends. I knew too much, so I had to be eliminated."

"What did you know?" Bourne asked.

"What does it matter, Cain? You won't remember any of it."

"Tell me."

The killer shrugged. "They sent me on a mission. A mission that went horribly wrong. A mission called *Defiance*."

Bourne blinked. The gun grew slippery in his hand with sweat. That word—it erupted in his head like fireworks! The roaring filled his ears, a wrenching pressure in his skull that he felt whenever the memories tried to come back. *Defiance*. He knew that word. It was not a lie. But he didn't know what it *meant*!

Or did he?

Yes. It meant death. Vengeance. Betrayal. And yet wherever that mission was in his mind, there was nothing but blackness. Everything about it had been wiped clean. He remembered nothing.

"It must be strange," Lennon said, as if reading his mind. "To look back into a blank space."

"What was Defiance?"

"Sorry, Cain. If you want to know any more than that, you'll have to go looking for it. Or who knows? Maybe the truth will find you. We both know the past is never really over. Not for us."

Bourne tried to hold the gun steady, to not let himself lose focus. Lennon was taunting him. Playing with him, a cat with a mouse. The assassin had no intention of giving up his secrets. He was dangling the truth in front of Jason like a shiny object, but all the while, he was really stalling. For what? What was going to happen next?

Kill him now.

That was what he needed to do. Forget the past. *Shoot!*

"You see, that's your weakness," Lennon said, watching his hesitation. "You can't let go, can you? You know the past is coming back to haunt you, to steal away anyone you love. And yet you can't stop. You could have walked away tonight, you could have been free, but here you are. I knew you'd come. I *told* them you'd come, no matter how much they threatened you, no matter how many times they told you to stay away. That's why we're ready for you. That's why this was the perfect place to spring the trap."

Jason felt a cold, clammy horror work its way up his back. It brought him back to where he was, in an estate owned by a billionaire who was lying in a pool of blood on the floor. Varak was dead. Genesis was dead.

But why had they used *Lennon* to kill him?

Why do a deal with the devil?

"The Pyramid hired you," Bourne said, suspicion filling his voice. "Why would you agree to betray them? That's not like you, to turn on the person paying the bills. An assassin can't afford that reputation. Particularly one who does work for the Russians."

Lennon shook his head. "The Pyramid didn't hire me. *Genesis* hired me."

"But you killed him. You shot him."

"I shot *Varak*," Lennon replied calmly.

Jesus! Suddenly, Bourne understood. He recognized the illusion they'd created. The theater, the art of deception. They had a billionaire to take the fall. Kill him, and pretend the Pyramid had been destroyed. But the Pyramid was not destroyed, not over. With Varak dead, it could go underground and create a new identity. It could stay in the shadows, manipulating events the way it had for years.

"Varak wasn't Genesis," Bourne said.

Lennon shrugged. "No."

"He never was."

"Of course not. Varak was a loyal servant. He played

his part, but he knew the end would come for him sooner or later. He always said he would gladly give his life for the cause, just as his father did."

"Then who is? Who is Genesis?"

A voice spoke from the shadows of the doorway behind him.

"I am."

Bourne spun, knowing it was too late, knowing Lennon was pointing a gun at him now, knowing he had nowhere to run. He'd risked everything for this moment, and he'd lost.

Obsessions like that come with a terrible price.

Walden Thatcher walked into the room. The old man held a gun, which was pointed at the head of Abbey Laurent.

41

"PLEASE PUT YOUR GUN ON THE FLOOR," THATCHER SAID.
"Don't let my age deceive you. I'm quite a good shot,
and as fond as I am of Abbey, I really would have no
hesitation about pulling the trigger."

Bourne stared at Abbey. She was gagged, unable to
speak, and her wrists were tied in front of her. Her ankles
were tied, too, barely allowing her to walk. Her hair,
which she'd taken from black back to red during their
week in New York, hung messily in her face. Their eyes
met across the darkness of the sunroom. He saw no fear
from her, only sadness and guilt. As if this situation were
her fault, when in reality, all the blame was his.

He'd killed her. He'd violated the first rule, the *only* rule,
by getting involved. For that sin, they would both die.

Jason knelt and put the gun on the stone floor.

"Kick it away now, will you? Toward Lennon, please."

Bourne did. Lennon retrieved the other gun from the floor, and the assassin's gun was rock-solid, pointed toward Jason's chest.

"Excellent," Thatcher said. "Thank you."

The professor nudged Abbey into the room. They went as far as the body of Varak, and Thatcher looked down at the billionaire with something like regret. "Such a shame, truly. We spent a long time building the cover for Varak. Steering contracts to his company, making sure he established a fortune. Nurturing his reputation as a philanthropist. He really was the perfect symbol for us, not bound to any cause or government. Of course, as Lennon says, Varak knew this day might come. He had a single-minded devotion to the Pyramid. And to me."

Thatcher glanced at Abbey, who studied him with fire in her eyes. "Ah, yes, I've disappointed you, my dear. I understand how you feel. Let's get rid of that gag, shall we? It doesn't matter now."

He undid the gag and eased it down her neck. Abbey worked out the kinks in her jaw and then stared at Jason.

"I'm so sorry," she told him, her voice raspy.

Bourne shook his head. "None of this was you. I did this."

"How very sweet," Thatcher said. "But you really shouldn't blame yourself, Cain. It was always going to end this way. I love Abbey, but she's simply too smart, too determined, for her own good. Tom Blomberg thought she might be dissuaded if we simply took away her reputation, but I knew her too well for that. The young journalist in the front row of my class was never going to give up, once she thought she had a story. That was why canceling her wasn't going to be enough."

"Christ, Thatcher, *why*?" Bourne demanded. "Why bring her back into this now? You could have let her go. It was done. She would never have known the truth about Varak. You could have killed me and put an end to it. Why kill Abbey, too?"

"A very noble sentiment," Thatcher replied. "I wish that were possible, because I'm not lying, Abbey. I have always been enormously fond of you. Proud of you, too, almost like you were a daughter to me. But that's also why I knew you'd never let it go. Varak dying wouldn't be enough to satisfy you that the Pyramid was gone. If Jason didn't come back, you'd pursue the truth and push and push until you found out everything. I'm afraid that was a risk we couldn't allow."

Abbey shook her head in disgust. "How could you be a part of this, Walden? *You*. It goes against everything you ever taught me."

The professor shrugged. "Ideals are for younger men. I told you that we faced a choice, Abbey. Not an easy choice, but one that had to be made. No one will thank you for your principles if you hold to them while the world is crumbling around you. And it *is* crumbling, my dear. We are spinning out of control in so many ways. Division is leaving us weak at a time when we need to be strong. When we need to have a unity of purpose to overcome the existential challenges to this country and to the world."

"And the way to unity is by lying to people?" Abbey

demanded. "By murdering those who get in the way of your plan?"

The professor stiffened. Harshness entered his voice, a ruthless certainty. Bourne had heard that tone before. It was the harshness of the radical so convinced of his own rightness that he can justify any evil to take power.

"Do sacrifices need to be made?" Thatcher asked. "Unpleasant ones? Violent ones? Yes, and I wish that weren't true. But what's the alternative, Abbey? Letting the world burn? Letting disease wipe out the population? Letting the country descend into civil war? No, I'm sorry. We may not like saying that the ends justify the means, but in this case, they do. They do, Abbey."

"How did *you* get involved?" Bourne asked him. "How did you become Genesis?"

Thatcher looked down again at the body of Varak on the floor. "I knew the men of the original Inver Brass decades ago. One of them was a university president. I was his senior aide back then. So I dealt with all of them. Genesis, Banner, Bravo, Paris, Venice, brilliant men who weren't appreciated for their selfless determination. I knew Varak, too. The father to the son. I was the one who set the boy up with the family in Iceland, who made sure his upbringing would prepare him for the future. Because one day, I knew Inver Brass would have to come back. A few years ago, as I watched the world going crazy, I convened several of my former students. People who'd taken their place as senior leaders in government, media, and business. I described the Inver Brass of the past, and I told them it needed to return in a new form. We would form the nucleus of the Pyramid, with Varak as the man in the middle, with an institute created by him as the means to put our plans into action. You may think we're the enemy, but I won't apologize for the work we've done, for the *progress* we've made. If you think you've stopped us, Cain—you and Abbey and Saira Kohli and Oskar Vogel— you are quite wrong. The faces may change, but the work goes on."

"And that's why Lennon had to go after Varak," Bourne concluded. "Not me. The rot goes deep into the government. They couldn't risk me finding out."

"Indeed. But Lennon assured us you'd come anyway, and he knows you well. I suppose that's not a sur- prise, given your *history*."

Outside the estate, they heard the throb of an engine, growing louder. Bourne knew what it was. As if he'd come full circle from that night in Iceland, he heard a helicopter descending toward the landing pad on the grounds of the estate. A helicopter that would take Len- non and Walden Thatcher to safety, with Varak left be- hind. The death of the old Pyramid, the beginning of the new.

And with Jason and Abbey both dead, too.

Lennon spoke into a microphone. "Perimeter, draw in. It's time to go."

Bourne felt the warmth of the plastic transmitter hid- den in his palm. He flipped up the acrylic cover with his thumb, and the red button waited beneath it. The mus- cles in his body tensed.

"With that, I'm afraid our time has come to an end,"

Thatcher said. "I wish there were some other way, Abbey. Truly, I do. As for you, Cain, well, I assume you always knew your life would end in a moment like this. Some things are inevitable."

Abbey was crying tears of fury. "Fuck you, Walden."

"Brave to the end, my dear, just as I would expect," the professor said. Then he nodded at Lennon. "If you would, sir. The satisfaction of dealing with Cain once and for all belongs to you. But let's make it quick, shall we?"

The assassin stood up from the chair. His arm was rigid, pointing the gun at Bourne's head. His mouth twisted into a cruel smile. "Years ago, you tried to kill me, and you failed, Cain. I told you, I was always the superior agent. By the way, I usually like to whistle a Beatles song as I do this. Any requests?"

Bourne shrugged. "How about 'Maxwell's Silver Hammer'? For old time's sake."

"Because you think something will fall down upon my head?"

"Yes, I do."

Jason pushed the button.

Outside, the IED erupted in the backpack. The first explosion rumbled like thunder and shook the walls of the house, but in the next instant, the gas line blew, and the earthquake threw all of them into the air and slapped them down. Every window in the room shattered, spraying a cloud of glass like broken teeth across the floor. Debris crashed from the ceiling. Bourne was ready. He shook off the impact, then scrambled to his feet and hoisted Abbey's body into his arms. She was stunned, almost unconscious. He glanced at Lennon and saw the killer recovering from the first blow, hunting for his gun on the floor. The man was between Bourne and the broken doors that led outside, so Jason stumbled the opposite way, carrying Abbey toward the main part of the house. In the hallway, he kicked the door shut and dived for the ground, just as a fusillade of bullets seared through the wood over their heads.

He grabbed for the backup gun strapped to his ankle, and he spun on his back, firing blindly through the door. Then he slapped Abbey's face gently, trying to rouse her from the impact of the blast. They needed to get away *now*.

"Abbey, get up, you need to get up, we need to run."

Her eyes blinked slowly, stirring from the shock wave. She pushed herself to her knees, then stood up dizzily as Bourne helped her. The two of them limped down the hallway, feeling the entire house shudder and groan around them. Black smoke filled the corridor, stinging their eyes and making them choke. The house was on fire, flames on the other side of the walls roaring like a beast fighting to get free. Jason took Abbey's hand, pulling her along, because they could barely see.

Stairs. They were at the *stairs*!

Bourne went first, guiding them, and Abbey steadied herself on the railing. A haze filled in around them like a cloud. Then, bursting out of that haze, one of Lennon's men shot up the stairs. Seeing Bourne above him, he began to raise the rifle in his hands, but Bourne lashed out with a kick that caught the man in the stomach and sent him reeling back down to the foyer. They found him on the floor, unconscious, and they stepped over him and headed for the door. The fire chased them, burning along the floors and walls; the ceiling began to come down in huge beams and fragments of stone from above.

"Out!" he shouted to Abbey. "Outside! Hurry!"

The two of them shoved open the front door into the fresh air. The dark night had turned to day, lit by flames. Next to them, the perpendicular wing of the house didn't exist anymore; it was a burning mound of wood and brick, leveled by the gas explosion, and the rest of the house was already being engulfed by a wave of destruction. They ran to put distance between themselves and the conflagration, but as he led Abbey toward the old Hamptons highway, he had to pull her to the ground again as bullets banged around them. Two men charged up the driveway, semiautomatic rifles in hand, peppering the air with gunfire. Bourne used his pistol to fire back, buying a few seconds.

"The back!" he shouted. "We need to get to the back!"

He lifted Abbey up and stayed behind her to shield her from the incoming fire. The bullets came close, and then closer, one searing his calf, another ricocheting off debris and sending up a fragment of metal that sliced his arm. He fired back again, over his shoulder, and then they crossed the corner of the house and were momentarily out of view. Ahead of them was the huge stretch of lawn, dancing with the reflected yellow glow of the flames. Smoke rose in billowing clouds. Only the bracing, incoming ocean gales kept the sparks and poison out of their faces.

"Stay there," he told Abbey. "Don't move. I'll be right back."

The entire rear of the house was aflame. Cinders shot in the air and landed around him like tiny meteors. He pushed through the smoke, bent over at the waist, and made his way to the remains of the porch steps. He found the M4 there, where he'd left it, the metal of the gun now blazing hot to the touch. Bourne slung it over his shoulder and made his way back to Abbey, and as he reached her, he spotted two of Lennon's men rounding the corner. They were barely twenty yards away, their rifles already firing.

"Jason!" Abbey screamed, ducking, diving.

He braced the carbine, aimed, and unleashed a deadly stream of automatic fire that practically cut both men in half.

"Come on!" he called again.

They ran for the water. Around them, glass exploded and blew like hail, and wood and stone shot from the house in a rain of shrapnel. As Jason glanced over his shoulder, he saw the entire rear wall shudder and collapse, shooting off fireworks that landed on their clothes and burned through to their skin. Abbey screamed at the pain. A fragment of wood hit her thigh like a knife, and she tripped and toppled to the ground. He turned to help her, but then, behind him, came the growl of an engine, even louder than the roar of the dying mansion.

Bourne looked back toward the ocean. Near the cliff-side, the helicopter began to rise from the helipad, an insect climbing into the sky. Lennon and Walden Thatcher were already on board. Escaping. Free. He turned the M4 up and fired, tracers of bullets whipping through the air, but he was too far away to do any damage. The helicopter kept getting higher and higher, soaring out of range.

He threw the M4 down to the ground and headed for Abbey, who was getting up now, pushing herself to her feet. She stood alone on the green grass, surrounded by pockets of fire, framed by the estate ablaze behind her. Her skin glowed, but her face was covered with dirt and blood. She favored one leg, and he could see that she couldn't walk. But that was okay. He would carry her if he had to.

And then light bloomed around her.

A cone of light from over their heads. A searchlight.

The helicopter lit up Abbey from above, and by instinct, she looked up in confusion, her face turned toward the sky.

Lennon.

Bourne felt his breath leave his chest. He was at least twenty feet from Abbey. Twenty feet that felt like twenty miles. He pushed off at a run, desperate, screaming at her to duck, to move, to throw herself away from that light. Ten feet. And there it was—the tiny dot of light appearing on Abbey's forehead, the laser scope from the sniper rifle that Lennon was aiming from the helicopter. She stared at Jason, her eyes uncomprehending, her lips bent into a strange little smile.

Jason threw himself off the ground.

At the same moment, the crack of the gunshot rippled through the air, following the bullet that tore into bone.

42

FOUR MONTHS. FOUR MONTHS HAD GONE BY.

Abbey awakened in the soft bed and reached out, but Jason wasn't there. The sheet was cold. He'd been gone for a while.

She got out of bed and slipped on a robe. There was still a half-full mug of coffee on the worktable near the window, but that was a leftover from the middle of the night. Her laptop was open, and the table was filled with yellow pads covered over in Peter Chancellor's spidery handwriting. That was his rhythm, to work in longhand—in pencil!—and to take volumes of notes and ideas, outlining every chapter, every thread of the story, every character. And then they would talk it over, and Abbey would take over in the late evening hours, turning the notes into prose until it was nearly three in the morning.

They'd been working that way since Abbey and Jason had arrived at the Pennsylvania house.

Now nearly half the book was done. The story that could only be told as fiction. *Pyramid!*

The upcoming novel by Peter Chancellor and Abbey Laurent.

Was it fact or fiction? That was up to the reader to decide. The only reality that had made it to the headlines was that Varak was dead and his institute had been shut down. There had been no mention of Walden Thatcher, who was still missing. Nor of the Pyramid. Nor of Lennon.

Abbey went to the window and opened it, letting in the fall air, which was cool and sweet. The view looked out across miles of national forest. A hawk made circles in the sky, going in and out of the dazzling sun. Below her, where the backyard of the Chancellor estate sprawled across the high ground, she saw Jason staring out over green hilltops that rolled toward the horizon. He had his hands in his pockets, and the breeze rustled his brown hair. But the white gauze pad on the side of his head was still visible, where Lennon's bullet had penetrated his skull. Nearly killing him, but not killing him.

That was the way it had happened once before, in the waters off Marseilles, when he'd been shot and lost his past. When everything had been erased. The question for both of them now was, how much would he remember this time?

Jason had awakened after two weeks in the hospital

and not known her. For another two weeks after that, she'd been a stranger to him. He'd remembered nothing, not of what had happened at Varak's estate, not of his life for the past several years. Not of Treadstone, or Nova, or the things he'd done. Not of meeting Abbey and falling in love with her. He was once again a man with no identity, wrestling with who he was.

And then slowly, oh, so slowly, memories had started to come back.

She hadn't told him her name. She wanted him to remember it on his own. And a month after he'd nearly died to save her life, his eyes fluttered open in a New York hospital, and he'd said the word that nearly made her heart leave her chest.

"Abbey."

They'd gone to Peter Chancellor's estate not long after that. Ever since, day by day and week by week, more pieces in the puzzle had begun to take shape in his mind. There was a little bit more whenever he awakened. Jason rested and remembered, and Abbey sat with Peter Chancellor and wrote.

She never wanted it to end.

"Good morning."

Abbey turned around and saw Peter's wife, Alison MacAndrew, standing in the doorway of the bedroom. She had fresh coffee and a freshly baked scone on a silver tray. They'd become close in the months that Abbey had been here. She'd learned that the reserve this beautiful woman used with other people was a defense mechanism, not dissimilar to her own. Partly to protect herself.

Partly to protect her husband. It was also obvious that Alison loved Peter Chancellor as much as the writer loved her.

Alison joined her at the window. She followed Abbey's stare to Jason, who was still absorbed in the hills.

"We both have men who would do anything for us," Alison said. "That's a rare gift. But sometimes those men also need us to rescue them."

"I don't think Jason needs anyone," Abbey murmured.

Alison gave a sparkling laugh. "Oh, you couldn't be more wrong about that. You don't see how he watches you when you're not looking."

Abbey smiled and felt warm at that thought.

Then Alison's face turned serious. "He remembered something this morning."

"What?" Abbey looked at her with concern. "How do you know?"

"He told me as he was going out."

"Did he say what it was?"

"No, but there was a darkness about him. That was new."

"I need to go," Abbey said, feeling an urgency to be with him.

"Yes, of course."

Alison left the bedroom, and Abbey rushed to get dressed. She drank coffee, she took a bite of the scone, and she checked through the window to see that Jason hadn't moved. She hurried downstairs, slipped a light jacket over shoulders, and then walked out into the cool air. She crossed through the wet grass and came up beside Jason. He didn't react as she joined him, but she saw that Alison was right.

There was something in his face. Something she didn't like. Darkness. Memory.

They didn't talk, not at first. She slipped a hand through his as they stared at the mountains, and she held on tightly.

Finally, she asked, "Are you okay?"

"Yes."

His eyes narrowed. He was staring far off into the hills, but Abbey didn't know what he was seeing.

"Is anything wrong?" she asked.

Jason didn't answer that question. Instead, he said, as if he were seeing it in his head for the first time, "I walked away from you that night in Quebec City."

"Yes, you did."

"That was a mistake. I was wrong to do that, Abbey."

"I know."

"I was trying to protect you. I still am."

"I'd rather be at risk than not have you with me," Abbey said. "Don't ever walk away from me again."

Jason turned and stared at her. "You may regret that. We both might. The rule says to never get involved."

"I don't care about rules," Abbey replied.

He was silent as he turned back to the hills. The hawk continued to soar in circles, hunting for prey hiding in the green fields.

"Alison said you remembered something," she went on.

Still silent, Jason nodded.

"Tell me," Abbey said. "What is it? Is it something about us?"

"I already remember everything about us. Every single second. No, this is new. This is from the past. From *before*."

The wind blew, and Abbey shivered, feeling a chill. Her face turned dark, like his. "Jason?"

He slid a hand into the pocket of his jacket and came out with his gun, which he rubbed between his fingers, checking it, arming it, disarming it. It didn't matter where they were, or how safe they were, or whether it was day or night. The gun was always with him. Danger was always with him. She was going to have to live with that.

"Jason?" she said again. "What did you remember?"

Bourne aimed his gun at the hills, as if strangers were always watching them.

"Things they wanted me to forget," he said.

TURN THE PAGE FOR AN EXCERPT

Around the world, Treadstone agents are being hunted down and murdered. Someone high up in the U.S. government is erasing all evidence of a shocking mission from Jason Bourne's past known as Defiance—including trying to erase the existence of Bourne himself. Staying one step ahead of a team of killers, Bourne follows a global trail that leads him to one of the government's darkest secrets—and brings him face-to-face with his archenemy, the assassin known as Lennon, for a final deadly confrontation.

Tskhinvali, South Ossetia Region
The past

THE FIVE-DAY WAR BETWEEN RUSSIA AND GEORGIA HAD
taken place years earlier, but the Treadstone agent known
as Cain still saw the aftereffects of the conflict around
him. He passed abandoned farmhouses with their roofs
caved in by mortar fire. Tall grass grew around bombed-
out rubble, and the stone walls of a lonely Orthodox
church bore the pockmarks of bullets. The area felt emptied of people. Many of the refugees of the region had
fled south to Tbilisi and never come home again, leaving
ruins of their old lives behind them.

Cain knew he was on the right path. He could follow
the trail of blood and footprints. His target was wounded,
probably dying. Initially, there had only been a few tiny
red drops in the white snow, but the evidence of blood
came more frequently now, the stains larger. Abel was
slowing down, losing strength. He couldn't be far away.

The pursuit had taken Cain north out of the town of Gori. Abel's left rear tire had blown near Tergvisi, and since then, he'd proceeded on foot through the rural countryside, making a run for Russian-occupied territory. Cain had gotten close enough to him in one of the empty farm fields to land a bullet in the man's back, but then Abel had struggled to his feet and disappeared into the trees again.

Cain and Abel.

Holly Schultz, who'd assigned the code names, had a malevolent sense of humor. She'd teamed them on Treadstone missions for years. They'd saved each other's lives often enough that they were almost like brothers. Cain had thought he knew the man well. He'd trusted him. But under the jokes, under the disguises, under the Beatles songs he whistled before a kill, Abel had been an agent with a deadly secret.

Abel was a traitor. A Russian asset.

And now Cain had been sent to kill him.

He stopped in the forest, listening to the hiss of November wind and feeling the wet flakes of snow on his eyelashes and inside his heavy boots. The snow made the whole world quiet, and in the silence, he heard movement—branches snapping—close by. It wasn't Abel. The blood trail didn't lead in the direction of the noise. He was more concerned that it was a Russian soldier. He wasn't sure which side of the border he was on, and the Russian base at Eredvi was just a few kilometers away.

Cain leveled his Makarov, a Russian pistol he'd acquired upon arrival in Georgia. The assassination needed to be done with a foreign gun; Holly had been clear about that. There could be no evidence of American involvement. He snapped his shoulders from side to side, his eyes hunting for movement in the trees. Then he saw a tiny face, and lowered his weapon. It was a boy, no more than nine or ten years old.

The boy came out of the trees, not looking scared. He had a dirty face, greasy brown hair that was raggedly cut, and intense blue eyes. He wore a pullover shirt that resembled a burlap sack, plus torn jeans and red rubber boots that were caked with mud. The boy took note of the gun in Cain's hand.

"You hunt that man?" the boy asked in Georgian.

Cain nodded.

"He is Russian?"

Close enough, Cain thought, so he nodded again.

The boy pointed through the trees. "I saw him go in a farmhouse over there. He's bleeding, but he has a gun, too, like you. Be careful. You kill him, okay? Shoot him dead. Kill the fucking Russians."

Cain dug some coins from his pocket and handed them to the boy. Then he nodded his head for him to run in the opposite direction. The boy thumped his chest twice with his fist in a gesture of solidarity, then vanished silently through the snow.

The farmhouse was close, not even a hundred yards away. The wooden front door was open, hanging from one hinge. It was a small structure, mostly destroyed by bombs, and he circled the place to confirm that there were no other doors, just the one way in and out. Cain

smelled the smoke of a fire and the stink of boiled cab-
bage. As he neared the door, he heard singing from inside.

"Back in the U.S.S.R."

Abel wasn't hiding his location. He knew Cain was
out there. Between the lyrics, his voice broke in alternate
fits of laughing and coughing. Then he called out, his
words slurring as he got weaker, "Come on in, Cain. We
might as well get this over with."

Cain led with the Makarov. He moved fast, expecting
a battle, but there was no gunfire as he spun through the
door. Instead, he saw Abel sitting in the corner of the
main room, lost in the shadows on the wooden floor.
He wasn't alone. His legs were spread wide, and he had
one arm around the waist of a black-haired teenage girl
sitting in front of him. With his other hand, he held his
pistol to the terrified girl's head.

"Hey, Cain. This is Tatiana. Say hello, Tatiana."

When the girl said nothing, Abel shoved the gun hard
into her dark hair and repeated in guttural Russian, *"Say
hello."*

"Hello," she gasped.

Tatiana was undernourished, her arms and legs skinny.
Her plain face was winter-pale, and tears leaked from her
dark eyes. Her whole body trembled. She couldn't have
been more than fifteen.

"Let her go, Abel," Cain murmured, aiming the Makarov at the man who'd once been his friend. But he
didn't have a clean shot, not without risking the teenager's life. "Hurting her won't change how this ends."

"Oh, I think you're wrong. See, I know you too well, Cain. You're always a hero when it comes to women. It's your fatal flaw."

"Let her go," he repeated.

Abel managed a laugh. He leaned forward and kissed the back of the girl's head, keeping his face barely visible. It was clear that Abel had a wary appreciation for the accuracy of Cain's shooting, even with a foreign gun.

"So here we are," Abel said. "You and me. Brothers-in-arms."

"Here we are."

Cain studied the man's features in the shadows. Abel was a master of disguise and rarely looked the same way twice. He could be young, old, blond, redheaded, dark-haired, blue eyes, brown eyes, green eyes. About the only thing that gave him away was his walk when he thought no one was looking, a strange way of gliding so that his shoulders seemed to float above his hips. But here, at the end, he was simply himself. Tall, strong, blond, blue-eyed, smart, and arrogant when he smiled.

Yes, Cain thought, seeing the truth for the first time. *He's Russian.*

Abel had been a Russian mole from the beginning. A graduate of Putin's charm school, designed to blend in like a native and infiltrate the U.S. intelligence services. He'd played them all. Fooled them all. Cain included.

Tatiana struggled in Abel's grasp, but the man held her tight. Staring back, he seemed to read Cain's mind.

"You think they want me dead because I'm a traitor, don't you?"

Cain didn't answer.

"Well you're wrong," Abel went on. "Think about it. Why kill me? If that's what this is about, Holly would want me in a cell somewhere, so they can sweat out every secret I've given away. When they'd bled me dry, they'd trade me, use me as a bargaining chip. But send you out here to shoot me? No. They're scared, Cain. Somebody wants to shut me up. Make sure I don't talk."

More games. More *lies*!

But Cain couldn't stop himself from playing. "Talk about what?"

"*Defiance*."

A flash of puzzlement ran through Cain's eyes. "Defiance? That was a Treadstone mission."

"That's right, but what was the mission really about? Who ordered it? What was it covering up?"

"Are you saying you know?"

"I know enough for them to want me dead."

Cain shook his head. "You're stalling. It's too late for that. You've run out of time. Do you think the Russians are coming to save you?"

Abel's blue eyes glinted, as if laughing at a joke only he could hear.

At that moment, Cain felt a rumble under his feet. Vibration traveled through the ground and under the floor like an earthquake. He knew what that meant. The lonely woods around the farmhouse were located near the road to Eredvi, and heavy vehicles were thundering down that road. The Russians *were* coming. Soldiers would already be in the woods, zeroing in on their location.

"You activated a tracker," Cain concluded, thinking furiously, assessing his options.

"Of course I did. See, you're the one who's running out of time, Cain. Get out of here while you still can."

Cain tightened his grip around the Makarov. He tried to send a message to the girl, Tatiana, with his eyes, telling her to jerk sideways and give him a shot. But the teenager's face was flushed with panic, and he couldn't trust her not to swing back into his line of fire. Abel recognized his predicament. They knew each other too well.

"Go, Cain. Save yourself. You can't kill me without killing her, and I know you won't do that. If you stay, you're dead."

The thunder on the road deepened and got louder. The throb of engines carried to his ears on the still air. Through the open door, he heard men trampling noisily through the forest. There were shouts in Russian. Cain endured a moment of paralysis—*stay or go*—but then the decision was made for him. A man's body filled the farmhouse doorway. It was a soldier dressed in olive gear, with an AK-12 rifle braced against his shoulder.

The man didn't see Cain at first, and Abel shouted in Russian, "Left! Left! Left!"

In that fraction of a second, Cain swung the Makarov and fired a single shot that took down the Russian soldier between his eyes. At the same moment, he dropped to the ground, watching as Abel threw the girl sideways and aimed his gun at Cain. Abel squeezed off a shot but missed high, and Cain fired back, hurrying, choosing the fattest target. The bullet landed squarely in Abel's chest.

A fatal shot; it *had* to be fatal.

Wasn't it?

Always confirm your kill.

Treadstone.

But there was no time to do that. The cursing voices outside got louder. More soldiers were coming. Cain took three steps forward and dragged Tatiana from the floor, where she was huddled in a fetal position, and slung her over his shoulder. Together, they burst through the farmhouse door, and Cain saw another young soldier running toward them through the snow, drawn by the gunfire. The man froze, startled by their sudden appearance, and his hesitation let Cain get off a wild shot that hit the man's knee and took him down, screaming.

Cain bolted into the woods, where the trees gave him cover. He was barely aware of the weight of Tatiana draped over his shoulder. He ran, dodging around thick pines, hearing more shouts as men joined the hunt from the road. They hadn't brought in a helicopter, but he doubted he had more than a few minutes before the search headed to the sky. He reached an open farm field where there was no protection, and he sprinted across the frozen land, chased by weapons fire crackling from behind him.

One bullet seared his leg, but he didn't slow down. Another whistled past his ear. As he neared the next grove of trees past the field, the firefight intensified, and he zigzagged, feeling another near miss that sprayed blood from his neck. When he finally reached the shelter of the trees again, he sagged to his knees, letting the girl slump to the ground next to him. He expected to hear the voices closing on him, expected to see dozens of soldiers converging on his location through the snowy field.

Instead, the gunfire stopped.

The Russians all withdrew.

At first he was puzzled, but then he understood. He'd crossed the border. He wasn't in the South Ossetia province; he was back in Georgia, in unoccupied territory. The Russians weren't ready to start another war over a single spy.

"We're safe," he told Tatiana, as he exhaled in relief. "They won't come for us now."

The girl didn't answer. He looked at her for the first time since they'd reached the trees, and he saw that her eyes were open and fixed in a look of scared surprise. Her trembling had stopped; her body was motionless. When he turned her over, he saw that a single bullet from one of the Russian rifles had landed in the back of her skull. Her black hair was matted with blood. She was dead, killed instantly.

If he hadn't been carrying her, that bullet would have killed him.

Cain got to his feet. He stared down at the lifeless teenager and felt a crushing wave of exhaustion, the weight of the world slumping his shoulders. His blood was warm inside his clothes. He needed to go, but he found he couldn't move; he couldn't leave her, not yet. He shook his head in bitter regret, and not for the first time, he hissed out a curse against the life he led.

ONE WEEK LATER, CAIN WAITED OUTSIDE A CARGO HANGAR AT the airport in Antalya, Turkey, on the Mediterranean coast. The weather was unseasonably hot, almost eighty degrees. He wore a black formfitting T-shirt and cargo shorts as he waited for the arrival of the Treadstone jet. Sunglasses covered his eyes. By habit, he examined the faces around him, but he concluded that he wasn't being watched.

His wounds were healing now. At least the ones the doctors could treat.

Cain pressed the secure satellite phone to his ear. The signal was crystal clear. Holly Schultz, who was in Washington, could have been standing a few feet away.

"You haven't checked in about the mission," she chided him. "I had to hear from Nash that you called for the jet."

"I've been busy staying alive," Cain told her.

That silenced her complaints, but the truth was, he'd deliberately put off making his report. He'd taken three days to make his way south from Georgia, and then he'd spent the last four days at a Turkish beachside resort. He'd swum out in the sea until the land was just a smudge on the horizon. He'd drunk a lot of raki. He'd paid a prostitute to do nothing but sit in his room for an entire day and talk to him, even though he didn't speak the language. That was how Cain ran from his troubles.

But he couldn't run forever.

"Anyway, I'm back," he went on.

"And Abel?"

"I shot him."

"He's dead?"

Cain hesitated. "I think so. I didn't have time to check as the Russians moved in."

"That's unfortunate," Holly said.

"I had to act fast. I didn't figure you'd want an American agent captured in Russian-occupied territory."

"True enough," she admitted in a grudging voice. "We'll need to do a full debrief when you're back. I'll have someone meet the plane."

"Fine. Whatever." He didn't hide the hatred he felt at that moment. For her. For himself. For the whole world.

"Are you all right, David?" she asked, injecting a forced bit of sympathy into her tone. When she wanted to pretend she cared, she used his real name. David Webb. But he had been Cain for so long that his birth name had little meaning for him. There were days when he didn't even remember it.

"I'm fine," he replied, "but I had to take over one of Abel's covers as I made my escape."

"What identity are you using now?" Holly asked.

Cain squinted into the hot Turkish sunlight. "My name is Jason Bourne."

1

WHEN SAM YOUNG SPOTTED THE BLOND WOMAN IN THE *Norwegian Jewel* sweatshirt coming into his gallery, he knew they'd found him. Yes, she looked like any of the thousands of other tourists streaming off the cruise ships every day. Her eyes went to the cheap framed prints of Mendenhall Glacier, not the handcrafted Native sculptures. She carried a plastic bag stuffed with Chinese-made T-shirts from a discount gift shop near the port. If he took her in the back and searched her, he was sure he'd find a valid cruise ship ID and a matching passport with her name and photograph. Spies didn't make obvious mistakes like that.

But she was a fake.

Cruise passengers came and went every day, but once their ship left for the next port, they were gone for good. In by eight a.m., out by four thirty p.m., depending on the tide. But this woman had been here before. Not in the gallery. She was smart enough not to kiss the dog more than once. However, Sam had learned to study and remember faces, and he was certain he'd seen this same woman outside the shop in the last couple of days.

He'd know for sure if he got a buzz on his phone. Sam's tradecraft specialty was as a computer hacker, and even though he'd been inactive for Treadstone for two years, he still kept his hand in the game. That was partly for his own protection, because when it came to Treadstone, you were never really out. He kept surveillance cameras inside and outside his Franklin Street shop, as well as on the road near his house on Black Wolf Way. He'd written an app to isolate faces from the video feeds and maintain them in a database, and with each new entry, the program ran facial recognition to look for duplicates. When it found one, it sent the information to his phone.

Buzz.

Sam felt the vibration in his pocket. He took out his phone and examined the side-by-side photographs that appeared in the notification from his app. One was the thirtysomething woman standing in his shop right now, pretending to study a display of colorfully painted Russian nesting dolls. The other was a woman with dark hair and an oilskin jacket who'd passed on the sidewalk outside the shop three days earlier. Although the second image was less focused, and she'd changed her hair in between, it was definitely the same person.

Studying the picture again, Sam was also certain that

he'd seen her at a table at Mar y Sol when he'd had dinner there on Wednesday. She'd been watching him for a while.

Sam slipped his hands casually into his pockets, one hand curling around the grip of his Hellcat pistol, as he approached her. "Can I help you?"

The woman was good. A pro. She looked up with a false smile, but he could see her eyes take note of his hands, then flick up to the corner of the ceiling and spot the positioning of the security camera. He assumed there was a weapon hidden inside her gift bag. If she went for it, the question would be which one of them was faster. Sam didn't like his odds. There was something about the hawkish look in her blue eyes that made him think she'd be the better fighter.

But she was the advance scout, not the shooter. There was too much risk going after him in the middle of downtown.

"Oh, no, thank you," she replied pleasantly. "Just browsing. You have beautiful things here."

"Thank you."

"I suppose most of your business comes from the ships. It must get so quiet off season. Do you close up for the winter?"

"No, I'm open all year, but you're right. Most of the crowds disappear as soon as the cruise season ends."

"How did you come to be in a place like this?" she asked him.

Sam shrugged. He was sure she knew exactly where

he'd come from. "I don't know. How does anyone end up anywhere?"

"Oh, well, I guess you're right about that. Anyway, I wish I could afford to buy something, but you know, the family's always on a budget. T-shirts for the kids and not much else."

"That's okay," he told her. "Take your time and look around."

"I will, thanks."

She spent another five minutes in the shop, just to make it look good. As she was leaving, she called out to say goodbye, and her eyes shot another glance at the ceiling camera. Then, as the bell on the door chimed, she headed out to Franklin Street and turned toward the harbor. She didn't look through the window again. That would be the last time he saw her. But others would come soon. Tonight, most likely. She'd probably report that she'd been blown and that the assault team needed to assume he'd be waiting for them.

She hadn't fooled him, and he hadn't fooled her.

As soon as she was gone, Sam closed the shop. He assessed his options but decided there was only one thing to do. Get the hell out of Juneau right now. Whoever was after him, he'd be outgunned and outnumbered. He didn't know how they'd found him—there were no more than half a dozen people who knew that the Arizona hacker with the Treadstone code name Dax was now gift shop owner Sam Young in Alaska—but he didn't have time to worry about how his cover had been blown.

He'd had an escape strategy in place from day one. It was time to put it into play.

Sam emptied the cash from the register. There wasn't much, just a few hundred dollars. He thought about stopping at the bank to withdraw the money from his accounts, but he assumed if they were watching the store, they'd have someone watching his bank, too, to see whether he was making a run. It didn't matter. His bank had a branch in the town of Haines. Once he was clear of Juneau, he could stop there on his way into the back-country.

He locked the shop and hiked up the Franklin Street hill. He always parked several blocks away, which gave him time to identify any surveillance that might be waiting for him. It was a cold September day, gray and ominous, with low clouds clinging to the steep green hillsides. Drizzle spat on his face. He kept his hand around the Hellcat in his pocket, but his shoulders were hunched, just a man trudging along in the rain. His eyes took a close look at each parked car and each doorway. If they were watching him, they were keeping it under wraps. He saw no one.

Sam debated whether to go home. He had his go bag, his laptop, and more money hidden under the floor-boards in his living room. He could be in and out in ninety seconds, and then he'd be on the way to Statter Harbor, where he kept his Exhilarator speedboat gassed up and ready to go. As he'd developed an escape plan— knowing a day like this would come sooner or later—he'd thought about using a floatplane. That would give him more range and speed, but the flying weather around Juneau was too iffy day by day to guarantee he could get out of town on short notice. With the Exhilarator, he could head to Hoonah or race up the channel to Haines or Skagway. Once there, he could hide out in the woods or take an SUV over the Rockies on the Alaska Highway.

He found his red Honda parked at the top of the hill near 6th Street. From there, he could see the dark water of the harbor through mist and fog. The *Jewel* was the only cruise ship docked there today, and he knew it would be gone in less than two hours. Everyone in Alaska retail knew the port times of the ships. Sam made a show of dropping his wallet, which gave him a chance to check the undercarriage of his Accord, in case anyone had planted explosives or tracking devices. He also noted the tiny red threads he'd secured across the gaps of each car door. They were still there; no one had broken into the vehicle during the day.

Even so, he held his breath when he started the engine. It caught. He didn't blow up.

Sam headed north on the Glacier Highway. He watched the mirrors and didn't see anyone following him. He decided to stop home to grab his go bag, but ten minutes later, he changed his mind. A shrill alarm went off on the phone in his pocket, which was the signal that someone had broken one of the invisible laser barriers guarding the windows and doors of his house. There were people inside. Sam pulled onto the highway shoulder near the bridge at Lemon Creek, where wooded hilltops and snowcapped mountains went in and out of view through the clouds. His breath came quickly; adrenaline surged through him.

When he dug out his phone, he activated the cameras located in the house's ductwork, which gave him sound and video of the interior. He spotted four men, all dressed in black, all armed with semiautomatics and suppressors. The faces of the men were unfamiliar, but who they were didn't concern him. What mattered was that they would take him down as soon as he came through the door.

"Should we check the computer?" one of them said through the video feed.

"Don't bother," another replied. *"He's a hacker. He'll have it secured. We'll take it with us and let the pros crack it. But keep your eyes open. He's bound to have backups. Maybe electronic, maybe print."*

"What are we looking for?"

"Anything about Intelsat."

On the shoulder of the Glacier Highway, Sam closed his eyes and swore. Now he understood. Now it all made sense.

Intelsat. Of course.